The Last Vendee

ALEXANDRE
DUMAS

Volume II

Fredonia Books
Amsterdam, The Netherlands

The Last Vendée; or The She-Wolves of Machecoul Volume II

by
Alexandre Dumas

ISBN 1-58963-174-9

Reprinted from the 1894 edition

Fredonia Books
Amsterdam, The Netherlands
http://www.fredoniabooks.com

In order to make original editions of historical works available to scholars at an economical price, this facsimile of the original edition of 1894 is reproduced from the best available copy and has been digitally enhanced to improve legibility, but the text remains unaltered to retain historical authenticity.

THE LAST VENDÉE;

OR,

THE SHE-WOLVES OF MACHECOUL

VOLUME II.

CONTENTS.

THE LAST VENDÉE;

OR,

THE SHE-WOLVES OF MACHECOUL.

I.

IN WHICH IT APPEARS THAT ALL JEWS ARE NOT FROM JERUSALEM, NOR ALL TURKS FROM TUNIS.

"Hola ! hey ! my rabbits ! " called Maître Jacques, as he entered the open.

At the voice of their leader the obedient "rabbits" issued from the underbrush and from the tufts of gorse and brambles beneath which they had ensconced themselves at the first alarm, and came running into the open, where they eyed the two prisoners, as well as the darkness would allow, with much curiosity. Then, as if this examination did not suffice, one of them went down into the burrow, lighted two bits of pine, and jumping back put the improvised torches under the nose of Petit-Pierre and that of her companion.

Maître Jacques had resumed his usual seat on the trunk of a tree, and was peaceably conversing with Aubin Courte-Joie, to whom he related the incidents of the capture he had made, with the same circumstantial particularity with which a villager tells his wife of a purchase he has just concluded at a market.

Michel, who was naturally somewhat overcome by the affair and by his wound, was sitting, or rather lying, on the grass. Petit-Pierre, standing beside him, was gazing, with an attention not exempt from disgust, at the faces of the bandits; which was easy to do, because, having satisfied their curiosity, they had gone back to their usual pursuits, — that is to say, to their psalm-singing, their games, their sleep, and the polishing of their weapons. And yet, while playing, drinking, singing, and cleansing their guns, carbines, and pistols, they never lost sight for an instant of the two prisoners who, by way of precaution, were placed in the very centre of the open.

It was then that Petit-Pierre, withdrawing her eyes from the bandits, noticed for the first time that her companion was wounded.

"Oh, good God!" she exclaimed, seeing the blood which had run down Michel's arm to his hand; "you are shot?"

"Yes; I think so, Ma — mon —"

"Oh! for heaven's sake, say Petit-Pierre, and more than ever. Do you suffer much pain?"

"No; I thought I received a blow from a stick on the shoulder, but now the whole arm is getting numb."

"Try to move it."

"Well, in any case, there is nothing broken. See!"

And he moved his arm with comparative ease.

"Good! This will certainly win you the heart you love, and if your noble conduct is not enough, I promise to intervene in your behalf; and I have good reason to think my intervention will be effectual."

"How kind you are, Ma — Petit-Pierre! And whatever you order me to do, I'll do it after such a promise; even if I have to attack a battery of a hundred guns single-handed, I'll go, head down, to the redoubt. Ah, if you would only speak to the Marquis de Souday for me, I should be the happiest of men!"

"Don't gesticulate in that way; you will prevent the blood from stanching. So it seems it is the marquis you are particularly afraid of. Well, I 'll speak to him, your terrible marquis, on the word of — of Petit-Pierre. But now, as they have left us alone to ourselves, let us talk about our present affairs. Where are we ? — and who are these persons ?"

"To me," said Michel, "they look like Chouans."

"Do Chouans stop inoffensive travellers ? Impossible !"

"They do, though."

"I am shocked."

"Well, if they have not done it before, they have done it now, apparently."

"What will they do with us ?"

"That we shall soon know; for see, they are beginning to bestir themselves,— about us, no doubt !"

"Goodness !" exclaimed Petit-Pierre; "how odd it will be if we are in danger from my own partisans! But hush!"

Maître Jacques, after conferring for some time with Aubin Courte-Joie, gave the order to bring the prisoners before him.

Petit-Pierre advanced confidently toward the tree, on which the master of the burrow held his assizes; but Michel who, on account of his wound and his bound hands, found some difficulty in getting on his legs, took more time in obeying the order. Seeing this, Aubin Courte-Joie made a sign to Trigaud-Vermin, who, seizing the young man by the waist, lifted him with the ease another man would have had in lifting a child three years old, and placed him before Maître Jacques, taking care to put him in precisely the same attitude from which he had taken him, — a manœuvre Trigaud-Vermin accomplished by swinging forward Michel's lower limbs and poking him in the back before he let him fall at full length on the ground.

"Stupid brute !" muttered Michel, who had lost under the effect of pain some of his natural timidity.

"You are not civil," said Maître Jacques; "no, I repeat to you, Monsieur le Baron Michel de la Logerie, you are not civil, and the kindness of that poor fellow deserved a better return. But come, let 's attend to our little business!" Casting a more observing look at the young man, he added, "I am not mistaken; you are M. le Baron Michel de la Logerie, are you not?"

"Yes," replied Michel, laconically.

"Very good. What were you doing on the road to Légé, in the middle of the forest of Touvois at this time of night?"

"I might answer that I am not obliged to give an account of my actions to you, and that the highways are open to everybody."

"But you won't answer me in that way, Monsieur le baron."

"Why not?"

"Because, with due respect to you, it would be folly, and I believe you have too much sense to commit it."

"Very good; I won't discuss the point. I was going to my farm of Banlœuvre, which, as you know, is at the farther end of the forest of Touvois, in which we now are."

"Well done; that 's right, Monsieur le baron. Do me the honor to answer always in that way and we shall agree. Now, how is it that the Baron de la Logerie, who has so many good horses in his stables, so many fine carriages in his coach-house, should be travelling on foot with his friend, like a simple peasant, — like us, in short?"

"We had a horse, but he got away in an accident we met with, and we could not catch him."

"Well done again. Now, Monsieur le baron, I hope you will be kind enough to give us some news."

"I?"

"Yes. What is going on over there, Monsieur le baron?"

"How can things over our way interest you?" asked Michel, who not being quite sure to which party the man he was addressing belonged, hesitated as to the color he ought to give to his replies.

"Go on, Monsieur le baron," resumed Maître Jacques; "never mind whether what you have to say is useful to me or not. Come, bethink yourself. Whom did you meet on the way ?"

Michel looked at Petit-Pierre with embarrassment. Maître Jacques intercepted the look, and calling up Trigaud-Vermin, he ordered him to stand between the two prisoners, like the Wall in "Midsummer-Night's Dream."

"Well," continued Michel, "we met what everybody meets at all hours and on every road for the last three days in and about Machecoul, — we met soldiers."

"Did they speak to you ?"

"No."

"No ? Do you mean to say they let you pass without a word ?"

"We avoided them."

"Bah !" said Maître Jacques, in a doubtful tone.

"Travelling on our own business it did not suit us to be mixed up in affairs that were none of ours."

"Who is this young man who is with you ?"

Petit-Pierre hastened to answer before Michel had time to do so.

"I am Monsieur le baron's servant," she said.

"Then, my young friend," said Maître Jacques, replying to Petit-Pierre, "allow me to tell you that you are a very bad servant. In fact, peasant as I am, I am grieved to hear a servant answering for his master, especially when no one spoke to him." Turning to Michel, he continued, "So this lad is your servant, is he ? Well, he is a pretty boy."

And the lord of the burrow looked at Petit-Pierre with scrutinizing attention, while one of his men threw the light of a torch full on her face to facilitate the examination.

"Let us come to the point," said Michel; "what do you want? If it is my purse I sha'n't prevent you from having it. Take it; but let us go about our business."

"Oh, fie !" returned Maître Jacques; "if I were a gentleman, like you, Monsieur Michel, I would ask satisfaction for such an insult. Do you take us for highwaymen? That 's not flattering. I would willingly tell you my business, only, I fear I should make myself disagreeable. Besides, you say you have nothing to do with politics. Your father, nevertheless, whom I knew something of in the olden time, did meddle with politics, and did n't lose his fortune that way either. I must admit, therefore, that I expected to find you a zealous adherent of his Majesty Louis-Philippe."

"Then you 'd have been very much mistaken, my good sir," broke in Petit-Pierre, disrespectfully; "Monsieur le baron is, on the contrary, a zealous partisan of his Majesty Henri V."

"Indeed, my little friend!" cried Maître Jacques. Then, turning to Michel, "Come, Monsieur le baron," he continued, "be frank; is what your companion — I mean your servant — says the truth?"

"The exact truth," answered Michel.

"Ah, but this is good news! I, who thought I had to do with those horrid curs! — good God! how ashamed I am of the way I have treated you, and what excuses I ought to offer! Pray, receive them, Monsieur le baron; and take your share, my excellent young friend, — master and servant, please to accept them together. I 'm not too proud to beg your pardon."

"Well, then," said Michel, whose displeasure was not lessened by Maître Jacques's sarcastic politeness, "you have a very easy way of testifying your regret, and that is by letting us go our way."

"Oh, no!" cried Maître Jacques.

"Why not?"

"No, no, no! I cannot consent to let you leave us in that way. Besides, two such partisans of legitimacy as you and I, Monsieur le Baron Michel, have a great deal to say to each other about the grand uprising that is now taking place. Don't you think so, Monsieur le baron?"

"It may be so; but the interests of that cause require

that I and my servant should immediately reach the safety of my farm at Banlœuvre."

"Monsieur le baron, there is no spot in all this region as safe as the one where you now are in the midst of us. I cannot allow you to leave us without giving you some proof of the really touching interest I feel for you."

"Hum!" muttered Petit-Pierre, under her breath; "things are going very wrong."

"Go on," said Michel.

"You are devoted to Henri V.?"

"Yes."

"Very devoted?"

"Yes."

"Supremely devoted?"

"I have told you so."

"Yes, you have told me so, and I don't doubt your word. Well, I'll provide you with a way to manifest that devotion in a dazzling manner."

"Do so."

"You see my men," continued Maître Jacques, pointing to his troop,—"some forty scamps who look more like Callot's bandits than the honest peasants that they are. They don't ask anything better than to be killed for our young king and his heroic mother; only, they lack everything needful to attain that end,—shoes to march in, arms to fight with, garments to wear, money to lessen the hardships of the bivouac. You do not, I presume, Monsieur le baron, desire that these faithful servants, accomplishing what you yourself regard as a sacred duty, should be exposed to cold, hunger, and other privations in all weathers?"

"But," said Michel, "how the devil am I to clothe and arm your men? Have I a base of supplies at command?"

"Ah, Monsieur le baron," resumed Maître Jacques, "don't think I know so little of good manners as to dream of burdening you with the annoyance of such details. No, indeed! But I've a faithful follower here" (and he pointed to Aubin Courte-Joie) "who will spare you all trouble. Give him the money, and he will lay it out to the best advantage, all the while saving your purse."

"If that's all," said Michel, with the readiness of youth and the enthusiasm of his dawning opinions, "I'm very willing. How much do you want?"

"Come, that's good!" exclaimed Maître Jacques, not a little amazed at this readiness. "Well, do you think it would be pushing things too far to ask you for five hundred francs for each man? I should like them to have, besides the uniform, — green, you know, like the chasseurs of Monsieur de Charette, — a knapsack comfortably supplied. Five hundred francs, that's about half the price Philippe charges France for every man she gives him; and each of my men is worth any two of his. You see, therefore, that I am reasonable."

"Say at once the sum you want, and let us make an end of this business at once."

"Well, I have forty men, including those now absent on leave, but who are bound to join the standard at the first call. That makes just twenty thousand francs, — a mere nothing for a rich man like you, Monsieur le baron."

"So be it. You shall have your twenty thousand francs in two days," said Michel, endeavoring to rise; "I give you my word."

"Oh, no, no; I wish to spare you all trouble, Monsieur le baron. You have a friend in this region, a notary, who will advance to you that sum if you write him a pressing little note, a polite little note, which one of my men shall take at once."

"Very well; give me something to write with, and unbind my hands."

"My friend Courte-Joie here has pens, ink, and paper."

Maître Courte-Joie had already begun to pull an inkstand from his pocket. But Petit-Pierre stepped forward.

"One moment, Monsieur Michel," she said, in a resolute

tone. "And you, Maître Courte-Joie, as I hear you called, put up your implements. This shall not be done."

"Upon my word!" ejaculated Maître Jacques; "and pray, why not, servant, — as you call yourself?"

"Because such proceedings, monsieur, are those of bandits in Calabria and Estramadura, and cannot be tolerated among men who claim to be soldiers of King Henri V. Your demand is an actual extortion, which I will not permit."

"You, my young friend?"

"Yes, I."

"If I considered you as being really what you pretend to be, I should treat you as an impertinent lackey; but it strikes me that you have a right to the respect we owe to a woman, and I shall not compromise my reputation for gallantry by handling you roughly. I therefore confine myself, for the present, to telling you to mind your own business and not meddle with what does n't concern you."

"On the contrary, monsieur, this concerns me very closely," returned Petit-Pierre, with dignity. "It is of the utmost consequence to me that no one shall make use of the name of Henri V. to cover acts of brigandage."

"You take an extraordinary interest in the affairs of his Majesty, my young friend. Will you be good enough to tell me why?"

"Send away your men, and I will tell you, monsieur."

"Off with you to a little distance, my lads!" he said. "It is n't necessary," he continued, as the men obeyed him, "as I have no secrets from those worthy fellows; but I 'm willing to humor you, as you see. Come, now we are alone, speak out."

"Monsieur," said Petit-Pierre, going a step nearer to Maître Jacques, "I order you to set that young man at liberty. I require you to give us an escort instantly to the place where we are going, and I also wish you to send in search of the friends we are expecting."

"You require? — you order? Ah, *ça!* my little turtledove, you talk like the king upon his throne. If I refuse, what then ?"

"If you refuse I will have you shot within twenty-four hours."

"Upon my word ! one would think you were the regent herself."

"I am the regent herself, monsieur."

Maître Jacques burst into a roar of convulsive laughter. His men, hearing his shouts, came up to have their share in the hilarity.

"Ouf !" he cried, seeing them about him; "here 's fun ! You were amazed enough just now, my lads, were n't you ? — to hear a Baron de la Logerie, son of that Michel you wot of, declare that Henri V. had no better friend than he. That was queer enough; but this — oh ! this is queerer still, and even more incredible. Here 's something that goes beyond the most galloping imagination. Look at this little peasant. You may have taken him for anything you like; but I 've supposed him to be nothing else than the mistress of Monsieur le baron. Well, well, my rabbits, we are all mistaken, — you 're mistaken; I 'm mistaken ! This young man whom you see before you is neither more nor less than the mother of our king !"

A growl of ironical incredulity ran through the crowd.

"I swear to you," cried Michel, "it is true."

"Fine testimony, faith !" retorted Maître Jacques.

"I assure you — " began Petit-Pierre.

"No, no," interrupted Maître Jacques; "I assure you that if within ten minutes — which I grant to your squire for reflection, my wandering dame — he does n't do as agreed upon, I 'll send him to keep company with the acorns over his head. He may choose, but choose quick, — the money or the rope. If I don't have the one, he 'll have the other, that 's all !"

"But this is infamous !" cried Petit-Pierre, beside herself.

"Seize her !" said Maître Jacques.

Four men advanced to execute the order.

"Let no one dare to lay a hand on me!" said Petit-Pierre. Then, as Trigaud-Vermin, callous to the majesty of her voice and gesture, still advanced, "What!" she cried, recoiling from the touch of that brutal hand, and snatching from her head both hat and wig, "Is there no man among those bandits who is soldier enough to recognize me? What! Will God abandon me now to the mercy of such brigands?"

"No!" said a voice behind Maître Jacques; "and I tell this man his conduct is unworthy of one who wears a cockade that is white because it is spotless."

Maître Jacques turned like lightning and aimed a pistol at the new-comer. All the brigands seized their weapons, and it was literally under an arch of iron that Bertha — for it was she — advanced into the circle that surrounded the prisoners.

"The she-wolf!" muttered some of Maître Jacques's men, who knew Mademoiselle de Souday.

"What are you here for?" cried the master of the band. "Don't you know that I refuse to recognize the authority your father arrogates to himself over my troop, and that I positively decline to be a part of his division?"

"Silence, fool!" said Bertha. Then, going straight to Petit-Pierre, and kneeling on one knee before her, "I ask pardon," she said, "for these men who have insulted and threatened you, — you who have so many claims to their respect."

"Ah, faith," cried Petit-Pierre, gayly, "you have come just in time! The situation was getting critical; and here's a poor lad who will owe you his life, for these worthy people were actually talking of hanging him and of sending me to keep him company."

"Good heavens, yes!" said Michel, whom Aubin Courte-Joie, seeing how matters stood, had hastened to unbind.

"And the worst of it was," said Petit-Pierre, laughing and nodding at Michel, "that the young man deserved to live for the favor of a good royalist like yourself."

Bertha smiled and dropped her eyes.

"So," continued Petit-Pierre, "it is you who will have to pay my debts toward him; and I hope you will not object to my keeping a promise I have made him to speak to your father in his behalf."

Bertha bent low to take the hand of Petit-Pierre and kiss it, — a movement which concealed the rush of color to her cheeks.

Maître Jacques, mortified and ashamed of his mistake, now approached and stammered a few excuses. In spite of her repulsion for the man's brutality, Petit-Pierre knew it would be impolitic to do more than show a certain amount of resentment.

"Your intentions may have been excellent, monsieur," she said, "but your methods are deplorable, and tend to nothing less than making highwaymen of our supporters, like the Company of Jehu in the old war; and I hope you will abstain from such proceedings in future."

Then, turning away, as if such persons no longer existed for her, she said to Bertha, "Now tell me how you happened to come here just at the right moment."

"Your horse smelt his stable-mates," replied the young girl; "we caught him, and then turned aside, for we heard the chasseurs coming up. Seeing the two bundles of thorns tied to the poor beast, we thought that you wanted to be rid of the animal in order to mask your escape, and we all dispersed in different directions to find you, giving ourselves rendezvous at Banlœuvre. I came through the forest; the lights attracted my attention, then the voices. I left my horse at some distance, for fear he might betray me; you know the rest, Madame."

"Very good," said Petit-Pierre; "and now if monsieur will be good enough to give us a guide to Banlœuvre, Bertha, let us start; for, to tell you the truth, I am half-dead with fatigue."

"I will guide you myself, Madame," said Maître Jacques, respectfully.

Petit-Pierre bowed her head in assent; and Maître Jacques busied himself eagerly in his arrangements. Ten men marched in advance to see that the road was clear, while he himself with ten others escorted Petit-Pierre, who was mounted on Bertha's horse.

Two hours later, as Petit-Pierre, Bertha, and Michel were finishing their supper, the Marquis de Souday and Mary arrived, the former testifying the utmost joy at finding the person whom he called his "young friend" in safety. We must admit that the old gentleman's joy, sincere and genuine as it was, was expressed in the stiff, ceremonious sentences of the old school.

In the course of the evening Petit-Pierre had a long conference with the marquis in a corner of the large hall, which Bertha and Michel watched with deep interest; which was still further deepened when, on the sudden entrance of Jean Oullier, the marquis rose, came up to the young people, and taking Bertha's hand in his, said to Michel:

"Monsieur Petit-Pierre informs me that you aspire to the hand of my daughter Bertha. I may have had other ideas for her establishment, but in consequence of these gracious commands I can only assure you, monsieur, that after the campaign is over my daughter shall be your wife."

A thunderbolt falling at Michel's feet would not have stunned him more. While the marquis ceremoniously prepared to place Bertha's hand in his he turned to Mary, as if to implore her intervention; but her low voice murmured in his ears the terrible words, "I do not love you."

Overwhelmed with grief, bewildered and surprised, Michel mechanically took the hand the marquis presented to him.

II.

MAÎTRE MARC.

THE day on which all these events — namely, those in the house of the Widow Picaut, in the château de Souday, the forest of Touvois, and the farmhouse of Banlœuvre — took place, the door of a house, No. 19 rue du Château, at Nantes, opened about five in the afternoon to give exit to two individuals, in one of whom we may recognize the civil commissioner Pascal, whose acquaintance we have already made at the château de Souday, and who, after leaving it, as we related, with the Duchesse de Berry, poor Bonneville, and the other Vendéan leaders, had returned without difficulty to his official and private residence at Nantes.

The other, and this is the one with whom we are for the present concerned, was a man about forty years of age, with a keen, intelligent, and penetrating eye, a curved nose, white teeth, thick and sensual lips, like those which commonly belong to imaginative persons; his black coat and white cravat and ribbon of the Legion of honor indicated, so far as one might judge by appearances, a man belonging to the magistracy. He was, in truth, one of the most distinguished members of the Paris bar, who had arrived at Nantes the evening before and gone straight to the house of his associate, the civil commissioner. In the royalist vocabulary he bore the name of Marc, — one of the several names of Cicero.

When he reached the street door, conducted, as we have said, by the civil commissioner, he found a cabriolet awaiting him. The two men shook hands affectionately, and the Parisian lawyer got into the vehicle, while the driver, leaning over to the civil commissioner, asked him, as if aware that the traveller was ignorant on the subject: —

"Where am I to take the gentleman?"

"Do you see that peasant at the farther end of the street on a dapple-gray horse?" asked the civil commissioner.

"Yes."

"Then all you have to do is to follow him."

This information was hardly given before the man on the gray horse, as though he had overheard the words of the legitimist agent, started, went down the rue du Château, and turned to the right, so as to keep along by the bank of the river, which flowed to his left. The coachman whipped up his horse, and the squeaking vehicle on which we have bestowed the unambitious name of "cabriolet," began to rattle over the uneven pavement of the capital of the Loire-Inférieure, following, as best it could, the mysterious guide before it.

Just as it reached the corner of the rue du Château and turned in the direction indicated, the traveller caught sight of the rider, who, without even glancing behind him, began to cross the Loire, by the pont Rousseau, which leads to the high-road of Saint-Philbert-de-Grand-Lieu. Once on the road the peasant put his horse to a trot, but a slow trot, such as the cabriolet could easily follow. The rider, however, never turned his head, and seemed not only quite indifferent as to what might be happening behind him, but also so ignorant of the mission he himself was performing that the traveller began to fancy himself the victim of a hoax.

As for the coachman, not being trusted with the secrets of the affair, he could give no information capable of quieting the uneasiness of Maître Marc. Having asked of the civil commissioner, "Where am I to go?" and being told, "Follow the man on the dapple-gray horse," he followed the man on the dapple-gray horse, seeming no more concerned about his guide than his guide was concerned about him.

They reached Saint-Philbert-de-Grand-Lieu in about two hours and just at dusk. The man on the gray horse stopped at the inn of the Cygne de la Croix, got off his horse, gave the animal to the hostler, and entered the inn. The traveller in the cabriolet arrived five minutes later and entered the same inn. As he crossed the kitchen the rider met him, and without appearing to take notice of him, slipped a little paper into his hand.

The traveller entered the common room, which happened at the moment to be empty; there he called for a light and a bottle of wine. They brought him what he asked for. He did not touch the bottle, but he opened the note, which contained these words: —

"I will wait for you on the high-road to Légé; follow me, but do not attempt to join me or speak to me. The coachman will stay at the inn with the cabriolet."

The traveller burned the note, poured himself out a glass of wine, with which he merely wet his lips, told the coachman to stay where he was and expect him on the following evening, and left the inn on foot, without attracting the innkeeper's attention, or at any rate, without the innkeeper's attention seeming to be attracted to him.

At the end of the village he saw his man, who was cutting a cane from a hawthorn hedge. The cane being cut, the peasant continued his way, stripping the twigs off the stick as he walked along. Maître Marc followed him for a mile and a half, or thereabout.

By this time it was quite dark, and the peasant entered an isolated house standing on the right of the road. The traveller hastened on and went in almost at the same moment as his guide. No one was there when he reached the threshold except a woman in the room that looked out on the high-road. The peasant was standing before her, apparently awaiting the traveller. As soon as the latter apppeared the peasant said to the woman: —

"This is the gentleman to be guided."

Then, having said these words, he went out, not giving time to the traveller he had conducted to reward him with either thanks or money. When the traveller, who followed the man with his eyes, turned his astonished gaze on the mistress of the house, she merely signed to him to sit down, and then without taking further notice of his presence, and without addressing him a single word, she went on with her household avocations.

A silence of half an hour ensued, and the traveller was beginning to get impatient, when the master of the house returned home. Without showing any sign of surprise or curiosity, he bowed to his guest; but he looked at his wife, who repeated, *verbatim*, the words of the peasant: "This is the gentleman to be guided."

The master of the house then gave the stranger one of those uneasy, shrewd, and rapid glances, which belong exclusively to the Vendéan peasantry. Then, almost immediately, his face resumed its habitual expression, which was one of mingled good-humor and simplicity, as he approached his guest, cap in hand.

"Monsieur wishes to travel through this region?" he said.

"Yes, my friend," replied Maître Marc; "I am desirous of going farther."

"Monsieur has his papers, no doubt?"

"Of course."

"In order?"

"They cannot be more so."

"Under his war name, or his real name?"

"Under my real name."

"I am obliged, in order that I make no mistake, to ask monsieur to show me those papers."

"Is it absolutely necessary?"

"Yes; because until I have seen them I cannot tell monsieur whether he will be absolutely safe in travelling in these parts."

The traveller drew out his passport, which bore date the 28th of February.

"Here they are," he said.

The peasant took the papers, cast his eyes over them to see if the description tallied with the individual before him, refolded the papers, and returned them, saying: —

"It is all right. Monsieur can go everywhere with those papers."

"And will you find some one to guide me?"

"Yes, monsieur."

"I wish to start as soon as possible."

"I will saddle the horses at once."

The master of the house went out. In ten minutes he returned.

"The horses are ready," he said.

"And the guide?"

"He is waiting."

The traveller went out and found a farm-hand already in his saddle, holding another horse by the bridle. Maître Marc perceived that the led horse was intended for his riding, the farm-hand for his guide. In fact, he had scarcely put his foot in the stirrup before his new conductor started, not less silently than his predecessor. It was nine o'clock, and the night was dark.

III.

HOW PERSONS TRAVELLED IN THE DEPARTMENT OF THE LOWER LOIRE IN MAY, 1832.

After riding for an hour and a half, during which time not a word was exchanged between the traveller and his guide, they reached the gate of one of those buildings peculiar to that region, which are something between a farmhouse and a château. The guide stopped, and made a sign to the traveller to do likewise. Then he dismounted and rapped at the door. A servant opened it.

"Here is a gentleman who wishes to speak to monsieur," said the farm-hand.

"It is impossible," replied the servant. "Monsieur has gone to bed."

"Already!" exclaimed the traveller.

The servant came closer.

"Monsieur spent last night at a rendezvous, and has been nearly all day on horseback," he said.

"No matter," said the guide. "This gentleman must see him; he comes from Monsieur Pascal, and is going to join Petit-Pierre."

"In that case it is different," said the servant. "I will wake monsieur."

"Ask him," said the traveller, "if he can give me a safe guide; a guide is all I want."

"I do not think monsieur would do that," said the servant.

"Why not?"

"Because he will wish to guide monsieur himself," said the man.

He re-entered the house. In five minutes he returned.

"Monsieur wishes to know if monsieur will take anything, or whether he prefers to continue his journey without delay."

"I dined at Nantes and need nothing. I prefer to go on immediately."

The servant again disappeared. A few moments later a young man came out. This time it was not the servant, but the master.

"Under any other circumstances, monsieur," he said, "I should insist on your doing me the honor to rest a while under my roof; but you are no doubt the person whom Petit-Pierre expects from Paris?"

"I am, monsieur."

"Monsieur Marc, then?"

"Yes, Monsieur Marc."

"In that case, let us not lose a moment; you are expected with the utmost impatience." Turning to the farm-hand, he said, "Is your horse fresh?"

"He has only done five miles to-day."

"In that case I'll take him; my horses are all knocked up. Stay here and drink a bottle of wine with Louis. I'll be back in two hours. Louis, take care of your comrade." Then turning to the traveller, he added, "Are you ready, monsieur?"

At an affirmative sign from the latter they started. After a dead silence of a quarter of an hour a cry sounded about a hundred steps before them. Monsieur Marc started and asked what it was.

"It came from our scout," said the Vendéan leader. "He asks in his fashion if the road is clear. Listen, and you will hear the answer."

He stopped his horse and signed to Monsieur Marc to do the same. Almost immediately a second cry was heard coming from a much greater distance. It seemed the echo of the first, so exactly alike were the two sounds.

"We can safely go on; the road is clear," said the Vendéan leader.

"Then we are preceded by a scout?"

"Preceded and followed. We have a man two hundred steps before us and two hundred steps behind us."

"But who are they who answer the scouts?"

"Peasants, whose cottages are along the road. Look attentively at these cottages as you pass them, and you will see a small skylight open and the head of a man come up and remain there motionless, as if made of stone, until we are out of sight. If we were soldiers of some neighboring cantonment the man who looked at us would instantly leave his house by the back-door, and if there were any meeting or assemblage of any kind in the neighborhood warning would be given in time of the approach of the troops." Here the leader interrupted himself. "Listen!" he said.

The two riders stopped.

"This time," said the traveller, "I only heard one cry, I think, — that of our scout."

"You are right; no cry has answered his."

"Which means?"

"That troops are somewhere about."

So saying, he put his horse to a trot; the traveller did the same. Almost at the same moment they heard a hurried step behind them; it was that of their rear scout, who now reached them, running as fast as his legs could carry him. At a fork of the road they found the man who preceded them standing still and undecided. His cry had not been answered from either road, and he was not sure which way was best to take. Both led to the same destination, but the one to left was the longest. After a moment's deliberation between the chief and the guide the latter took the path to the right. The Vendéan and the traveller followed him in about five minutes and were in turn followed by their rear-guard after the same lapse of time. These distances were carefully kept up between the advanced guard, the army corps, and the rear-guard.

Three hundred steps farther on the two royalists found

their forward scout once more stationary. He made them a sign with his hand, requesting silence. Then, in a low voice, he said: —

"A patrol!"

Listening attentively they could hear, though at some distance, the regular tramp of marching men; it was, in fact, that of a small detachment of General Dermoncourt's column making a night inspection.

The traveller and the Vendéan leader were now in one of those sunken roads between banks and hedges so frequent in La Vendée at this period, and more especially during that of the great war, but which are now disappearing and giving place to well-constructed parish roads. The banks on either side were so steep that it would have been impossible to make the horses mount either of them, and there was no way of avoiding the patrol if they met it except by turning short round and gaining some open place where they might scatter to right or left. But in case of flight the patrol of foot-soldiers would, of course, hear the horsemen as plainly as the horsemen heard the foot-soldiers.

Suddenly the forward scout drew the attention of the Vendéan leader by a sign. He had seen, thanks to a momentary gleam of moonlight which instantly disappeared, the flash of bayonets; and his finger, pointing diagonally, showed the Vendéan leader and the traveller the course they ought to follow. The soldiers (to avoid the water which usually flowed through these sunken roads or lanes after rainy weather), instead of marching along the lane, had climbed the bank and were now behind the natural hedge which grew at the top of it. This was on the left of the horsemen. By continuing in this way they would pass within ten feet of the riders and the scouts, who were hidden below them in the sunken lane. If either of the two horses had neighed the little troop would have been taken prisoners; but, as if the animals understood the danger, they were as still as their masters, and the soldiers passed on, without suspecting that any one was near. When the sound of their footfalls died away the travellers breathed again, and once more resumed their march.

A quarter of an hour later they turned from the road and entered the forest of Machecoul. There they were more at their ease; it was not likely that the soldiers would enter the woods at night, or at any rate take any but the mainroads which, like great arteries, passed through it. By taking one of the wood-paths known to the country-people, they had little to fear.

The two gentlemen now dismounted, and left their horses in charge of one of the scouts, while the other disappeared rapidly in the darkness, rendered deeper still by the leafing out of the May foliage. The Vendéan leader and the traveller followed the same path. It was evident that they were nearing the end of their journey. The abandonment of the horses amply proved it.

In fact, Maître Marc and the Vendéan had hardly gone two hundred yards from the place where they left the horses before they heard the hoot of an owl. The Vendéan leader put his hands to his mouth, and in reply to the long, lugubrious howl, he gave the sharp and piercing cry of the screech-owl. The hoot of the horned owl answered back.

"There 's our man," said the Vendéan leader.

A few moments later the sound of steps was heard on the path before them, and their advanced scout came in sight, accompanied by a stranger. This stranger was no other than our friend Jean Oullier, sole and consequently first huntsman to the Marquis de Souday, who had temporarily renounced hunting, occupied as he was by the political events now developing around him.

In his previous introductions the traveller had noticed the use of one formula: "Here is a gentleman who wishes to speak to monsieur." This formula was now changed; and the Vendéan leader said to Jean Oullier, "Here is a gentleman who wishes to speak to Petit-Pierre."

To this Jean Oullier merely replied: —

"Let him follow me."

The traveller stretched out his hand to the Vendéan leader, who shook it cordially. Then he felt in his pocket, intending to divide the contents of his purse between the guides; but the Vendéan gentleman guessed his intention, and laying a hand on his arm, made him a sign not to do a thing which would seem to the worthy peasants an insult.

Maître Marc understood the matter, and a friendly grasp of their hands paid his debt to the peasants, as it had to their leader. After which, Jean Oullier took the path by which he had come, saying two words, with the brevity of an order and the tone of an invitation: —

"Follow me."

The traveller was beginning to get accustomed to these curt, mysterious ways, hitherto unknown to him, which revealed if not actual conspiracy, at least approaching insurrection. Shaded as the Vendéan leader and the guides were by their broad hats, he had scarcely seen their faces; and now in the darkness it was with difficulty that he made out even the form of Jean Oullier, although the latter slackened his pace, little by little, until he fell back almost to the traveller's side. Maître Marc felt that his guide had something to say to him, and he listened attentively. Presently he heard these words, uttered like a murmur: —

"We are watched; a man is following us through the wood. Do not be disturbed if you see me disappear. Wait for me at the place where you lose sight of me."

The traveller answered by a simple motion of the head, which meant, "Very good; as you say."

They walked on fifty steps farther. Suddenly Jean Oullier darted into the wood. Thirty or forty feet in the depths of it a sound was heard like that of a deer rising in affright. The noise went off in the distance, as though it were indeed a deer that had made it. Jean Oullier's steps were heard in the same direction. Then all sounds died away.

The traveller leaned against an oak and waited. At the end of twenty minutes a voice said beside him: —

"Now, we 'll go on."

He quivered. The voice was really that of Jean Oullier, but the old huntsman had come back so gently that not a single sound betrayed his return.

"Well ?" said the traveller.

"Lost time!" exclaimed Jean Oullier.

"No one there ?"

"Some one; but the villain knows the wood as well as I do."

"So that you did n't overtake him ?"

Oullier shook his head as though it cost him too much to put into words that a man had escaped him.

"And you don't know who he was ?"

"I suspect one man," said Jean Oullier, stretching his arm toward the south; "but in any case he is an evil one." Then, as they reached the edge of the woods, he added, "Here we are."

The traveller now saw the farmhouse of Banlœuvre looming up before him. Jean Oullier looked attentively to both sides of the road. The road was clear; he crossed it alone. Then with a pass-key he opened the gate.

"Come!" he said.

Maître Marc crossed the highway rapidly and disappeared through the gate, which closed behind him. A white figure came out on the portico.

"Who 's there ?" asked a woman's voice, but a strong, imperative voice.

"I, Mademoiselle Bertha," responded Jean Oullier.

"You are not alone, my friend ?"

"I have brought the gentleman from Paris who wishes to speak to Petit-Pierre."

Bertha came down the steps and met the traveller.

"Come in, monsieur," she said.

And she led the way into a salon rather poorly furnished, though the floor was admirably waxed and the curtains irreproachably clean. A great fire was burning, and near the fire was a table on which a supper was already served.

"Sit down, monsieur," said the young girl with perfect grace, which, however, was not without a certain masculine tone which gave it much originality. "You must be hungry and thirsty; pray eat and drink. Petit-Pierre is asleep; but he gave orders to be waked if any one arrived from Paris. You have just come from Paris, have you not?"

"Yes, mademoiselle."

"In ten minutes I will return."

And Bertha disappeared like a vision. The traveller remained a few seconds motionless with amazement. He was an observer, and never had he seen more grace and more charm mingled with strength of will than in Bertha's demeanor. She might be, thought he, the young Achilles, disguised as a woman, before he saw the blade of Ulysses. Absorbed in this thought or in others allied to it, the traveller forgot to eat or drink.

Bertha returned as she had promised.

"Petit-Pierre is ready to receive you, monsieur," she said.

The traveller rose; Bertha walked before him. She held in her hand a short taper, which she raised to light the staircase, and which lighted her own face at the same time. The traveller looked admiringly at her beautiful black hair and her fine black eyes, her ivory skin, with all its signs of youth and health, and the firm and easy poise of the figure, which seemed to typify a goddess.

He murmured with a smile, remembering his Virgil, — that man who himself is a smile of antiquity, — "Incessu patuit dea!"

The young girl rapped at the door of a bedroom.

"Come in," replied a woman's voice.

The door opened. The young girl bowed slightly and allowed the traveller to pass her. It was easy to see that humility was not her leading virtue.

The traveller then passed in. The door closed behind him, and Bertha remained outside.

IV.

A LITTLE HISTORY DOES NO HARM.

The room into which Maître Marc was now shown had been recently built; the plastered walls were damp, and the wainscot showed the fibre of its wood under the slight coating of paint that covered it. In this room, lying on a bedstead of common pine roughly put together, he saw a woman, and in that woman he recognized her Royal Highness the Duchesse de Berry.

Maître Marc's attention fixed itself wholly upon her. The sheets of the miserable bed were of the finest lawn, and this luxury of white and exquisite linen was the only thing about her which testified in any degree to her station in the world. A shawl with red and green checkers formed her counterpane. A paltry fireplace of plaster, with a small wooden mantel, warmed the apartment, the only furniture of which was a table covered with papers, on which were a pair of pistols, and two chairs, where lay the garments of a peasant-lad and a brown wig. The chair with the wig stood near the table, that with the clothes was near the bed.

The princess wore on her head one of those woollen *coifs* distinctive of the Vendéan peasant-women, the ends of which fell on her shoulders. By the light of two wax candles, placed on the shabby rosewood night-table (a relic, evidently, of some castle furniture), the duchess was looking through her correspondence. A large number of letters, placed on this table and held in place by a second pair of pistols, which served as a paper-weight, were still unopened.

Madame appeared to be awaiting the new-comer impatiently, for as soon as she saw him she leaned half out of her bed and stretched her two hands toward him. He took them, kissed them respectfully, and the duchess felt a tear from the eyes of her faithful partisan on the hand he kept longest in his own.

"Tears!" she said. "You do not bring me bad news, monsieur, surely?"

"They come from my heart, Madame," replied Maître Marc. "They express my devotion and the deep regret I feel in seeing you so isolated, so lost in this lonely Vendéan farmhouse, — you, whom I have seen —"

He stopped, for the tears choked his voice. The duchess took up his unfinished phrase.

"At the Tuileries, you mean, on the steps of a throne. Well, my good friend, I was far worse guarded and less well served there than I am here. Here I am guarded and served by a fidelity which shows itself in devotion, there I was served by the self-interest that calculates. But come, to business; it makes me uneasy to observe that you are delaying. Give me the news from Paris at once! Is it good news?"

"Pray believe, Madame," said Maître Marc, "I entreat you to believe in my deep regret at being forced to advise prudence, — I, a man of enthusiasm!"

"Ah! ah!" exclaimed the duchess. "While my friends in La Vendée are being killed for my sake, the friends in Paris are prudent, are they? You see I have good reason for telling you I am better served and guarded here than I ever was at the Tuileries."

"Better guarded, yes, Madame; better served, no! There are moments when prudence is the very genius of success."

"But, monsieur," said the duchess, impatiently, "I am as well informed on the state of Paris as you can be, and I know that a revolution is imminent."

"Madame," replied the lawyer, in a firm, sonorous voice,

"we have lived for a year and a half in the midst of riots and tumults, and none of them have yet been able to rise to the level of revolution."

"Louis-Philippe is unpopular."

"Granted; but that does not mean that Henri V. is popular."

"Henri V! Henri V! My son is not Henri V., monsieur; he is Henri IV. the Second."

"As for that, Madame, may I be allowed to say that he is still too young to enable us to be sure of his true name and nature. The more we are devoted to our leader the more we owe him the truth."

"The truth! yes, yes. I ask for it; I want it. But what is the truth?"

"Madame it is this. Unfortunately, the memories of a people are lost when their horizon is narrow. The French people — I mean that material, brute force which makes convulsions and sometimes (when inspired from above) revolutions — has two great recollections that take the place of all others. One goes back forty-three years, the other seventeen years. The first is the taking of the Bastille; in other words the victory of the people over royalty, — a victory that bestowed the tricolor banner upon the nation. The second memory is the double restoration of 1814 and 1815; the victory of royalty over the masses, — a victory which imposed the white banner on the nation. Madame, in great national movements all is symbolic. The tricolor flag is liberty to the people; it bears inscribed upon its pennant the thought, 'By token of this flag we conquer.' The white flag is the banner of despotism; it bears upon its double face the sign, 'By token of this flag we are conquered.'"

"Monsieur!"

"You asked for the truth, Madame; let me, therefore, tell it to you."

"Yes; but after you have told it you will allow me to reply."

"Ah, Madame, I should be glad indeed if your reply could convince me."

"Go on."

"You left Paris on the 28th of July, Madame; you did not witness the fury with which the populace tore down the white flag and trampled on the fleurs-de-lis."

"The flag of Denain and of Taillebourg! the fleurs-de-lis of Saint-Louis and of Louis XIV.!"

"Unhappily, Madame, the populace remember only Waterloo; they know only Louis XVI, — a defeat and an execution. Well, the great difficulty I foresee for your son, the descendant of Saint-Louis and of Louis XIV., is that very flag of Taillebourg and of Denain. If his Majesty Henri V., or Henry IV. the Second, as you so intelligently call him, returns to Paris bearing the white banner, he will not pass the faubourg Saint-Antoine; before he reaches the Bastille he is dead."

"And if he enters with the tricolor, — what then?"

"Worse still, Madame; he is dishonored."

The duchess bounded in her bed. But at first she was silent; then, after a pause, she said: —

"Perhaps it is the truth; but it is hard."

"I promised you the whole truth, and I keep my word."

"But, if that is your conviction, monsieur, why do you remain attached to a party which has no possible chance of success?"

"Because I have sworn allegiance with heart and lips to that white banner without which, and with which, your son can never return, and I would rather die than be dishonored."

The duchess was once more silent.

"But," she said presently, "all this that you tell me does not tally with the information which induced me to come to France."

"No, doubtless it does not, Madame; but you must remember one thing, — if truth does sometimes reach a reigning prince it is never told to a dethroned one."

"Permit me to say that in your capacity as a lawyer, monsieur, you may be suspected of cultivating paradox."

"Paradox, Madame, is one of the many facets of eloquence; only here, in presence of your Royal Highness, my purpose is not to be eloquent, but to be true."

"Pardon me, but you said just now that truth was never told to dethroned princes; either you were mistaken then or you are misleading me now."

The lawyer bit his lips; he was hoist with his own petard.

"Did I say *never*, Madame?"

"You said *never*."

"Then let us suppose there is an exception, and that I am permitted by God to be that exception."

"Agreed. And I now ask, why is truth not told to dethroned princes?"

"Because while princes on their thrones may have, at times, men of satisfied ambition about them, dethroned princes have only inordinate ambitions to satisfy. No doubt, Madame, you have certain generous hearts about you who devote themselves to your cause with complete self-abnegation; but there are, none the less, many others who regard your return to France solely as a path opened to their private ends, to their personal reputation, fortune, honor. There are, besides, dissatisfied men who have lost their position and are craving to re-conquer it and avenge themselves on those who turned them out of it. Well, all such persons take a false view of facts; they cannot perceive the truth of the situation. Their desires become hopes, their hopes beliefs; they dream incessantly of a revolution which may come possibly, but most assuredly not when they expect it. They deceive themselves and they deceive you; they began by lying to themselves, and now they are lying to you. They are dragging you into the danger they are rushing into themselves. Hence the error, the fatal error, into which you are now being hurried, Madame, — an error I implore you to recognize in

Portrait of Louis Philippe.

presence of the truth which I have, so cruelly perhaps, unveiled before your eyes."

"In short," said the duchess, all the more impatiently because these words confirmed those she had heard during the conference at the château de Souday, "what is it that you have brought in your toga, Maître Cicero? Is it peace or war? Out with it!"

"As it is proper that we maintain the traditions of constitutional royalty, I answer your Highness that it is for her, in her capacity as regent, to decide."

"Yes, indeed; and have my Chambers refuse me subsidies if I do not decide as they wish. Oh, Maître Marc, I know the fictions of your constitutional *régime*, the principal feature of which is to do the work, not of those who speak wisely, but of those who talk the most. But you must have heard the opinions of my faithful and trusty adherents as to the present opportunity for a great uprising. What is that opinion? What is your own opinion? We have talked of truth; truth is sometimes an awful spectre. No matter; woman as I am, I dare to evoke it."

"It is because I am convinced there is the stuff of twenty kings in Madame's head and heart that I have not hesitated to take upon myself a mission which I feel to be distressing."

"Ah, here we come to the point! Less diplomacy, if you please, Maître Marc; speak out firmly, as you should to one who is, what I am here, a soldier."

Then, observing that the traveller, taking off his cravat, was tearing it apart in search of a paper.

"Give it me! give it me!" she cried; "I can do that quicker than you."

The letter was written in cipher.

"I should lose time in making it out," said the duchess; "read it to me. It must be easy to you, who probably know what is in it."

Maître Marc took the paper from her hand and read, without hesitating, the following letter: —

"Those persons in whom an honorable confidence has been reposed cannot refrain from testifying their regret at unwise councils which have brought about the present crisis. Those councils were given, no doubt, by zealous men; but those men little understand the actual state of things, or the condition of the public mind.

They deceive themselves if they think there is any possibility of an uprising in Paris. It would be impossible to find twelve hundred men, not connected with the police, who would consent to make a riot in the streets and face a struggle with the National Guard and the faithful garrison.

They deceive themselves likewise about La Vendée, just as they deceived themselves about Marseille and the South. La Vendée, that land of devotion and sacrifice, is controlled by a numerous army supported by the population of the cities, which are almost wholly anti-legitimist; a rising of the peasantry could only end in devastating the country and in consolidating the present government by an easy victory.

It is thought that if the mother of Henri V. be really in France she should hasten her departure as much as possible, after exhorting all the Vendéan leaders to keep absolutely quiet. If, instead of organizing civil war, she appeals for peace, she would have the double glory of doing a grand and courageous deed and of preventing the effusion of French blood.

The true friends of Legitimacy, who have not been informed of present intentions, and not consulted on the perilous risks which are being taken, and who have known nothing of acts until they were accomplished, desire to place the responsibility of those acts on the persons who have advised and promoted them. They disclaim either honor or blame for whatever result of fortune may be the upshot."

During the reading of this communication Madame was a prey to the keenest agitation. Her face, habitually pale, was flushed; her trembling hand pushed back the woollen cap she wore, and was thrust through and through her hair. She did not utter a word or interrupt the reader in any way, but it was evident that her calm preceded a tempest. In order to divert it, Maître Marc said, as he folded the letter and gave it to her:—

"I did not write that letter, Madame."

"No," replied the duchess, unable to restrain herself any longer; "but he who brought it was capable of writing it."

Maître Marc felt sure that he should gain nothing in dealing with that eager, impressionable nature if he lowered his head. He therefore drew himself up to his full height.

"Yes," he said; "and he blushes for a moment's weakness. And he now declares to your Royal Highness that while he does not approve of certain expressions in the letter he shares the sentiment that dictated it."

"Sentiment!" cried the duchess. "Call it selfishness; call it caution, that comes very near to —"

"Cowardice, you mean, Madame. Yes, that heart is cowardly, indeed, that leaves all and comes to share a situation it never counselled. Yes, the man is selfish who stands here and says, 'You asked for the truth, Madame, and here it is; but if it pleases your Royal Highness to advance to a death as useless as it is certain I shall march beside you.'"

The duchess was silent for a few moments; then she resumed, more gently: —

"I appreciate your devotion, monsieur, but you do not understand the temper of La Vendée; you derive your information from those who oppose the movement."

"So be it. Let us suppose that which is not; let us suppose that La Vendée will surround you with battalions and spare neither blood nor sacrifices for the cause; nevertheless La Vendée is not France."

"Having told me that the people of Paris hate the fleur-de-lis and despise the white flag, do you now want me to believe that all France shares those feelings of the Parisian populace?"

"Alas! Madame, France is logical; it is we who are pursuing chimeras in dreaming of an alliance between the divine right of kings and popular sovereignty, — two things which howl and rend each other when coupled.

The divine right leads fatally and inevitably to absolutism, and France will no longer submit to absolutism."

"Absolutism! absolutism! a fine word to frighten children!"

"No, it is not a fine word; it is a terrible one. Perhaps we are nearer to the thing itself than we think; but I grieve to say to you, Madame, that I do not believe that God reserves to your royal son the dangerous honor of muzzling the popular lion."

"Why not, monsieur?"

"Because it is he whom that lion most distrusts. The moment it sees him approaching in the distance, the lion shakes his mane, sharpens his teeth and claws, and will suffer him to come nearer only for the purpose of springing upon him. No one could be the grandson of Louis XVI. with impunity, Madame."

"Then, according to you, the Bourbon dynasty has seen its last days."

"God grant that such an idea may never come to me, Madame. What I mean is that revolutions never go backward; I believe that if they once come to birth it is best not to stop their development. It is attempting the impossible; it is like trying to drive a mountain torrent backward to its source. Either our present revolution will be fruitful of national good,—in which case, Madame, I know the patriotism of your feelings too well not to be sure you would accept it, —or it will be a barren failure, and then the faults of those who have seized the sovereign power will serve your son far better than all our efforts could."

"But, in that case, monsieur, things may go on thus to the end of time."

"Madame, his Majesty Henri V. is a principle, and principles share with God the privilege of having their kingdom in eternity."

"Therefore, it is your opinion that I ought to renounce my present hopes, abandon my compromised friends, and three days hence, when they take up arms, leave them in the lurch and justify the man who tells them, 'Marie-Caroline, for whom you are ready to fight, for whom you are ready to die, despairs of her prospects and recoils at fate; Marie-Caroline is afraid.' Oh, no; never, never, never, monsieur!"

"Your friends will not be able to make you that reproach, Madame, for they will not take arms, as you suppose, a few days hence."

"Are you ignorant that the day is fixed for the 24th?"

"The order is countermanded."

"Countermanded!" cried the duchess; "when?"

"To-day."

"To-day!" she exclaimed, lifting herself up by her wrists. "By whom?"

"By the man you yourself commanded them to obey."

"The maréchal?"

"The maréchal, following the instructions of the committee in Paris."

"But," cried the duchess, "am I to be of no account?"

"You, Madame!" exclaimed the messenger, falling on one knee and clasping his hands, — "you are all. That is why we seek your safety; it is why we will not let you be sacrificed in a useless effort; that is why we fear to let you risk your popularity by a defeat."

"Monsieur, monsieur," said the duchess, "if Maria Theresa's counsellors had been as timid as mine she would never have re-conquered the throne of her son."

"It is, on the contrary, to secure, at a later period, your son's throne that we now say to you, Madame, 'Leave France; let the people know you as an angel of peace, not as a demon of war.'"

"Oh! oh!" exclaimed the duchess, pressing her clenched fists to her eyes; "what humiliation! what cowardice!"

Maître Marc continued as though he did not hear her, or rather as if his resolution to make known a truth to her mind was so fixed that nothing could change it.

"All precautions are taken to enable Madame to leave

France without molestation. A vessel is cruising in the bay of Bourgneuf; your Highness can be on board of her in three hours."

"Oh, noble land of Vendée!" cried the duchess; "could I have believed you would repulse me, drive me from you, — me who came to you in the name of your God and your king? Ah! I thought that Paris alone was unfaithful, ungrateful; but you, — you to whom I come seeking the recovery of a throne, you deny me so much as a place of burial! Oh, no, no; I never could have believed it!"

"But you will go, will you not, Madame?" said the messenger, still on his knees, with clasped hands.

"Yes, I will go," said the duchess. "I will leave France. But remember this, I shall never return, for I will never come with foreigners. They are only waiting, as you well know, for the right moment to form a coalition against Philippe. When that moment comes they will ask me for my son, — not that they care for him more than they cared for Louis XVI. in 1792, or Louis XVIII. in 1813, but he can be made the means of their having a party in Paris. Well, I say to you, no! they shall not have my son; no! they shall not have him, not for a kingdom! Rather than that I will fly with him to the mountains of Calabria. I tell you, monsieur, if he must buy the throne by the cession of a province, a town, a fortress, a house, a cottage like that I am now in, I swear as regent and as his mother, that he shall never be king of France. And now, that is all I have to say to you. Go back to those who sent you and repeat my words."

Maître Marc rose and bowed to the duchess, expecting that as he left she would offer one of the two hands she had stretched out to him when he came; but she was motionless, stern, her fists were closed, her brows knitted.

"God guard your Highness!" said the messenger, believing it was useless to stay longer, and thinking, not without reason, that as long as he was there not a muscle of that generous organization would give way.

He was not mistaken; but the door was scarcely closed behind him before Madame, exhausted by the strain, fell back upon her bed and sobbed aloud: —

"Oh, Bonneville! my poor Bonneville!"

V

PETIT-PIERRE RESOLVES ON KEEPING A BRAVE HEART AGAINST MISFORTUNE.

Immediately after the conversation we have just reported, the traveller left the farmhouse; he was anxious to be back at Nantes before the middle of the day. A few moments after his departure, though it was scarcely day-light, Petit-Pierre, dressed in her peasant's clothes, left her room and went to the hall on the ground-floor of the farmhouse.

This was a vast room, the dingy walls of which were denuded in many places of the plaster that originally covered them, while the beams across the ceiling were blackened by smoke. It was furnished with a large ward-robe of polished oak, the brass locks and handles of which sparkled in the shadow of the dull, brown masses about it. The rest of the furniture consisted of two beds, standing parallel, surrounded by curtains of green serge, two common pitchers, and a clock in a tall carved wooden case, the ticking of which was the only sign of life in the silence of the night.

The fireplace was broad and high, and its shelf was draped with a band of serge like that of the curtains; only, instead of fading to a rusty green, this piece of stuff, owing to the smoke, had changed to a dingy brown. On this mantel-shelf were the usual adornments, — a wax figure, representing the Child Jesus, covered by a glass shade; two china pots, containing artificial flowers, covered by gauze to protect them from flies; a double-barrelled gun; and a branch of consecrated holly.

This hall was separated from the stable by a thin board partition, and through this partition, in which were sliding panels, the cows poked their heads to eat the provender that was laid for them on the floor of the room.

When Petit-Pierre opened the door a man who was warming himself under the high mantel of the fireplace rose and walked away respectfully to leave his seat free to the new-comer. But Petit-Pierre made him a sign with one hand to resume his chair, gently pushing him with the other. Petit-Pierre then fetched a stool and sat down in the farther corner of the fireplace opposite to the man, who was no other than Jean Oullier. Then she leaned her head on her hand, put her elbow on her knee, and sat absorbed in reflection, while her foot, beaten with a feverish motion which communicated a tremulous movement to the whole body, showed that she was under the shock of some deep vexation.

Jean Oullier, who, on his side, had subjects for thought and anxiety, remained silent and gloomy, twisting his pipe, which he had taken from his mouth when Petit-Pierre entered the room, mechanically in his fingers, and issuing from his meditations only to give vent to sighs that seemed like threats, or to push the burning logs together on the hearth.

Petit-Pierre spoke first.

"Were not you smoking when I came in, my brave fellow?" she said.

"Yes," he replied, with a very unusual tone of respect in his voice.

"Why don't you continue?"

"I am afraid it may annoy you."

"Nonsense! We are bivouacking, or something very like it, my friend; and I am all the more anxious it should be comfortable for all, for it is our last night together."

Enigmatical as these words were to him, Jean Oullier did not allow himself to ask their meaning. With the wonderful tact which characterizes the Vendéan peasantry, he refrained from profiting by the permission given, but without showing by look or sign that he knew the real rank and quality of Petit-Pierre.

In spite of Petit-Pierre's own pre-occupations, she noticed the clouds which darkened the peasant's face. She again broke silence.

"What is the matter, my dear Jean Oullier?" she asked. "Why do you look so gloomy when I should expect, on the contrary, to see you joyful?"

"Why should I be joyful?" asked the old keeper.

"Because a good and faithful servant like you shares in the happiness of his masters; and I think your young mistress looks happy enough to have a little of her joy reflected in your face."

"God grant her joy may last!" replied Jean Oullier, with a doubtful smile.

"Why, Jean, surely you do not object to marriages of inclination! For my part, I love them; they are the only ones I have ever, in all my life, been willing to help on."

"I have no objection to such marriages," replied Jean Oullier; "but I have a great objection to this husband."

"Why?"

Jean Oullier did not reply.

"Speak," said Petit-Pierre.

The Vendéan shook his head.

"Tell me, I beg of you, my dear Jean. I know your young ladies, and I know now that they are like your own children to you; you need not have any secrets from me. Though I am not the Holy Father himself, you know very well that I have power to bind and unbind."

"I know that you can do much," said Jean Oullier.

"Then tell me why you disapprove of this marriage?"

"Because disgrace attaches to the name every woman must bear if she marries Monsieur Michel de la Logerie; and this woman ought not to give up one of the noblest names in the land to take it."

"Ah, my dear Jean," said Petit-Pierre, with a sad

smile, "you are doubtless ignorant that in these days children do not inherit as a tradition either the virtues or the faults of their ancestors."

"Yes, I was ignorant of that," said Jean Oullier.

"It is task enough," continued Petit-Pierre, "or so it appears, for each man to answer for himself in our day. See how many fail! — how many are missing from our ranks, where the name they bear ought to have kept them! Let us, therefore, be grateful to those who, in spite of their father's example, in spite of their family ties, or the temptations to their personal ambition, come to our banner with the old chivalric sentiment of devotion and fidelity in misfortune."

Jean Oullier raised his head and said, with a look of hatred he did not attempt to conceal: —

"You may be ignorant — "

Petit-Pierre interrupted him.

"I am not ignorant," she said. "I know the crime you lay to the Logerie father; but I know also what I owe to the son, wounded for me and still bleeding from that wound. As to his father's crime, — if his father really committed it, which God alone can decide, — he expiated that crime by a violent death."

"Yes," replied Jean Oullier, lowering his head; "that is true."

"Who dares to penetrate the judgments of Providence? Can you venture to say that when he, in his turn, appeared before that Judgment-seat, pale and bloody from a violent death, the Divine mercy was not laid upon his head? Why, then, if God himself may have been satisfied, should you be more stern, more implacable than God?"

Jean Oullier listened without replying. Every word of Petit-Pierre made the religious chords of his heart vibrate, and shook his resolutions of hatred toward Baron Michel, but did not uproot them altogether.

"Monsieur Michel," continued Petit-Pierre, "is a good and brave young man, gentle and modest, simple and devoted; he is rich, which certainly does no harm. I think that your young mistress, with her rather self-willed character and her habits of independence, could not do better. I am convinced she will be perfectly happy with a man of his nature. Why ask more of God, my poor Jean Oullier? Forget the past," added Petit-Pierre, with a sigh. "Alas! if we remembered all, we could love nothing."

Jean Oullier shook his head.

"Monsieur Petit-Pierre," he said, "you speak well and like a good Christian; but there are things that cannot be driven from the memory, and, unfortunately for Monsieur Michel, my connection with his father is one of them."

"I do not ask your secrets, Jean," replied Petit-Pierre, gravely; "but the young baron, as you know, has shed his blood for me. He has been my guide; he has given me a refuge in this house, which is his. I feel something more than regard for him, — I feel gratitude; and it would be a real grief to me to think that dissensions existed among my friends. So, my dear Jean Oullier, in the name of the devotion you have shown to my person, I ask you, if not to abjure your memories, — for, as you say, we cannot always do that, — at any rate, to stifle your hatred until time, until the sight of the happiness the son of your enemy bestows upon the child you have brought up and loved, has effaced that hatred from your soul."

"Let that happiness come in the way God wills, and I will thank Him for it; but I do not believe it will enter the château de Souday with Monsieur Michel."

"Why not, if you please, my good Jean?"

"Because the closer I look, Monsieur Petit-Pierre, the more I doubt whether Monsieur Michel loves Mademoiselle Bertha."

Petit-Pierre shrugged her shoulders impatiently.

"Permit me, my dear Jean Oullier," she said, "to doubt your perspicacity in love."

"You may be right," said the old Vendéan; "but if this marriage with Mademoiselle Bertha — the greatest honor to which that young man can aspire — really fulfils his wishes, why did he make such haste to leave the farm-house; and why has he been roaming all night in the woods, like a madman?"

"If he has been wandering all night, as you say," said Petit-Pierre, smiling, "it is because happiness will not let him rest; if he has really left the farm, it is probably on some business for the cause."

"I hope so. I am not of those who think only of themselves; and though I am quite determined to leave the family when the son of Michel enters it, I will none the less pray God, night and morning, to promote the child's happiness. At the same time, I shall watch that man. If he loves her, as you say he does, I will try to prevent my presentiments from being realized, — presentiments, I mean, that instead of happiness he will only bring despair upon his wife."

"Thank you, Jean Oullier. Then, I may hope — you promise me, don't you? — that you will not show your teeth to my young friend?"

"I shall keep my hatred and my distrust in the depths of my heart, and only bring them forth in case he justifies them; that is all I can promise you. Do not ask me to like him, or respect him."

"Unconquerable race!" muttered Petit-Pierre, in a low voice; "it is that which has made thee so strong, so grand."

"Yes," replied Jean Oullier to this aside, said loud enough for the old Vendéan to overhear it, — "yes; we of this region, we have but one love and one hatred. Can you complain of that?"

And he looked fixedly at Petit-Pierre, with a sort of respectful challenge.

"No," said the latter; "and I complain of it the less because it is nearly all that remains to Henri V. of his heritage of fourteen centuries, — and it is powerless, they say."

"Who says so?" cried the Vendéan, rising, in a tone that was almost threatening.

"You will soon know. We have talked of your interests, Jean Oullier, and I am not sorry, for our talk has been a truce to thoughts that were sad indeed. Now I must return to my own affairs. What time is it?"

"Half-past four."

"Then wake up our friends. Their political anxieties allow them to sleep; not so with me, for my politics are of one sole thing, — maternal love. Go, friend!"

Jean Oullier went out. Petit-Pierre, with bowed head, walked up and down the room; sometimes she stamped with impatience, and wrung her hands in despair. Presenty she returned to the hearth. Two big tears were rolling down her cheeks, and her emotion seemed to choke her. Then she fell on her knees, and clasping her hands, prayed to God, the Giver of all good, the Dispenser of crowns, to enlighten and guide her resolutions and to grant her either an indomitable power to fulfil her task or the resignation to endure defeat."

VI.

HOW JEAN OULLIER PROVED THAT WHEN THE WINE IS DRAWN IT IS BEST TO DRINK IT.

Some minutes later Gaspard, Louis Renaud, and the Marquis de Souday entered the room. Seeing Petit-Pierre on her knees, absorbed in prayer and meditation, they paused on the threshold; and the Marquis de Souday, who had thought proper to salute the reveille, as in the good old times, with a song, stopped short in his tune respectfully.

But Petit-Pierre had heard the opening of the door. She rose and addressed those who stood there.

"Come in, gentlemen, and forgive me for disturbing you so early," she said; "but I have important determinations to announce to you."

"On the contrary, it is we who ought to ask your Royal Highness's pardon for not foreseeing her wishes and for having slept while we might have been useful to her," said Louis Renaud.

"A truce to compliments, my friend," interrupted Petit-Pierre. "That appanage of royalty is ill-timed now that royalty is deserted and engulfed for the second time."

"What can you mean ?"

"I mean, my good and dear friends," resumed Petit-Pierre turning her back to the fireplace, while the Vendéans stood in a circle round her, — "I mean that I have called you to me that I may now give back your promises and bid you farewell."

"Give back our promises! bid us farewell!" cried her astonished partisans. "Your Royal Highness is surely not thinking of leaving us ?"

Then, all together, looking at each other, they cried out: —

"It is impossible!"

"Nevertheless, I must."

"Why so?"

"Because I am advised, — more than that, I am adjured to do so."

"By whom?"

"By those whose judgment and intelligence I cannot doubt, any more than I distrust their devotion and fidelity."

"But for what reasons? — under what pretexts?"

"It seems that the royalist cause is despaired of even in La Vendée; the white banner is a rag which France repudiates. I am told there are not in Paris twelve hundred men who, for a few francs, would begin a riot in the streets; that it is false to say that we have sympathizers in the army, false that certain of the government are true to us, false that the Bocage is ready to rise as one man to defend the rights of Henri V. — "

"But," interrupted the noble Vendéan who had for the time changed a name illustrious in the great war for that of Gaspard, and who seemed incapable of longer controlling himself, "who gives such advice? Who speaks of La Vendée with such assurance? Who measures our devotion, and says, 'Thus far and no farther shall it go'?"

"Various royalist committees that I need not name to you, but whose opinion we must regard."

"Royalist committees!" cried the Marquis de Souday. Ha! *parbleu!* I know them; and if Madame will believe me, we had better treat their advice as the late Marquis de Charette treated the advice of the royalist committees of his day."

"How was that, my brave Souday?" said Petit-Pierre.

"The respect I have for your Royal Highness," replied the marquis, with magnificent self-possession, "will not, unfortunately, allow of my specifying further."

Petit-Pierre could not help smiling.

"Ah!" she said; "we no longer live in the good old times, my poor marquis. Monsieur de Charette was an autocratic sovereign in his own camp, and the Regent Marie-Caroline will never be anything but a very constitutional regent. The proposed uprising can succeed only on condition of complete agreement among all those who desire its success. Now, I ask you, does that complete agreement exist when, on the eve of the uprising, notice is given to the general that three fourths of those on whom he counted would not take part in it?"

"What matter for that?" cried the Marquis de Souday; "the fewer we are at the rendezvous, the greater the glory to those who appear."

"Madame," said Gaspard, gravely, "they went to you, and they said to you, — when perhaps you had no thought of re-entering France, — 'The men who deposed King Charles X. are held at arm's length by the present government and reduced to impotence; the ministry is so composed that you will find few if any changes necessary to make there; the clergy, a stationary and immovable power, will lend its whole influence to the re-establishment of the legitimate royalty by divine right; the courts are still administered by men who owe their all to the Restoration; the army, fundamentally obedient, is under the orders of a leader who has said that in public policy there should be more than one flag; the people, made sovereign in 1830, has fallen under the yoke of the most idiotic and most inept of aristocracies. Come, then,' they said, 'your entry into France will be another return from Elba. The population will everywhere crowd around you to hail the last scion of our kings whom the nation desires to proclaim!' On the faith of these words you have come to us, Madame; and at your coming we have risen to arms. I hold it, therefore, an error for our cause and a shame for ourselves that this retreat, which would impeach your own political sagacity and prove our personal powerlessness, has been demanded of you."

"Yes," said Petit-Pierre, who by a singular turn of fate found herself called upon to defend a course which was breaking her heart, — "yes; all you say is true. I was promised all that; but it is neither your fault nor mine, my brave, true friends, if fools have taken baseless hopes for realities. Impartial history will say that when I was accused of being a faithless mother (and I have been so accused) I answered, as I was bound to answer, 'Here I am, ready to make all sacrifices!' History will also say of you, my loyal friends, that the more my cause seemed hopeless and abandoned the less you hesitated in your devotion to it. But it is a matter of honor with me not to put that devotion to the proof uselessly. Let us talk plainly, friends. Let us come down to figures; they are practical. How many men do you think we can muster at this moment?"

"Ten thousand at the first signal."

"Alas!" said Petit-Pierre; "that is many, but not enough. Louis-Philippe has at least four hundred and eighty thousand unemployed troops, not to speak of the National Guard."

"But think of the defections of the officers who will resign," said the marquis.

"Well," said Petit-Pierre, addressing Gaspard, "I place my destiny and that of my son in your hands. Tell me, assure me, on your honor as a gentleman, that we have two chances in ten of success, and instead of ordering you to lay down your arms, I will stay among you to share your perils and your fate."

At this direct appeal, not to his feelings but to his convictions, Gaspard bent his head and made no answer.

"You see," resumed Petit-Pierre, "that your judgment and your heart are not in unison. It would be a crime in me to use a chivalry which common-sense condemns. Let us, therefore, not discuss that which has been decided, — wisely decided, perhaps. Let us rather pray God to send me back to you in better times and under more favorable auspices. Meantime, let us now think only of my departure."

No doubt the gentlemen present felt the necessity of this resolution, little as it agreed with their feelings. Believing that the duchess was fully determined on it, they answered nothing and only turned away to hide their tears. The Marquis de Souday walked about the room with an impatience he did not attempt to disguise.

"Yes," said Petit-Pierre, bitterly, after a long silence, — "yes, some have said, like Pilate, 'I wash my hands of it,' and my heart, so strong in danger, so strong to meet death, has yielded; for it cannot face in cold blood the responsibility of failure and the useless shedding of blood. Others — "

"Blood that flows for the faith is never uselessly shed," said a voice from the chimney-corner. "God himself has said it, and, humble as I am, I dare to repeat the words of God. Every man who believes and dies for his belief is a martyr; his blood enriches the earth and hastens the harvest."

"Who said that?" asked Petit-Perre, eagerly, rising on the tips of her toes.

"I," said Jean Oullier, simply, getting up from the stool on which he was sitting, and entering the circle of nobles and leaders.

"You, my brave fellow!" cried Petit-Pierre, delighted to find a reinforcement at the very moment she seemed to be abandoned by all. "Then you don't agree with the Parisian gentlemen. Come here, and speak your mind. In these days Jacques Bonhomme is never out of place, even at a royal council."

"I am so little of the opinion that you ought to leave France," said Jean Oullier, "that if I had the honor to be a gentleman, like those present, I should lock the door and bar your way and say, 'You shall not leave us!'"

"But your reasons? I am eager to hear them. Speak, speak, my Jean!"

"My reasons? — my reasons are that you are our flag; and so long as one of your soldiers is left standing, be he the humblest of your army, he should bear it aloft and steady until death makes it his winding-sheet."

"Go on, go on, Jean Oullier! You speak well."

"My reasons? — one is that you are the first of your race who have come to fight with those who fight for its cause, and it would be a shameful thing to let you go without a sword being drawn from its scabbard."

"Go on, go on, Jacques Bonhomme!" cried Petit-Pierre, striking her hands together.

"But," interrupted Louis Renaud, alarmed at the attention the duchess gave to Jean Oullier, "the withdrawals we have just heard of deprive the movement of all chance of success; it will be nothing more than a mere skirmish."

"No, no; that man is right!" cried Gaspard, who had yielded with great reluctance to Petit-Pierre's arguments. "An attempt, if only a skirmish, is better than the non-existence into which we should drop. A skirmish is a date, a fact; it will stand in history, and the day will come when the people will forget all except the courage of those who led it. If it does not lead to the recovery of the throne it will at least leave traces on the memory of nations. Who would remember the name of Charles Edward were it not for the skirmishes of Preston-Pans and Culloden? Ah, Madame, I long to do as this brave peasant advises!"

"And you would be all the more right, Monsieur le comte," said Jean Oullier, with an assurance which showed that these questions, apparently above his level, were familiar to him, — "you would be all the more right because the principal object of her Royal Highness, that to which she is even willing to sacrifice the monarchy confided to her regency, — I mean the welfare of the people, — will otherwise fail."

"How do you mean?" asked Petit-Pierre.

"The moment Madame withdraws and the government

knows she is safely out of the country, persecutions will begin; and they will be the more keen, the more violent, because we shall have shown ourselves daunted. You are rich, you gentlemen, — you can escape by flight, you can have vessels to wait for you at the mouths of the Loire and the Charente. Your country is everywhere, in many lands. But as for us poor peasants, we are tethered like the goats to the soil that feeds us; we would rather face death than exile."

"And your conclusion is, my brave Jean Oullier — "

"My conclusion is, Monsieur Petit-Pierre," said the Vendéan, "that when the wine is drawn it is best to drink it; we have taken arms, and having taken them, we ought to fight without delay."

"Let us fight!" cried Petit-Pierre, enthusiastically. "The voice of the people is the voice of God. I have faith in that of Jean Oullier."

"Let us fight!" echoed the marquis.

"Let us fight!" said Louis Renaud.

"Well then, what day shall we decide on for the first outbreak?" asked Petit-Pierre.

"Why," said Gaspard, "I thought it was decided for the 24th!"

"Yes; but these gentlemen in Paris have countermanded the order."

"Without informing you?" cried the marquis. "Don't they know that men are shot for less than that?"

"I forgave them," said Petit-Pierre, stretching out her hand. "Besides, those who did it are civilians, not soldiers."

"This counter-order and delay are most unfortunate," said Gaspard, in a low tone; "had I known of it — "

"What?" asked Petit-Pierre.

"I might not have agreed in the opinion of that peasant."

"Oh, nonsense!" cried Petit-Pierre; "you heard what he said, dear Gaspard, — when the wine is drawn it is best to drink it. Let us drink it gayly, gentlemen, even though it be that with which the lord of Beaumanoir refreshed himself at the fight of the gallant Thirty. Come, Marquis de Souday, find me pen, ink, and paper in this farmhouse where your future son-in-law has given me hospitality."

The marquis hastened to search for what Petit-Pierre wanted; and while opening drawers and closets and rummaging the clothes and linen of the farmer, he contrived to wring Jean Oullier's hand and whisper: —

"You talked gold, my brave *gars;* never one of your tally-hos rejoiced my heart like that "boot-and-saddle" you 've just rung out."

Then, having found what he wanted he carried it to Petit-Pierre. The latter dipped the pen into the ink-bottle, and in her firm, bold, large handwriting, she wrote as follows: —

MY DEAR MARÉCHAL, — I remain among you. Be so good as to come to me.

I remain, inasmuch as my presence has already compromised many of my faithful followers, and it would be cowardice on my part to abandon them. Besides, I hope, in spite of this unfortunate counter-order, that God will grant us victory.

Farewell, Monsieur le maréchal: do not give in your resignation, for Petit-Pierre will not give in hers.

PETIT-PIERRE.

"And now," said Petit-Pierre, folding the letter, "what day shall we fix for the uprising ?"

"Thursday, May 31," said the marquis, thinking that the nearest time was the best, "if that is satisfactory to you."

"No," said Gaspard; "excuse me, Monsieur le marquis, "but it seems to me best to choose the night of Sunday, the 3d to the 4th of June. On Sunday, after high mass, the peasants of all the parishes assemble in the porches of their different churches, and the captains will have an opportunity to communicate the order without exciting suspicion."

"Your knowledge of the manners and customs of this

region is a great help, my friend," said Petit-Pierre, "and I agree to your advice. Let the date be therefore the night of the 3d to the 4th of June."

Whereupon, she began at once to write the following order: —

Having resolved not to leave the provinces of the West, but to confide myself to their fidelity, — a fidelity so often proved, — I rely upon you, monsieur, to take all necessary measures in your division for the call to arms which is appointed to take place during the night of the 3d and 4th of June.

I summon to my side all faithful hearts. God will help us to save the country; no danger, no fatigue, shall discourage me. I shall be present at the first engagement.

To this document Petit-Pierre signed her name as follows: —

MARIE-CAROLINE,
Regent of France.

"There, the die is cast!" cried Petit-Pierre. "Now it remains to conquer or die."

"And now," added the marquis, "if twenty counter-orders are sent to me, I 'll ring that tocsin on the 4th of June, and then — yes, damn it, after us the deluge!"

"One thing is absolutely necessary," said Petit-Pierre, showing her order. "This order must immediately and infallibly reach the various division commanders so as to neutralize the bad effects of the manifesto sent from Nantes."

"Alas!" said Gaspard; "God grant that luckless counter-order may reach the country districts in time to paralyze the first movement and yet leave vigor for the second. I fear the reverse; I am terribly afraid that many of our brave fellows will be the victims of their courage and their isolation."

"That is why I think we ought not to lose a moment, messieurs," said Petit-Pierre, "but use our legs while waiting to use our arms. You, Gaspard, inform the divisions of Upper and Lower Poitou. Monsieur le Marquis de Souday will do the same in the Retz and Mauges regions. You, my dear Louis Renaud, must explain it all to your Bretons. But who will undertake to carry my despatch to the maréchal? He is at Nantes; and your faces are far too well known there to allow me to send any of you on this errand."

"I will go," said Bertha, who had heard, in the alcove where she was resting with her sister, the sound of voices, and had risen to share in the discussion. "That is one of my functions as aide-de-camp."

"Certainly it is; but your dress, my dear child," replied Petit-Pierre, "will not meet the approval of the Nantes people, charming as I myself think it."

"Therefore my sister will not go to Nantes, Madame," said Mary, coming forward; "but I will, if you permit me. I can wear the dress of a peasant-woman, and leave your Royal Highness her first aide-de-camp."

Bertha wished to insist; but Petit-Pierre, whispering in her ear, said: —

"Stay, my dear Bertha; I have something to say to you about Baron Michel. We will plan a project he will not oppose, I am very sure."

Bertha blushed, lowered her head, and left her sister to take possession of the letter and convey it to Nantes.

VII.

HEREIN IS EXPLAINED HOW AND WHY BARON MICHEL DECIDED TO GO TO NANTES.

We have mentioned already, incidentally, that Michel had left the farmhouse; but we did not dwell sufficiently on this caper, nor on the circumstances that accompanied it.

For the first time in his life Michel acted slyly and even showed duplicity. Under the shock of emotion produced by Petit-Pierre's speech to the marquis, and by the vanishing (through Mary's unexpected declaration) of all the hopes he had been cherishing so complacently, he was utterly crushed down and annihilated. Fully aware that the fancy Bertha had so liberally shown for him separated him from her sister far more than any aversion on the latter's part, he reproached himself for having encouraged that fancy by his silence and his foolish timidity. But there was no use scolding himself now; he knew that in the depths of his soul he had not the necessary strength to cut short a misunderstanding which fatally interfered with an affection that was dearer to him than life itself. There was not in his nature resolution enough to bring the matter to a frank, categorical explanation; he felt it to be impossible to say to that handsome girl, to whom he had perhaps owed his life a few hours earlier, "Mademoiselle, it is not you whom I love."

During all that evening, although occasions to open his heart honestly to Bertha were not lacking, — for she, very uneasy about a wound which if given to herself she would hardly have noticed, persisted in dressing it, — Michel remained passive in a situation the difficulties of which increased every moment. He tried to speak to Mary; but Mary took as much pains to prevent this as he did to accomplish it, and he renounced the idea, which he indulged for a moment, of making her his intermediary. Besides, those fatal words, 'I do not love you,' sounded in his ears like a funeral knell.

He profited by a moment when no one, not even Bertha, had an eye upon him to retire, or rather to flee to his own room. There he flung himself on the straw bed which Bertha with her own white hands had prepared for him; but he soon got up, his head on fire, his heart more and more convulsed, to bathe his burning face in water and bind a wet towel round his head. This done, he profited by his sleeplessness to search for some method of release.

After an actual travail of imagination which lasted nearly an hour an idea came to him. It was this, — that he might have courage to write what he could not say. This, Michel felt, was the highest point his strength of character could reach. But in order to get any good out of such a letter he felt he could not be present in the house when Bertha received it and read the revelation of his secret thoughts; for not only do timid persons dread being made to suffer, but they also dread making others suffer.

The result of Michel's reflections was that he would leave the farmhouse; but not for long, be it understood; for he intended, as soon as the position was plainly defined and the ground cleared, to return and take his place beside the sister he really loved. The Marquis de Souday would surely not refuse him the hand of Mary, since he had given him that of Bertha, as soon as he was made aware that it was Mary and not Bertha whom he loved. The father could have no possible reason for refusal.

Much encouraged by this prospect, Michel rose and with profound ingratitude cast off the towel to which he owed (thanks to the quiet its cool refreshment had restored to his brain), the good idea he was now intent on putting into execution. He went down to the yard of the farmhouse and began to lift the bars at the stable entrance. But just as he had lifted and pushed back the first of these bars and was beginning on the second, he saw, under a shed, a bale of straw, and out of that bale of straw came a head which he recognized as that of Jean Oullier.

"The devil!" said the latter in his gruffest tone; "you are pretty early this morning, Monsieur Michel."

At that instant two o'clock rang from the steeple of a neighboring village.

"Have you any errand to do?" asked Jean Oullier.

"No," replied the baron, for he fancied that the Vendéan's eye could penetrate into the deepest recesses of his soul, — "no; but I have a dreadful headache, and I thought the night air might still it."

"I warn you that we have sentinels all around us, and if you have not the password you may be roughly used."

"I!"

"Damn it! you as well as others. Ten steps from here you 'll find out you are not the master of this house."

"But that password, — do you know it, Monsieur Jean?"

"Of course."

"Then tell me."

Jean Oullier shook his head.

"That 's the Marquis de Souday's affair. Go up to his room; tell him you want to go away, and in order to do so you must have the password. He 'll give it to you, — that is, if he thinks proper to do so."

Michel took good care to do nothing of the kind, and he remained standing where he was, with his hand on the bar. As for Jean Oullier, he again buried himself in the straw.

After a while Michel, wholly discomfited, went and sat down on an overturned trough, which formed a kind of seat at the inner gate of the farmyard. There he had leisure to continue his meditations; but although the pile of straw did not move again, Michel fancied that an aperture was made in its thickest part, and that in the depths of that cavity he could see something glitter, which was, doubtless, the eye of Jean Oullier. And alas! he knew there was no chance of eluding the eye of that watch-dog.

Luckily, as we have said, meditation was on this occasion singularly useful to the young baron. The question now was how to find a pretext to get away from Banlœuvre in a proper manner. Michel was still seeking that pretext when the first rays of the rising sun began to light up the horizon and gild the thatch of the cottage-roof and color with its opal tints the panes of the narrow windows.

Little by little life was renewed around Michel. The cattle lowed for their food; the sheep, impatient for the fields, bleated and poked their gray-white muzzles through the bars of their pen; the hens fluttered down from their perches and stretched their wings and clucked on the manure heap; the pigeons came out of the cote and flew to the roof, to coo their hymn of love eternal; while the ducks, more prosaic, stood in a long line by the farmyard gate and filled the air with discordant noises, — noises which, in all probability, expressed their surprise at finding that gate closed when they were in such a hurry to go and dabble in the pond.

At the sound of these various noises, forming the matutinal concert of a well-managed farm, a window just above the bench on which Michel was sitting opened softly, and Petit-Pierre's head appeared within it. She did not, however, see Michel; her eyes were turned to heaven, and she seemed entirely absorbed either by inward thought or by the glorious spectacle the dawn presented to her. Any eye — above all, that of a princess unaccustomed to watch the rising of the sun — would have been dazzled by the jets of flame which the king of day was sending along the plain, where they sparkled like thousands of precious stones upon the wet and quivering leaves of the forest-trees and the dewy herbage of the fields; presently an invisible hand softly raised the veil of vapor from the valley, disclosing, one by one, like a modest virgin, its beauty, grace, and splendor.

Petit-Pierre gave herself up to the contemplation of this scene for several minutes. Then, resting her head on her hand, she murmured sadly: —

"Alas! bare as this poor cottage is, those who live in it are more fortunate than I."

These words struck the young baron's brain like a magic wand and elicited the idea, or rather the pretext, he had been vainly searching for the last two hours. He kept quite still against the wall, to which he had clung when the window opened, and he did not move until a sound told him the window was shut and he could leave his station without being seen.

He went straight to the shed.

"Monsieur," he said to Jean Oullier, "Petit-Pierre opened his window — "

"So I saw," said the Vendéan.

"He spoke; did you hear what he said?"

"It did not concern me, and therefore I did not listen."

"Being nearer to him, I heard what he said, without intending to listen."

"Well?"

"Well, our guest thinks this house unpleasant and inconvenient; it lacks many things which are a necessity to a person of his aristocratic habits. Could n't you — I giving you the money, of course — could n't you procure some of these necessary things?"

"Where, I should like to know?"

"Why, in the nearest town or village, — Légé or Machecoul."

Jean Oullier shook his head.

"Impossible," he said.

"Why so?" asked Michel.

"Because if I were to buy articles of luxury just now in either of those places, where not a gesture of certain persons is unobserved, I should awaken dangerous suspicion."

"Could n't you go as far as Nantes ?"

"No," said Jean Oullier, curtly; "the lesson I got at Montaigu has taught me prudence, and I shall not leave my post. But," he continued, in a slightly ironical tone, "you who want the fresh air to cure your headache, — why don't you go to Nantes ?"

Seeing his scheme thus crowned with success, Michel blushed to the whites of his eyes; and yet he trembled, now that it came to putting it into execution.

"Perhaps you are right," he stammered; "but I am afraid, too."

"Pooh! a brave man like you ought to have no fear," said Jean Oullier, emerging from the straw, and shaking it off as he walked toward the gate, leaving the young man time to reflect.

"But —" said Michel.

"What ?" asked Jean Oullier, impatiently.

"Will you undertake to explain the reasons of my departure to Monsieur le marquis, and present my excuses to —"

"Mademoiselle Bertha ?" said Jean Oullier, sarcastically. "Yes; don't trouble yourself."

"I shall be back to-morrow," said Michel, as he passed through the gate.

"Don't hurry; take your time, Monsieur le baron. If not to-morrow, the next day will do." So saying, he closed the heavy gate behind the young man.

The sound of the gate barricaded against him gave a painful shock to Michel's heart. At that moment he thought less of the difficulties he was seeking to escape than of his total separation from the one he loved. It seemed to him that the worm-eaten gate was an iron barrier which he should ever find in future between the gentle form of Mary and himself.

So, instead of starting on his way, he again sat down,

this time by the roadside, and wept. There was a moment when, if he had not feared Jean Oullier's sarcasms (inexperienced as he was, he could not be ignorant of the man's malevolence), he would have rapped on the gate and asked for re-admittance to see once more his tender Mary; but an inward impulse of — we were about to say false shame; let us rather say — true shame withheld him, and he at last departed, without very well knowing whither he went.

He was, however, on the road to Légé, and before long the sound of wheels made him turn his head. He then saw the diligence which ran from Sables-d'Olonne to Nantes coming toward him. Michel felt that his strength, lessened by the loss of blood, though his wound was slight, would not enable him to walk much farther. The sight of the vehicle brought him to a resolution. He stopped it, got into one of the compartments, and reached Nantes a few hours later.

But when he got there all the melancholy of his situation came over him. Habituated from childhood to live the life of others, to obey a will that was not his own, and still maintained in that mental servitude by the very substitution that had just taken place within him, — having, as we may say, changed masters by abandoning his mother to follow the woman whom he loved, — liberty was to him so novel that he did not feel its charm, whereas his solitude and isolation were unbearable to him.

For hearts that are deeply wounded there is no such cruel solitude as that of a city; and the larger and more populous it is, the greater the solitude. Isolation in the midst of a crowd, the nearness of the joy and the heedlessness of those they meet, contrasting with the sadness and anxiety in their own minds, become unendurable to them. So it was now with Michel. Finding himself, almost without the action of his own will, on the road to Nantes, he hoped to find there some distraction to his anxious grief; on the contrary, he found it far more keen and agonizing.

Mary's image followed him; he seemed to see her in every woman he met, and his heart dissolved into bitter regrets and impotent desires.

In this condition of mind he presently turned back to the inn at which the coach had stopped, where he shut himself up in a room and again began to weep. He thought of returning instantly to Banlœuvre, flinging himself at Petit-Pierre's feet, and asking her to be his mediator between the two sisters. He blamed himself for not having done so that morning, and for weakly yielding to the fear of wounding Bertha's pride.

This current of ideas brought him naturally back to the object, or rather the pretext, of his journey, — that is, the articles of luxury he had proposed to purchase. Those purchases once made, — to serve as a legitimate reason for his absence, — he would write the terrible letter which was, in truth, the one only and true cause of his flight to Nantes.

Presently he decided that he had better begin by writing that letter. This resolution taken, he did not lose a moment in carrying it out. He seated himself at the table and composed the following letter, on which fell as many tears from his eyes as words from his pen: —

Mademoiselle, — I ought to be the happiest of men, and yet my heart is broken, and I ask myself whether death were not more tolerable than the suffering I endure.

What will you think of me, what will you say when this letter tells you that which I can no longer conceal without being utterly unworthy of your goodness to me? I need the memory of that goodness, the certainty of the grandeur and generosity of your soul, but, above all, I need the thought that it is the being you love best in the world who separates us, before I can summon courage to take this step.

Mademoiselle, I love your sister Mary; I love her with all the power of my heart; I love her so that I do not wish to live — I cannot live without her! I love her so much that at this moment, when I am guilty toward you of what a less noble character than yours might perhaps consider a cruel wrong, I stretch to you my supplicating hands and say: Let me hope that I may obtain the right to love you as a brother loves a sister!

It was not until this letter was folded and sealed that Michel thought of how it might be made to reach Bertha. No one in Nantes could be sent with it; the danger was too great either for a faithful messenger, or for themselves if the messenger were treacherous. The only means he could think of was to return to the country and find some peasant in the neighborhood of Machecoul on whose fidelity he could rely, and wait himself in the forest for the reply on which his future hung. This was the plan on which he decided.

He spent the remainder of the evening in making the different purchases for the comfort of Petit-Pierre, which he packed in a valise, putting off till the next morning the buying of a horse, — an acquisition which was necessary to him in future if he was, as he hoped, to continue the campaign he had already begun.

The next day, about nine o'clock in the morning, Michel, mounted on an excellent Norman beast, with his valise behind him, was preparing to start on his way back to the Retz region.

VIII.

THE SHEEP, RETURNING TO THE FOLD, TUMBLES INTO A PIT-FALL.

It was market-day, and the influx of countrymen was considerable in the streets and along the quays of Nantes. At the moment when Michel reached the pont Rousseau the road was blocked by a compact line of heavy vehicles loaded with grain, carts heaped with vegetables, horses, mules, peasants, and peasant-women, all carrying in baskets, hods, or tin-pails the produce they were bringing to the town.

Michel's impatience was so great that he did not hesitate to plunge into the midst of the crowd; but just as he was pushing his horse into it he caught sight of a young girl leaving it in a direction opposite to his own course, and something in her aspect made him quiver.

She was dressed, like other peasant-women, in a blue-and-red striped petticoat and a cotton mantle with a hood to it; her head was covered by a *coif*, with falling lappets of the commonest kind. Nevertheless, in spite of this humble costume, she closely resembled Mary, — so closely that the young baron could not restrain a cry of astonishment.

He tried to turn back; but, unfortunately, the commotion he made in the crowd by the stopping and turning of his horse raised such a storm of oaths and cries that he had no courage to brave it. He let his beast continue its way, swearing to himself at the obstacles which hindered his advance. Once over the bridge, however, he jumped from his horse and looked about for some one to hold it.

while he went back to see if his eyes had deceived him, or whether it were possible that Mary had come to Nantes.

At that instant a voice, nasal like that of all the beggars of that region, asked alms of him. He turned quickly, for he thought he knew the voice. Leaning against the last post of the bridge were two individuals, whose countenances were far too marked and characteristic to have escaped his memory. They were Aubin Courte-Joie and Trigaud-Vermin, who, apparently, were there for no other purpose than to work upon the pity of the crowd, though, in all probability, they had some object not foreign to the political and commercial interests of Maître Jacques.

Michel went eagerly up to them.

"You know me?" he asked.

Aubin Courte-Joie winked.

"My good monsieur," he said, "have pity on a poor cartman who has had both legs crushed under the wheels of his cart, coming down the hill by the springs of Baugé."

"Yes, yes, my good man," said Michel, understanding instantly.

He went close up to the pair as he gave them alms, and the alms were a piece of gold, which he slipped into the capacious paw of Trigaud-Vermin.

"I am here by order of Petit-Pierre," he said, in a low voice, to the false and the real mendicant; "hold my horse for a few moments while I do an important errand."

The cripple made a sign of assent. Baron Michel tossed the bridle of the horse to Trigaud and turned to re-cross the bridge. Unfortunately for him, if the passage was difficult for a horseman, it was still more difficult for a foot-passenger. Michel in vain attempted some assumption, and tried to make his timid nature more aggressive. He punched with his elbows, and glided where he could through interstices; he risked his life a dozen times under the wheels of hay-carts and cabbage-carts, but finally he was forced to resign himself to follow the stream and go with the torrent, though it was evident the young peasant woman would be far out of sight by the time he reached the place where he had seen her.

He thought, sagaciously enough, that she must, like other peasant-women, have gone toward the market, and he took that direction, looking at all the countrywomen he passed with an anxious curiosity that earned him some jests and came near causing a quarrel or two. None of them was she whom he sought. He rushed through the market and the adjacent streets, but saw nothing that recalled to him the graceful apparition he had seen on the bridge.

Completely discouraged, he was thinking of returning on his steps and remounting his horse, when, as he turned the corner of the rue du Château he saw, not twenty steps distant from him, the identical petticoat of blue-and-red stripes and the very cotton mantle of which he was in search. The carriage and step of the woman who wore that dress had all the elegance of Mary's own bearing. It was surely her slender and delicate form the outline of which he saw through the folds of the coarse material she wore. Those were the curves of her graceful neck, which made the lappets of her common *coif* an adornment; and the knot of hair which came below the *coif*, surely it was braided of the same fair golden hair which Michel had so often admired.

No, he could not be deceived; that young peasant-woman and Mary were one and the same person, and Michel was so sure of it that he dared not pass her and look into her face as he had into that of others. He contented himself by simply crossing the street. The result of that strategic movement assured him he was not mistaken.

But why was Mary in Nantes; and being there, why was she thus disguised? These questions Michel put to himself without being able to solve them, and he was, after a violent struggle with himself, just about to approach the young girl and speak to her, when he saw her stop at No. 17 of this very rue du Château, push the gate of the house, and as the gate was not locked, pass through it, enter an alley, close the gate behind her, and disappear.

Michel went eagerly to the gate; but it was now locked. He stood before it in deep and painful stupefaction, not knowing what to do next, and half-inclined to believe he was dreaming.

Suddenly he felt a tap upon his arm; he shuddered, so far was his mind at that moment from his body. Then he turned round. The notary, Loriot, was beside him.

"You here!" exclaimed the latter, in a tone that denoted surprise.

"Is there anything so very astonishing in my being at Nantes, Maître Loriot?" asked Michel.

"Come, speak lower, and don't stand before that door as if you had taken root there; I advise you not."

"Goodness! what 's the matter with you? I knew you were cautious, but not to that extent."

"One can't be too cautious. Come, let 's talk as we walk; then we sha'n't be remarked upon." Passing his handkerchief over his face, which was bathed in perspiration, he added, "Though it will compromise me horribly."

"I swear, Maître Loriot, I don't know what you are talking about," exclaimed Michel.

"You don't understand what I mean, unfortunate young man? Don't you know that you are down on the list of suspected persons, and that a warrant has been issued for your arrest?"

"Well, let them arrest me!" cried Michel, impatiently, trying to turn the notary back toward the house into which Mary had disappeared.

"Arrest you! Hey! you take it gayly enough, Monsieur Michel. All right; call it philosophy. I ought to tell you that this same news, which seems to you so unimportant, has produced such a dreadful effect upon your mother that if chance had not thrown you in my way here I should have gone immediately to Légé to find you."

"My mother!" cried the young man, whom the notary

was touching on his weak spot, — "what has happened to my mother?"

"Nothing has happened, Monsieur Michel. Thank Heaven, she is as well as persons can be when their minds are full of uneasiness and their hearts of grief. I must not conceal from you that that is your mother's condition at this moment."

"Good God! what do you mean?" said Michel, sighing dolefully.

"You know what you are to her, Monsieur Michel; you can't have forgotten the care she took of your youth, and the solicitude she continues to bestow upon you, though you are now of an age when lads begin to slip through their mother's fingers. You can, therefore, imagine what her tortures are in knowing that you are exposed every day to the terrible dangers that surround you. I do not conceal from you that I considered it my duty to inform her of what I suppose to be your intentions, and I have fulfilled that duty."

"Oh, what have you said to her, Maître Loriot?"

"I told her, in plain language, that I believed you to be desperately in love with Mademoiselle Bertha de Souday —"

"Goodness!" exclaimed Michel; "he, too!"

"And," continued the notary, without noticing the interruption, "that, to all appearance, you intend to marry her."

"What did my mother say?" asked Michel, with visible anxiety.

"Just what all mothers say when they hear of a marriage they disapprove. But come, let me question you myself, my young friend; my position as notary of both families ought to give me some influence with you. Have you seriously reflected on what you are about to do?"

"Do you share my mother's prejudices?" demanded Michel. "Do you know anything against the reputation of the Demoiselles de Souday?"

"Nothing whatever, my young friend," replied Maître

Loriot, while Michel gazed anxiously at the windows of the house into which Mary had entered, — "nothing whatever! On the contrary, I consider those young ladies, whom I have known from childhood, as among the purest and most virtuous in the land, in spite of the malicious nickname a few evil tongues have applied to them."

"Then," said Michel, "why is it you disapprove of what I do?"

"My young friend," said the notary, "please observe that I have given no opinion; I simply advise prudence. You will have to make three times as much effort to succeed in what must be called from a certain point of view — pray excuse the word — a folly, as it would cost you to renounce the attachment now; though I don't say but what the fine qualities of the young lady justify it."

"My dear Monsieur Loriot," said Michel, who at a safe distance from his mother was not sorry to burn his vessels, "the Marquis de Souday has been so good as to grant me his daughter's hand; there 's no getting over that."

"Oh, that indeed is another thing," said Maître Loriot. "If you have reached that point in the affair, I have only one word to say and one advice to give. Remember that it is always a serious matter legally to marry in defiance of the will of parents. Persist in your intention; that 's very right. But go and see your mother; don't give her the chance to complain of your neglect. Try to overcome her prejudices."

"Hum!" muttered Michel, who felt the wisdom of these remarks.

"Come," persisted Loriot, "will you promise me to do as I ask you?"

"Yes, yes!" replied the young man, who wanted to get rid of the notary, for he thought he heard steps in the alley, and feared that Mary might come out while Maître Loriot was there.

"Good!" said the latter. "Remember, also, that you

are safer at La Logerie than elsewhere. Your mother's name and influence with the administration can alone save you from the consequences of your late conduct. You have been committing various pranks for some time past which no one would have suspected you to be capable of; you must admit that, young man."

"Yes, yes; I admit it," cried Michel, impatiently.

"That 's all I want. The sinner who confesses is half-repentant. There! now I must say good-bye; I leave Nantes at eleven o'clock."

"Are you going back to Légé?"

"Yes; with a young lady who is to meet me presently at my hotel, and to whom I am to give a seat in my cabriolet, which I would otherwise offer to you."

"You would go out of your way a mile or two to do me a service, would n't you?"

"Of course; with the greatest pleasure, my dear Monsieur Michel," said the notary.

"Then, go by way of Banlœuvre, and give this letter to Mademoiselle Bertha."

"So be it; but for God's sake," cried the notary, with a frightened look, "be more cautious in your way of handing it to me."

"I notice you are not yourself, my dear Monsieur Loriot; when those people passed us just now you jumped off the pavement as if they had the plague. What 's the matter with you? Come, Mr. Notary, speak up!"

"I 'd change my practice at this very moment for the poorest practice in the Sarthe or the Eure departments. I feel such terrible emotions that if they go on much longer my days will be numbered; that 's what 's the matter with me. Monsieur Michel," continued the notary, lowering his voice, "think of it; they have put four pounds of gunpowder in my pockets, against my will. I tremble as I walk along the pavement; every cigar that comes along puts me into a fever. Well, good-bye; take my advice and go back to La Logerie."

Michel, whose agonies, like those of Maître Loriot, grew worse and worse, let the notary depart, having got from him all he wanted, — namely, the certainty that his letter would reach Banlœuvre. No sooner was Loriot out of sight than his eyes, returning naturally to the house he was watching, fixed themselves on a window where he fancied he saw the curtain move, and the vague silhouette of a face looking at him through the glass. He thought it might be on account of his persistency in standing before the house that the young girl watched him; he therefore moved in the direction of the river, and hid behind the angle of a house, not, however, losing sight of all that happened in the rue du Château.

Presently the gate of No. 17 opened, and the same young peasant-girl appeared; but she was not alone. A young man, dressed in a long blouse, and affecting rustic manners, accompanied her. Rapidly as they passed him, Michel noticed that the man was young, and the distinction of his face was in marked contrast to his peasant's clothes; he saw, too, that he was jesting with Mary on a footing of equality, offering, apparently, to carry her basket, — an attention the young girl was refusing, with a laugh.

The serpents of jealousy gnawed his heart. Convinced, as he remembered what Mary had whispered to him, that these disguises hid some amorous as well as some political intrigue, he rushed away toward the Rousseau bridge, which lay in exactly the opposite direction to that taken by Mary and her friend. The crowd on the bridge was no longer so great. He crossed it easily; but when he reached the further end, and began to look round for Courte-Joie, Trigaud, and his horse, all three had disappeared.

Michel was so upset in mind that it did not occur to him to search the neighborhood. Remembering, too, what the notary had said, he thought it would be dangerous to lodge a complaint, which might bring about his own arrest, and reveal, besides, his acquaintance with the two mendicants. He therefore made up his mind to do nothing to recover his horse, but to go home on foot; and he accordingly took his way toward Saint-Philbert-de-Grand-Lieu.

Cursing Mary, and shedding tears over the betrayal of which he believed himself the victim, he had no other thought than to do as Maître Loriot advised, — that is to say, return to La Logerie and fling himself into the arms of his mother, toward whom the sight he had just seen impelled him far more than the remonstrances of the notary.

Thus preoccupied, he reached the height of Saint-Corentin without hearing the footsteps of two gendarmes who were walking behind him.

"Your papers, monsieur," said one of them, a corporal, after examining him from head to foot.

"My papers?" exclaimed Michel, in astonishment, the inquiry being addressed to him for the first time in his life, — "I have none."

"And why have you none?"

"Because I never supposed that any passport was required to come from my house into Nantes."

"Where is your house?"

"It is the château de la Logerie."

"What is your name?"

"Baron Michel."

"Baron Michel de la Logerie?"

"Yes."

"If you are Baron Michel de la Logerie, I arrest you," said the corporal.

Then, without more ado, and before the young man could think of flight, which from the nature of the ground was quite possible, the corporal collared him, while the other gendarme, minion of equality before the law, slipped the hand-cuffs on his wrists.

This operation over, — and it lasted only a few seconds, thanks to the stupefaction of the prisoner and the dexterity of the gendarme, — the two agents of the armed forces conducted Baron Michel to Saint-Colombin, where they locked him into a sort of cellar, belonging to the barracks of the troops stationed there, which was used as a temporary prison.

IX.

TRIGAUD PROVES THAT IF HE HAD BEEN HERCULES, HE WOULD PROBABLY HAVE ACCOMPLISHED TWENTY-FOUR LABORS INSTEAD OF TWELVE.

It was about four in the afternoon when Michel, thrust into the lock-up of the guard-house at Saint-Colombin, became aware of the delights of that abode. On entering what seemed to be a dungeon, the young man's eyes, accustomed to the brilliant light without, could distinguish nothing around him. Little by little they grew accustomed to the darkness, and then their owner was able to make out the sort of lodging he was in.

It was partly under and partly above the surface of the ground; its walls were of thicker and more solidly constructed masonry than was usual in such buildings, for the reason that it supported the walls of the house above it. The floor was bare earth; and as the place was very damp, that earth was nearly mud. The ceiling was of beams, placed very near together. The light usually entered through a grating placed just above the level of the ground; but owing to the necessities of its present use this aperture was closed inside by heavy planks, and outside by an enormous mill-stone placed vertically in front of it. A hole in the centre of the stone gave entrance to a feeble ray of light, of which two thirds was intercepted by the plank shutters, so that it only cast a single weird gleam into the middle of the cellar.

In the track of that gleam lay the fragments of a cider-press, — that is to say, the branch of a tree squared at one end, and now half-rotten, and a circular trough of freestone decorated with silvery arabesques by the slimy and capricious promenades of slugs and snails.

To any other prisoner than Michel the inspection of his surroundings might have seemed desperately discouraging, for it plainly showed there were few, if any, chances of escape; but the young baron was moved to make it by nothing more than a feeling of vague curiosity. The first anguish his heart had ever felt plunged him into a state of prostration where the soul is indifferent to all outside things; and in the first shock of discovering that he must renounce the sweet hope of being loved by Mary, palace or prison were alike to him.

He sat down on the edge of the trough, wondering who could be the young man he had seen with Mary; then, after the violence of his jealous transports subsided, he turned to recollections of his first intercourse with the sisters. But his anguish was as great from the one emotion as from the other; for, says the Florentine poet, that great painter of infernal torture, "There is no greater pain than to recall a happy time in wretchedness."

But let us now leave the young baron to his grief, and see what was happening in other parts of the guard-house of Saint-Colombin.

This guard-house, materially speaking, which had been occupied for the last few days by a detachment of troops of the line, was a vast building, with a front toward the courtyard, while its rear looked out upon the country road that leads from Saint-Colombin to Saint-Philbert-de-Grand-Lieu, about a kilometre from the first of these two villages and a stone's throw from the high-road between Nantes and the Sables-d'Olonne.

This building, constructed on the ruins and with the fragments of an old feudal fortress, occupied an eminence that commanded the whole neighborhood. The advantages of the position had struck Dermoncourt as he returned from his expedition to the forest of Machecoul. Accordingly, he left a score of men to hold it. It answered the purpose of a block-house, where expeditionary columns could find, on occasion, a resting-place or a refuge, and at the same time it might be made a sort of station for prisoners, where they could be collected until a sufficiently imposing force was mustered to escort them to Nantes, without danger of rescue.

The accommodations of the guard-house consisted solely of a somewhat vast hall and a barn. The hall, over the cellar in which Michel was confined, and consequently five or six feet above the ground, served as the guard-room. It was reached by a flight of steps, made with the old stones of the fortress, placed parallel with the wall.

The barn was used as barracks for the men; they slept there on straw. The post was guarded with all military precautions. A sentry stood before the gate of the courtyard which opened to the road, and a lookout was stationed in an ivy-covered tower, the sole remains left standing of the old feudal castle.

Now, about six o'clock in the evening, the soldiers who formed the little garrison were seated on some heavy rollers which had been left at the foot of the outside wall of the house. It was a favorite spot for their siesta; there they enjoyed the gentle warmth of the setting sun and a splendid view of the lake of Grand-Lieu in the distance, the surface of which, tinted by the beams of the star of day, resembled at that hour an immense sheet of scarlet tin. At their feet ran the road to Nantes, like a broad ribbon through the midst of the verdure which at that season covered the plain; and we must admit that our heroes in red trousers were more interested in what happened on that road than in all the beauties which Nature spread before them.

On the evening of which we write, the laborers leaving the fields, the flocks returning to their stables made the road a somewhat lively and varied panorama. Each heavy hay-cart, each group returning from the Nantes market, and, above all, every peasant-woman in her short skirt was a text for remark and jocularity, which, it must be owned, were not restrained.

"Goodness!" cried one of the men, suddenly, "what 's that I see down there?"

"A fellow with bagpipes," said another.

"Bagpipes, indeed! Do you think you are still in Brittany? Down here they don't groan bagpipes; they only whine complaints."

"What has he got on his back, then, if it is n't his instrument?"

"That 's an instrument, sure enough," said a fourth soldier; "it must be an organ."

"Queer organ!" said a fifth. "I tell you that 's a sack; the man 's a beggar. You can tell him by his clothes."

"Then his sack has eyes and a nose, like the rest of us. Why, look at him, Limousin!"

"Limousin's arm is long, but his sight is short," said another; "you can't have everything."

"Pooh!" said the corporal; "I see what it is. It is one man carrying another on his shoulders."

"The corporal is right!" chorused the soldiers.

"I am always right," said he of the woollen stripes, "first as your corporal, next as your superior; and if there are any of you who doubt after I have once said a thing, he is going to be convinced now, for here come the men straight toward us."

As he spoke, the tramp who had roused the discussion (in whom our readers have no doubt recognized Trigaud-Vermin, as in his bagpipe, organ, or sack, they have also recognized his rider, Aubin Courte-Joie) turned off the main-road to the left, and came up the flight of steps which led to the guard-house.

"What a pair of brigands!" said one of the soldiers. "If they caught us alone, behind a hedge, either of those rascals would clip us a shot, would n't he, corporal?"

"Like enough," responded the latter.

"But as we are all here together they come and beg, — ha, the cowards !"

"I 'll be shot if I give 'em a penny," said the soldier who had spoken first.

"See here !" said another, picking up a stone; "I 'll put something into his hat."

"I forbid you," said the corporal.

"Why so ?"

"Because he has n't any hat."

The soldiers burst out laughing at the joke, which was recognized at once as very choice.

"Let 's have a look," said a soldier, "at what the fellow is really carrying; don't discourage him. For my part, I don't find such delight in this beggarly guard-house that I despise any sort of fun that comes along."

"Fun?"

"Yes, any kind, — music perhaps. Every tramp in this region is a sort of troubadour. We 'll make him sing what he knows, and a good deal he does n't know; it will help pass the evening."

By this time the mendicant, now no longer an enigma to the soldiers, was close beside them, holding out his hand.

"You were right, corporal; he has got another man perched on his shoulders."

"I was wrong," responded the corporal.

"How so ?"

"That is n't a man, — only a section of humanity."

The soldiers laughed at the second joke as heartily as they laughed at the first.

"He can't spend much on trousers," said one.

"And less for boots," added the facetious corporal.

"Are n't they hideous ?" said the Limousin. "Upon my word, you might think 'em a monkey mounted on a bear."

While these poor waggeries were flying about and reaching Trigaud's ear, he stood immovable, holding out his hand and giving a most pitiable expression to his face, while Aubin Courte-Joie, in his capacity as orator of the association, repeated, in his nasal voice, the unvarying formula: —

"Charity, if you please, my good gentlemen! — charity for a poor cartman with both legs taken off by his cart, coming down the hill at Ancenis."

"What ignorant savages they must be to expect alms of soldiers in garrison. Scamps! I 'll bet if we searched their pockets we 'd find double what we have got in our own."

Hearing which suggestion, Aubin Courte-Joie modified the formula, and came down to a precise request: —

"A bit of bread, just a bit of bread, if you please, my good gentlemen," he said. "If you have n't any money you have surely a bit of bread."

"Bread!" said the corporal. "Yes, you shall have bread, my good man; and with the bread, soup, and with the soup a bit of meat. We 'll do that for you; but I should like to know what you 'll do for us."

"My good gentlemen, I 'll pray God for you," replied Courte-Joie, in his nasal whine, which formed the treble to his partner's bass.

"That will do no harm," said the corporal, — "no, certainly, there 's no harm in that; but it is n't enough. Come, have n't you anything funny in your sack?"

"How do you mean?" asked Courte-Joie, assuming ignorance.

"I mean, villanous old black-birds that you are, you must be able to whistle an air or two; in which case, let 's have the music first. That will pay for the soup and the bread and the meat."

"Ah, yes, yes; I understand. Well, we don't refuse. On the contrary, officer," said Aubin, flattering the corporal, "it is fair enough that if you give us the charity of the good God we should try to amuse you and your company as best we can."

"Good; the more the better. You can't go too far, for we are dying of dulness in your devilish land."

"All right," said Courte-Joie; "we 'll begin by showing you something you never saw before."

Although the promise was nothing more than the usual exordium of clowns at a circus, it roused the curiosity of the soldiers, who clustered round the mendicants in silence, with an eagerness that was almost respectful. Courte-Joie, who until then had kept his seat on Trigaud's shoulders, made a movement of his body, indicating that he wished to be deposited on the ground, and Trigaud, with that passive obedience which he practised to the will of his master, seated him on a fragment of the old battlement half-buried in nettles, which lay near the rollers on which the men were seated.

"Hey! how neatly that was done!" cried the corporal. "I 'd like to recruit that fellow and turn him over to the fat major, who can't find a cob fit to carry him."

During this time Courte-Joie had picked up a stone, which he gave to Trigaud. The latter, without further directions, closed and then opened his hand, showing the stone reduced to fragments.

"Good Lord! he 's a Hercules! You must tackle him, Pinguet," said the corporal, addressing the soldier we have hitherto called the Limousin.

"All right," said the latter, jumping up; "we 'll see about it."

Trigaud, taking no notice of the words or actions of Pinguet, continued his exercises. He seized two soldiers by the straps of their knapsacks, gently raised and held them aloft at arm's-length for a few seconds, and then as gently put them down, with perfect ease.

The soldiers cheered him loudly.

"Pinguet! Pinguet!" they cried, "where are you? Here 's some one who can knock you into a cocked-hat."

Trigaud continued his performances as if these experiments on his strength were a pre-arranged matter. He invited two other soldiers to seat themselves astride of the shoulders of the first two, and he carried all four with almost as much ease as if there were but two. As he put them down, Pinguet arrived with a gun on each shoulder.

"Bravo, Limousin! bravo!" cried the soldiers.

Encouraged by the acclamations of his comrades, Pinguet cried out: —

"All that is mountebank business. Here, you braggart, let me see you do what I am going to do."

Putting a finger of each hand into the muzzle of a gun, he held the weapons out before him, at arm's-length.

"Pooh!" said Courte-Joie, while Trigaud looked on with a movement of the lips that might pass for a smile at Pinguet's feat, — "pooh! bring two more guns."

When the guns were brought Trigaud put all four muzzles on the fingers of one hand and raised them to the level of his eye, without any contraction of the muscles that betrayed an effort. Pinguet was distanced forever in the struggle.

Then rummaging in his pocket, Trigaud brought out a horse-shoe, which he folded in two as easily as an ordinary man would fold a leather strap. After each of his experiments he turned his eyes to Courte-Joie, asking for a smile; then Courte-Joie would signify by a nod that he was satisfied.

"Come," said Aubin, "you 've only earned our suppers so far; now you must get us a night's lodging. Is n't that so, my good gentlemen? If my comrade does something more wonderful still, won't you give us a little hay and a corner in the stable to lie on?"

"As for that, it is impossible," said the sergeant of the company, who, being attracted by the shouts and plaudits of the soldiers, had come to share the sight; "the orders are strict."

This answer seemed to discourage Courte-Joie greatly; his weasel-face grew serious.

"Never mind," said one of the men; "we 'll club

together, and get you ten sous, which will pay for a bed at the nearest tavern, and that will be softer than buckwheat hay."

"If the ox you ride has legs as solid as his arms," said another, "a mile or two farther won't trouble you."

"First, let 's see the performance!" cried the soldiers. "Show us his best thing."

There was no repelling this enthusiasm, and Courte-Joie yielded with an alacrity which showed his confidence in his comrade's biceps.

"Have you a grindstone here, or anything that weighs about twelve or fifteen hundred pounds?" he asked.

"There 's the block of stone you are sitting on," said a soldier.

Courte-Joie shrugged his shoulders.

"If that stone had a handle Trigaud would pick it up for you with one hand."

"There 's that millstone we tipped up before the grating of the dungeon," said a soldier.

"Why not tell him to lift the whole building at once?" said the corporal. "It took six of you men to put it where it is, and with levers, too. I was furious that my rank forbade me from lending a hand to what I called a pack of idlers."

"Besides, you must not touch that millstone," interposed the sergeant; "that 's also against orders. There 's a prisoner in the cellar."

Courte-Joie gave Trigaud a glance, and the latter, paying no attention to the sergeant's remark, went straight to the millstone.

"Don't you hear me?" said the sergeant, raising his voice, and catching Trigaud by the arm; "you are not to touch it."

"Why not?" said Courte-Joie. "If he moves it he 'll replace it; don't be afraid."

"Besides," said a soldier, "if you look at the mouse they have got in the trap you 'll see it would never run away if it could, — a poor little monsieur who might be taken for a woman in disguise. I thought at first he was the Duchesse de Berry herself."

"Yes, and he 's too busy crying to think of escape," said the corporal, who was evidently burning with the desire to see the feat. "When we took him his food, Pinguet and I, — that is, I and Pinguet, — he burst into tears; I declare if his eyes were n't two faucets!"

"Well, well," said the sergeant, who was no less curious than the rest to see how the tramp would accomplish his Titanic task, "I will take the responsibility of allowing it."

Trigaud profited by the permission. He seized the millstone between his arms at its base, leaned his shoulder on its centre, and with a powerful effort tried to raise it. But the weight of this enormous mass of stone had sunk it into the ground on which it rested to the depth of some four or five inches, and the adherence of this earth socket, thus hollowed, neutralized Trigaud's efforts.

Courte-Joie, who had entered the circle of soldiers by creeping on his hands and knees, like a huge scarabœus, called attention to the nature of the difficulty; then with a large flat stone which he picked up, and partly also with his hands, he grubbed out the earth which hindered the success of Trigaud's feat. The giant then applied himself once more to the work. Soon he raised the huge block and held it up for a few seconds, resting against his shoulder and also against the wall, about a foot from the ground.

The enthusiasm of the soldiers knew no bounds. They pressed around Trigaud and overwhelmed him with congratulations to which he seemed perfectly insensible; they shouted in frantic admiration, which was shared by the corporal, and then, through the natural hierarchy of rank, by the sergeant himself. They talked of carrying Trigaud in triumph to the sutler's, where the reward of his vigor awaited him, swearing by every oath known to the sons of Mars that Trigaud deserved not only the bread and soup and meat promised by the corporal, but the rations of a general, or indeed of the king of France, which would be none too much to maintain the strength required for such prowess.

As we have said, Trigaud seemed in no way puffed-up by his triumph; his countenance remained as impassible as that of an ox allowed to breathe after some powerful exertion. His eyes, however, sought those of Aubin Courte-Joie, as if to ask "Master, are you satisfied?"

Courte-Joie, on the other hand, looked radiant, possibly because of the impression made upon the spectators by a strength he considered his own, though it far exceeded that which Nature had originally bestowed upon him. Perhaps, however, his satisfaction was really caused by the success of a little manœuvre he had cleverly performed while the attention of all was concentrated on his companion,—a manœuvre which consisted in slipping under the millstone the large flat stone he held in his hand, placing it in such a way that the enormous mass which closed the grating of the cellar was so poised upon its smooth surface that the strength of a child would suffice to displace it.

The two beggars were taken to the sutler's, and there Trigaud furnished still another text of admiration to the soldiers. After he had swallowed an enormous canful of soup, four rations of beef and two loaves of bread were placed before him. Trigaud ate the first loaf with the first two rations; then, as if by changing his method of deglutition he changed and improved the taste of the objects swallowed, he took his second loaf, split it in two, scooped out and ate, by way of pastime, the crumb within it, placed the meat in the cavity, put the two halves of the crust together, and proceeded to bite through the whole with a coolness and force of jaw which brought down thunders of applause from the delighted audience.

After about five minutes of this exercise nothing remained of either bread or meat but a few crumbs of the loaf, which Trigaud, apparently ready to begin all over again, carefully collected. His admirers hastened to bring him a third loaf, which, though stale and dry, Trigaud treated like the first two.

The soldiers were not yet satisfied; they would have liked to push their investigations still further, but the sergeant thought it more prudent to bring their scientific curiosity to an end. Courte-Joie had now become thoughtful, and his expression was noticed by the soldiers.

"Ah, *ça!*" said the corporal; "here you are, eating and drinking on the earnings of your comrade. That 's not fair; it seems to me you might give us a song, if only to pay your scot."

"Unquestionably," said the sergeant.

"Yes, yes, a song!" cried the soldiers, "and then the affair will be complete."

"Hum!" muttered Courte-Joie. "I know some songs, of course I do."

"All right then, sing away!"

"But my songs may n't be to your liking."

"Never mind, — so long as it is n't a fugue for the devil's funeral, anything will be fun to us; we are not hard to please at Saint-Colombin."

"Yes," said Courte-Joie, "I can see that; you are horribly bored."

"Monstrously," said the sergeant.

"We don't expect you to sing like Monsieur Nourrit," observed a Parisian.

"Make it a bit quizzical," said another man, "and the more the better."

"As I have eaten your bread and drunk your wine," said Courte-Joie, "I have no right to refuse you anything; but, I repeat it, my songs will probably not be to your taste."

And thereupon, he trolled out the following stanza: —

"Look! look! my *gars*, down there! down there!
Don't you see the infernal band?
Spread out, spread out, surprise them there,
Behind the gorse, across the land.
Spread out! I say, my *gars!* my *gars!*
Await the Blues with steady hand."

Courte-Joie got no farther. After a moment of surprised silence at his first words a roar of indignation arose; ten soldiers sprang upon him and the sergeant, seizing him by the collar, threw him on the ground.

"Villain!" he cried, "I 'll teach you to come here in our midst and sing praises to your brigands."

But before the words were well out of his mouth (words to which he added a variety of adverbs that were customary with him) Trigaud, his eyes flashing with anger, made his way through to Courte-Joie, pushed back the sergeant and stood before his comrade in so threatening an attitude that the soldiers remained for some moments silent and uncertain.

But soon, mortified at being held at bay by an unarmed man, they drew their sabres, and rushed upon the beggars.

"Kill them! kill them!" they cried; "they are Chouans!"

"You asked me for a song; I warned you that the songs I knew were not to your taste," cried Courte-Joie, in a voice that rose high above the tumult. "You ought not to have insisted. Why do you complain?"

"If you only knew such songs as you have just sung you are a rebel, and I arrest you peremptorily."

"I know such songs as please the people of the towns and villages whose alms are my living. A poor cripple like me and an idiot like my comrade can't be dangerous. Arrest us if you choose; but such captures won't do you any honor."

"That may be," replied the sergeant, "but meantime you 'll sleep in the lock-up. You were puzzled where to go for a night's lodging, my fine fellow; well, I 'll give you one. Come, men, seize and search them, and let us lock them up incontinently."

But, as Trigaud still maintained a threatening attitude, no one hastened to execute the sergeant's order.

"If you don't go with a good grace," said the latter, "I 'll send for some loaded muskets, and we will see if your skin is bullet-proof."

"Come, Trigaud, my lad," said Courte-Joie, "if we must resign ourselves, we must; besides, it can't matter, they won't detain us long. Their fine prisons are not built for poor devils like us."

"That 's right," said the sergeant, much pleased at the pacific turn the affair was taking. "You will be searched, and if nothing suspicious is found upon you, and you behave properly during the night, we 'll see about letting you out to-morrow morning."

The two beggars were searched, but nothing was found upon them except a few copper coins; which confirmed the sergeant in his ideas of clemency.

"After all," he said, pointing to Trigaud, "that great ox is not guilty; I see no reason why I should lock him up."

"If you do," said the Limousin, "he might take it into his head, like his forefather Samson, to shake the walls and bring them down about our ears."

"You are right, Pinguet," said the sergeant, "because that 's my opinion, too. We should only embarrass ourselves by holding the pair. Come, off with you, friend, and quick too!"

"Oh! my good monsieur, don't separate us," cried Courte-Joie, in a tearful voice. "We can't do without each other; he walks for me, and I think for him."

"Upon my word," said a soldier, "they are worse than lovers."

"No," said the sergeant to Courte-Joie. "I shall make you pass the night in the dungeon to punish you, and to-morrow the officer of the day will decide what is to be done with your carcass. Come, to the cellar!"

Two soldiers approached Courte-Joie; but he with an agility not to be expected in so helpless a body, sprang upon Trigaud's shoulders, and the giant walked peacefully along toward the door of the dungeon, under escort of the soldiers.

On the way Aubin put his lips close to the ear of his comrade and said some words in a low voice. Trigaud deposited his master at the cellar-door, through which the sergeant thrust the cripple, who made his entrance by rolling forward like an enormous ball.

The soldiers then took Trigaud outside the courtyard gate, which they closed behind him. The giant stood for a few moments motionless and bewildered, as if he did not know what course to decide upon. He tried at first to sit down on the rollers, where, as we have seen, the soldiers took their siesta. But the sentry made him understand that that was impossible, and the beggar departed in the direction of the village of Saint-Colombin.

X.

GIVING THE SLIP.

About two hours after Aubin Courte-Joie's incarceration the sentry of the post heard a cart coming up the road which led past the guard-house. "Qui vive?" he cried; and when the cart was only a short distance from him he ordered it to halt. The cart, or rather the cartman, obeyed.

The corporal and four soldiers came out of the guard-room to inspect both man and vehicle. The cart was a harmless one, loaded with hay, and was like all the others that were plodding along the road to and from Nantes during the evening. Only one man was with it; he explained that he was going to Saint-Philbert with hay for his landlord, — adding that he went by night to economize time, which was precious at this season of the year. The corporal gave orders to let him pass.

But this permission was wasted on the poor fellow. His cart, drawn by a single horse, had stopped at the steepest part of the rising ground about the guard-house, and in spite of the efforts made by horse and cartman it was impossible to start the heavy vehicle again.

"There is n't any sense," said the corporal, "in overburdening a beast like that! Don't you see that your horse has double the load he can draw?"

"What a pity," remarked one of the soldiers, "that the sergeant let that big ox of a fellow we had here go. We might have harnessed him to the horse and I 'll warrant he 'd have pulled to the collar."

"That 's supposing he would have let himself be harnessed."

If the man who spoke last had looked behind the cart, he would have seen good reason why Trigaud should not allow himself to be harnessed to the front of the cart to pull it forward; he would also have understood the difficulty the horse found in starting the cart. For this difficulty was chiefly owing to Trigaud himself. The giant, completely hidden in the darkness and behind the hay, was dragging at the rear bar of the cart and opposing his strength to that of the horse, with as much success as he had won when exhibiting his prowess in the evening.

"Shall we lend you a hand ?" said the corporal.

"Wait till I try again," said the driver, who had turned his cart obliquely, to lessen the sharpness of the acclivity, and now, grasping the horse by the bridle, prepared for a final effort to disprove the blame the corporal laid upon him.

He whipped his beast vigorously, exciting him by voice and pulling on the bridle, while the soldiers joined their cries to his. The horse stiffened all four legs for the effort, making the sparks fly from his heels among the stones of the road; then, he suddenly fell down, and at the same moment, as if the wheels had encountered some obstacle which disturbed their equilibrium, the cart swayed over to left and upset against the building.

The soldiers ran forward and helped to release the horse from the harness and get him on his legs. The result of their friendly eagerness was that none of them saw Trigaud, who, satisfied no doubt with a result to which he had powerfully contributed by slipping under the cart and hoisting it on his Herculean shoulders, until it lost its centre of gravity, now retired composedly behind a hedge to await events.

"Shall we help you to set your cart back on its pin ?" said the corporal to the driver. "If so, you must get an additional horse."

"Faith, no !" cried the cartman. "To-morrow I 'll see about it. It is evident the good God does n't mean me to keep on, — must n't go against His will."

So saying, the peasant threw the reins on the crupper of his horse, pushed up the collar, mounted the animal, and departed, after wishing good-night to the soldiers, and saying he should be back in the morning to remove the hay. Two hundred yards from the guard-house Trigaud joined him.

"Well," said the peasant, "was that done to your liking? Are you satisfied?"

"Yes," replied Trigaud, "that was just as *gars* Aubin Courte-Joie ordered."

"Good luck to you, then! As for me, I'll put the horse back where I found it. But when the cartman wakes up to-morrow and looks for his cart and his hay he'll be rather surprised to find it up there."

"Well, tell him it is for the good of the cause, and he won't mind," replied Trigaud.

The two men parted.

Trigaud, however, did not leave the place; he roamed about its neighborhood till he heard the stroke of twelve from the steeple of Saint-Colombin. Then he returned to the guard-house, *sabots* in hand, and without making the slightest noise, or rousing the attention of the sentry, who was pacing up and down, he crept to the grating of the dungeon. Once there he softly drew the hay into a thick heap beside the millstone, which he then, as softly, turned over upon it. Then he leaned behind it to the grating, wrenched off the boards that closed it, drew out first Courte-Joie, whom Michel pushed behind, then the young baron by the hands; after which, putting one on each shoulder, Trigaud, still barefooted, walked rapidly away from the neighborhood of the guard-house, making, in spite of his immense size and the weight he carried, no more noise than a cat on a carpet.

When he had gone about five hundred yards he stopped; not that he was tired but because Aubin Courte-Joie signed to him. Michel slipped to the ground and feeling in his pocket pulled out a handful of money, among it a few gold coins which he deposited in Trigaud's capacious hand.

The giant made as though he were about to put them in a pocket twice as capacious as the hand itself, but Aubin Courte-Joie stopped him.

"Return that to monsieur," he said; "we don't take pay from both sides."

"Both sides!" exclaimed Michel, "what do you mean?"

"Yes; we have n't obliged you personally as much as you think for," said Courte-Joie.

"I don't understand you, friend."

"My young gentleman," said the cripple, "now that we are safely outside that cellar I 'll frankly admit that I lied to you just now, when I said I had got myself locked up merely to get you out of that hole. But, don't you see, I wanted your help; I could never have clambered up alone to that grating. Now, however, thanks to your good-will and my friend Trigaud's wrists, we 've given 'em the slip successfully, and I feel bound to tell you that you have only exchanged one captivity for another."

"What does that mean?"

"It means that just now you were in a damp unhealthy prison, and now, though you are in the midst of the fields, on a calm, still night, you are none the less in prison."

"In prison?"

"Well, a prisoner."

"Whose prisoner?"

"Mine, of course!"

"Yours?" said Michel, laughing.

"Yes, for the time being. Oh, you need n't laugh! You are a prisoner, I tell you, till I consign you to the hands that want you."

"Whose hands are they?"

"As for that, you can find out for yourself. I fulfil my errand, neither more nor less. You need n't be frightened; you might have fallen into worse hands, that 's all I shall tell you."

"But —"

"Well, in return for services that have been done, and in consideration of a good sum of money for my poor Trigaud, I took the order of a person who said: 'Help M. le Baron Michel de la Logerie to escape, and bring him to me.' I have helped you to escape, and now I am taking you to that person, Monsieur le baron."

"Listen," said the young man, who did not comprehend one word of all the tavern-keeper was telling him: "Here is my purse, well-filled; put me on the road to La Logerie, where I desire to be this evening, and take the purse and my thanks to boot."

Michel fancied that his two liberators did not think the price paid sufficient.

"Monsieur," said Courte-Joie, with all the dignity of which he was capable, "my comrade Trigaud cannot accept your reward because he has been already paid for doing exactly the contrary of what you wish. As for me, I am not aware if you know who I am, and therefore it is best to tell you. I am an honest trader, whom differences of opinion with the government have compelled to close his business; but, miserable as my external appearance may be, let me tell you that I give my services to others, I don't sell them."

"But where the devil are you taking me?" demanded Michel, who certainly did not expect such sensitive feelings in his strange conductor.

"Be so good as to follow us, and in less than an hour you will find out."

"Follow you, indeed! when you say I am your prisoner! Not I! I am not so amiable as all that."

Courte-Joie made no answer; but a single touch on Trigaud's arm told the giant what he had to do, and the young man had scarcely uttered the words and made a hasty step in advance, before Trigaud, flinging out his arm like a grapnel-iron, seized him by the collar. Michel tried to shout, preferring to be retaken by the soldiers rather than be Trigaud's prisoner. But with his free hand the giant grasped the baron's face and silenced him as successfully as the famous gag of Monsieur de Vendôme might have done it. In this condition Michel was rushed, with the rapidity of a race-horse, across the fields for a distance of some seven or eight hundred yards, half suspended in space by the arm of the colossus, so that he touched the ground with the points of his toes only.

"That will do, Trigaud," said Courte-Joie, who was in his usual place on the shoulders of his human steed, who seemed to care little for the double burden; "that will do; the young baron is disgusted enough by this time with the idea of going back to La Logerie. Besides, we were cautioned to take care of him; it won't do to spoil the merchandise." Then as Trigaud halted obediently, Aubin said to Michel, who was nearly suffocated, "Will you be docile now?"

"You are the stronger, and I have no arms," said the baron. "I am therefore obliged to submit to your ill-treatment."

"Ill-treatment! Ha! don't you say that, or I'll appeal to your honor to say if it is n't true that you have urged me all along, both in the dungeon of the Blues and here in the fields, to let you go back to La Logerie, and that it was only your obstinacy which obliged me to use violence."

"Well, at any rate, tell me the name of the person who ordered you to come after me and take me to him."

"I am positively forbidden to do so," said Courte-Joie, "but, without transgressing orders, I can tell you that it is one of your very best friends."

A cold chill ran through Michel's heart. He thought of Bertha. He fancied she had received his letter. It was doubtless an angry "she-wolf" who awaited him, and, painful as the interview would be, he felt that he could not, in honor, refuse it.

"Very good," he said; "I know now who it is."

"You know, do you?"

"Yes, it is Mademoiselle de Souday."

Aubin Courte-Joie did not answer; but he looked at Trigaud with an air that seemed to say, "Faith! he 's guessed it!" Michel intercepted the look.

"Let us walk on," he said.

"You won't try to get away?"

"No."

"On your word of honor?"

"On my word of honor."

"Well, as you are now sensible, we 'll give you the means of getting along without skinning your feet among the briers or gluing them to this cursèd sticky soil, which adds at least seven pound weight to our boots."

These words were soon explained to Michel, for after crossing the highway behind Trigaud, and going a hundred yards into the woods that bordered the road he heard the whinnying of a horse.

"My horse!" he exclaimed, not concealing his surprise.

"Did you think we had stolen it?" asked Courte-Joie.

"Why did n't you stay at the place where I gave it to you?"

"Confound it!" replied Aubin. "I 'll tell you: we noticed a lot of men walking round us and watching us with an interest that was too deep not to be disquieting; and as inquisitive folk are not to my taste, and time went by and you did n't return, we thought we had better take your beast to Banlœuvre, where we supposed you had gone, if not arrested; and it was only as we went along we discovered that if not actually arrested you soon would be."

"Soon would be?"

"Yes, and so you were."

"Were you near me when the gendarmes arrested me?"

"My young gentleman," replied Courte-Joie in his jeering, sarcastic way, "you must have little experience in life or you would n't go along the high-roads dreaming of your own affairs, instead of looking about you and seeing who go and come and what they are doing. You might have heard the trot of those gendarmes ten minutes before they came up with you; we heard them, and you might easily have gone into the woods as we did."

Michel took care not to say what was filling his mind to the exclusion of every other thought at the moment the gendarmes arrested him; he contented himself by giving a deep sigh at this reminder of his sufferings. Then he mounted his horse, which Trigaud had unfastened and presented to him awkwardly enough, though Courte-Joie endeavored to show his henchman how to hold a stirrup properly. Then they took once more to the high-road, and the giant, with his hand on the withers of the horse, accompanied Michel easily at whatever pace the latter chose to ride.

A mile and a half farther on they struck into a cross-road, and Michel fancied, dark as it was, that he recognized the path from certain shapes in the dark masses of the trees. Presently they reached a crossway at sight of which the young man quivered. He had passed that place on the evening when for the first time he walked home with Bertha from Tinguy's cottage. A minute more and they were making their way to the cottage itself, where, in spite of the lateness of the hour, a light was sparkling; at that instant a little cry, apparently a call, came from behind the hedge that ran along the road.

Aubin Courte-Joie answered it.

"Is that you, Monsieur Courte-Joie?" asked a woman's voice, and at the same moment a white form showed itself above the hedge.

"Yes, but who are you?"

"Rosine, Tinguy's daughter; don't you remember me?"

"Rosine!" exclaimed Michel, confirmed in the thought that Bertha was awaiting him by the sight of her young maid.

Courte-Joie with his monkey-like agility slid down Trigaud's body, and went to the hedge-bank with a movement a good deal like that of a frog's jump, leaving Trigaud to keep guard over Michel.

"Pest, little one!" he cried, "the night is so dark one may well take white for gray. But," he added, lowering his voice, "why are not you at home, where we were told to find you?"

"Because there are people in the cottage, and it won't do to take Monsieur Michel there."

"People? Ah, *ça!* those damned Blues get a footing everywhere."

"There are no soldiers there; it is only Jean Oullier, who has spent the day going round the country, and has brought a few of the Montaigu men with him."

"What are they doing?"

"Only talking. Go in, and drink a cup of cider with them, and warm yourself a bit."

"Well, but our young gentleman, my dear, what shall we do with him?"

"Leave him with me. That was agreed upon, you know, Maître Courte-Joie."

"We were to give him to you in your house, where there 's a cellar or a garret to put him in; and that 's easy enough to do, for he is not hard to manage, poor fellow, — but here in the open fields there 's a risk of losing him; he 'll slip away from you like an eel."

"Pooh!" said Rosine, with a smile which since the deaths of her father and brother seldom came upon her lips, "do you think he would make more objection to following a pretty girl than two old fellows like you?"

"But suppose the prisoner carries off his keeper?" said Courte-Joie, still dissatisfied.

"Oh! don't trouble yourself about that; I 've a good foot, a good eye, and an honest heart. Besides, Baron Michel is my foster-brother; we 've known each other this long while, and I know he is no more capable of forcing the virtue of a girl than the bolts of a prison. Besides, what were you told to do?"

"Release him if we could and bring him, willingly or unwillingly, to your father's house, where we were to find you."

"Well, here I am, and there 's the house; the bird is out of his cage; that 's all that was asked of you, was n't it ?"

"Hang it ! yes, I believe so."

"Then, good-night."

"Look here, Rosine, for greater security, don't you want us to put a rope round his paws ?" said Courte-Joie, sarcastically.

"Thank you, no, Maître Courte-Joie," said Rosine, going toward Michel; "better put one on your own tongue."

Michel, in spite of the distance at which he stood, had distinguished Rosine's name and perceived, as we have said, the connivance which evidently existed between her and his captors. He was more and more confirmed in the belief that he owed his deliverance to Bertha. Courte-Joie's proceedings, the sort of violence he had used toward him, by means of his auxiliary Trigaud, the mystery in which the tavern-keeper had wrapped the origin and reason of his devotion to a man whom he scarcely knew,—all these things agreed wonderfully with the irritation which the letter he had sent by the notary was calculated to rouse in the violent and irascible heart of the young girl.

"Oh ! Rosine, is that you ?" he exclaimed, raising his voice as soon as he saw through the darkness his foster-sister coming toward him.

"Good !" cried Rosine, "you are not like that wretch of a Courte-Joie, who did n't choose to recognize me at first. You knew me at once, did n't you, Monsieur Michel ?"

"Yes, of course. Tell me, Rosine, where is she ?"

"Who ?"

"Mademoiselle Bertha."

"Mademoiselle Bertha ?"

"Yes."

"I don't know," said Rosine, with a simplicity which Michel knew to be sincere.

"What! you don't know?" he repeated.

"I suppose she is at Souday."

"You don't know, you only suppose?"

"Bless me —"

"Have you seen her to-day?"

"No, Monsieur Michel; I only know that she was to go to the château to-day with Monsieur le marquis; but I 've been at Nantes myself."

"At Nantes!" cried the young man, "were you at Nantes this morning?"

"Yes."

"What time were you there?"

"It was striking nine as we crossed the pont Rousseau."

"You say *we?*"

"Yes, of course."

"Then you were not alone?"

"Why, no! I went there to accompany Mademoiselle Mary; it was sending to the château for me that delayed her journey."

"But where is she now,— Mademoiselle Mary?"

"Now, this minute?"

"Yes."

"On the little island of La Jonchère; and that 's where I am going to take you. But how queer of you to ask me all this, Monsieur Michel!"

"Are you really going to take me to her?" cried Michel, beside himself with joy. "Then come along, come quick, my little Rosine."

"Good! and that old fool Courte-Joie, who said I could n't manage you! What idiots men are!"

"Rosine, my dear, for heaven's sake don't lose time."

"I 'm ready; but had n't you better take me up behind? and then we can go faster."

"Of course we can," said Michel, whose heart, at the

mere idea of seeing Mary, abjured all its jealous suspicions, and glowed with the thought that she whom he loved was really the one who had so effectually managed his release. "Come, come on!"

"Here I am! give me your hand," said Rosine, resting her wooden shoe on the young man's foot. Then, making her spring, "There! I'm all right," she said, settling herself. "Now then, turn to the right."

The young man obeyed, with no more thought of Courte-Joie and Trigaud than if they did not exist. To him, there was no one at this moment in the world but Mary.

"Rosine," he said, after he had gone a little way, longing to talk about Mary, "how did mademoiselle know I was arrested by the gendarmes?"

"Bless me! I should have to tell you what happened before that, Monsieur Michel."

"Tell me all you can, my dear, good Rosine; only, do speak up. I'm burning with impatience. Ah! how good it is to be free," cried the young man; "and to be going to Mary!"

"Then I must tell you that mademoiselle came from Banlœuvre to Souday very early this morning; she borrowed my Sunday clothes and put them on, and then she said 'Rosine, you are to go with me.'"

"Go on, Rosine, do! I'm listening."

"Well, then we started, with eggs in our baskets like real peasant-women. At Nantes while I sold eggs mademoiselle did her errand."

"What was that errand, Rosine?" asked Michel, before whose eyes the form of the young man disguised as a peasant now loomed like a spectre.

"Oh, that I don't know, Monsieur Michel." Then, without pausing to notice the heavy sigh with which Michel received her words, she added: "As mademoiselle was very tired we asked Monsieur Loriot, the Légé notary, to drive us back in his carriole. We stopped half way to bait the horse and while the notary was gossiping with the innkeeper we went into the garden to get away from the people who stared at mademoiselle, — who is really much too beautiful for a peasant-woman. There she read a letter, which made her cry dreadfully."

"A letter!" exclaimed Michel.

"Yes, a letter Monsieur Loriot gave her as we came along."

"My letter!" murmured Michel; "she has read my letter to her sister! Oh!"

He stopped his horse abruptly, not knowing whether to rejoice or to be terrified at this fact.

"What 's the matter?" asked Rosine, who of course, did not understand the sudden halt.

"Nothing, nothing," replied Michel, shaking the reins and putting the horse to a trot.

Rosine resumed her tale.

"Well, she was crying over the letter when some one called us from the other side of the hedge: it was Aubin Courte-Joie, and Trigaud with him. He told us your adventure, and asked mademoiselle what he had better do with your horse. Then, poor young lady, she seemed to feel worse than when she read that letter. She was all upset, and said such a lot of things to Courte-Joie — who, indeed, is under great obligations to Monsieur le marquis — that she persuaded him to rescue you from the soldiers. You 've got a good friend in her, Monsieur Michel."

Michel listened delightedly; he was almost beside himself with joy and satisfaction, and would gladly have paid a piece of gold for every syllable Rosine uttered. He began to think his horse went much too slowly, and cutting a branch from a nut-tree he endeavored to excite the animal to a pace in keeping with the pulses of his heart.

"But," he asked, "why did n't she wait for me in your father's cottage, Rosine?"

"We did intend to, Monsieur le baron; in fact, we made Monsieur Loriot leave us there, telling him we would walk to Souday. Mademoiselle had charged Courte-Joie to take you to my house, and on no account let you go to Banlœuvre until she had seen you; but as ill-luck would have it, the cottage, which since father's death has been quite deserted, was to-night as full of people as an inn. Jean Oullier has got a meeting there of all the leaders of his district. So Mademoiselle Mary hid herself in the barn, and asked me to take her to some place where she could see you alone as soon as Courte-Joie brought you. Here we are on a level with the mill of Saint-Philbert; we shall see the lake of Grand-Lieu in a moment."

Rosine's last words brought a more emphatic blow with the nut-stick on the horse's quarters than any that preceded it. Michel felt that an end was coming to the difficult position in which he stood. Mary now knew the strength of his love; she knew that it was powerful enough to make him reject the proffered marriage; she was evidently not offended by it, since her regard for him had led her to do him a signal service and even to risk her reputation by doing it. Timid, reserved, and backward as Michel was, his hopes now rose to the level of these proofs, as he thought them, of Mary's affection. It seemed to him impossible that a young girl who braved public opinion, her father's anger, her sister's reproaches, to secure the safety of a man whose love and whose hopes she thoroughly well knew, could deny herself to that love or disappoint those hopes. He saw his future through a misty horizon still, but the mists were roseate as he began to descend the hill which locks in the lake of Grand-Lieu to the southeast.

"Are we getting there ?" he said to Rosine.

"Yes," she replied, slipping from the horse's back, "follow me."

Michel dismounted and the pair entered a little thicket of osiers, in the middle of which stood a willow, to which Michel tied his horse. Then they pushed their way for a hundred yards or so through the flexible branches, until they came out upon the bank of a sort of creek which flowed to the lake. Rosine jumped into a little boat with a flat bottom. Michel offered to take the oars, but Rosine, knowing that he was a novice at such performances, pushed him back and took her seat on the thwart with an oar in each hand.

"No, no!" she said, "I can manage better than you; I have often rowed my poor father when he cast his nets into the lake."

"But," said Michel, "are you sure you can hit the island of Jonchère in this darkness?"

"Look!" she said, without turning round, "can't you see anything on the water?"

"Yes," replied the young man, "I see what looks like a star."

"Well, that star is Mademoiselle Mary, who is holding a lamp in her hand. She must have heard the oars, and is coming to meet us."

Michel would gladly have flung himself into the sea to precede the boat, for, in spite of Rosine's nautical skill, it progressed very slowly. He began to think he should never get over the distance between himself and that light, which was now seen to grow brighter and brighter every moment.

But, alas! contrary to the hopes which Rosine had inspired, when they were near enough to the island to distinguish the one willow which adorned it Michel did not see Mary awaiting him on the shore; the glow came from a fire of rushes which she had doubtless lighted and left to burn slowly out upon the shore.

"Rosine," cried Michel, aghast, jumping up in the boat which he nearly overset, "I don't see Mademoiselle Mary."

"She is probably in the duck-shooters' hut," replied the girl, pulling in her oars. "Take one of those burning sticks; you'll find the hut on the other side toward the offing."

Michel sprang ashore, did as he was told, and hurried away in the direction of the hut.

The island of Jonchère is some two or three hundred yards square. It is covered with reeds on the low ground, which is overflowed in winter by the waters of the lake. About fifty feet square of dry land rise above the level of this inundation; on this elevation old Tinguy had built for himself a little hut, to which he came on winter nights to watch for wild-duck. This was the place to which Rosine had taken Mary.

Whatever his hopes might be, Michel's heart beat almost to bursting when he came in sight of the little building. As he laid his hand on the latch of the door the oppression became so great that he hesitated.

During that momentary pause his eyes rested on a pane of glass introduced into the upper half of the entrance door, through which it was possible to look into the cabin. There he beheld Mary, sitting on a heap of reeds, her head bending forward on her breast.

By the feeble light of a lantern which was placed on a stool he fancied he saw two tears glittering on the long, fringed eyelashes of the young girl, and the thought that those tears were shed for him made him lose all diffidence. He opened the door and rushed to her feet, crying out:

"Mary, Mary, I love you!"

XI.

MARY IS VICTORIOUS AFTER THE MANNER OF PYRRHUS.

However firm Mary's resolution to control herself may have been, Michel's entrance was so sudden, his voice vibrated with such an accent, there was in his cry so much of love, so passionate a prayer, that the gentle creature was unable to repress her own emotion; her breast heaved, her fingers trembled, and the tears the young baron fancied he saw on her eyelids detached themselves and fell, drop by drop like liquid pearls, on Michel's hands which were grasping hers. The poor lover himself was too overcome with his own emotion to notice Mary's, and the girl had time to recover herself before he spoke. She gently pushed him aside and looked about her. Michel's eyes followed Mary's and then fixed themselves anxiously and inquiringly on her face.

"How is it that you are alone, monsieur?" she asked. "Where is Rosine?"

"And you, Mary," said the young man, in a voice full of sadness, "how is it that you are not, as I am, full of the happiness of our meeting?"

"Ah! my friend," said Mary, dwelling on the word, "you have no cause — now especially — to doubt the interest I take in your safety."

"No," said Michel, trying to regain the hand she had drawn away from him. "No, indeed, for it is you to whom I owe my liberty, and probably my life."

"But," interrupted Mary, trying to smile, "all that does not make me forget that we are alone together. Do me the kindness to call Rosine, for there are certain social conventions I do not wish to disregard."

Michel sighed and remained on his knees, while two large tears escaped his eyelids. Mary turned away her head that she might not see them; then she made a motion as if to rise. But Michel retained her. The poor lad had not enough experience of the human heart to observe that Mary had never before manifested any reluctance to be alone with him, and to draw from her present action a deduction favorable to his love. On the contrary, all his beautiful visions went up in smoke, and Mary seemed to him even colder and more indifferent than she had been of late.

"Ah!" he cried, in a tone of melancholy reproach, "why did you rescue me from the hands of the soldiers? They might have shot me, but I would meet that fate rather than live to know you do not love me!"

"Michel! Michel!" cried Mary.

"Oh!" he exclaimed, "I repeat it, I would rather die."

"Don't talk so, naughty child that you are!" said Mary, striving to assume a maternal tone. "Don't you see that it distresses me?"

"You do not care!" said Michel.

"You cannot doubt," continued Mary, "that my friendship for you is true and most sincere."

"Alas! Mary," said the young man, sadly, "that feeling is not enough to satisfy the passion that consumes my heart ever since I have known you; I do feel certain of your friendship, but my heart wants more."

Mary made a supreme effort.

"My friend, what you ask of me, Bertha will give you; She loves you as you wish to be loved, as you deserve to be loved;" said the poor child, in a trembling voice, striving to put her sister's name as a barrier between herself and the man she loved.

Michel shook his head and sighed.

"Oh, not her! not her!" he said.

"Why —" said Mary as if she did not see his gesture of refusal or hear that cry from his heart. "Why did you write her that letter, which would have filled her with despair had it reached her?"

"That letter; then it was you who received it?"

"Alas! yes," said Mary, "and painful as it was to me, it is most fortunate that I did so."

"Did you read it through?" asked Michel.

"Yes," said the young girl, lowering her eyes before the supplicating glance with which he enfolded her as he asked the question. "Yes, I read it — all; and it is because I did so, dear friend, that I wished to speak to you before you see my sister again."

"But, Mary, do you not see that that letter is truth itself from the first line to the last, and that if I love Bertha at all it can only be as a sister?"

"No, no," cried Mary; "I only know that my future would be horrible if I caused unhappiness to my poor sister whom I love so well."

"But," said Michel, "what do you ask of me?"

"I ask you," replied Mary, clasping her hands, "to sacrifice a feeling which has not had time to strike deep roots into your heart; I ask you to forget a fancy nothing justifies, to renounce an attachment which can have no good result for you and must be fatal to all three of us."

"Ask my life, Mary; I can kill myself, or let myself be killed, — nothing is easier; but to ask me not to love you! Good God! what would my poor heart be if deprived of its love for you?"

"And yet it must be so, dear Michel," said Mary, in her winning voice; "for never — no never — will you obtain from me a word of encouragement for the love you speak of in that letter. I have sworn it."

"To whom, Mary?"

"To God and to myself."

"Oh!" exclaimed Michel, sobbing, "and I dreamed she loved me!"

Mary thought that the more warmth he put into his words and actions, the colder it behooved her to be.

"All that I have now said to you, my friend," she continued, "is dictated not only by common-sense, but by the strong interest I feel in your future. If I were indifferent to you, I should simply express my feelings and let the matter end; but as a friend I cannot do so, — as a friend, I say to you, Michel, forget the woman who can never be yours and love the woman who loves you and to whom you are virtually betrothed."

"Oh, but you know very well how that betrothal, as you call it, took me by surprise; you know that in making that proposal Petit-Pierre mistook my feelings. Those feelings you well know. I expressed them to you that night when the general and the soldiers were at the château. You did not repulse them; I felt your hands press mine; I knelt at your feet, Mary, as I do now; you bent your head to mine; your hair, your beautiful, adored hair touched my forehead. I did wrong not to tell Petit-Pierre who it was I loved; but how could I expect what has happened? It never crossed my mind she could suppose I loved any one but Mary. It is the fault of my timidity, which I curse; but, after all, it is not so grievous a fault that it ought to separate me forever from the woman I love, and chain my life to one I do not love."

"Alas! my friend, the fault that seems to you so light seems to me irreparable. Whatever happens, and even though you repudiate the promise made in your name and in which you acquiesced by silence, you must understand that I can never be yours, for I will never rend the heart of my beloved sister with the sight of my happiness."

"Good God!" cried Michel, "how wretched I am!"

He put his face in his hands and burst into tears.

"Yes," said Mary, "I know you suffer now; but take courage. Call up your virtue, your courage, my friend. Listen willingly to my advice; this feeling will, little by little, be effaced from your heart. If necessary, I will go away for a time that you may cure yourself."

"Go away! separate yourself from me! No, Mary, never, never! no, don't leave me, for I swear that the day you leave, I leave; where you go, I go. Good God! what would become of me, deprived of your dear presence? No, no, no; don't go, I implore you, Mary."

"So be it; I will stay, but only to help you to do whatever may be painful and sad in your duty; and when that is done, when you are happy, when you are Bertha's husband —"

"Never! never!" muttered Michel.

"Yes, my friend, for Bertha is more fitted to be your wife than I am; her love for you, — and I can swear this for I have heard her express it, — is greater than you suppose; her tenderness will satisfy the craving for love which now consumes you, and my sister's strength and energy, which I do not possess, will clear your path in life of the thorns and briers you might not of yourself be able to put aside. So, if there is really a sacrifice on your part, that sacrifice, believe me, will be well-rewarded."

In saying these words Mary affected a calmness which was far indeed from being in her heart, the real condition of which was betrayed by her paleness and agitation. As for Michel, he listened in feverish agitation.

"Don't talk so!" he cried as she ended. "Do you suppose the current of human affections is a thing to be managed and directed as we please, like a river which an engineer forces between the banks of a canal, or a vine which the gardener trains as he will? No, no; I tell you again, I repeat it and I will repeat it a hundred times, — it is you, you alone whom I love, Mary. It would be impossible for my heart to name any other name than yours, even if I wished it, and I don't wish it. My God! my God!" continued the young man, flinging up his arms to heaven with a look of agonized despair; "what would become of me if I saw you the wife of another man?"

"Michel," said Mary, with passionate fervor, "if you will do as I ask you, I swear by all that is most sacred that, as I cannot be your wife, I will belong to none but God; I will never marry. All my affection, my tenderness shall remain yours; and this affection will not be of the vulgar kind that years destroy or a mere chance kills. It will be the deep, unutterable affection of a sister for a brother; it will be a gratitude which will forever bind me to you. I shall owe to you the happiness of my sister, and all my life shall be spent in blessing you."

"Your love for your sister misleads you, Mary," replied Michel. "You think only of her; you do not think of me when you seek to condemn me to the horrible torture of being chained, for life, to a woman I do not love. Oh, Mary! it is cruel of you, — you for whom I would give my life, — it is cruel to ask of me a thing to which I can never resign myself."

"Oh, yes, you can, my friend," persisted the girl; "you can surely resign yourself to what, though it may be the result of fate, is also most assuredly, a generous and magnanimous action; you can resign yourself because you know that God would never suffer a sacrifice like that to go unrewarded, and the reward will be — yes, it will be — the happiness of two poor orphans."

"Oh, Mary," said Michel, quite beside himself, "don't talk to me like that. Oh, it is plain that you don't know what it is to love! You tell me to give you up! but remember that you are my heart, my soul, my life, — it is simply asking me to tear my heart from my breast, forswear my soul, blast my happiness, dry up my very existence at its source. You are the light for which and by which the world, to my eyes, is a world; the day you cease to shine upon my life I shall fall into a gulf the darkness of which horrifies me. I swear to you, Mary, that since I have known you, since that moment when I first saw you and felt your hands cooling my wounded forehead, you have been so identified with my being that there is not a thought in my mind that does not belong to you, all that is within me refers to you, and if my heart were to lose you, it would cease to beat as if the principle of life were taken from it. You see, therefore, that it is impossible I should do as you ask."

"And yet," cried Mary, in a paroxysm of despair, "Bertha loves you, and I do not love you."

"Ah! if you do not love me, Mary, if, with your eyes in my eyes, your hands in my hands, you have the courage to say, 'I do not love you,' then, indeed, all is over."

"What do you mean by that,— how is it all over?"

"Simply enough, Mary. As truly as those stars in heaven see the chastity of my love for you, as truly as that God who is above those stars knows that my love for you is immortal, Mary, neither you nor your sister shall ever see me again."

"Oh, don't say that, Michel."

"I have but to cross the lake and mount my horse, which is there among the osiers, and gallop to the first guard-house; once there, I have only to say, 'I am Baron Michel de la Logerie,' to be shot in three days." Mary gave a cry. "And that is what I will do," added Michel, "as surely as the stars look down upon us, and God himself is above them."

The young man made a movement to rush from the hut. Mary threw herself before him and clasped him round the body, but her strength gave way, her hold loosened, and she slipped to his feet.

"Michel," she murmured, "if you love me as you say you do, you will not refuse my entreaty. In the name of your love I implore you, — I whom you say you love, — do not kill my sister, grant me her life; grant her happiness to my prayers and tears. God will bless you for it; and every day my soul shall rise to Him, imploring happiness for one who has helped me to save a sister I love better than myself. Michel, forget me, — I ask it of your mercy, Michel, — do not reduce my Bertha to despair."

"Oh, Mary, Mary, you are cruel!" cried the young man, grasping his hair with both hands; "you are asking my very life. I shall die of this."

"Courage, friend, courage," said the girl, weakening herself.

"I could have courage for all, except renouncing you; but the simple thought of that makes me feebler than a child, — more despairing than a soul in hell."

"Michel, my friend, will you do as I ask of you?" stammered Mary, her voice half drowned in tears.

"I — I —"

He was about to answer that he would, but he stopped.

"Ah," he cried, "if you suffered as I suffer!"

At that cry of utter selfishness and yet of infinite love, Mary, beside herself, panting for breath, half maddened, clasped him in her nervous arms and said in a sobbing voice: —

"Would it comfort you to know that my heart is torn with an anguish like yours?"

"Yes, yes; oh, yes!"

"Would hell be a paradise if I were by your side?"

"An eternity of suffering with you, Mary, and I could bear all."

"Well, then," cried Mary, losing control of herself; "be satisfied, cruel man! your sufferings, your anguish — I feel them all. Like you, I am dying of despair at the sacrifice our duty is wringing from us."

"Then you love me, Mary?" said the young man.

"Oh, faithless heart!" she cried; "oh, faithless man, who can see my tears, my tortures, and cannot see my love!"

"Mary, Mary!" exclaimed Michel, staggering, breathless, mad, and drunken at once; "after killing me with grief, will you kill me with joy?"

"Yes, yes, I love you!" repeated Mary. "I love you! I needs must say the words that have choked me long. Yes, I love you as you love me. I love you so well that when I think of the sacrifice we both must make, death would be dear to me could it come at this moment when I tell you the truth."

Saying these words in spite of herself, and as if attracted by magnetic power, Mary approached her face to that of the young man, who looked at her with the eyes of one whom a sudden hallucination has flung into ecstasy; her blond hair touched his forehead; their breaths mingled and intoxicated both. As if overcome by this amorous effluence, Michel closed his eyes, his lips touched Mary's, and she, exhausted by her struggle so long sustained against herself, yielded to the impulse that moved her. Their lips united, and thus they stayed for several moments, lost in a gulf of dolorous felicity.

Mary was the first to recover herself. She rose quickly, pushed Michel away from her, and began to cry bitterly.

At that instant Rosine entered the hut.

XII.

BARON MICHEL FINDS AN OAK INSTEAD OF A REED ON WHICH TO LEAN.

Mary felt that Rosine's coming was a help sent to her from above. Alone, without other support than her own heart, which had yielded so utterly, she felt herself at the mercy of her lover. Seeing Rosine, she ran to her and caught her hand.

"What is it, my child?" she said. "What have you come to say?"

She passed her hands over her forehead and eyes to efface, if possible, the signs of her emotion.

"Mademoiselle," said Rosine, "I think I hear a boat."

"In which direction?"

"Toward Saint-Philbert."

"I thought your father's boat was the only one on the lake."

"No, mademoiselle, the miller of Grand-Lieu has one; it is half-rotten to be sure, but some one has no doubt taken it to come over here."

"Well," said Mary, "I'll go with you and see who it is?"

Then, without paying the slightest heed to the young man, who stretched out his arms to her in a supplicating way, Mary, who was not sorry to leave Michel in order to gather up her courage, sprang from the hut. Rosine followed her.

Michel was left alone, completely crushed; he felt that happiness had escaped him, and he doubted the possibility of recovering it. Never again would another such scene bring another such avowal.

When Mary returned, after listening in all directions without hearing anything more than the lapping of the water on the shore, she found Michel sitting on the reeds with his head in his hands. She thought him calm, — he was only depressed; she went to him. Michel, hearing her step, raised his head, and seeing her as reserved on her return as she was emotional before she left him, he merely held out his hand and shook his head sadly.

"Oh, Mary, Mary!" he said.

"Well, my friend?" she replied.

"Repeat to me, for Heaven's sake — repeat to me those dear words you said just now! Tell me again that you love me!"

"I will repeat it, dear friend," said Mary, sadly; "and as often as you wish it, if the conviction that my love is watching tenderly your sufferings and your efforts can in any way inspire you with courage and resolution."

"What!" cried Michel, wringing his hands, "are you still thinking of that cruel separation? Can you expect me, with the knowledge of my love for you, and the certainty of your love for me, — can you still expect me to give myself to another woman?"

"I expect us both to accomplish the duty that lies before us, my friend. That is why I do not regret having opened my heart to you. I hope that my example will teach you to suffer, and inspire you with resignation to the will of God. A fatal chain of circumstances, which I deplore as much as you, Michel, has separated us; we cannot belong to each other."

"But why not? I have made no pledge. I never said one word of love to Mademoiselle Bertha."

"No; but she told me that she loved you. I received her confidence as long ago as that evening when you met her at Tinguy's cottage, and walked home with her."

"But whatever I said to her that night that may have

seemed tender referred to you," said the luckless young man.

"Ah! friend, a heart which bends is soon filled; poor Bertha deceived herself. As we returned to the château that night and I was thinking in the depths of my heart, 'I love him,' she said those very words to me aloud. To love you is only to suffer, but to be yours, Michel, would be a crime."

"Ah! my God, my God!"

"Yes, God will give us strength, Michel,—the God whom we invoke. Let us bear heroically the consequences of our mutual timidity. I do not blame you for yours, be sure of that; but, at least, spare me the remorse of feeling that I have made my sister's unhappiness without benefit or advantage to myself."

"But," said Michel, "your project is senseless; the very thing you seek to avoid would surely come of it. Sooner or later Bertha must discover that I do not love her, and then —"

"Listen to me, friend," interrupted Mary, laying her hand on Michel's arm; "though very young, I have strong convictions on what is called love. My education, the direct opposite of yours, has, like yours, its drawbacks, but also some advantages. One of these advantages — a terrible one, I admit — is a practical view of realities. Accustomed to hear conversations in which the past disguised nothing of its weakness, I know, through what I have learned from my father's life, that nothing is more fugitive than the feelings which you now express to me. I therefore hope that Bertha will have taken my place in your heart before she has time to perceive your indifference. That is my hope, Michel, and I pray you not to destroy it."

"You ask an impossibility, Mary."

"Well, if it must be so, it must. You are free not to keep the engagement which binds you to my sister; free to reject the prayer I make to you on my knees; it will be only another wound and shame inflicted on two poor girls already unjustly treated by the world. My poor Bertha will suffer, I know that; but at least I shall suffer with her, and with the same pain as hers; but take care, Michel, lest our sufferings, increased by each seeing that of the other, end by cursing you."

"I implore you, Mary, I conjure you do not say such words, — they break my heart."

"Listen, Michel; the hours are passing, the night is nearly gone, day will soon be here; we must now separate, and my resolution is irrevocable. We have both dreamed a dream which we must both forget. I have told you how you can deserve, — I will not say my love, for you have it, — but the eternal gratitude of your poor Mary. I swear to you," she added, in a deeper tone of supplication than she had yet used; "I swear to you that if you will devote yourself to the happiness of my sister, I will have but one thought, one prayer, in my heart, — that of beseeching God to reward you here below, and in heaven above. If, on the contrary, you refuse me, Michel, if your heart cannot rise to the level of my own abnegation, you must renounce the sight of us, you must go far away; for, I repeat, and I swear it before God, I will never, my friend, *never* be yours!"

"Mary, Mary, do not take that oath; leave me some hope, at least. The obstacles around us may lessen."

"To leave you any hope would be doing wrong, Michel; and since the certainty that I share your sufferings has not given you — as you promised me it should — the firmness and resignation which strengthen my own heart, I bitterly regret the confession I have made this night. No," she added, passing her hand across her forehead, "we must have no more dreams; they are too dangerous. I have made you a request, a prayer; you will not listen to it; there is nothing left but to bid you an eternal farewell."

"Never to see you, Mary! Oh, rather death! I will do what you exact — "

He stopped, unable to say the words.

"I exact nothing," said Mary. "I have asked you on my knees not to break two hearts instead of one, and, on my knees, I once more ask it."

And she did, in fact, slip down to the feet of the young man.

"Rise, rise!" he cried. "Yes, Mary, yes, I will do what you want. But you must be there, you must never leave me; and when I suffer too much I must draw my strength and courage from your eyes. Promise me that, Mary, and I will obey you."

"Thank you, friend, thank you. That which gives me strength to ask and accept this sacrifice, is my conviction that nothing is lost for your happiness as well as Bertha's."

"But yours, yours?" cried the young man.

"Do not think of me, Michel." A groan escaped him. "God," she continued, "has given consolations to sacrifice of which the soul knows nothing till it sounds those depths. As for me," said Mary, veiling her eyes with her hand as though she feared they might deny her words, "I shall endeavor to find the sight of your happiness sufficient for me."

"Oh, my God, my God!" cried Michel, wringing his hands; "is it all over,— am I condemned to death?"

And he flung himself face down upon the floor.

At that moment Rosine entered.

"Mademoiselle," she said, "the day is breaking."

"What is the matter, Rosine?" asked Mary; "you are trembling!"

"I am sure I heard oars in the lake; and just now I heard footsteps behind me."

"Footsteps on this lonely islet! you are dreaming, child."

"I think so myself, for I have searched everywhere and seen no one."

"Now we must go," said Mary.

A sob from Michel made her turn to him.

"We must go alone, my friend," she said, "but in an hour Rosine shall come back for you with the boat. Don't forget what you have promised me. I rely upon your courage."

"Rely upon my love, Mary," he said. "The proof you exact is terrible; the task you impose immense. God grant I may not fail under the burden of it."

"Remember, Michel, that Bertha loves you, that she cherishes every glance you give her. Remember, too, that I would rather die than have her discover the true state of your heart."

"Oh, my God! my God!" murmured the young man.

"Courage! courage! Farewell, friend!"

Profiting by the moment when Rosine turned to open the door and look outside, Mary laid a kiss on Michel's forehead. It was a different kiss from that she had given him half an hour earlier. The first was the jet of flame, which darts from the heart of the lover to that of the loved one; the second was the chaste farewell of a sister to a brother.

Michel understood the difference, and it wrung his heart. Tears sprang again to his eyes. He went with the two young girls to the shore, and when he had seen them in the boat he sat down upon a stone and watched the little bark till it was lost in the morning mist that was rising from the lake.

The sound of oars still lingered in his ear; he was listening, as though to some funeral knell which told him that his illusions were vanishing like phantom dreams, when a hand was lightly laid upon his shoulder. He turned and saw Jean Oullier close beside him.

The Vendéan's face was sadder than usual, but it seemed to have lost the expression of hatred which Michel had so often seen there. His eyelids were moist, and two big drops were hanging to the beard which formed a collar round his face. Were they dew? Could they be tears from the eyes of the old follower of Charette?

He held out his hand to Michel, a thing he had never done before. The latter looked at him in surprise, and took, with some hesitation, the hand that was offered to him.

"I heard all," said Jean Oullier.

Michel sighed and dropped his head.

"Noble hearts ! both of you," said the Vendéan; "but you were right. It is a terrible task that poor child has set you. May God reward her devotion ! As for you, when you feel that you are weakening, let me know, Monsieur de la Logerie, and you 'll find out one thing, and that is, if Jean Oullier hates his enemies he can also love those he does love."

"Thank you," replied Michel.

"Come, come !" continued Jean Oullier, "no more tears; it is n't manly to cry. If necessary, I 'll try to make that iron head, called Bertha, listen to reason; though I admit to you, in advance, it is n't easy."

"But in case she won't hear reason, there is one thing else you can help me in, — an easy thing."

"What is that ?"

"To get myself killed."

Michel said it so simply that it was evidently the expression of his thought.

"Oh, oh !" muttered Jean Oullier; "he really looks, my faith, as if he 'd do it." Then he added aloud, addressing the young man: "Well, so be it; if the necessity comes, we 'll see about it."

This promise, melancholy as it was, gave Michel a little courage.

"Now, then," said the old Chouan, "come with me. You can't stay here. I have a miserable boat, but by taking some precautions I think we can both of us get safely ashore."

"But Rosine was to return in an hour and row me over," objected the young man.

"She will come on a useless errand, that 's all;" replied

Jean Oullier. "It will teach her to gossip on the high-road about other people's affairs as she did with you to-night."

After these words, which explained how Jean Oullier came to visit the island of Jonchère, Michel followed him to the boat, and presently, avoiding the road taken by Mary and Rosine, they took to the open country in the direction of Saint-Philbert.

XIII.

THE LAST KNIGHTS OF ROYALTY.

As Gaspard had clearly foreseen, and as he had predicted to Petit-Pierre at the farm-house of Banlœuvre, the postponement of the uprising till the 4th of June was a fatal blow to the projected insurrection. In spite of every effort and every activity on the part of the leaders of the Legitimist party, who all, like the Marquis de Souday, his daughters, and adherents, went themselves to the villages of their divisions to carry the order for delay, it was too late to get the information sent to the country districts, and these conflicting plans defeated the whole movement.

In the region about Niort, Fontenay, and Luçon, the royalists assembled; Diot and Robert, at the head of their organized bands, issued from the forests of the Deux-Sèvres, to serve as kernel to the movement. This was instantly made known to the military leaders of the various surrounding detachments, who at once assembled their forces, marched to the parish of Amailloux, defeated the peasantry, and arrested a large number of gentlemen and royalist officers who were in the neighborhood, and had rushed into the fight on hearing the firing.

Arrests of the same kind were made in the environs of the Champ-Saint-Père. The post of Port-la-Claye was attacked, and although, because of the small number of assailants the royalists were easily repulsed, it was evident from the audacity and vigor of the attack that it was made, or at any rate led, by other than mere refractories, — deserting recruits.

On one of the prisoners taken at the Champ-Saint-Père a list was found of the young men forming the *corps d'élite* of the royalist forces. This list, these attacks made on various sides at the same time, these arrests of men known for the enthusiasm of their Legitimist opinions, naturally put the authorities on their guard, and made them regard as imminent the dangers they had hitherto treated lightly.

If the countermand of the uprising did not reach the country districts of La Vendée in time, still less could the provinces of Brittany and Maine receive the order; and there the standard of revolt was openly unfurled. In the first, the division of Vitré took the field, and even won a victory for the Bretons at Bréal, — an ephemeral victory, which was changed to defeat the following day at Gaudinière.

In Maine Gaullier received the countermand too late to stop his *gars* from making a bloody fight at Chaney, which lasted six hours; and besides that engagement (a serious one in its results) the peasantry, unwilling to return to their homes after beginning the insurrection, kept up a daily guerilla warfare with the various columns of troops which lined the country.

We may boldly declare that the countermand of May 22, the headlong and unsupported movements which then took place, the want of cohesion and confidence which naturally resulted, did more for the government of July than the zeal of all its agents put together.

In the provinces where these premature attempts were made it was impossible to revive the ardor thus chilled and wasted. The insurgent peasantry had time to reflect; and reflection, often favorable to calculation, is always fatal to sentiment. The leaders, whose names were now made known to the government, were easily surprised and arrested on returning to their homes.

It was still worse in the districts where the peasantry had openly taken the field. Finding themselves abandoned by their own supporters, and not receiving the reinforcements on which they counted, they believed themselves betrayed, broke their guns in two, and returned, indignantly, to their cottages.

The Legitimist insurrection died in the womb. The cause of Henri V. lost two provinces before his flag was raised; but such was the courage of these sons of giants that, as we are now about to see, they did not yet despair.

Eight days had elapsed since the events recorded in our last chapter, and during those eight days the political turmoil going on around Machecoul was so violent that it swept into its orbit all the personages of our history whose own passions and interests might otherwise have kept them aloof from it.

Bertha, made uneasy at first by Michel's disappearance, was quite reassured when he returned; and her happiness was shown with such effusion and publicity that it was impossible for the young man, unless he broke the promise he had made to Mary, to do otherwise than appear, on his side, glad to see her. The many services she had to render to Petit-Pierre, the many details of the correspondence with which she was intrusted, so absorbed Bertha's time that she did not notice Michel's sadness and depression, or the constraint with which he yielded to the familiarity her masculine habits led her to show to the man whom she regarded as her betrothed husband.

Mary, who had rejoined her father and sister two hours after leaving Michel on the islet of Jonchère, avoided carefully all occasions of being alone with her lover. When the necessities of their daily life brought them together she took every possible means to put her sister at an advantage in Michel's eyes; and when her own eyes encountered those of the young baron she looked at him with so supplicating an expression that he felt himself gently but relentlessly held to the promise he had given.

If, by accident, Michel seemed to authorize by his

silence the attentions with which Bertha overwhelmed him, Mary affected a joyous and demonstrative pleasure, which, though doubtless far from her own heart, was agonizing to that of Michel. Nevertheless, in spite of all her efforts, it was impossible for her to conceal the ravages which the struggle she was making against her love wrought in her appearance. The change would certainly have struck every one about her had they been less pre-occupied,— Bertha with her love, Petit-Pierre and the marquis with the cares of State. Poor Mary's healthy freshness disappeared; dark circles of bluish bistre hollowed her eyes, her pale cheeks visibly grew thinner, and slender lines appearing on her beautiful forehead contradicted the smile that was ever on her lips.

Jean Oullier, whose loving solicitude could not have been deceived, was absent. The very day he returned to Banlœuvre the marquis despatched him on a mission to the East, and, inexperienced as he was in matters of the heart, he had departed almost easy in mind, having no real conception, in spite of all he had heard, that the trouble was so deep.

The 3d of June had now arrived. On that day a great commotion took place at the Jacquet mill in the district of Saint-Colombin. From early morning the going and coming of women and beggars had been incessant, and by nightfall the orchard which surrounded the mill had all the appearance of an encampment.

Every few minutes men in blouses or hunting-jackets, armed with guns, sabres, and pistols, kept coming in; some through the fields, others by the roads. They said a word to the sentries posted around the farm, on which word they were allowed to pass. They stacked their guns along the hedge which separated the orchard from the courtyard, and prepared, as they severally arrived, to bivouac under the apple-trees. Each and all came full of devotion; few with hope.

The courage and loyalty of such convictions make them

sacred and worthy of respect. No matter to what opinions we may belong, we must be proud of finding such loyalty, such courage, among friends, and glad to recognize them among adversaries. That political faith for which men did not shrink from dying may be rebuked and denied; God was not with it and it fell. Nevertheless, it has won the right to be honored, even in defeat, without discussion.

Antiquity declared, "Ills to the vanquished!" but antiquity was pagan. Mercy never reigned among false gods.

As for us, — not concerning ourselves in the sentiments or convictions which animated them, — we feel it was a noble and chivalric devotion which these Vendéans of 1832 held up to France, then beginning to be invaded by the narrow, sordid, commercial spirit which has since then absorbed it. And above all it seems noble and chivalrous when we reflect that most of these Vendéans had no illusion as to the outcome of their struggle; they advanced without hope to certain death. However mistaken they may have been, whatever may be said of their action, the names of those men belong to history; and we here join hands with history, if not to glorify them, at least to absolve them, although their actual names must not be mentioned in our narrative.

Inside the Jacquet mill the concourse, though less numerous than without, was not less noisily busy. Some of the leaders were receiving their last instructions and concerting with each other for the morrow; others were relating the occurrences of the day, which had not been uneventful. A gathering had taken place on the moors of Les Vergeries, and several encounters with the government troops had occurred.

The Marquis de Souday made himself conspicuous among the various groups by his enthusiastic loquacity. Once more he was a youth of twenty. In his feverish impatience it seemed to him that the sun of the morrow would never dawn; and he was profiting by the time the earth consumed in making its revolution to give a lesson in military tactics to the young men about him.

Michel, sitting in the chimney-corner, was the only person present whose mind was not completely absorbed in the events that were impending. His situation was growing more complicated every moment. A few friends and neighbors of the marquis had congratulated him on his approaching marriage with Mademoiselle de Souday. At every step he made he felt he was entangling himself more and more in the net he had blindly entered head foremost; and at the same time he felt that all his efforts to keep the promise Mary had wrung from him were hopeless. He knew it was in vain to attempt to drive from his heart the gentle image that had taken possession of it.

His sadness grew deeper and heavier, and presented at this moment a curious contrast with the eager countenances of those about him. The noise and the excitement soon became intolerable to him, and he rose and went out without exciting notice. He crossed the courtyard and passing behind the mill-wheel entered the miller's garden, followed the water-course, and finally sat down on the rail of a little bridge some two or three hundred yards from the house.

He had been sitting there about an hour, indulging in all the dismal ideas which the consciousness of his unfortunate position suggested to him, when he noticed a man who was coming toward him along the path he himself had just taken.

"Is that you, Monsieur Michel ?" asked the man.

"Jean Oullier!" cried Michel. "Jean Oullier ! Heaven has sent you. When did you get back ?"

"Half an hour ago."

"Have you seen Mary ?"

"Yes, I have seen Mademoiselle Mary."

And the old keeper raised his eyes to heaven and sighed. The tone in which he said the words, the gesture, and the sigh which accompanied them, showed that his deep solicitude was not blind to the cause of the young girl's fading appearance, and also that he fully appreciated the gravity of the situation.

Michel understood him; he covered his face with his hands and merely murmured: —

"Poor Mary!"

Jean Oullier looked at him with a certain compassion; then, after a moment's silence he said: —

"Have you decided on a course?"

"No; but I hope that to-morrow a musket-ball will save me the necessity."

"Oh," said Jean Oullier, "you can't count on that; balls are so capricious, — they never go to those who call them."

"Ah, Monsieur Jean!" exclaimed Michel, shaking; "we are very unhappy."

"Yes, so it seems; you are making terrible trouble for yourselves, all of you. What you call love is nothing but unreasonableness. Good God! who could have told me that these two children, who thought of nothing but roaming the woods bravely and merrily with their father and me, would fall in love with the first hat that came in their way, — and that, too, when the man it covered was more of a girl in his sex than they were in theirs!"

"Alas! it is fatality, my good Jean."

"No," said the Vendéan, "you need n't blame fate; it was I. But come, as you have n't the nerve to face that foolish Bertha, and speak the truth, how do you expect to remain an honest man?"

"I shall do all I can to get nearer to Mary; you can count on me for that so long as you act in that direction."

"Who says anything about your keeping near to Mary? Poor child! she has more good sense than all of you. She cannot be your wife, — she told you so the other day, or rather the other night; and she was perfectly right, — only, her love for Bertha is carrying her too far. She is condemning herself to the torture she wishes to spare her sister; and that is what neither you nor I must allow."

"How can we help it, Jean Oullier?"

"Easily. As you cannot be the husband of the woman you love, you must not be the husband of the woman you don't love. Now it is my opinion that Mary's grief will get easier when that pain is taken away from her. For she may say what she pleases; there 's always a touch of jealousy at the bottom of a woman's heart, however tender it may be."

"Renounce both the hope of making Mary my wife and the consolation of seeing her? Impossible! I can't do it. I tell you, Jean Oullier, that to get nearer to Mary I would go through hell-fire."

"Phrases, my young gentleman, phrases! The world has been consoled for being turned out of paradise, and at your age a man can always forget the woman he loves. Besides, the thing that ought to separate you from Mary is something else than hell-fire. It may be the dead body of her sister; for you don't yet know what an undisciplined child it is that goes by the name of Bertha, nor of what she is capable. I don't understand, poor fool of a peasant that I am, all your fine sentiments; but it seems to me the grandest of them ought to pause before an obstacle of this sort."

"But what can I do, my friend? What shall I do? Advise me."

"All the trouble comes, as I think, from your not having the character of your sex. You must now do what a person of the sex to which by your manners and your weakness you seem to belong would do under the circumstances. You have not known how to master the situation in which fate placed you; and now you must flee from it."

"Flee from it! But did you hear Mary say the other day that if I renounced her sister she would never see me again?"

"What of that, if she respects you?"

"But think of all I shall have to suffer!"

"You won't suffer at a distance more than you will suffer here."

"Here, at least, I can see her."

"Do you think the heart knows distance? No, not even when those we are parted from have bid us their last farewell. Thirty years ago and over I lost my poor wife, but there are days when I see her as plain as I now see you. Mary's image will remain on your heart, and you will hear her voice thanking you for what you now do."

"Ah! I would rather you talked to me of death."

"Come, Monsieur Michel, make an effort. I 'd go on my knees to you if necessary — I who have many a cause of hatred against you; I beg you, I implore you, give peace, as far as it is now possible, to those poor creatures!"

"What do you want me to do?"

"I want you to go. I have said it, and I repeat it."

"Go? Go away? You can't mean it. Why, they fight to-morrow, and to go to-day would be deserting, — it would be dishonor."

"No, I don't want you to dishonor yourself. If you go it shall not be desertion."

"How so?"

"In the absence of a captain of the Clisson division I have been appointed to take his command; you shall come with me."

"Oh, I hope the first ball to-morrow may carry me off."

"You will fight under my eyes," continued Jean Oullier; "and if any one doubts your bravery, I 'll bear witness to it. Will you come?"

"Yes," replied Michel, in so low a voice that the old man could scarcely hear him.

"Good! in three hours we start."

"Start! without bidding her farewell?"

"Yes. In the face of such circumstances she might not have the strength to let you go. Come, take courage!"

"I will take it, Oullier; you shall be satisfied with me."

"Then I can rely upon you?"

"You can. I give you my word of honor."

"I shall be waiting at the crossways of Belle-Passe in three hours from now."

"I will be there."

Jean Oullier made Michel a farewell sign that was almost friendly; then springing across the little bridge, he went to the orchard and mingled with the other Vendéans.

XIV.

JEAN OULLIER LIES FOR THE GOOD OF THE CAUSE.

THE young baron remained for several minutes in a state of utter prostration. Jean Oullier's words rang in his ears like a knell sounding his own death. He thought he dreamed, and he kept repeating, as if to convince himself of the reality of his sorrow, "Go away? Go away?"

Presently, the chill idea of death, which he had lately invoked as a succor from heaven, an idea adopted as we fasten upon such thoughts at twenty, passed from his brain to his heart and froze him. He shuddered from head to foot. He saw himself separated from Mary, not merely by a distance he dared not cross, but by that wall of granite which incloses a man eternally in his last abode.

His pain grew so intense that he thought it a presentiment. He now accused Jean Oullier of cruelty and injustice. The sternness of the old Vendéan in refusing him the consolation of a last farewell seemed to him intolerable; it was surely impossible that he should be actually denied a last look. He rebelled at the thought, and resolved to see Mary, no matter what might come of it.

Michel knew the internal arrangements of the miller's house. Petit-Pierre's room was the miller's own, above the grindstones. This was, naturally, the place of honor in the establishment. The sisters slept in a little room adjoining this chamber. A narrow window in the smaller room looked down upon the outside mill-wheel which kept the machinery at work. For the present, however, all was still, lest the noise should prevent the sentries from hearing other sounds.

Michel waited till it was dark,—an hour perhaps; then he went to the buildings. A light could be seen in the narrow window. He threw a plank on a paddle of the wheel and managed, by resting his body against the wall, to climb spoke by spoke to the highest point of the wheel; there he found himself on a level with the narrow casement. He raised his head and looked into the tiny room.

Mary was alone, sitting on a stool, her elbow resting on the bed, her head in her hands. Now and then a heavy sigh escaped her; from time to time her lips moved as though she were murmuring a prayer. The young man tapped against a window-pane. At the sound she raised her head, recognized him through the glass, and ran to him.

"Hush!" he said.

"You! you here!" cried Mary.

"Yes, I."

"Good God! what do you want?"

"Mary, it is more than a week since I have spoken to you, almost a week since I have seen you. I have come to bid you farewell before I go to meet my fate."

"Farewell! and why farewell?"

"I have come to say farewell, Mary," said the youth, firmly.

"Oh, you do not mean to die?"

Michel did not answer.

"No, no; you will not die," continued Mary. "I have prayed so much that God must hear me. But now that you have seen me, now that you have spoken to me, you must go,—go!"

"Why must I leave you so soon? Do you hate me so intensely that you cannot bear to see me?"

"No, you know it is not that, my friend;" said Mary. "But Bertha is in the next room; she may have heard you come. She may be hearing what you say. Good God! what would become of me—of me who have sworn to her that I did not love you!"

"You may have sworn that to her, but to me you swore otherwise. You swore that you loved me, and it was upon the faith of that love that I consented to conceal my own."

"Michel, I entreat you, go away!"

"No, Mary, I will not go until your lips have repeated to me again what they said on the island of Jonchère."

"But that love is almost a crime!" said Mary, desperately. "Michel, my friend, I blush, I weep, when I think of that momentary weakness."

"Mary! I swear to you that to-morrow you shall have no such remorse, you shall shed no tears of that kind."

"Oh, you mean to die! No, no; do not say it! Leave me the hope that my sufferings may bring you a better fate than mine. Hush! Don't you hear? Some one is coming! Go, Michel; go, go!"

"One kiss, Mary!"

"No."

"Yes, yes; a last kiss — the last!"

"Never, my friend."

"Mary, it is to a dying man!"

Mary gave a cry; her lips touched his forehead; but the instant they had done so, and while she was closing the window hastily, Bertha appeared in the door-way.

When the latter saw her sister, pale, perturbed, scarcely able to support herself, she rushed, with the terrible instinct of jealousy, to the window, opened it violently, leaned out, and saw a shadow disappearing in the darkness.

"Michel was with you, Mary!" she cried, with trembling lips.

"Sister," said Mary, falling on her knees; "I swear —"

Bertha interrupted her.

"Don't swear, don't lie. I heard his voice."

Bertha pushed Mary away from her with such violence that the latter fell flat upon the floor. Then Bertha, springing over her sister's body, furious as a lioness deprived of her young, rushed from the room and down the stairs, crossed the mill, and reached the courtyard. There, to her astonishment, she saw Michel sitting on the doorstep beside Jean Oullier. She went straight up to him.

"How long have you been here?" she said in a curt, harsh voice.

Michel made a gesture as if to say, "I leave Jean Oullier to reply."

"Monsieur le baron and I have been talking here for the last half hour or more."

Bertha looked fixedly at the old Vendéan.

"That is singular!" she said.

"Why singular?" asked Jean Oullier, fixing his own eyes steadily upon her.

"Because," said Bertha, addressing Michel and not Jean Oullier, "because I thought I heard you talking with my sister at her window, and saw you climbing down the mill-wheel which you had mounted to reach her."

"Monsieur le baron does n't look as if he had just performed such an acrobatic feat," said Jean Oullier, sarcastically.

"Then who do you suppose it was, Jean?" said Bertha, stamping her foot impatiently.

"Oh, some of those drunkards over there, who were playing a trick."

"But I tell you that Mary was pale and trembling."

"With fright," said Jean Oullier. "She has n't got your iron nerves."

Bertha grew thoughtful. She knew the feelings that Jean Oullier cherished against the young baron; therefore she could hardly suppose he was in league with him against her. After a moment's silence her thoughts reverted to Mary, and she remembered that she had left her almost fainting.

"Yes," she said; "yes, Jean Oullier, you are right. The poor child must have been frightened, and I, with my rough ways, have made matters worse. Oh," she muttered, "this love is making me beside myself!"

Then, without another word to Michel or Jean Oullier, she rushed into the mill.

Jean Oullier looked at Michel, who lowered his eyes.

"I shall not reproach you," he said to the young man, "but you must see now on what a powder-barrel you are stepping. What would have happened if I had not been here to lie, God forgive me! as if I were a liar born."

"Yes," said Michel, "you are right, Jean,—I know it; and the proof is that I swear to follow you, for I see plainly I can't stay here any longer."

"That 's right. The Nantes men will start in a few moments; the marquis joins them with his division; start yourself at the same time, but fall behind and join me, you know where."

Michel went off to fetch his horse, and Jean Oullier, meantime, obtained his last instructions from the marquis. The Vendéans camping in the orchard now formed in line, their arms sparkling in the shadows. A quiver of repressed impatience ran through the ranks.

Presently Petit-Pierre, followed by the principal leaders, came out of the house and advanced to the Vendéans. She was hardly recognized before a mighty cry of enthusiasm burst from every mouth. Sabres were drawn to salute her for whose cause each man was prepared to die.

"My friends," said Petit-Pierre, advancing, "I promised I would be present at the first armed meeting; and here I am, never to leave you. Fortunate or unfortunate, your fate shall be mine henceforth. If I cannot — as my son would have done — rally you to where my white plume shines, I can — as he would — die with you! Go, sons of giants, go where duty and honor call you!"

Frantic cries of "Vive Henri V! Vive Marie-Caroline!" welcomed this allocution. Petit-Pierre addressed a few more words to those of the leaders whom she knew; and then the little troop on which rested the fate of the oldest monarchy in Europe took its way in the direction of Vieille-Vigne.

During this time Bertha had been showering attentions on her sister, all the more eager because of her sudden change of feeling. She carried her to her bed and bathed her face in cold water. Mary opened her eyes and looked about her in a bewildered way, murmuring in a low voice Michel's name. Her heart revived before her reason.

Bertha shuddered. She was about to ask Mary to forgive her violence, but Michel's name on her sister's lips stopped the words in her throat. For the second time the serpents of jealousy were gnawing at her heart.

Just then the acclamations with which the Vendéans welcomed the address of Petit-Pierre reached her ears. She went to the window of the next room and saw the waving line of a dark mass among the trees, lighted here and there with flashes. It was the column just beginning its march. The thought struck her that Michel, who was certainly with that column, had gone without bidding her good-bye; and she returned, thoughtful, uneasy, and gloomy to her sister's bedside.

XV.

JAILER AND PRISONER ESCAPE TOGETHER.

At daybreak on the 4th of June the tocsin sounded from all the bell-towers in the districts of Clisson, Montaigu, and Machecoul. The tocsin is the drum-call of the Vendéans. Formerly, that is to say in the days of the great war, when its harsh and sinister clang resounded through the land the whole population rose in a mass and ran to meet the enemy.

How many noble things those people must have done to enable us to forget, almost forget, that their enemy was — France!

Happily, — and this proves the immense progress we have made in the past forty years, — happily, we say, in 1832 the tocsin appeared to have lost its power. If a few peasants, answering its impious call, left their ploughs and seized the guns hidden in the hedges, the majority continued calmly along the furrows, and contented themselves by listening to the signal for revolt with that profoundly meditative air which suits so well with the Vendéan cast of countenance.

And yet, by ten o'clock that morning, a rather numerous body of insurgents had already fought an engagement with the regular army. Strongly intrenched in the village of Maisdon, this troop sustained a strong attack directed against it, and had only given way before superior numbers. It then effected its retreat in better order than was customary with the Vendéans even after a slight or momentary reverse.

The reason was, and we repeat it, that La Vendée was no longer fighting for the triumph of a great principle, but simply from a great devotion. If we are now making ourselves the historian of this war (after our usual fashion of writing history) it is because we hope to draw from the very facts we relate the satisfactory conclusion that civil war will soon be impossible in France.

Now, this devotion of which we speak was that of men of noble, elevated hearts, who felt themselves bound by their fathers' past, and who gave their honor, their fortunes, and their life in support of the old adage, *Noblesse oblige.* That is the reason why the retreat was made in good order. Those who executed it were no longer undisciplined peasants, but gentlemen; and each man fought not only from devotion but also from pride,—pride for himself, and, in a measure, for others.

The Whites were immediately attacked again at Château-Thébaud by a detachment of fresh troops sent by General Dermoncourt to pursue them. The royalists lost several men at the passage of the Maine, but having succeeded in putting that river between themselves and their pursuers, they were able to form a junction on the left bank with the Nantes men, whom we lately saw departing, full of enthusiasm, from the Jacquet mill, and who since then had been reinforced by the men from Légé and the division of the Marquis de Souday. This reinforcement brought the effective strength of this column, which was under Gaspard's command, to about eight hundred men.

The next morning it marched on Vieille-Vigne, hoping to disarm the National Guard at that point; but learning that the little town was occupied by a much superior force, to which would be added in a few hours the troops assembled at Aigrefeuille (where the general had collected a large body for the purpose of throwing them on any point in case of necessity), the Vendéan leader determined to attack the village of Chêne, intending to capture and occupy it.

The peasants were scattered through the neighborhood. Hidden among the wheat, which was already of a good height, they worried the Blues with incessant sharp-shooting, following the tactics of their fathers. The men of Nantes and the country gentlemen formed in column and prepared to carry the village by main force, attacking it along the chief street which runs from end to end of it.

At the end of that street ran a brook; but the bridge had been destroyed the night before, nothing remaining of it but a few disjointed timbers. The soldiers, withdrawn into the houses and ambushed behind the windows, protected with mattresses, poured a cross-fire down upon the Whites, which repulsed them twice and paralyzed their onset, until, electrified by the example of their leaders, the Vendéan soldiers flung themselves into the water, crossed the little river, met the Blues with the bayonet, hunted them from house to house, and drove them to the extremity of the village, where they found themselves face to face with a battalion of the 44th of the line which the general had just sent forward to support the little garrison of Chêne.

The sound of the firing reached the mill, which Petit-Pierre had not yet quitted. She was still in that room on the first floor where we have already seen her. Pale, with eager eyes, she walked up and down in the grasp of a feverish agitation she could not quell. From time to time she stopped on the threshold of the door, listening to the dull roll of the musketry which the breeze brought to her ears like the rumbling of distant thunder; then, she passed her hand across her forehead, which was bathed in sweat, stamped her feet in anger, and at last sat down in the chimney-corner opposite to the Marquis de Souday, who, though no less agitated, no less impatient than Petit-Pierre, only sighed from time to time in a dolorous way.

How came the Marquis de Souday, whom we have seen so impatient to begin all over again his early exploits in the great war, to be thus tied down to a merely expectant position? We must explain this to our readers.

The day of the engagement at Maisdon Petit-Pierre, in accordance with the promise she had given to her friends, made ready to join them and share in the fight itself. But the royalist chiefs were alarmed at the great responsibility her courage and ardor threw upon them. They felt that the dangers were too many under the still uncertain chances of this war, and they decided that until the whole army were assembled they could not allow Petit-Pierre to risk her life in some petty and obscure encounter.

Respectful representations were therefore made to her, all of which failed to change her strong determination. The Vendéan leaders then took counsel together and decided among themselves to keep her as it were a prisoner, and to appoint one of their own number to remain beside her, and prevent her, by force if necessary, from leaving her quarters.

In spite of the care the Marquis de Souday (who was of the council) took in voting and intriguing to throw the choice on one of his colleagues, he himself was selected; and that is why he was now, to his utter despair, compelled to stay in the Jacquet mill beside the miller's fire, instead of being at Chêne and under the fire of the Blues.

When the first sounds of the combat reached the mill Petit-Pierre endeavored to persuade the marquis to let her join her faithful Vendéans; but the old gentleman was not to be shaken; prayers, promises, threats, were all in vain against his strict fidelity to orders received. But Petit-Pierre could plainly see on his face the deep annoyance he felt; for the marquis, who was little of a courtier by nature, was unable to conceal it. Stopping short before him just as one of the sighs of impatience we have already mentioned escaped him, she said: —

"It seems to me, marquis, that you are not extraordinarily delighted with my companionship?"

"Oh!" exclaimed the marquis, endeavoring, but without success, to give a tone of shocked denial to his interjection.

"Yes," said Petit-Pierre, who had an object in persisting, "I think you are not at all pleased with the post of honor assigned to you."

"On the contrary, I accepted that post with the deepest gratitude; but — "

"Ah! there 's a *but?* I knew it!" said Pêtit-Pierre, who seemed determined to fathom the old gentleman's mind on this point.

"Is n't there always a *but* in every earthly thing?" replied the marquis, evasively.

"What is yours?"

"Well, I regret not to be able, while showing myself worthy of the trust my comrades have laid upon me, I certainly do regret not being able to shed my blood on your behalf, as they are doing, no doubt, at this very moment."

Petit-Pierre sighed heavily.

"I have no doubt," she said, "that our friends are even now regretting your absence. Your experience and tried courage would certainly be of the utmost help to them."

The marquis swelled with pride.

"Yes, yes," he said; "I know they 'll repent of it."

"I am sure of it. My dear marquis, will you let me tell you, with my hand on my conscience, the whole truth as I see it?"

"Oh, yes; I entreat you."

"Well, I think they distrusted you as much as they did me."

"Impossible!"

"Stop! you don't see what I mean. They said to themselves: 'A woman would hinder us in marching; we should have to think of her if we retreat. In any case we must devote to the security of her person a troop of soldiers we could better employ elsewhere.' They did not choose to believe that I have succeeded in conquering the weakness of my body, and that my courage is equal to the greatness of my task; if they think so of me, can you wonder if they think it of you?"

"Of me!" cried Monsieur de Souday, furious at the mere suggestion. "I have given proofs of courage all my life!"

"All the world knows that, my dear marquis; but perhaps, remembering your age, they may have thought that your bodily vigor, like mine, was no longer equal to the ardor of your spirit."

"Oh, that 's too much!" cried the old soldier of former days in a tone of the deepest indignation. "Why! there has n't been a day for the last fifteen years that I have n't been six or eight hours in the saddle, — sometimes ten, sometimes twelve! In spite of my white hairs I can stand fatigue as well as any man. See what I can do still!"

Seizing the stool on which he was sitting, he struck it with such violence against the stone chimney-piece that he shattered the stool to bits and made a deep gash in the mantel. Brandishing above his head the leg of the hapless stool which remained in his hand, he cried out: —

"How many of your young dandies, Maître Petit-Pierre, could do that?"

"I never doubted your powers, my dear marquis; and that is why I say those gentlemen have made a great mistake in treating you like an invalid."

"An invalid! I? God's death!" cried the marquis, more and more exasperated, and totally forgetting the presence of the person with whom he was speaking. "An invalid! I? Well, this very evening, I 'll tell them I renounce these functions, which are those, not of a gentleman, but a jailer."

"That 's right!" interjected Petit-Pierre.

"Functions, which for the last two hours," continued the marquis, striding up and down the room, "I have been sending to all the devils."

"Ah, ha!"

"And to-morrow, yes, I say to-morrow, I 'll show them who 's an invalid, that I will!"

"Alas!" said Petit-Pierre in a melancholy tone, "to-morrow may not belong to us, my poor marquis; you are wrong to count upon it."

"Why so?"

"You know very well the uprising is not as general as we hoped it might be. Who knows whether the shots we now hear may not be the last fired in defence of the white flag?"

"Hum!" growled the marquis, with the fury of a bull-dog tugging at his chain.

Just then a call for help from the farther end of the orchard put an end to their talk. They both ran to the spot, and there saw Bertha, whom the marquis had stationed as an outside lookout, bringing in a wounded peasant, whom she had scarcely strength enough to support. Mary and Rosine had also rushed out at the cry. The peasant was a young *gars* from twenty to twenty-two years of age, with his shoulder shattered by a ball. Petit-Pierre ran up to him and placed him on a chair, where he fainted.

"For heaven's sake, retire," said the marquis to Petit-Pierre; "my daughters and I will dress the poor devil's wound."

"Pray, why should I retire?" said Petit-Pierre.

"Because the sight of that wound is not one that everybody can stand; I am afraid it is more than you have strength to bear."

"Then you are like all the rest; and you lead me to suppose that our friends were right in the judgment they formed on you as well as on me."

"I don't see that; how so?"

"You think, as they do, that I am wanting in courage." Then, as Mary and Bertha were beginning to examine the wound, "Let the poor fellow's wound alone," she continued, "I — and I alone, do you hear me? — will dress it."

Taking her scissors Petit-Pierre slit up the sleeve of the Vendéan's jacket, which was stuck to the arm by the dried blood, opened the wound, washed it, covered it with lint and deftly bandaged it. Just as she was finishing her work the wounded peasant opened his eyes and recovered his senses.

"What news?" asked the marquis, unable to restrain himself a moment longer.

"Alas!" said the man; "our *gars*, who were conquerors at first, are now repulsed."

Petit-Pierre, who did not blanch while attending to the wound, grew as white as the linen she was using for bandages; and putting in a last pin to hold it, she seized the marquis by the arm and drew him toward the door.

"Marquis," she said, "you, who saw the Blues in the great war, tell me, what was done when the nation was in danger?"

"Done?" cried the marquis. "Why, everybody ran to arms."

"Even the women?"

"Yes, the women; even the old men, even the children."

"Marquis, it may be that the white flag will fall to-day never to rise again. Why do you condemn me to making barren and impotent prayers and vows in its behalf?"

"But just reflect," said the marquis; "suppose a ball were to strike you."

"Oh! do you think my son's cause would be injured if my bloody and bullet-riddled clothing were carried on a pike in front of our battalions?"

"No, no!" cried the marquis, passionately. "I would curse my native soil if the stones themselves did not rise at such a sight."

"Then come with me and let us join our troops."

"But," replied the marquis, with less determination than he had previously shown against Petit-Pierre's entreaties, —as if the idea of being regarded as an invalid had shaken the firmness with which he executed his orders, — "but I promised you should not leave the mill."

"Well, I release you from that promise," said Petit-Pierre; "and I, who know your valor, order you to follow me. Come, marquis, we may still be in time to rally victory to our flag; if not, if we are too late, we can at least die with our friends."

So saying, Petit-Pierre darted through the courtyard and orchard, followed by Bertha and by the marquis, who thought it his duty to renew, from time to time, his remonstrances; although, in the depths of his heart, he was delighted with the turn affairs were taking.

Mary and Rosine remained behind to care for the wounded.

XVI.

THE BATTLEFIELD.

The Jacquet mill was about three miles from the village of Chêne. Petit-Pierre, guided by the noise of the firing, did half the way running; and it was with great difficulty that the marquis stopped her as they neared the scene of action, and succeeded in inspiring her with some prudence, lest she should plunge head-foremost into the government troops.

On turning one of the flanks of the line of sharp-shooters, whose firing, as we have said, was her guide, Petit-Pierre, followed by her companions, came upon the rear of the Vendéan army, which had, in truth, lost all the ground we saw it gain in the morning, and was now driven back some distance beyond the village of Chêne. On catching sight of Petit-Pierre, as, with flying hair and gasping breath she came up the hill toward the main body of the Vendéans, the whole of the little army burst into a roar of enthusiasm.

Gaspard, who, together with his officers, was firing like a common soldier, turned round at the shout and saw Petit-Pierre, Bertha, and the Marquis de Souday. The latter, in the rapidity of their course, had lost his hat, and now appeared with his white hair flying in the wind. It was to him that Gaspard spoke first.

"Is this how the Marquis de Souday keeps his word?" he said in an irritated tone.

"Monsieur," replied the marquis, sharply, "it is not of a poor invalid like me that you ought to ask that question."

Petit-Pierre hastened to intervene. Her party was not strong enough to allow of dissensions among its leaders.

"Souday is bound, as you are, to obey me," she said; "I seldom claim the exercise of that right; but to-day I have thought proper to do so. I assume my place as generalissimo, and ask, how goes the day, lieutenant?"

Gaspard shook his head significantly.

"The Blues are in force," he said, "and my scouts report that reinforcements are reaching them."

"So much the better," cried Petit-Pierre; "they will be so many more to tell France how we died."

"You cannot mean that, Madame!"

"I am not Madame here; I am a soldier. Fight on, without regard to me; advance your line of skirmishers and double their fire."

"Yes; but first, to the rear!"

"To the rear! who?"

"You, in God's name!"

"Nonsense! to the front you mean."

Snatching Gaspard's sword, Petit-Pierre put her hat on the point of it as she sprang in the direction of the village crying out:—

"Those who love me, follow me!"

Gaspard vainly attempted to restrain her, and even caught her arm; but Petit-Pierre, light and agile, escaped him and continued her way toward the line of houses whence the soldiers, observing the renewed movement on the part of the Vendéans, were beginning a murderous fire.

Seeing the danger that Petit-Pierre was incurring, all the Vendéans rushed forward to make a rampart of their bodies, and the effect of such a rush was so sudden, so powerful, that in a few seconds they were over the brook and into the village, where they came face to face with the Blues. The clash was almost instantly followed by a terrible *mêlée*. Gaspard, his mind wholly occupied by one thing, the safety of Petit-Pierre, succeeded in reaching her and flinging her back among his men. So intent was he on saving the august life he felt that God himself had intrusted to him, that he gave no thought to his own safety, and did not see that a soldier posted at the corner of the first house was aiming at him.

It would have been all over with the Chouan leader if the marquis had not observed the threatened danger. Slipping along the wall of the house he threw up the muzzle of the weapon just as its owner fired it. The ball struck a chimney; the soldier turned furiously on the marquis, and tried to stab him with his bayonet, which the latter evaded by throwing back his body. The old gentleman was about to reply with a pistol-shot when a ball broke the weapon in his hand.

"So much the better!" he cried, drawing his sabre and dealing so terrible a blow that the soldier rolled at his feet like an ox felled by a club; "I prefer the white weapon." Then, brandishing his sabre he cried out: "There, General Gaspard, what do you think of your invalid now?"

Bertha had followed Petit-Pierre, her father and the Vendéans; but her thoughts were much less on the soldiers than on what was passing immediately about her. She looked for Michel, striving to distinguish him in the whirlwind of men and horses that passed beside her.

The government troops, surprised by the suddenness and vigor of the attack, retreated step by step; the National guard of Vieille-Vigne had retired altogether. The ground was heaped with dead. The result was that as the Blues no longer replied to the straggling fire of the *gars* posted in the vineyards and gardens around the village, Maître Jacques, who commanded the skirmishers, was able to assemble his men in a body. Putting himself at their head he led them through a by-way which skirted the gardens and fell upon the flank of the soldiers.

The latter, whose resistance was becoming by this time more resolute, sustained the attack valiantly, and forming in line across the main street of the village, presented a front to their new assailants. Soon a pause of hesitation appeared among the Vendéans, the Blues regained the advantage, and their column having, in its charge, passed the opening of the little by-way by which Maître-Jacques and his men had debouched, the latter with five or six of his "rabbits," among whom figured Aubin Courte-Joie and Trigaud-Vermin, found themselves cut off from the body of their comrades. Whereupon Maître Jacques, rallying his men about him, set his back to a wall to protect his rear, and sheltering beneath the scaffolding of a house which was just being built at the corner of the street, prepared to sell his life dearly.

Courte-Joie, armed with a small double-barrelled gun, fired incessantly on the soldiers; each of his balls was the death of a man. As for Trigaud, his hands being free, for the cripple was strapped to his shoulders by a girth, he manœuvred with wonderful adroitness a scythe with its handle reversed, which served him as lance and sabre both.

Just as Trigaud, with a backward blow, brought down a gendarme whom Courte-Joie had only dismounted, great shouts of triumph burst from the government ranks, and Maître Jacques and his men beheld a woman in a riding-habit in the hands of the Blues, who seemed, even in the midst of the fight, to be transported with joy. It was Bertha, who, still preoccupied by her search for Michel, had imprudently advanced too far and was captured by the soldiers. They, being deceived by her dress, mistook her for the Duchesse de Berry; hence their joy.

Maître Jacques was misled like the rest. Anxious to repair the blunder he had made in the forest of Touvois, he made a sign to his men, and together they abandoned their defensive position, and rushing forward, thanks to a great swathe mown down by Trigaud's terrible scythe, they reached the prisoner, seized her, and placed her in their midst.

The soldiers, disappointed, renewed their efforts, and flung themselves on Maître Jacques and his men, who had promptly regained their shelter against the wall of the house; and the little group became a centre toward which converged the points of twenty-five bayonets, and a continuous fusillade from the circumference of the circle. Already two Vendéans were dead; Maître Jacques, struck by a ball which broke his wrist, was forced to drop his gun and take to his sabre, which he wielded with his left hand. Courte-Joie had exhausted his cartridges; and Trigaud's scythe was almost the only protection left to the four surviving Vendéans, — an efficacious protection hitherto, for it laid the assailants on the ground in such serried ranks that the soldiers no longer dared to approach the terrible mendicant.

But Trigaud, wishing to strike a direct blow at a horseman, missed his aim. The scythe struck a stone and flew into a thousand bits; the giant fell to his knees, so violent was the force of his impulsion; the girth which fastened Courte-Joie to his shoulders broke, and the cripple rolled into the midst of the fray.

A loud and joyous hurrah greeted this accident, which delivered the formidable giant into the hands of his enemies; and a National guard was in the act of raising his bayonet to stab the fallen cripple, when Bertha, taking a pistol from her belt, fired upon the man and brought him down upon the body of Courte-Joie.

Trigaud had risen with an agility scarcely to be expected of so enormous a bulk; his separation from Courte-Joie and the danger the latter was in increased his strength tenfold. Using the handle of his scythe, he disposed of one man and disabled another. With a single kick he sent to a distance of several feet the body of the man who had fallen upon his friend, and taking the latter in his arms, as a nurse lifts a child, he joined Bertha and Maître Jacques beneath the scaffolding.

While Courte-Joie lay on the pavement, his eyes, roving about him with the rapidity and acuteness of a man in peril of death, seeking on all sides for a chance of escape, fell on the scaffolding where they noticed a heap of stones collected by the masons for the construction of the wall.

"Get under shelter in the doorway," he said to Bertha, when, thanks to Trigaud, he found himself beside her; "perhaps I can return the service you have just done me. As for you, Trigaud, let the red-breeches come as near as they please."

In spite of Trigaud's thick brain he at once understood what his companion wanted of him; for, little as the sound was in harmony with the situation, he broke into a peal of laughter that resembled the braying of trumpets.

The soldiers, seeing the three disarmed men, and wishing, at any cost, to recapture the woman whom they still supposed to be the Duchesse de Berry, came nearer, calling out to the Vendéans to surrender. But, just as they stepped beneath the scaffolding, Trigaud, who had placed Courte-Joie near Bertha, sprang to one of the joists that supported the whole erection, seized it with both hands, shook it, and tore it from the ground. In an instant the planks tipped, and the stones piled upon them followed their incline and fell like hail, beyond Trigaud, upon eight or ten of the foremost soldiers.

At the same moment the Nantes men, led by Gaspard and the Marquis de Souday, making a desperate effort, firing, sabring, bayoneting hand to hand, had driven back the Blues, who now retreated to their line of battle in the open country, where their superiority in numbers and also in weapons would infallibly give them the victory.

The Vendéans, rash as the effort was, were about to risk an attack, when Maître Jacques, whom his men had rejoined, and who, in spite of his wound, still continued to fight, said a few words in Gaspard's ear. The latter immediately, and in spite of the commands and entreaties of Petit-Pierre, ordered a retreat and again took up the position he had occupied an hour earlier on the other side of the village.

Petit-Pierre was ready to tear her hair with anger, and urgently demanded explanations, which Gaspard did not give her until he had ordered a halt.

"We are now surrounded by five or six thousand men," he said, "and we ourselves are scarcely six hundred. The honor of the flag is safe, and that is all we can hope for."

"Are you certain of that ?" asked Petit-Pierre.

"Look for yourself," he replied, taking her to a rise in the ground from which could be seen, converging on all sides toward the village of Chêne, dark masses topped with bayonets which sparkled in the rays of the setting sun. There, too, they heard the sound of drums and bugles approaching from all the points of the horizon.

"You see," continued Gaspard, "that in less than an hour we shall be completely surrounded, and no resource will then remain to these brave men — who, like myself, cannot away with Louis Philippe's prisons — but to get themselves killed upon the spot."

Petit-Pierre stood for some moments in gloomy silence; then, convinced of the truth of what the Vendéan leader told her, beholding the destruction of the hopes which a few moments earlier had seemed to her ardent mind so strong and dauntless, she felt her courage desert her, and she became, what she really was, a woman; she, who had so lately braved fire and sword with the nerve of a hero, sat down by the wayside and wept, disdaining to conceal the tears which furrowed her cheeks.

XVII.

AFTER THE FIGHT.

GASPARD, having rejoined his companions, thanked them for their services, told them of the state of things, and dismissed them for better times,— advising them to disperse at once, and thus escape all pursuit by the soldiers. Then he returned to Petit-Pierre, whom he found in the same place, and around her the Marquis de Souday, Bertha, and a few Vendéans who would not think of their own safety till certain of hers.

"Well," asked Petit-Pierre when Gaspard returned to her alone, "have they gone?"

"Yes; they could do no more than they have done."

"Poor souls! what troubles await them!" said Petit-Pierre. "Why has God refused me the consolation of pressing them to my heart? But I should never have had the strength; they do right to leave me without farewell. Twice to suffer thus in life is too much agony. Those days at Cherbourg!— I hoped I might never see their like again."

"Now," said Gaspard, "we must think of your safety."

"Oh, never mind me personally," replied Petit-Pierre; "my sole regret is that the balls did not choose to come my way. My death would not have given you the victory, that is true; but at least the struggle would have been glorious. And now what are we to do?"

"Wait for better days. You have proved to the French people that a valiant heart is beating in your bosom. Courage is the principal virtue they demand of their rulers; they will remember your action, never fear."

"God wills it!" said Petit-Pierre, rising and leaning on Gaspard's arm, who led her from the hilltop into the road across the plain. The government troops, who did not know the country, were forced to keep to the main roads.

Gaspard guided the little company, which ran no risk in the open country, except from scouts — thanks to the knowledge Maître Jacques possessed of paths that were almost impassable; they reached the neighborhood of the Jacquet mill without so much as seeing a tricolor cockade.

As they went along, Bertha approached her father and asked him whether in the midst of the *mêlée* he had seen or heard of Baron Michel; but the old gentleman, horrified at the issue of the insurrection prepared with so much care and so quickly stifled, was in the worst of humors, and answered gruffly that for the last two days no one knew what had become of the Baron de la Logerie; probably he was frightened, and had basely renounced the glory he might have won and the alliance which would have been the reward of his glory.

This answer filled Bertha with consternation. Useless, however, to say that she did not believe one word of what her father said; but her heart trembled at an idea which alone seemed to her probable, — namely, that Michel had been killed, or at any rate grievously wounded. She resolved to make inquiries of every one until she discovered something as to the fate of the man she loved. She first questioned all the Vendéans. None of them had seen Michel; but some, impelled by the old hatred against his father, expressed themselves about the son in terms that were not less vehement than those of the marquis himself.

Bertha grew frantic with distress; nothing short of palpable, visible, undeniable proof could have forced her to admit that she had made a choice unworthy of her, and, though all appearances were against Michel, her love, becoming more ardent, more impetuous under the pressure of such accusations, gave her strength to regard them as calumnies. A few moments earlier her heart was torn, her brain maddened under the idea that Michel had met his death in the struggle; and now that glorious death had become a hope, a consolation to her grief. She was frantic to acquire the cruel certainty, and even thought of returning to Chêne, visiting the battle-field, in search of her lover's body, as Edith sought that of Harold; she even dreamed of avenging him on his murderers after vindicating his memory from her father's aspersions. The girl was reflecting on the pretext she could best employ to remain behind the rest and return to Chêne, when Aubin Courte-Joie and Trigaud, the rear-guard of the company, came up and were about to pass her. She breathed more freely; they, no doubt, could throw some light upon the matter.

"You, my brave friends," she said, "can you give me news of Monsieur de la Logerie ?"

"Yes, indeed, my dear young lady," replied Courte-Joie.

"Ah !" cried Bertha, with the eagerness of hope, "he has not left the division as they say he has, has he ?"

"He has left it," replied Courte-Joie.

"When ?"

"The evening before the fight at Maisdon."

"Good God !" cried Bertha, in a tone of anguish. "Are you sure ?"

"Quite sure. I saw him meet Jean Oullier at the Croix-Philippe; and we walked a little way together."

"With Jean Oullier !" cried Bertha. "Oh ! then I am satisfied; Jean Oullier was not deserting. If Michel is with Jean Oullier he has done nothing cowardly or dishonorable."

Suddenly a terrible thought came into her mind. Why this sudden interest on Jean Oullier's part for the young man ? Why had Michel followed Jean Oullier rather than the marquis ? These questions, which the young girl put to herself, filled her heart with sinister forebodings.

"And you say you saw the two on their way to Clisson ?" she said to Courte-Joie.

"With my own eyes."

"Do you know what is going on at Clisson?"

"It is too far from here to have got the details as yet," replied Courte-Joie; "but a *gars* from Sainte-Lumine overtook us just now and said that a devilish firing had been going on since ten o'clock in the morning over against Sèvre."

Bertha did not answer; her ideas had taken another course. She saw Michel led to his death by Jean Oullier's hatred; she fancied the poor lad wounded, panting, abandoned, lying helpless on some lonely and bloody moor, calling on her to save him.

"Do you know any one who could guide me to Jean Oullier?" she asked Courte-Joie.

"To-day?"

"Now, this instant."

"The roads are covered with the red-breeches."

"The woodpaths are not."

"But it is almost night."

"We shall be all the safer. Find me a guide; if not, I shall start alone."

The two men looked at each other.

"No one shall guide you but me," said Aubin Courte-Joie. "Do I not owe your family a debt of gratitude? Besides, Mademoiselle Bertha, you did me, no later than to-day, a service I shall never forget, — in knocking up the bayonet of that National guard who was going to split me."

"Very good; then drop behind and wait for me here in this wheat-field," said Bertha. "I shall be back in fifteen minutes."

Courte-Joie and Trigaud lay down among the wheat ears, and Bertha, hastening her steps, rejoined Petit-Pierre and the Vendéans just as they were about to enter the mill. She went rapidly up to the little room she occupied with her sister, and hurriedly changed her clothes, which were covered with blood, for the dress of a peasant-woman. Coming down, she found Mary busy among the wounded, and told her, without explaining her plan, not to feel uneasy if she did not see her again till the next day. She then returned to the wheat-field.

Reserved as she was in what she said to her sister, her face was so convulsed and agitated that Mary read upon it plainly the thoughts that filled her soul; she knew of Michel's disappearance, and she did not doubt that Bertha's sudden departure was caused by it. After the scene of the previous evening Mary dared not to question her sister; but a new anguish was added to those which already rent her heart, and when she was called to mount and attend Petit-Pierre in search of another refuge, she knelt down and prayed to God that her sacrifice might not be useless, and that it would please Him to protect both the life and honor of Bertha's affianced husband.

XVIII.

THE CHÂTEAU DE LA PÉNISSIÈRE.

While the Vendéans were making their useless but not inglorious fight at Chêne, forty-two of their number were sustaining a struggle at Pénissière de la Cour, of which the memory survives in history.

These forty-two royalists, who were part of the Clisson division, left that town intending to march to the village of Cugan, and there disarm the National Guard. A frightful storm forced them to find shelter in the château de la Pénissière, where a battalion of the 29th regiment of the line, informed of their movements, lost no time in besieging them.

La Pénissière is an ancient building, with a single story between the ground-floor and garret. It has fifteen irregularly shaped windows. The chapel backs against one corner of the château. Beyond it, joining the valley, are meadow-lands divided by evergreen hedges, which heavy rains sometimes transform into a lake. A battlemented wall, built by the Vendéans, surrounded the building.

The commanding officer of the battalion of the line had no sooner reconnoitred the situation than he ordered an immediate attack. After a short defence the exterior wall was abandoned, and the Vendéans retreated to the château, within which they barricaded themselves. Each man took his place on the ground-floor, and on the main-floor; and on both floors a bugler was stationed, who never ceased to sound his instrument throughout the combat, which began with rapid volleys from the windows, so well directed and so vigorous as to conceal the small number of the besieged.

Picked men and the best shots were chosen to fire; they discharged, almost without stopping, the heavy blunderbusses which their comrades reloaded and handed back to them. Each blunderbuss carried a dozen balls. The Vendéans fired five or six at once; the effect was that of a discharge of grape-shot. Twice the regular troops attempted an assault; they came within twenty paces of the château, but were forced to retreat.

The commander ordered a third attack, and while it was preparing, four men, assisted by a mason, approached the château by a gable-end, which had no outlook on the garden, and was therefore undefended. Once at the foot of the wall, the soldiers raised a ladder, and reaching the roof uncovered it, flung down into the garret inflammable substances, to which they set fire, and then retreated. Immediately a column of smoke burst from the roof, through which the flames soon forced their way.

The soldiers, uttering loud cries, again marched eagerly to the little citadel, which seemed to be flying a flag of flame. The besieged had discovered the conflagration, but there was no time to extinguish it; besides, the flames were pouring upward, and they trusted that after destroying the roof the fire might burn out of itself. Accordingly they replied to the shouts of their assailants with a terrible fusillade, — the bugles never ceasing for a single instant to sound their joyous and warlike notes.

The Whites could hear the Blues saying to each other: "They are not men, they are devils!" and this military praise inspired them with fresh ardor.

Nevertheless, a reinforcement of fifty men having reached the besiegers, the commanding officers ordered the drummers to beat the charge; and the soldiers, emulous of each other, rushed for the fourth time upon the château. This time they reached the doors, which the sappers began to batter in. The Vendéan leaders ordered their men on the ground-floor up to the first floor; the men obeyed; and while one half of the besieged continued the firing, the other half pulled up the boards and broke through the ceilings, so that when the soldiers entered the building they were greeted with a volley at close quarters, poured down upon them from above through the rafters. Again, and for the fourth time, they were forced to retreat.

The commander of the battalion then ordered his men to do on the ground-floor what they had done in the attic. Fascines of gorse and dried fagots were thrown through the windows into the rooms of the lower floor; lighted torches were flung after them, and in a few moments the Vendéans were inclosed in fire above and below them. And still they fought. The volumes of smoke which issued from the window were striped, every second or two, with the scarlet flame of the blunderbusses; but the firing now became the vengeance of despair rather than an effort of defence. It seemed impossible for the little garrison to escape death.

The place was no longer tenable; beams and joists were on fire and were cracking beneath the feet of the Vendéans; tongues of flame began to dart here and there through the floor; at any moment the roof might fall in and crush them from above, or the floor give way and precipitate them into a gulf of flame. The smoke was suffocating.

The Vendéan leaders took a desperate resolution. They determined to make a sortie; but to give it any chance of success, the firing would have to be kept up to protect the movement. The leaders asked if any would volunteer to sacrifice themselves for the safety of their comrades.

Eight men stepped forward.

The troop was then divided into two squads. Thirty-three men and a bugler were to gain, if possible, the farther extremity of the park, which was closed by a hedge only; the eight others, among them the second bugler, were left to protect the attempt.

In consequence of these arrangements, and while those who volunteered to remain were running from window to window and keeping up a vigorous fire, the others broke through the wall on the opposite side to where the soldiers were attacking, issued in good order with the bugler at their head, and made their way at a quick step toward the end of the park where the hedge stood. The soldiers fired upon them and rushed to intercept them. The Vendéans fired back, knocked over those who opposed them, escaped through the hedges, leaving five of their number dead, and scattered over the meadows, which were then under water. The bugler, who received three wounds, never ceased to sound his bugle.

As for the men who remained in the château, they still held out. Each time that the soldiers attempted to approach, a volley issued from the brazier and cut a swathe through their ranks. This lasted for half an hour. The bugle of the besieged never ceased to sound through the rattling of the volleys, the crackling of the flames, the rumbling of the falling timbers, like a sublime defiance hurled by these men at Death standing before them.

At last, an awful crash was heard; clouds of smoke and sparks rose high in air; the bugle was hushed, the firing ceased. The flooring had fallen in, and the little garrison were doubtless swallowed up in the burning gulf beneath them — unless a miracle had happened.

Such was the opinion of the soldiers, who, after watching the ruins for some moments, and hearing no cry or moan that betrayed the presence of a living Vendéan, abandoned the furnace which was burning up the bodies of both friends and enemies; so that nothing remained on the scene of the struggle, lately so turbulent and noisy, but the red and smoking flames dying down in silence, and a few dead bodies lighted by the last glare of the conflagration.

Thus the scene remained for several hours of the night. But about one o'clock a man of more than ordinary height, gliding beside the hedges, or crawling when obliged to cross a path, inspected cautiously the surroundings of the château. Seeing nothing that warranted distrust, he made the round of the devastated building, examining attentively all the bodies he found; after which he disappeared among the shadows. Presently, however, he returned, carrying a man upon his back and accompanied by a woman.

These men and this woman, as our readers are of course aware, were Bertha, Courte-Joie, and Trigaud.

Bertha was pale; her firmness and her habitual resolution had given way to a sort of restless bewilderment. From time to time she hurried before her guides, and Courte-Joie was obliged to recall her to prudence. When the three debouched from the wood into the meadow lately occupied by the soldiers, and saw in front of them the fifteen openings which stood out, red and gaping, from the blackened wall, like so many vent-holes out of hell, the young girl's strength gave way; she fell upon her knees and cried out a name which her agony transformed into a sob. Then, rising like a man, she rushed to the burning ruins.

On her way she stumbled over something; that something was a dead body. With a horrible expression of anguish she stooped to look at the livid face, turning it toward her by the hair. Then, seeing other bodies scattered on the ground, she went wildly from one to another as if beside herself.

"Alas! mademoiselle," said Courte-Joie, "he is not here. To spare you this dreadful sight, I had already ordered Trigaud, who came here first, to look at those bodies. He has seen Monsieur de la Logerie two or three times, and idiot though he be, you can be sure he would have recognized him were he here among the dead."

"Yes, yes, you are right; and if he is anywhere —" cried Bertha, pointing to the ruins; and before the two men could stop her, she sprang upon the sill of a window on the ground-floor, and there, standing on the heated stone, she looked down into the gulf of fire still belching at her feet, into which it almost seemed as though she were about to fling herself.

At a sign from Courte-Joie Trigaud seized the girl round her waist and placed her at some distance on the grass. Bertha made no resistance, for an idea had just crossed her brain which paralyzed her will.

"My God!" she cried, as if with a last expiring sigh of her former strength, "you denied me the power to defend him or to die with him; and you now deny me the consolation of giving burial to his body."

"But mademoiselle," said Courte-Joie, "if it is the will of the good God you must resign yourself to it."

"Never! never! never!" cried Bertha, with the excitement of despair.

"Alas!" said the cripple, "my heart is heavy too; for if Monsieur de la Logerie is down there, so is poor Jean Oullier."

Bertha groaned; in the selfishness of her grief she had never once thought of Jean Oullier. "It 's true," continued Courte-Joie, "he dies as he wished to die — with arms in his hand; but that does n't console me for thinking he is down there."

"Is there no hope?" cried Bertha. "Could n't they have escaped in some way? Oh, let us look! let us search!"

Courte-Joie shook his head.

"I think it is impossible. After what that man of the thirty-three others who did escape told us, it does not seem possible. Five of those who made the sortie were killed."

"But Jean Oullier and Monsieur Michel were among those who remained," said Bertha.

"No doubt; and that is why I have so little hope. See," said Courte-Joie, pointing to the walls, which rose from their foundations to the eaves without a fissure, and then recalling Bertha's eyes by a gesture to the furnace of the ground-floor, where the roof and the floors were still burning; "see, there is nothing left but charred remains and walls that threaten ruin. Courage, mademoiselle, courage, for there is not one chance in a hundred that your lover and Jean Oullier have escaped that wreck."

"No, no!" cried Bertha, rising. "No! I say he cannot, he shall not be dead! If it needed a miracle to save him God has performed it. I will dig those embers, I will sound those walls. I will have him, dead or living! I say I will; do you hear me Courte-Joie?"

Seizing in her white hands a beam which protruded its charred end through a window, Bertha made superhuman efforts to draw it toward her, as if with that lever she could lift the enormous mass of material and discover what it concealed.

"Don't think of it!" cried Courte-Joie, desperately; "the work is beyond your strength, mademoiselle, and above mine and even Trigaud's. Besides, we have n't time for it; the soldiers will return by daybreak, and they must n't find us here. Let us go, mademoiselle; for Heaven's sake let us go at once!"

"You may go if you like," said Bertha, in a tone that allowed of no objections. "I shall stay here."

"Stay here!" exclaimed Courte-Joie, horrified.

"I shall stay. If the soldiers return it will no doubt be for the purpose of searching the ruins. I will throw myself at the feet of their commander; my prayers, my tears will persuade them to let me share in the work, and I shall find him—oh, yes, I shall find him!"

"You are mistaken, mademoiselle; the red-breeches will know you as the daughter of the Marquis de Souday. If they don't shoot you, they 'll take you prisoner. Come away! it will be daylight soon. Come, and if necessary," added Courte-Joie, alarmed at the girl's determination, "if necessary, I promise to bring you back to-morrow night."

"No, I tell you, no,—I will not go away!" answered the young girl. "Something tells me here" (and she struck her breast) "that he is calling me, he wants me."

Then, as Trigaud advanced, on a sign from Courte-Joie,

apparently to seize her, she cried out, springing once more to the sill of the window: —

"Come a step nearer, and I will jump into that furnace."

Courte-Joie, perceiving that nothing could be obtained of Bertha by force, was about to resort to prayers, when Trigaud, who had remained standing with his arms stretched out in the position he had taken to seize the young girl, made a sign to his companion to be silent.

Courte-Joie, who knew by experience the extraordinary acuteness of the poor fool's senses, obeyed him. Trigaud listened.

"Are the soldiers returning?" asked Courte-Joie.

"No; it is not that," replied Trigaud.

Then, unbinding Courte-Joie, who was strapped as usual to his shoulders, he lay down flat on his stomach with his ear to the ground. Bertha, without coming down from her present post, turned her head to the mendicant and watched him. The movement he had made, the words he had said, caused her heart, she knew not why, to beat violently.

"Do you hear anything extraordinary?" asked Courte-Joie.

"Yes," replied Trigaud.

Then he made a sign to Courte-Joie and Bertha to listen likewise. Trigaud, as we know, was stingy of words.

Courte-Joie lay down with his ear to the earth. Bertha sprang down from the window, and it was but a second after she had laid her ear to the ground before she rose again, crying out: —

"They are alive! they are alive! Oh, my God, I thank thee!"

"Don't let us hope too soon," said Courte-Joie; "but I do hear a dull sound which seems to come from the depths of those ruins. But there were eight of them; we can't be sure the sound comes from the two we seek."

"Not sure, Aubin! My presentiment, which would not let me go away when you begged me, makes me sure of it.

Our friends are there, I tell you; they found a shelter in some cellar where they are now imprisoned by the fall of these materials."

"It may be so," replied Courte-Joie.

"It is certainly so!" cried Bertha. "But how can we release them? How shall we reach the place where they are?"

"If they are in a vault, the vault must have an opening; if they are in a cellar, the cellar has a window."

"Well, then, if we can't find either we must dig out the earth and through the foundation-wall."

So saying, Bertha began to go round the building, dragging aside with frenzied motions the beams, stones, tiles, and other fragments which had fallen beside the outer wall and now hid its base.

Suddenly she gave a cry. Trigaud and Courte-Joie ran to her, — one on his great legs, the other on his stumps and hands, with the rapidity of a batrachian.

"Listen!" said Bertha, triumphantly.

Sure enough, on the spot where she stood they heard distinctly a dull but continued sound coming from the depths of the ruined building, — a sound like that of some tool or instrument striking steady and regular blows on the foundations.

"This is the place," said Bertha, pointing to an enormous pile of rubbish heaped against the wall. "We shall find them here."

Trigaud set to work. He began by pushing away a whole section of the roof which had slid down outside the building and now lay vertically against the wall. Then he threw aside the loose stones piled there by the fall of a window-casing on the first floor; and finally, after wonderful feats of strength, he laid bare an opening through which the sounds of the labor of the buried men came to them distinctly.

Bertha wanted to pass through the opening as soon as it was practicable; but Trigaud held her back. He took a fallen lath, lit it by the embers, fastened the girth, which usually held Courte-Joie to his shoulders, round the latter's waist, and lowered him into the cavity.

Bertha and Trigaud held their breaths. Courte-Joie's voice was heard, speaking to some one; then he gave a signal to be hoisted up. Trigaud obeyed with the alacrity of a well-fed animal.

"Living? are they living?" cried Bertha, in anguish.

"Yes, mademoiselle, but for God's sake don't attempt to go down there; they are not in the cellar, but in a sort of niche beyond it. The opening through which they got there is blocked. We must break through the wall to reach them; and I am very much afraid that may bring down the roof of the cellar upon them. Let me direct Trigaud."

Bertha fell on her knees and prayed. Courte-Joie collected a number of dry laths and returned to the cellar; Trigaud followed him.

At the end of ten minutes, which seemed to Bertha as many centuries, a loud noise of crashing stones was heard. A cry of anguish escaped her; she darted to the opening and there met Trigaud coming up, bearing on his shoulder the body of a man bent double, whose pale face was hanging down upon the giant's breast. Bertha recognized Michel.

"He is dead! Oh, my God! he is dead!" she cried, not daring to go up to him.

"No, no," said a voice from below, which Bertha recognized as that of Jean Oullier, "no, he is not dead."

At these words the girl sprang forward, took Michel from Trigaud's hands, laid him on the grass, and quite reassured by the beating of his heart, endeavored to bring back his senses by bathing his forehead with water from a pool.

XIX.

THE MOOR OF BOUAIMÉ.

WHILE Bertha endeavored to bring Michel from his swoon (which was chiefly caused by suffocation) Jean Oullier reached the outer air, followed by Courte-Joie, whom Trigaud drew up by the same means he had used to lower him. A moment more and all three were safely outside.

"Ah *ça!* were you the only ones in there?" said Courte-Joie to Jean Oullier.

"Yes."

"And the others?"

"They took refuge under the stairway; the ceiling fell before they had time to get to us."

"Are they dead?"

"I don't think so; for about an hour after the soldiers left we heard the stones moving and voices. We called to them, but they did not hear."

"It is a lucky chance we came."

"That it is; without you I could never have got through that wall, especially with the young baron in such a state. Ha! I 've made a fine campaign of it, faith," muttered Jean Oullier, shaking his head as he looked at Bertha, who, having drawn Michel's head and shoulders on her knees and brought him to his senses, was now expressing to him all the happiness she felt in recovering him.

"And it is not over yet," said Courte-Joie, ignorant of the meaning the old Vendéan gave to his words, and anxiously looking to the east, where a broad purple line announced that the day was breaking.

"What do you mean?" asked Jean Oullier.

"I mean that two hours more of darkness would have mightily helped our safety; a cripple, a fainting man, and a woman are not so easy to manœuvre on a retreat. Besides, the victors in yesterday's fight will swarm upon the roads to-day — if they don't beat the woods."

"Yes; but I 'm at ease now. I don't have that roof over my head."

"You are only half saved yet, my good Jean."

"Well, let us take precautions."

So saying, Jean Oullier began to search for the cartridge-boxes of the dead, and took their contents. Then he loaded his gun as coolly as though he were starting on a hunt, and went up to Bertha and Michel. The eyes of the latter were closed as if he were unconscious.

"Can you walk ?" Jean Oullier said to him.

Michel did not answer. When he first opened his eyes he saw Bertha, and closed them hastily, conscious of the difficulties of his position.

"Can you walk ?" repeated Bertha, in a tone which the latter could no longer pretend not to hear.

"I think so," he replied.

In point of fact he had only a flesh wound in the arm; the bone was not injured.

Bertha had examined the wound and slung the arm about his neck with her white silk cravat.

"If you can't walk," said Jean Oullier, "I 'll carry you."

At this fresh proof of the change in Jean Oullier's feelings to the young baron, Bertha went up to him.

"You must explain to me why you took away my betrothed husband," she said, emphasizing the last two words; "and why you persuaded him to leave his post and be dragged into this affair which has exposed him, in spite of all the dangers he may have met, to serious and shameful accusations."

"If Monsieur de la Logerie's reputation has suffered through me," replied Jean Oullier, gently, "I will repair it."

"You?" said Bertha, more and more astonished.

"Yes," said Jean Oullier; "for I can and will say openly that with all his effeminate ways, this young man has shown himself to be full of courage and constancy."

"Will you really do that, Jean Oullier?" cried Bertha.

"Not only will I do it," said the old Vendéan, "but if my testimony is not enough I will get that of the brave men beside whom he fought, — for I now desire that his name be counted honorable and honored."

"Is it possible that you say that, Jean Oullier?"

Jean Oullier nodded.

"You who would rather see me dead than bearing that name?"

"That 's how things change in this world, Mademoiselle Bertha. I desire now to see Monsieur Michel my master's son-in-law."

Jean Oullier said the words with a look so expressive and a voice so sad and meaning, that Bertha felt her heart tighten, and she thought involuntarily of Mary. She was about to question the old keeper, but, at that moment, the sound of trumpets came down upon the wind from the direction of Clisson.

"Courte-Joie was right!" exclaimed Jean Oullier. "The explanation you ask of me, Bertha, you shall have as soon as circumstances permit; for the present we must think of our own safety." Then, listening attentively, he added: "Come, let us start! there 's not an instant to lose, I 'll answer for that."

Passing his hand through Michel's well arm to support him, he gave the signal to depart. Courte-Joie was already perched on Trigaud's shoulders.

"Which way shall we go?" he asked.

"Better make for the lonely farmhouse of Saint-Hilaire," replied Jean Oullier, who felt Michel staggering under his first few steps. "It is quite impossible that Monsieur Michel should do the twenty miles to Machecoul."

"Straight for Saint-Hilaire, then," said Courte-Joie.

In spite of their slow advance, by reason of Michel's feebleness in walking, they were not more than a few hundred steps from the farm, when Trigaud showed his rider with some pride a sort of club he had been peeling and polishing with his knife as he walked along. It was made from the stem of a wild apple-tree, of suitable length, which Trigaud had spied in the orchard at Pénissière; he thought it admirably suited to replace the terrible scythe he had shattered at Chêne.

Courte-Joie gave a cry of anger. Evidently he did not share the satisfaction with which his companion flourished the knotty bulk of his new weapon.

"The devil take that animal to the lowest hell!" he cried.

"What's the matter?" asked Jean Oullier, leaving Michel to Bertha's care and hurrying on to join Courte-Joie and Trigaud.

"Matter!" cried Courte-Joie, "the matter is that this brute has put the whole band of the red-breeches on our track! May the plague choke me for not having thought of it before! Ever since we left La Pénissière he has been a regular Tom Thumb; and, unluckily for us, it is n't bread crumbs he has strewn along the way, but the twigs, leaves, bark of his tree. Those scoundrelly soldiers, who, I have n't a doubt, will find out that we dug among the embers, are by this time at the other end of the trail this animal has provided for them. Ah, double, treble, quadruple, brute!" concluded Courte-Joie, by way of peroration.

Joining action to words he brought down his fist with all his might on the skull of the giant, who seemed no more conscious of the blow than if Courte-Joie had merely passed his hand through his hair.

"Damn it!" said Jean Oullier, "what's to be done now?"

"Give up the farm at Saint-Hilaire, where they'd catch us like mice in a trap."

"But," said Bertha, quickly, "Monsieur Michel cannot possibly go any farther. See how pale he is!"

"Let us bear to the right," said Jean Oullier, "and make for the Bouaimé moor, where we can hide among the rocks. To walk faster and leave fewer tracks, I 'll take Monsieur Michel on my shoulders. We 'll walk in file, and Trigaud's steps will hide the rest."

The Bouaimé moor, toward which Jean Oullier now guided the little troop, lies about three miles from the village of Saint-Hilaire; the river Maine must be crossed to reach it. It extends on the north as far as Rémouillé and Montbert; the lay of the land is very uneven and it is strewn with granite rocks, some evidently placed there by the hand of man. Druidic stones and dolmens lift their brown heads crowned with moss amid tufts of heather and the yellow flowers of the gorse and broom. It was to one of the most remarkable of these stones that Jean Oullier now guided the little caravan. This stone was flat, and rested on four enormous corner-stones of granite. Ten or a dozen persons could easily have lain in its shadow.

Michel was no sooner there than he gave way entirely, and would have fallen flat on the ground if Bertha had not supported him. She hastened to gather ferns, which she spread beneath the dolmen; and Michel was no sooner laid upon them than, in spite of the gravity of the situation, he fell soundly asleep.

Trigaud was stationed as sentinel on the dolmen; aboriginal statue on an aboriginal pedestal, he called to mind by his mighty outline the giants of two thousand years ago, who raised that altar. Courte-Joie, unstrapped, lay down to rest near Michel, whom Bertha would not leave, in spite of the exhaustion, both moral and physical, which the fatigues of the previous day and night had entailed upon her. Jean Oullier walked away, partly to reconnoitre the situation, and partly to obtain provisions, of which they stood greatly in need.

For about two hours Trigaud's eyes had roved over the broad expanse of the savanna before and around him. Not a sound had reached his ear, attentively listening, except the monotonous hum of bees and wasps pilfering sweetness from the broom and the wild thyme. The mists which the sun was drawing from the earth began to assume to Trigaud's eyes a variety of rainbow tints, the shimmerings of which, added to the rays of the sun, which were now falling plumb on his tufts of red hair, benumbed his brain; various somniferous combinations were about to plunge him into a siesta, not induced, unfortunately for him, by any meal, when the sudden report of a fire-arm roused him from his torpor.

He looked in the direction of Saint-Hilaire and saw the white vapor produced by the shot. Next, he saw a man running at full speed, apparently making for the dolmen. With one bound Trigaud was off his pedestal. Bertha, who had resisted sleep, heard the shot and immediately waked up Courte-Joie.

Trigaud took the cripple in his arms and hoisted him above his head till he was fully ten feet off the ground, saying but two words, which, however, needed no commentary: —

"Jean Oullier."

Courte-Joie shaded his eyes with his hand and had no difficulty in recognizing the old Vendéan; but he noticed that instead of making direct for the dolmen, Jean Oullier had taken to the opposite hill and was heading for Montbert. He also observed that instead of running on the slope of the hill, where he might have been sheltered from the eyes of his pursuers, the old huntsman had chosen the most exposed places, keeping in full view of whoever was within three miles of him.

Jean Oullier, he knew, was far too wary to act heedlessly; he must have some good reason for his present behavior; no doubt he was attracting the enemy's attention to himself in order to divert it from the rest of the party. Courte-Joie therefore concluded that the wisest thing for him and his companions to do was to stay in their present shelter and await events, carefully watching, meantime, all that happened.

Whenever intelligence was needed instead of senses, Courte-Joie no longer trusted to Trigaud. He had himself hoisted to the top of the dolmen, although, small as his truncated body was, he thought best not to display it too openly on that pedestal. He therefore lay down flat on his stomach with his face turned in the direction of the hill up which Jean Oullier was proceeding.

Soon, at the very place whence the Vendéan had issued, he saw a soldier, then another, then a third; he counted them up to twenty. They did not seem eager to measure speed with their game; they simply spread over the moor to cut off his retreat in case he attempted to return. These equivocal tactics increased Courte-Joie's watchfulness; for they led him to think that the soldiers had some other object in view than the mere pursuit of the Vendéan. The hill which the latter was mounting ended, about half a mile from the point where Jean Oullier then was, in a sharp point of rocks, at the foot of which was a bog. It was on that spot, no doubt because Jean Oullier was aiming for it, that Courte-Joie's attention was now fixed.

"Hum!" said Trigaud, suddenly.

"What is it?" asked Courte-Joie.

"Red-breeches," replied the other, pointing to the bog.

Courte-Joie followed the direction of Trigaud's finger and saw the barrel of a gun in the midst of the reeds; then a form. It was that of a soldier, and he, like the one first seen on the heath, was followed by twenty others. Courte-Joie saw them crouching among the reeds like sportsmen on the watch. Their game was Jean Oullier. If he descended by the point of rocks, as he was evidently about to do, he must fall into the ambush.

There was not a moment to be lost in warning him. Courte-Joie did not hesitate; he seized his gun and fired it, taking care to hold the muzzle below the bushes and to fire behind the dolmen. Then he looked hastily back to the scene of action.

Jean Oullier had heard the signal and knew the ring of Courte-Joie's little gun; he was not mistaken for a moment as to the reasons that constrained his friend to abandon the concealment he was preserving for them at such cost to himself. Instantly he made a half turn, and instead of continuing his way to the steep descent and the bog, he rapidly descended the hill he had been climbing. He no longer ran, he flew; no doubt some plan had occurred to him, and he was hurrying to put it into execution. At the rate he was coming down he would join his friends in a few moments.

But in spite of Courte-Joie's precautions to conceal the smoke of his shot, the soldiers had seen the direction from which it came, and those on the moor as well as those in the bog joined forces behind Jean Oullier (who was still coming down at a great pace), and seemed to be consulting together while awaiting orders.

Courte-Joie glanced about him, apparently studying each point of the horizon; he wet a finger and lifted it to discover the direction of the wind, and felt the heather anxiously, to be sure that the sun, which was hot, and the wind, which was keen, had dried it thoroughly.

"What are you doing?" asked Bertha, who had watched the different phases of this prologue, fully aware of the imminence of the danger, and was now helping Michel, who seemed more depressed than suffering, to get on his feet.

"What am I doing, — or rather what am I going to do, my dear young lady?" replied the cripple. "I am going to make a glorious bonfire; and you can boast to-night, if the fire saves you, as I hope it will, that you never saw the like before."

So saying, he gave Trigaud several lighted bits of tinder, which the latter stuck into bundles of dried herbage, which he placed at intervals of ten feet among the heather, blowing each of them into a flame with his powerful lungs. He was placing his last bundle as Jean Oullier came up the slope which led to the dolmen.

"Up! up!" cried the latter. "I am not ten minutes in advance of them."

"Yes, but this will give us twenty," said Courte-Joie pointing to the twigs of heather which were beginning to curl and crackle with the flames, while a dozen or more spiral lines of smoke were rising in the air.

"That fire won't burn fast enough or hot enough to stop them," said Jean Oullier. "Besides," he added, after studying the condition of the atmosphere, "the wind will send the flame in the direction that we must take."

"Yes; but flame, *gars* Oullier, carries smoke," said Courte-Joie, triumphantly; "and that 's what I 'm counting on. The smoke will hide how few we are and where we are going."

"Ah! Courte-Joie, Courte-Joie," muttered Oullier between his teeth, "if you had your legs what a poacher you 'd be!"

Then, without saying another word, he picked Michel up and put him on his shoulders (in spite of the young man's assurance that he could walk well enough, and did not wish to cause that additional fatigue to the old Vendéan), and followed Trigaud, who had already started with his rider on his back.

"Take mademoiselle's hand!" called Courte-Joie to Jean Oullier; "and tell her to shut her mouth and take in a long breath; in ten minutes we sha'n't be able to see or breathe."

In fact the ten minutes had not expired before the ten columns of smoke were blended into one and formed a dense sheet stretching to right and left five hundred feet, while the flames roared sullenly behind them.

"Can you see sufficiently to guide us?" said Jean Oullier to Courte-Joie; "for the most important thing of all is not to go astray, and next, not to get separated."

"We have no other guide than the smoke," replied Courte-Joie. "Let us follow that boldly and it will take us where we want to go; but don't lose sight of Trigaud as head of the column."

Jean Oullier was one of those men who know the value of words and time; he therefore contented himself with saying: —

"Forward, march!" giving the example and seeming no more hindered by Michel's weight than Trigaud was by Courte-Joie's.

They walked thus for fifteen minutes without getting out of the smoke which their conflagration, spreading with amazing rapidity under the force of the wind, rolled up about them. Once or twice Jean Oullier muttered to Bertha, who was half suffocated: —

"Can you breathe?"

To which she replied with an almost inarticulate yes. As for Michel, the old keeper cared not at all; he was certain to keep up with the rest, inasmuch as he, Jean Oullier, had him on his shoulders.

Suddenly Trigaud, who marched at their head guided by Courte-Joie, and utterly indifferent to where he went, stepped back abruptly. He had set his feet in water, which the smoke had prevented him from seeing, and he was now knee-deep in it. Aubin uttered a cry of joy.

"We 've done it!" he said; "the smoke has led us as straight as the best-broken hound ever led a sportsman."

"Ah!" exclaimed Jean Oullier.

"You understand now, don't you, my *gars?*" said Courte-Joie, in a tone of triumph.

"Yes; but how shall we reach the island?"

"How? Why, there 's Trigaud."

"True; but when the soldiers miss us won't they suspect the trick?"

"Of course, if they do miss us; but I intend they sha'n't."

"Go on."

"They don't know how many we are. We will put Mademoiselle Bertha and the wounded man in safety, and then, as if we had made a mistake and found our way blocked by the pond, you and I and Trigaud will land, and show them by a few shots where we are. After that, being free of incumbrance, we can easily get into the woods of Gineston, and return to the island after dark."

"But these poor children will be left without food!"

"Pooh!" said Courte-Joie, "it won't kill them to go twenty-four hours without eating."

"So be it." Then, with a sort of sad contempt for his want of intelligence, "Last night," he continued, "must have addled my brain, or I should have thought of all this myself."

"Don't expose yourselves uselessly," said Bertha, half joyous at the thought of the *tête-à-tête* which these strange circumstances were giving her with the man she loved.

"Don't trouble about that," replied Jean Oullier.

Trigaud took Michel in his arms, without unhorsing Courte-Joie (which would have made him lose time) and entered the pond. He walked thus till the water was up to his middle; then he hoisted Michel to his head in case the water mounted higher. It stopped, however, at the level of the giant's breast. He crossed the pond to a sort of island about twelve feet square, which seemed in the midst of that stagnant water to be nothing more than a vast duck's-nest. It was covered with a forest of reeds.

Trigaud deposited Michel among the reeds and returned for Bertha, whom he carried in the same manner and put down, as he might a bird, beside the young Baron de la Logerie.

"Lie down flat among the reeds in the middle of the island!" called Jean Oullier from the shore. "Lift the reeds you have just bent down, and I can promise that no one will find you!"

"Very good," replied Bertha; "and now, my friends, think only of yourselves."

XX.

THE FIRM OF AUBIN COURTE-JOIE AND CO. DOES HONOR TO ITS PARTNERSHIP.

It was high time for the three Chouans to finish what they had to do on the borders of the pond. The flames were rolling onward with terrifying rapidity; they ran along the flowery tops of the broom and heather like gold and purple birds swept forward by the wind, as if they preferred to play among the twigs and branches before they seized upon the stems. Their mutterings, like the roar of ocean, increased in all directions round the fugitives, and the smoke grew denser and more suffocating.

But the steel muscles possessed by Jean Oullier and Trigaud were a match for the flames, and the trio were soon safe from all danger of fire. They turned obliquely to the left, and soon reached a dip in the valley which was almost free of the smoke which so far had been their main protection,—serving to hide their number, the direction of their flight, and the manœuvre by which Michel and Bertha were now in a place of safety.

"Let us crawl; we must crawl now, Trigaud," cried Jean Oullier. "The soldiers must n't see us till we know where they are and what they are doing."

The giant bent down as though he were going on all fours; and it was lucky for him he did so, for no sooner had he stooped than a ball, which he would otherwise have received in his breast, whizzed harmlessly through the air.

"The devil!" cried Courte-Joie; "you did n't give that advice a bit too soon, *gars* Oullier."

"They have guessed our trick and have surrounded us — on this side at least," said Jean Oullier.

They now saw a file of soldiers posted at a hundred paces from each other, all the way from the dolmen to a distance of a mile and a half, evidently waiting, like huntsmen, till the quarry should reappear.

"Shall we rush upon them ?"

"That 's my advice; but wait till I have made a gap."

Putting his gun to his shoulder (but without leaving his horizontal position) Jean Oullier fired on the soldier who was now reloading his gun. The man, struck in the breast, twirled round upon himself and fell head foremost to the ground.

"That 's one!" said Jean Oullier.

Then aiming at the next soldier as calmly as he would at a partridge, he fired. The second man fell like the first.

"A double-shot!" exclaimed Courte-Joie. "Bravo, *gars* Oullier, bravo!"

"Forward! forward!" cried Oullier, springing to his feet with the agility of a panther. "Forward! and spread a little to give less chance for the balls they 'll rain upon us!"

The Vendéan was right. The three comrades had scarcely advanced ten steps before six or eight successive discharges were heard; and one of the balls splintered the club which Trigaud was carrying in his hand. Happily for the fugitives, the soldiers hurrying on all sides to the help of their wounded companions, and coming up out of breath, had fired unsteadily. Nevertheless they closed the way and it is probable that Jean Oullier and his friends would not have had time to escape through their line without a hand-to-hand fight.

As it was, just as Jean Oullier, who held the left, was about to spring across a little ravine, a shako rose on the other side, and he saw a soldier awaiting him with fixed bayonet. The rapidity of his rush prevented the Vendéan from reloading his gun, but he calculated that as his adversary contented himself with his bayonet he was probably in the same condition as himself. Risking all, he drew his knife, put it between his teeth, and continued his way with headlong speed. On the edge of the ravine he stopped short, and putting up his gun took aim at his adversary. The soldier, thinking the Vendéan's gun was loaded, flung himself flat on his stomach to escape the shot. An instant after, and as if the pause he made had not diminished the impulsion of his spring, Jean was across the ravine, over the body of the soldier, and away like lightning on the other side.

Trigaud was equally fortunate; and save for a ball which grazed his shoulder and added more rags to those he wore, he and his partner Courte-Joie got safely across the line. The two fugitives (Trigaud and Courte-Joie count as one) now turned diagonally, one to right, the other to left, so as to meet at the point of the angle. At the end of five minutes they were within speaking distance.

"Are you all right?" said Jean Oullier to Courte-Joie.

"All right!" answered the cripple; "and in twenty minutes, if we don't have a limb lopped off by those rascally Blues, we 'll be in the fields; and once we are behind a hedge the devil himself can't touch us. That was a bad idea of ours, taking to the moor, *gars* Oullier."

"Pooh! we 'll soon be away from it; and the young folks are much safer where they are than if we had put them in the thickest forest. You are not wounded?"

"No; and you, Trigaud? I thought I felt a sort of shudder on your hide."

The giant showed the gash the ball had made in his club; evidently, this misfortune, which destroyed the symmetry of the work at which he had fondly labored all the morning, troubled him far more than the damage done to his clothing or to his deltoid, which was slightly injured by the passage of the ball.

"Oh, be joyful!" cried Courte-Joie; "here are the fields."

In truth, not a thousand steps away from the fugitives, at the bottom of a slope which was so gentle as to be almost imperceptible, fields of wheat were visible, their ears already yellowing and swaying to the breeze in their dull-green sheaths.

"Suppose we stop to breathe a minute," said Courte-Joie, who seemed to feel the fatigue that Trigaud felt.

"Yes," said Jean Oullier, "and give me time to reload. Meantime, do you look about."

Jean Oullier reloaded his gun, and Courte-Joie turned his eyes in a circle around him.

"Oh, ten million thunders!" exclaimed the cripple suddenly, just as the Vendéan was ramming in his second ball.

"What now?" said Jean Oullier, turning round.

"Forward! all the devils of hell! forward! I don't see anything yet, but I hear something that bodes no good."

"Whew! they are doing us the honor of cavalry, *gars* Courte-Joie. Quick, quick, lazy-bones!" he added, addressing Trigaud.

The latter, as much to relieve his lungs as to make answer to Jean Oullier, gave vent to a sort of bellow which a lusty Poitevin bull might have envied him, and then with a single stride he jumped an enormous stone which lay on his way; as he did so a cry of pain burst from Jean Oullier.

"What 's the matter?" asked Courte-Joie, looking back to the latter, who had stopped and was leaning on his gun with his foot raised.

"Nothing, nothing," replied Oullier; "don't trouble about me."

He tried to walk, gave another cry, and sat down.

"Oh," said Courte-Joie, "we shall not go on without you. Tell me, what 's the matter?"

"Nothing, I say."

"Are you wounded?"

"Oh, for that bone-setter of Montbert!" exclaimed Jean Oullier.

"What 's that?" said Courte-Joie, who did not catch his meaning.

"I 've either broken or turned my ankle by stepping into a hole; at any rate, I can't take another step."

"Trigaud will take you on one shoulder and me on the other."

"Impossible! you could never reach the hedges."

"But if we leave you behind they 'll kill you, my Jean."

"Maybe so," said the Vendéan, "but I 'll kill a few of them before I die; and by way of a beginning, look at that fellow."

A young officer of chasseurs, better mounted than the rest, appeared at the top of a rise about three hundred paces from the fugitives. Jean put his musket to his shoulder and fired. The young man threw up his arms and fell from his saddle. Jean Oullier reloaded his gun.

"Can't you walk at all?" asked Courte-Joie.

"I might limp a dozen steps; but what 's the good of that?"

"Then here we 'll stay, Trigaud."

"You won't do such a foolish thing, I hope?" cried Jean Oullier.

"Yes, by my faith, I will. Where you die we die, old friend; but, as you say, we 'll bring down a few of them first."

"No, no, Courte-Joie; that sha'n't be so. You must live to look after those young ones we left over there — What are you about, Trigaud?" he suddenly asked, looking at the giant, who had gone down into a ravine and was lifting a block of granite.

"Don't scold him!" said Courte-Joie; "he is n't wasting time."

"Here, here!" cried Trigaud, showing a hollow made by the flow of water under the stone.

"Faith, he 's right. I declare if he has n't the mind of a monkey this day, my *gars* Trigaud! Here, Jean Oullier, here, get under! get under!"

Jean Oullier dragged himself to the stone and rolled into the excavation, where he curled himself into a ball with the water to his middle. Trigaud then replaced the stone, leaving just enough space to give air and light to the living being it covered like a tombstone.

The giant had just concluded this work when the horsemen appeared at the top of the slope; and after convincing themselves that the young officer was really dead, dashed down in pursuit of the Chouans at full gallop.

Nevertheless, all hope was not lost. Trigaud and Courte-Joie were scarcely fifty steps from a hedge beyond which they would be safe from horsemen; and as for the foot-soldiers, they appeared to have relinquished their pursuit.

But a subaltern officer admirably mounted pressed them so hard that Courte-Joie felt the hot breath of the animal on his legs. The rider, determined to end the matter, rose in his stirrups and aimed such a blow with his sabre at the cripple's head that he would certainly have split it in two; but the horse, which he did not have well in hand, swerved to the left, while Trigaud instinctively flung himself to the right. The weapon therefore missed its mark and merely made a flesh wound on the cripple's arm.

"Face about!" cried Courte-Joie to Trigaud, as though he were commanding a company. The latter pivoted round, absolutely as though his body were riveted to the ground with an iron screw.

The horse, passing beside him, struck him in the breast, but did not shake him. At the same instant Courte-Joie, firing one barrel of his little gun, knocked over the subaltern, who was dragged to some distance by the impetus of his horse.

"One!" counted Trigaud, in whom the imminence of danger seemed to develop a loquacity which was not habitual with him.

During the moment that this affair lasted the other horsemen were rapidly approaching; a few horse's-lengths alone separated them from the two Vendéans, who could hear, above the tramp of their galloping steeds, the sharp cocking of their pistols and musketoons. But that moment had sufficed Courte-Joie to judge of the resources offered him by the place in which he found himself.

They were now at the farther end of the moor of Bouaimé, a few steps from a crossway whence several roads diverged. Like all such open spaces in Brittany and La Vendée, this crossway had its crucifix; and the cross, which was of stone, and dilapidated on one side, offered a temporary refuge which might soon become untenable. To right were the first hedges of the fields; but there was no chance whatever of reaching them, for three or four horsemen, forestalling their intention, had obliquely advanced to thwart it. Opposite to them and flowing to their left was the river Maine, which made a bend at this place; but Courte-Joie knew it was useless to even think of putting the river between himself and the soldiers, for the opposite bank was a face of rock rising from the water; and in following the current to find a spot to land, the two Chouans would have been simply a target for the enemy.

It was, therefore, the refuge of the cross on which Courte-Joie decided, and in that direction Trigaud, under his master's orders, proceeded. But just as he reached the column of stone and turned it to put its bulk between the soldiers and themselves, a ball struck an arm of the cross, ricochetted, and wounded Courte-Joie in the cheek,—not, however, preventing the cripple from replying to it in turn.

Unfortunately, the blood which poured from the wound fell on Trigaud's hands. He saw that blood, gave a roar of fury, — as though he felt nought but that which injured his companion, — and charged madly on the soldiers like a wild-boar on its hunters.

In an instant Courte-Joie and Trigaud were surrounded; a dozen sabres whirled above their heads, a dozen pistol muzzles threatened their bodies, and one gendarme seized

Courte-Joie. But Trigaud's club descended; it fell upon the leg of the gendarme and crushed it; the hapless rider uttered a terrible cry and fell from his horse, which fled across the moor.

At the same instant a dozen shots were fired; Trigaud had a ball in the breast, and Courte-Joie's right arm, broken in two places, hung helpless at his side. The giant seemed insensible to pain; with his trunk of a tree he made a moulinet which broke two or three sabres and warded others.

"To the cross! to the cross!" cried Courte-Joie. "It is well to die there."

"Yes," muttered Trigaud; hearing his master speak of dying he brought down his club convulsively on the head of a horseman, who fell like a log. Then, executing the order he had received, he walked backward to the cross — to cover as much as possible the body of his friend with his own body.

"A thousand thunders!" shouted a corporal; "we are wasting time and lives and powder on those beggars."

So saying, he spurred his horse and forced it with one bound upon the two Vendéans. The horse's head struck Trigaud full in the chest, and the shock was so violent that it brought the giant to his knees. The soldier profited by the chance to strike Courte-Joie a blow which entered his skull.

"Throw me at the foot of the cross and escape if you can!" said Courte-Joie, in a failing voice. "It is all over with me." Then he began the prayer: "Receive my soul, O God!"

But the colossus no longer obeyed him; maddened with blood and fury he uttered hoarse, inarticulate cries, like those of a lion at bay; his eyes, usually dull and lifeless, cast out flames; his lips drew up, exposing the clenched and savage teeth ready to render craunch for craunch with a tiger. The gallop of the horse had carried the soldier who wounded Courte-Joie to some distance. Trigaud could not reach him; but he measured the space with his eye, and whirling the club above his head, he flung it hissing through the air as if from a catapult.

The rider forced his horse to rear, and so avoided the blow; but the horse received it on his head. The creature beat the air with his forefeet as he fell over backward, and rolled with his rider on the ground.

Trigaud uttered a cry of joy more terrible and horrible than a cry of pain; the rider's leg was caught beneath the animal. He flung himself upon him, parried with his arm, which was deeply gashed, a sabre-cut; seized the soldier by the leg; dragged him from the body of the horse; and then, twirling him in the air, as a child does a sling, he dashed out his brains upon an arm of the cross.

The byzantine stone shook to its base, and remained bent over to one side, and covered with blood. A cry of horror and of vengeance burst from the troops, but this specimen of the giant's strength deterred the soldiers from approaching him; they stopped where they were, to reload their guns.

During this time Courte-Joie breathed his last, saying, in a loud voice: —

"Amen!"

Then Trigaud, feeling his beloved master dead, and utterly ignoring the preparations the chasseurs were making to kill him, — Trigaud sat down at the foot of the cross, unfastened the body of Courte-Joie from his shoulders and laid it on his knees, as a mother might handle the body of her child; he gazed on the livid face, wiping with his sleeve the blood that blurred it, while a torrent of tears — the first that being, indifferent to all the miseries of life, had ever shed — flowed thick and fast from his eyes, mingling with the blood he was piously and absorbedly removing.

A violent explosion, two new wounds, and the dull thud produced by three or four balls striking the body which Trigaud was holding in his arms and pressing to his breast, roused him from his grief and his insensibility. He rose to his full height; and this movement, which made the soldiers think he meant to spring upon them, caused them to gather up the reins of their horses, while a visible shudder ran through their ranks.

But Trigaud never looked at them; he thought of them no longer; he was seeking a means of not being parted from his friend by death; was he searching for a spot which promised him a union throughout eternity?

He walked toward the river. In spite of his wounds, in spite of the blood which flowed down his body from the holes of several pistol-balls and left a rivulet of blood behind him, Trigaud walked firm and erect. He reached the river-bank before a single soldier thought of preventing him; there he stopped at a point overlooking a black pool of water, the stillness of which proclaimed its depth. Clasping the body of the cripple still tighter to his breast, and gathering up his last remaining strength, he sprang forward into its depths without uttering a word.

The water dashed noisily above the mighty mass it now engulfed, boiling and foaming long over the place where Trigaud and his friend had disappeared; then it subsided into rings, which widened, widened ever till they died upon the shore.

The soldiers had ridden up. They thought the beggar had thrown himself into the water to reach the other bank, and pistol in hand they held themselves ready to fire the moment he came to the surface of the stream.

But Trigaud never reappeared; his soul had gone to join the soul of the only being he had loved in this world, and their bodies lay softly together on a bed of reeds in a pool of the river Maine.

XXI.

IN WHICH SUCCOR COMES FROM AN UNEXPECTED QUARTER.

During the week which had just elapsed Maître Courtin kept prudently quiet and out of sight in his farmhouse at La Logerie. Like all diplomatists, Courtin had no great fancy for war; he calculated, very justly, that the period of pistol-shots and sabre-cuts must soon pass by, and he wished to be fresh and lively for the succeeding period, when he might be useful to the cause — and to himself — according to the petty means which Nature allotted to him.

He was not without some uneasiness, the cautious farmer, as to the consequences which might result to him from the part he had taken in the arrest of Jean Oullier and the death of Bonneville; and at this moment when hatred, rancor, vengeance of all kinds had put the country under arms, he thought it wisest not to foolishly risk his person within their range. He was even afraid of meeting his young master, Baron Michel (inoffensive as he knew him to be), ever since a certain night when he had cut the girths of the baron's saddle.

In fact, the day after that performance, thinking that the best way to escape being killed was to seem half dead, he took to his bed and gave out, by his servant-woman, to his neighbors and administrators that a malignant fever like that of poor old Tinguy had brought him to death's door.

Madame de la Logerie, in her distress at Michel's flight, had sent twice for her farmer; but danger paralyzed Courtin's desire to please her, and the proud baroness, goaded by anxiety, was forced to go herself to the peasant's house.

She had heard that Michel was a prisoner, and was about to start for Nantes to use all her influence with the authorities to get him released, and all her authority as a mother to take him far away from this disastrous neighborhood. Under no circumstances would she return to La Logerie, where further sojourn seemed to her dangerous by reason of the conflict about to take place; and she was anxious to see Courtin and leave him in charge of the château and her interests.

Courtin promised to be worthy of her confidence, but in so weak and dolorous a voice that the baroness left the farmhouse with a heart full of pity for the poor devil, even in the midst of her own personal anxieties.

After this came the fights at Chêne and La Pénissière. On the days of their occurrence the noise of the musketry, as it reached the farmer's ears, caused a relapse in his illness. But no sooner had he heard of the result of those fights than he rose from his bed entirely cured. The next day he felt so vigorous that, in spite of his woman's remonstrance, he determined to go to Montaigu, his market-town, and get the orders of the sub-prefect as to his future course. The vulture smelt the carnage, and wanted to be sure of his little share of the spoil.

At Montaigu Maître Courtin learned that his trip was useless; the department had just been placed under military authority. The sub-prefect advised the mayor of La Logerie to go to Aigrefeuille and get his instructions from the general, who was there at that moment.

Dermoncourt, fully occupied with the movement of his columns, and having, as a brave and loyal soldier, little liking for men of Courtin's character, received the latter's denunciations, made under the guise of necessary information, with an abstracted air, and, in fact, showed a coldness to the mayor of La Logerie which greatly chilled that functionary's hopes. Nevertheless the general accepted a proposal which Courtin made him, to put a garrison in the château de la Logerie; for the position seemed to him an excellent one from which to hold the whole region in hand, from Machecoul to Saint Colombin.

Heaven owed the farmer some compensation for the general's want of sympathy, and, with its usual justice, soon bestowed it.

As he left the house which served as headquarters, Maître Courtin was approached by a man whom he had no recollection of ever having met, but who, nevertheless, showed him the utmost civility and a friendliness that was altogether touching. This individual was a man about thirty years of age, dressed in black clothes, the cut of which resembled that of priestly garments worn in a city. His forehead was low, his nose hooked like the beak of a bird of prey. His lips were thin; and yet, in spite of their thinness, they were prominent, owing to a peculiar formation of the jaw; his pointed chin protruded at an angle which was more than sharp; his hair, of a leaden black, was plastered along his temples, and his gray eyes, often dropped, seemed to see through his winking eyelids. It was the countenance of a Jesuit grafted on the face of a Jew.

A few words said by this unknown man to Courtin appeared to remove the distrust with which the latter was inclined to receive advances which seemed to him at first suspicious. He even accepted with a good grace an invitation to dinner at the hôtel Saint-Pierre, which the stranger gave him; and after two hours passed *tête-à-tête* in a private room, where the individual we have described ordered the table to be laid, such mutual sympathy had been developed that they treated each other, Courtin and he, as old friends; exchanging, when they parted, many shakings of the hand, while the mayor of La Logerie, as he struck his spurs into his pony's flanks, promised his new acquaintance that he should not be long without hearing from him.

Toward nine o'clock that evening Maître Courtin was jogging along, with the tail of his beast toward Aigrefeuille and its nose toward La Logerie; he seemed quite lively and joyous, and was flirting his whip by its leather handle right and left on the flanks of his little steed, with a jollity and ease that were not characteristic of him.

Maître Courtin's brain was evidently larded with *couleur-de-rose* ideas. He was thinking how on the morrow he should have, at a stone's throw from his farm, a detachment of fifty soldiers, whose presence would relieve him of anxiety, not only about the consequences of what he had done, but also about those of certain things that he wanted to do; he was thinking, too, that in his capacity as mayor he could use those fifty bayonets according to the needs of his private animosities. This idea gratified his self-love and his hatred together.

But, seductive as this idea of a Pretorian guard which could, if cleverly managed, be turned into his private guard, might be, it was surely not sufficient to give Maître Courtin — a practical man if ever there was one — his present exuberant satisfaction.

The mysterious unknown had no doubt dazzled his eyes with something more than the glitter of an ephemeral glory, — in fact, it was neither more nor less than piles of gold and silver which Maître Courtin was beholding in his mind's eye through the mists of the future, and toward which he was mechanically stretching out his hand with a smile of covetousness.

Under the control of these agreeable hallucinations, and somewhat hazy from the fumes of wine which his new friend had poured for him generously, Maître Courtin let himself drop into a state of gentle somnolence; his body swayed to right and left, according to the caprices of his ambling pony, until at last, the quadruped having stumbled over a stone, Maître Courtin pitched forward and remained doubled over on the pommel of his saddle.

The position was uncomfortable, but Maître Courtin was

careful not to change it; he was then in the midst of so delightful a dream that, for all the world, he would not lose it by awaking. He thought he was meeting his young master, who said to him, waving his hand over the domain of La Logerie, "All this is thine!"

The gift was proving more considerable than Courtin at first thought it; untold riches were developing. The trees in the orchard were laden down with gold and silver fruit; all the poles in the neighborhood would not suffice to hinder the branches from breaking under the weight of such wealth. The wild-roses and hawthorns were bearing, instead of their usual haws, jewels of all colors, which sparkled in the sun like so many carbuncles; and there was such a quantity of them that, although he knew they were precious stones, Courtin saw, with an eye of equanimity, a small marauder filling his pockets with them.

The farmer entered his own stable. In that stable he beheld a file of fat and well-fed cows extending out of sight so far, so far, that the one which was nearest the door seemed to be of the size of an elephant, while the one in the farthest distance was no bigger than a worm. Under each of these cows was a young girl milking. The first two had the features of the "she-wolves," the daughters of the Marquis de Souday. From the teats of the cows they were milking ran a white and yellow liquid, brilliant as two metals in fusion. As it fell into the copper pails of the two girls it produced that delightful sound which is music to the ear, — the sound of gold and silver coins piling one above the other.

As he looked into the pails the happy farmer saw that they were more than half full of rare and precious coins of various effigies. He stretched out his eager, grasping, quivering hands to seize these treasures, and as he did so a violent shock accompanied by a cry of agony put to flight his soft illusions.

Courtin opened his eyes and saw in the darkness a

peasant-woman with torn clothes and dishevelled hair stretching out her hands to him.

"What do you want?" cried Maître Courtin, assuming a gruff voice and raising his stick in a threatening manner.

"Your help, my good man; I implore it in God's name!"

Finding that pity alone was asked for, and certain now that he had only a woman to deal with, Maître Courtin, who at first had looked about him in a terrified manner, was completely reassured.

"You are committing a misdemeanor, my dear," he said. "You have no right to stop persons on the high-road and ask for alms!"

"Alms! who said anything about alms?" returned the woman, in a refined and haughty tone of voice which arrested Courtin's attention. "I want you to help in rescuing an unfortunate man who is dying of fatigue and exposure! I want you to lend me your horse to take him to some farmhouse in the neighborhood."

"Who is it I am to help?"

"You seem by your dress to belong to the country people. I shall therefore not hesitate to tell you the truth, for I am sure, whatever your political opinions may be, you will not betray us, — he is a royalist officer."

The voice of the unknown woman excited Courtin's curiosity to the utmost. He leaned from his saddle striving to see in the darkness the face of her to whom the voice belonged; but he did not succeed in doing so.

"Who are you, yourself?" he asked.

"What is that to you?"

"Do you expect me to lend my horse to persons I don't know?"

"I have made a mistake; your answer proves that I was wrong to treat you as a friend or a generous enemy. I had better have employed another means. Give me your horse at once!"

"Indeed!"

"You have two minutes for decision."

"And if I refuse ?"

"I will blow your brains out!" said the woman, pointing a pistol at Courtin and clicking the trigger to let him know the execution of the threat would follow promptly.

"Ah, good! I recognize you now," said Courtin. "You are Mademoiselle de Souday."

Then, without allowing his questioner time to say more, the mayor of La Logerie got off his pony.

"Very good!" said Bertha, for it was she. "Now tell me your name, and to-morrow the horse shall be sent home to you."

"No need, for I 'll go with you and help you."

"You! why this sudden change ?"

"Because I take it the person you want me to help is the owner of my farm."

"His name ?"

"Monsieur Michel de la Logerie."

"Ah ! you are one of his tenants. Then we can go to your farmhouse for concealment."

"But," stammered Courtin, who was far from comfortable at the thought of meeting the young baron, especially when he reflected that if he took him with Bertha under his roof Jean Oullier would be certain to come there after them, "you see I am the mayor, and — "

"You are afraid of compromising yourself in serving your master !" exclaimed Bertha, in a tone of the deepest contempt.

"Oh, no, not that! I 'd give my blood for the young man; but we are to have a garrison of soldiers in the château de la Logerie."

"So much the better; they will never suspect that Vendéans, insurgents, would take refuge so near them."

"But I think, in the interest of Monsieur le baron, that Jean Oullier could find you a safer retreat than my house, where the soldiers are likely to be, morning, noon, and night."

"Alas! poor Jean Oullier is not likely to help any of his friends in future."

"How so?"

"We heard this morning some brisk firing in the direction of the moor; we did not stir from where we were, as he told us to wait till he returned. But we waited, and waited, in vain! Jean Oullier is either dead or a prisoner, for he is not one of those who desert their friends."

If it had been daylight Courtin could not have concealed the joy this news, which relieved him of his worst anxieties, caused him. But, though he was not master of his countenance, he was of his words; and he answered Bertha, who had spoken in an agitated voice full of feeling, with a mournful ejaculation which rather reconciled her to him.

"Let us walk faster," said Bertha.

"I 'm willing. What a smell of burning there is here!"

"Yes, they set fire to the heath."

"Ah! How came Monsieur le baron to escape the fire? He is in the direction of it."

"Jean Oullier put us among the reeds in the Fréneuse pond."

"Ah! that 's why when I touched you just now I felt you were all wet?"

"Yes; as Jean Oullier did not return I crossed the pond to seek for help. Finding no one, I took Baron Michel on my shoulders and brought him ashore. I hoped to carry him to the nearest house, but I have not the strength. I have been obliged to leave him among the bushes and come to the high-road myself. We have had nothing to eat for twenty-four hours."

"Ha! you 're a stalwart girl!" cried Courtin, who, in the uncertainty he felt as to how his young master might receive him, was not sorry to conciliate Mademoiselle Bertha's good-will. "You are just the helpmate Monsieur le baron needs in these stirring times."

"It is my duty to give my life for him," said Bertha.

"Yes," said Courtin, emphatically; "and that duty no

one, I swear to God, understands as you do. But be calm and don't walk so fast!"

"But he suffers! he may be calling for me — if he comes out of his swoon."

"Did he swoon?" cried Courtin, eagerly, seeing in that small detail the chance of escaping an immediate explanation.

"Yes, poor fellow! he is badly wounded, too."

"Good God!"

"Just think! for twenty-four hours, in his state, he has had no proper care! for my help has been powerless, I may say."

"Good heavens!"

"And think, too! he has been all day in the burning sun in the middle of the reeds; and to-night, in spite of my precautions, the fog has wet him through and through, and he has had a chill.

"Good Lord!"

"Ah! if evil happens to him I'll expiate my fault in penance all my life for having urged him into dangers for which he was unfit!" cried Bertha, whose political sentiments vanished before the loving anguish Michel's sufferings caused her.

As for Courtin, Bertha's assurance that Michel was not in a state to talk to him seemed to double the length of his legs. The girl no longer needed to hasten him on; he walked at his top speed, with a vigor he seldom showed, pulling the pony after him by the bridle, the beast being recalcitrant over the rough and heated road.

Relieved for ever and aye of Jean Oullier, Courtin believed it would be easy to excuse himself to his young master, — in fact, that the matter would settle itself.

They soon reached the spot where the girl had left Michel. He, with his back against a stone, his head dropped on his breast, was, if not actually unconscious, in such a state of utter prostration that he had only a dim and confused sense of what was passing about him. He paid no heed to Courtin; and when the latter, with Bertha's help, hoisted him on the pony, he pressed Courtin's hand, as he did that of Bertha, without knowing what he was about.

Courtin and Bertha walked on either side of the pony to support Michel, who, without their help, would have fallen to left or right.

They reached the farmhouse. Courtin woke up his servant-woman, on whom he knew he could rely, took his own mattress (the only one the house afforded) into a sort of lean-to above his bedroom, where he installed his young master with such zeal, self-devotion, and eager protestations that Bertha ended by regretting the opinion she had formed of him on the high-road.

When Michel's wound was dressed, and he was safely in the bed improvised for him, Bertha went to the servant's room to seek her rest.

Left alone, Maître Courtin rubbed his hands; he had done a good night's work. Violent behavior had not answered hitherto; gentleness, he was sure, was more likely to succeed. He had done better than enter the enemy's camp — he had brought the enemy's camp into his own house, which gave him every likelihood of detecting the secrets of the Whites, especially those concerning Petit-Pierre.

He went over in his brain all the injunctions given to him by the mysterious man at Aigrefeuille; the most important of which was to send him immediate information if he contrived to discover the retreat of the heroine of La Vendée, and not to communicate any facts to the generals, — men who cared nothing for the art of diplomacy, and were altogether below the level of great political machinations.

Courtin now thought it possible, through Michel and Bertha, to discover Madame's retreat; he began to believe that dreams were not always lies, and that, thanks to the two young people, the wells of gold and silver and precious stones, the streams of metallic milk, would become to him a reality.

XXII.

ON THE HIGHWAY.

DURING all this time Mary had no news of Bertha. Since the evening on which the latter left the Jacquet mill, announcing her resolve to search for Michel, Mary knew nothing of Bertha's movements. Her mind was lost in conjecture. Had Michel spoken? Had Bertha, reduced to despair, done some fatal deed? Was he wounded? Was he killed? Had Bertha herself been shot in one of her adventurous undertakings? Such were the gloomy alternatives Mary feared for the two objects of her affections; both left her a prey to the keenest anxiety, the sharpest anguish.

In vain she told herself that the wandering life she now led with Petit-Pierre, forced each evening to leave the shelter of the night before, made it very difficult for Bertha to recover their traces. Making all such allowances it seemed to Mary that, unless some misfortune had happened to her, Bertha would surely have sent some news of her whereabouts through the channels of communication which the royalists possessed among the peasantry. Mary's courage was already weakened by the many shocks she had just endured; and she herself, unsupported, isolated, deprived of her lover's presence, which had secretly sustained her in the hour of struggle, now gave way to gloomy distress, and broke down utterly under her trouble. She spent her days, which she ought to have employed in resting after the fatigues of the night, in watching for Bertha or for some messenger who never came; for hours at a time she sat silently absorbed in her grief, speaking only when spoken to.

Mary certainly loved her sister; the immense sacrifice to which she had resigned herself for Bertha's sake abundantly proved it — and yet she blushed, owning to herself, honestly, that it was not Bertha's fate that chiefly filled her mind. However warm, however sincere was the affection Mary felt for her sister, another and more imperious emotion had glided into her soul, and fed on the pain it brought there. In spite of all the poor girl's efforts, the sacrifice of which we speak had never detached her from him who was the occasion of it. Now that Michel was separated from her, she fancied she could indulge without danger the thoughts she had struggled to put away from her; and little by little Michel's image had so gained possession of her heart that it no longer left it, even for a moment.

In the midst of the sufferings of her life, the pain these remembrances of her lover gave her seemed comforting; she flung herself into it with a sort of passion. Day by day he had an ever-increasing share in the tears and anxiety caused by the strange and long-protracted absence of her sister. After yielding, without reserve, to her despair, after exhausting every gloomy supposition, after evoking all the cruel alternatives of the uncertainty in which each passing hour left her, after anxiously counting all the minutes of those hours, little by little Mary fell into regret, — regret intermingled with self-reproach.

She went over in her memory the smallest incidents of her relation and that of her sister with Michel. She asked herself whether she were not doing wrong in breaking the heart of the poor lad while she broke her own; whether she had the right to force the disposal of his love; whether she were not responsible for the misery into which she was plunging Michel by compelling him to be a sharer in the immense sacrifice she was offering to her sister. Her thoughts returned, with irresistible inclination, to the night spent on the islet of Jonchère. She saw once more those reedy barriers; she fancied she heard that softly harmonious voice, which said: "I love thee!" She closed her eyes, and again she felt the young man's breath as it touched her hair, and his lips laying on her lips the first, the only, but ah! the ineffable kiss she had received from him.

Then the renunciation which her virtue, her tenderness for her sister urged upon her seemed greater than her strength could bear. She blamed herself for rashly attempting a superhuman task, and Love regained so vigorously a heart all love, that Mary, — ordinarily pious, submissive, accustomed to seek, in view of a future life, the path of patient courage, — Mary had no longer the strength to look to heaven only; she was crushed. In the anguish of her passion she gave herself up to impious despair, asking God if this fleeting memory of the touch of those lips was all she was to know of the happiness of being loved; and whether life were worth the pain of living thus disinherited of joy.

The Marquis de Souday at last perceived the great alteration produced on Mary's face by these grievous emotions; but he naturally attributed it to the great bodily fatigue the young girl was now enduring. He was himself much depressed in seeing all his fine dreams vanishing, and all the predictions made to him by the general realized. He saw with dread a return of his exiled days without even having seen, as it were, the dawn of a struggle. Still, he felt it his duty to force his courage and resolution to the level of the misfortune which overwhelmed him, and that duty the marquis would have died rather than not fulfil; for was it not a soldier's duty? Little as he cared for social duties and proprieties, the more he stickled for those which concerned his military honor. Therefore, notwithstanding his inward depression, he showed no outward sign of it, and even found in the vicissitudes of their adventurous life the text of many a joke with which he tried to distract the minds of his companions from the anxiety and disappointment consequent on the failure of the insurrection.

Mary had told her father of Bertha's departure; and the worthy old gentleman had intelligently guessed that the girl's anxiety about the conduct and fate of her betrothed was at the bottom of it. As eye-witnesses had already brought him word that Michel, far from failing in his duty, had heroically contributed to the defence of La Pénissière, the marquis, — who supposed that Jean Oullier, on whose care and prudence he implicitly relied, was with his daughter and future son-in-law, — the marquis did not think it necessary to be more uneasy at Bertha's absence than a general might have been about an officer dispatched on an expedition. Nevertheless, the marquis could not explain to himself why Baron Michel had preferred to fight so well under Jean Oullier's orders rather than under his own, — and he was inclined to be annoyed at the preference.

Surrounded by Legitimist leaders, Petit-Pierre, on the very evening of the fight at Chêne, left the Jacquet mill, where the danger of a surprise was imminent. The main-road, which was not far distant, was covered at intervals by bodies of soldiers escorting prisoners. Petit-Pierre and her body-guard started, therefore, as soon as it was dark.

Wishing to follow the highway as much as possible, the little troop encountered a detachment of the government troops, and was forced to crouch in a wayside ditch, which was filled with brambles, for over an hour, while the detachment filed by. The whole region was so patrolled by these movable columns that it was only by following the most impassable wood-paths that the fugitives could be sure of escaping their vigilance.

Petit-Pierre's uneasiness was extreme; her physical appearance betrayed her mental sufferings, but her words, her behavior, never! In the midst of this hazardous life, so disturbed and often so gloomy, the same bright gayety sparkled from her, and held its own with that the marquis was assuming. Pursued as they were, the fugitives never had a full night's rest; and no sooner had the daylight dawned than danger and fatigue awoke when they did. These terrible night marches were sometimes dangerous, and always horribly fatiguing to Petit-Pierre. Sometimes she went on horseback, oftener on foot,—through fields divided by hedges and embankments, which could only be crossed after darkness had fallen; through vineyards, which, in that region, trail their vines on the ground, where they catch the feet and threaten a fall at every moment; through cow-paths trampled into mud by the constant passage of the cattle, — mud which came to the knees of foot-passengers and horses.

Petit-Pierre's companions were now very anxious as to the results of this life of incessant emotion and bodily fatigue on the health of their precious charge. They deliberated on the best means of putting her, once for all, in safety. Opinions differed; some were for taking her to Paris, where she might be lost in the midst of a vast population; others proposed Nantes, where a safe concealment was already prepared; a third party counselled immediate embarkation, not thinking it possible to ensure her safety so long as she stayed in France, where search would be only the more active because the actual insurrection was at an end.

The Marquis de Souday was of the latter opinion; to which objection was made that a vigorous watch was kept along the coast, and that it would be absolutely impossible to embark from any port, however insignificant, without a passport.

Petit-Pierre cut short the discussion by declaring that she should go to Nantes, and would enter it on the morrow in full daylight, dressed as a peasant-woman. As the great change and depression visible in Mary's appearance had not, as may well be supposed, escaped her, and as she supposed, like the marquis, that they were due to the great fatigue the girl was enduring, —and as this fatigue would continue if she stayed with her father, —Petit-Pierre proposed to the marquis to take his daughter with her. The marquis accepted the offer gratefully.

Mary did not readily resign herself. Shut up in a town she was not so likely to obtain news of Bertha and Michel, which she was now awaiting from hour to hour with feverish anxiety. On the other hand, refusal was impossible, and she therefore yielded.

On the morrow, which was Saturday, and market-day, Petit-Pierre and Mary, dressed as peasant-women, started for the town at six in the morning; they had about ten miles to go. After walking for half an hour the wooden shoes, but, above all, the woollen socks, to which Petit-Pierre was not accustomed, hurt her feet. She tried to keep on; but knowing that if she blistered her feet she would be unable to continue the journey, she sat down by the wayside, took off her shoes and stockings, stuffed them into her capacious pockets, and started again barefooted.

Presently, however, she noticed, as other peasant-women passed her, that the whiteness and delicacy of her skin might betray her; she therefore turned off the road a little way, took some dark, peaty earth, and rubbed it on her feet and legs till they were stained with it, and then resumed her way.

They had just reached the top of the hill at Sorinières when they saw in front of a roadside tavern two gendarmes who were talking with a peasant like themselves, who was on horseback.

Mary and Bertha were at this moment in the midst of a group of five or six peasant-women, and the gendarmes paid no attention to any of them. But Mary, who watched every one she passed, thinking some information as to Bertha and Michel might chance to reach her, — Mary fancied that the mounted peasant looked at her with peculiar attention. A few moments later she turned her head and saw that the peasant had left the gendarmes, and was hurrying his pony as if to overtake the group of peasant-women.

"Take care of yourself," she whispered hastily to Petit-Pierre; "there 's a man I don't know who just examined me with great attention and then started to follow us. Go on alone, and seem not to know me!"

"Very good; but suppose he joins you, Mary?"

"I can answer him; don't be afraid."

"In case we are forced to separate, shall you know where to find me?"

"Yes; but don't let us say another word to each other — he is coming."

The horse's hoofs were now ringing on the paved centre of the road. Without appearing to do so Mary lagged behind the group of peasant-women. She could not help quivering when she heard, as she expected, the voice of the man addressing her.

"So we are going to Nantes, my pretty girl?" he began, pulling in his horse when he reached Mary's side, and again looking at her attentively.

"So it appears," she said, seeming to take the matter gayly.

"Don't you want my company?" asked the rider.

"Oh, no, thank you," replied Mary, imitating the speech of the Vendéan peasant-women; "I 'll keep on with the rest from our parts."

"The rest from your parts? You don't expect me to believe that all those girls before us are from your village?"

"Whether they are or not, what 's that to you?" retorted Mary, evading a question which was evidently insidious.

The man saw through her purpose.

"I 'll make you a proposal," he said.

"What sort of proposal?"

"Get up behind me."

"Yes, that 's likely!" replied Mary; "a pretty sight it would be to see a poor girl like me holding on to a man who looks like a gentleman."

"Especially as you are not accustomed to hug those who look and are such."

"What do you mean by that?" asked Mary.

"I mean that you may pass for a peasant-girl in the eyes of gendarmes; but my eyes are another thing. You are not what you are trying to seem, Mademoiselle Mary de Souday."

"If you have no evil intentions toward me why do you say my name in a loud voice on the public highway?" asked the young girl, stopping short.

"What harm is there in that?" said the rider.

"Only that those women may have heard you; and if I wear these clothes you must know it is because my interests or my safety oblige me."

"Oh!" said the man, winking one eye and affecting a knowing air; "those women you pretend to be afraid of know all about you."

"No, they do not!"

"One of them does, any how."

Mary trembled in spite of herself; but summoning all her strength of will, she replied: —

"Neither one nor all. But may I ask why you are putting these questions to me?"

"Because, if you are really alone, as you say you are, I shall ask you to stop here for a few minutes."

"I?"

"Yes."

"For what purpose?"

"To save me a long search I should have made to-morrow if I had not met you now."

"Search for what?"

"Why, for you!"

"Do you mean that you are seeking me?"

"Not on my own account, you must understand."

"But who sent you on such an errand?"

"Those who love you." Then lowering his voice he added: "Mademoiselle Bertha and Monsieur Michel."

"Bertha? Michel?"

"Yes."

"Then he is not dead!" cried Mary. "Oh, tell me, tell me, monsieur, I implore you, what has become of them?"

The terrible anxiety betrayed by the tone in which Mary said the words, the agitation of her face as she awaited the answer, which seemed to be one of life or death to her, were noticed with curiosity by Courtin, on whose lips flickered a diabolical smile. He took pleasure in delaying his answer in order to prolong the young girl's anguish.

"No, no!" he said at last, "don't be uneasy; he 'll get over it!"

"Get over it! is he wounded?" asked Mary, vehemently.

"Did n't you know it?"

"Oh, my God! my God! Wounded!" cried Mary, with her eyes full of tears.

"Pooh!" said Courtin, "his wound won't keep him long in bed or hinder his marriage!"

Mary felt that she turned pale in spite of herself. Courtin's words reminded her that she had not asked news of her sister.

"And Bertha?" she said, "you have told me nothing about her."

"Your sister? Ha! she 's a dashing girl! When she hooks her arm into her husband's she may well say she has earned him."

"But she is not ill, she is not wounded, is she?"

"She is a trifle ill, but that 's all."

"Poor Bertha!"

"She did too much. I tell you there 's many a man would have died of the strain if he had done what she did."

"Good God!" cried Mary; "both ill, and both without care!"

"Oh, as for that, no; they are caring for one another. You ought to see how your sister, ill as she is, cossets the young baron. Some men have the luck of it, that 's a fact; Monsieur Michel is just as much petted by his lady-love as he was by his mother. . He 'll have to love her well, if he does n't want to be ungrateful."

Mary's agitation increased at these words, — a fact which did not escape the rider's notice, and he smiled.

"Shall I tell you something that I think I have discovered ?" he said.

"What is it ?"

"Why, that Monsieur le baron, in the matter of color, prefers fair hair to black."

"What do you mean ?" asked Mary, quivering.

"If you wish me to explain, I 'll tell something that you know as well as I do; and that is, that he loves you. And if Bertha is the name of his betrothed, Mary is the name of his heart's love."

"Oh!" cried Mary, "you are inventing all that; Monsieur de la Logerie never told you any such thing."

"No; but I have seen it for myself; and as I cherish him like my own flesh and blood, I want to see him happy, the dear lad ! Therefore I said to myself yesterday, when your sister asked me to get word to you about her, that I 'd clear my conscience of the matter and tell you what I think."

"You are mistaken in your thoughts, monsieur," replied Mary. "Monsieur Michel does not care for me; he is my sister's betrothed husband, and he loves her deeply; I can assure you of that."

"You are wrong not to trust me, Mademoiselle Mary. Do you know who I am? I am Courtin, Monsieur Michel's head farmer, and I may say, his confidential man; and if you choose — "

"Monsieur Courtin, you will oblige me extremely," interrupted Mary, "if you would choose — "

"What ?"

"To change the conversation."

"Very good; but allow me to renew my offer. Won't y u ride behind me? — it would ease your journey. You are going to Nantes, I suppose ?"

"Yes," replied Mary, who, little as she liked Courtin, thought she had better not conceal her destination from the Baron de la Logerie's confidential man.

"Well," continued Courtin, "as I am going there myself we had better go together, unless — If you are going to Nantes on an errand, and I could do it for you, I 'd willingly undertake it, and save you the trouble."

Mary, in spite of her natural truthfulness, felt compelled to dissimulate; for it was all-important that no one should even guess at the cause of her journey.

"No," she replied; "it is impossible. I am on my way to join my father, who has taken refuge in Nantes, where he is now concealed."

"Dear, dear!" said Courtin, "Monsieur le marquis hiding in Nantes! that 's a clever idea. They are looking for him the other way, and talk of turning the château de Souday inside out to its foundations."

"Who told you that?" asked Mary.

Courtin saw that he had made a blunder by seeming to know the plans of the government agents; he tried to repair it as best he could.

"It was chiefly to prevent you from going back there that Mademoiselle Bertha sent me in search of you," he said.

"Well, you see," said Mary, "that neither my father nor I are at Souday."

"Ah, that reminds me!" exclaimed Courtin, as if the thought had just come naturally into his head; "if Mademoiselle Bertha and Monsieur de la Logerie want to communicate with you, how are they to address you?"

"I don't know myself as yet," replied Mary. "I am to meet a man on the pont Rousseau who will take me to the house where my father is concealed. After I get there and have seen him I will write to my sister."

"Very good; if you have any communication to make, or if Monsieur le baron and your sister want to join you, and need a guide, I will undertake to manage it." Then, with a meaning smile, he added: "I 'll answer for one thing; Monsieur Michel will be sending me more than once."

"Enough!" said Mary.

"Ah! excuse me. I did n't know it would make you angry."

"It does; your suppositions are offensive both to your master and to me."

"Pooh!" said Courtin, "all that is only talk. Monsieur le baron has a fine fortune, and there is n't a young lady the country round, whether she is an heiress or not, who would turn up her nose at it. Say the word, Mademoiselle Mary," continued the farmer, who believed that everybody worshipped money as he did; "only say the word and I 'll do my best to make that fortune yours."

"Maître Courtin," said Mary, stopping short, and looking at the farmer with an expression in her eye he could not mistake; "it needs all my sense of your attachment to Monsieur de la Logerie to keep me from being seriously angry. I tell you again, and once for all, you are not to speak to me in that manner!"

Courtin expected a different reply, — his conception of a "she-wolf" not admitting of such delicacy. He was all the more surprised because he saw very plainly that the young girl shared the love his prying eyes had detected in the depths of the young baron's heart. For a moment he was disconcerted. Then he reflected that he might lose all by hurrying matters; better let the fish get thoroughly entangled in the net before he pulled it in.

The mysterious man at Aigrefeuille had told him it was probable that the leaders of the Legitimist insurrection would seek shelter in Nantes. Monsieur de Souday — Courtin believed this — was there already; Mary was on her way; Petit-Pierre would probably follow. Michel's love for the young girl might be used, like Ariadne's thread, to lead the way to her retreat, which would probably be that of Petit-Pierre; and the capture of Petit-Pierre was the real end and object of Courtin's ambitious hopes. If he persisted in accompanying Mary he would rouse her suspicions; and although he was most desirous to succeed that very day in his enterprise, prudence and strategy prevailed, and he resolved to give Mary some proof which might reassure her completely as to his intentions.

"Ah!" said he, "I see you despise my horse; but all the same it hurts me to see your little feet cut to pieces on those stones."

"Well, it can't be helped," replied Mary. "I shall be less noticed on foot than if I were mounted behind you; and, if I dared, I would ask you not to keep at my side. Anything that draws attention to me is dangerous. Let me walk alone and join those peasant-women just in front of us. I run less risk in their company."

"You are right," said Courtin; "and all the more because the gendarmes are behind and will overtake us soon."

Mary started; true enough, two gendarmes were really following them about a thousand feet back.

"Oh! you need n't be afraid," said Courtin; "I 'll detain them at that tavern. Go on alone; but tell me, first, what I am to say to your sister?"

"Tell her that all my thoughts and prayers are for her welfare."

"Is that all?"

The girl hesitated; she looked at the farmer; doubtless the expression of his countenance betrayed his secret thoughts, for she lowered her head and answered: —

"Yes, that is all."

Courtin was well aware that although Mary did not utter Michel's name, he was the first and last thought of her heart.

The farmer stopped his horse. Mary, on the other hand, hastened her steps and joined the other peasant-women, who had gained some distance ahead while she talked with Courtin. As soon as she reached them she walked on by Petit-Pierre and told her what had happened, — suppressing, of course, that part of the conversation that related to the young baron.

Petit-Pierre thought it wise to evade the curiosity of the man; for his name recalled in a vague way some unpleasant memory. She therefore dropped behind the other women with Mary; and when they were fairly out of sight — thanks to a turn in the road — the two fugitives slipped into a wood at a short distance from the highway, from the edge of which they could see who passed it. After about fifteen minutes they saw Courtin hurrying, as best he could, his stubborn pony. Unfortunately, the farmer passed too far from the place where they were hidden to allow of Petit-Pierre's recognizing him as the man who had visited Pascal Picaut's house, and cut the girths of Michel's horse.

When he was out of sight Petit-Pierre and her companion returned to the high-road and continued their way to Nantes. The nearer they came to the town, where Petit-Pierre was promised a safe retreat, the more their fears diminished. She was now quite used to her costume, and the farmers who passed them did not seem to perceive that the little peasant-woman who tripped so lightly along the road was other than she seemed to be. It was surely a great thing to have deceived an instinct so penetrating as that of the country-folk, who have no masters, and perhaps no rivals, in this respect except soldiers.

At last they came in sight of Nantes. Petit-Pierre put on her shoes and stockings, preparatory to entering the town. One thing, however, made Mary uneasy. Courtin would doubtless be watching for her on the bridge; therefore, instead of entering by the pont Rousseau, the two women took advantage of a boat to cross the Loire to the other side of the town.

As they passed the Bouffai a hand was laid on Petit-Pierre's shoulder. She started and turned round. The person who had taken that alarming liberty was a worthy old woman on her way to market, who had put down her basket of apples in order to rest herself, and was not able to lift it alone and replace it on her head.

"My dears," she said to Petit-Pierre and Mary, "do help me, please, to get up my basket, and I'll give you each an apple."

Petit-Pierre took one handle, motioned to Mary to take the other, and the basket was quickly replaced and balanced on the head of the old woman, who began to walk away without bestowing the promised reward. But Petit-Pierre caught her by the arm, saying: —

"Look here, mother, where's my apple?"

The market-woman gave it to her. Petit-Pierre set her teeth into it and was munching it with an appetite sharpened by a ten-mile walk, when, lifting her head, her eyes fell on a notice posted on the walls upon which appeared in large letters these words :—

STATE OF SIEGE.

It was a ministerial decree placing four departments in La Vendée under martial law.

Petit-Pierre went up to the notice and read it through from end to end tranquilly, in spite of Mary's entreaties to go as quickly as possible to the house where she was expected. Petit-Pierre very justly remarked that the matter was of such importance to her that she was right in obtaining a thorough knowledge of it.

Presently, however, the two women went their way into the dark and narrow streets of the old Breton city.

XXIII.

WHAT BECAME OF JEAN OULLIER.

Though it was next to impossible for the soldiers to discover Jean Oullier in the hiding-place poor Trigaud's herculean strength had made for him, nevertheless, now that Courte-Joie and his companion were dead, Jean Oullier had only exchanged the prison into which the Blues would have thrust him, had he fallen into their hands, for another prison more terrible, a death more awful than any his captors could inflict upon him. He was buried alive; and in this deserted region there was little hope that any human being would hear his cries.

Toward the middle of the night which followed his parting from his two associates, finding they did not return, he felt certain that some fatal event had overtaken them; evidently, they were either dead or prisoners. The mere idea of the position in which he himself was placed was enough to freeze the blood in the veins of the bravest man; but Jean Oullier had one of those strongly religious natures which continue a struggle in faith when the bravest despair. He commended his soul to God in a short but fervent prayer, and then set to work as ardently as he had done in the burning ruins of La Pénissière.

Up to this time he had been crouching, bent double, with his chin on his knees ; it was the only position the cramped quarters of the excavation allowed. He now endeavored to change it, and after many efforts he succeeded in getting on his knees. Then bracing himself on his hands and applying his shoulders to the heavy stone, he endeavored to raise it. But that which was child's play to Trigaud was impossible to any other man. Jean Oullier could not even shake the enormous mass which the giant had placed between him and the heavens.

He felt the ground beneath him; it was not earth but rock, — rock to right, rock to left, above and below him, rock only.

The slab of granite which Trigaud had laid like a monstrous cover on the stone box, slanted forward and left an open space about four inches wide between the bed of the rivulet and the imprisoned man, through which the air could reach him.

It was on this side that Jean Oullier, after fully reconnoitring his position, decided to apply his efforts.

He broke the point of his knife against the rock and made a chisel of it. The butt-end of his pistol answered for a hammer, and he set to work to widen the aperture. He spent twenty-four hours at this labor, without other sustenance than that contained in his huntsman's brandy-flask, from which he sipped from time to time some drops of the strengthening liquor it contained. During those twenty-four hours his courage and force of will did not desert him for a single instant.

At last, on the evening of the second day, he succeeded in passing his head through the aperture he had cut in the base of his prison; before long his shoulders could follow his head; and then, clasping the rock and making a vigorous effort, he drew out the rest of his body.

It was indeed high time that he did so; his strength was exhausted. He rose to his knees, then to his feet, and attempted to walk. But his injured ankle had swelled to such a frightful extent during the thirty-six hours he had spent in that horribly constrained position that at the first step he took all the nerves of his body quivered as if they were wrung. He uttered a cry and fell gasping on the heather, mastered at last by the terrible pain.

Night was coming on. Listen as he might, Jean Oullier could hear no sound. The thought came to him that this night, now beginning to wrap the world in its shadows, would be his last. Again he commended his soul to God, praying him to watch over the two children he had loved so well, and who, but for him, would long ago have been orphaned through their father's indifference. Then, determined to neglect no chances, he dragged himself by his hands, or rather crept, in the direction where the sun had set, which he knew to be that of the nearest dwellings.

He had gone in this way nearly a mile when he reached a little hill, whence he could see the lights in a few lonely houses scattered on the moor. Each of them was to him a pharos, beckoning to life and safety; but, in spite of all his courage, his strength now deserted him and he could do no more. It was sixty hours since he had eaten anything. The stumps of the brambles and the gorse, cut down in the haying season and sharpened by the scythe, had torn his hands and chest, and loss of blood from these wounds still further weakened him.

He allowed himself to roll into a ditch by the wayside; determined to go no farther, but to die there. Intense thirst possessed him, and he drank a little water which was stagnant in the ditch. He was so weak that his hand could scarcely reach his mouth; his head seemed absolutely empty. From time to time he fancied he heard in his brain a dull, lugubrious roar, like that of the sea making a breach over a ship and about to engulf it; a sort of veil seemed to spread before his eyes, and behind that veil coursed myriads of sparks, which died away and sparkled again like phosphorescent gleams.

The unfortunate man felt that this was death. He tried to shout, not caring whether enemies or friends came to his relief; but his voice died away in his throat, and he scarcely heard himself the hoarse cry which he managed to emit.

Thus he remained for over an hour, in a dying condition. Then, little by little, the veil before his eyes thickened and took prismatic tints; the humming in his brain had strange modulations, and for a time he lost consciousness of all about him.

But his powerful being could not be annihilated without a further struggle; the lethargic stillness in which he remained for some time allowed the heart to regulate its pulses, the blood to circulate less feverishly. The torpor in which he now lay did not lessen the acuteness of his senses. Presently he heard a sound which his huntsman's ear did not mistake for a single instant. A step was coming across the heather, and that step he knew to be a woman's.

That woman could save him! Torpid as he was, Jean Oullier understood it. But when he tried to call or make a movement to attract her attention he was like a man in a trance, who sees the preparations for his funeral and is unable to arrest them; he perceived with terror that nothing remained of him but his intelligence, and that his body, completely paralyzed, refused to obey him. As the hapless being nailed in his coffin makes frantic efforts to burst the iron barrier which parts him from the world, so Jean Oullier strained at every spring which Nature puts at the service of man's will to conquer matter. In vain.

And yet, the steps were coming nearer; each minute, each second made them more distinct, more unmistakable to his ear. He fancied that every pebble they displaced rolled to his heart; his agony from the multiplicity of his abortive efforts grew intense; his hair rose on his head; an icy sweat stood on his brow. It was worse and more cruel than death itself, for death feels nothing.

The woman passed.

Jean Oullier heard the thorns on the briers catch and scrape her dress as if even they wished to stop her; he saw her shadow lying dark upon the bushes; then she passed away, and the sound of her steps was lost in the sighing of the wind among the reeds.

The unfortunate man believed he was doomed; and the moment hope abandoned him the awful struggle he had fought against himself came to an end. He recovered calmness and mentally prayed to God, commending his soul to Him.

This prayer so absorbed him that it was not until he heard the noisy breathing of a dog, which passed its head through the bushes scenting an emanation, that he noticed the coming of an animal. He turned, with an effort, not his head, that was impossible, but his eyes in the direction of the creature, and there saw a cur gazing at him with frightened but intelligent eyes.

Catching Jean Oullier's gaze the animal retreated to a little distance and began to bark. At this instant Jean Oullier fancied that he heard the woman calling to her dog; but the creature did not choose to leave its post, continuing to bark. It was a last hope, — a hope that was not balked.

Tired of calling to her dog, and curious to know what excited it, the woman retraced her steps. Chance, or Providence, willed that this woman should be the widow of Pascal Picaut. As she neared the bushes she saw a man; stooping over him she recognized Jean Oullier.

At first she thought him dead; then she saw his eyes, unnaturally wide open, fixed upon her. She laid her hand upon the huntsman's heart and felt it beating; she lifted him to a sitting posture, threw a little water on his face, and poured a few drops through his clenched teeth. Then — as if through contact with a living being he recovered contact with life itself — Jean Oullier felt the enormous weight which lay upon him lightening; warmth returned to his torpid limbs; he felt its glow steal softly to each extremity; tears of gratitude welled from his eyelids and rolled down his sunken cheeks; he caught the woman's hand and carried it to his lips, wetting it with tears.

She, on her side, was greatly moved. Philippist as she was, the good woman highly esteemed the old Chouan.

"Well, well," she said, "don't take on so, my Jean Oullier! It is all natural, what I am doing! I 'd do as much for any Christian; and all the more for you, who are a man after God's own heart ! "

"That does n't prevent — " said Jean Oullier.

He could say no more, his breath failed him.

"Does n't prevent what ? " asked the widow.

Oullier made an effort.

"Does n't prevent — that I owe you my life," he said.

"Oh, nonsense ! " exclaimed Marianne.

"It is as I say. Without you, I should have died."

"Without my dog, Jean. You see it is n't me, but the good God you have to thank." Then noticing with horror that he was covered with blood, "Why, you are wounded!" she exclaimed.

"Oh, no, nothing but scratches. My worst trouble is that I have dislocated my ankle; and besides, I have n't eaten anything for nearly three days. It is chiefly weakness that is killing me."

"Good gracious ! but see here, I was just carrying dinner to some men who are getting litter for me on the moor. You shall have their soup."

So saying, the widow put down the basket she was carrying, untied the four corners of a cloth in which were several porringers full of soup and bouilli smoking hot. She gave several spoonfuls to Jean Oullier, who felt his strength returning as every mouthful of the warm and succulent broth got down into his stomach.

"Ah ! " he said; and he breathed noisily.

A smile of satisfaction crossed the grave, sad face of the widow.

"Now," she said, sitting down opposite to him, "what are you going to do ? Of course you know the red-breeches are after you ? "

"Alas ! " said Jean Oullier; "I have lost all power with my poor leg. It will be months before I can roam the woods as I must to escape a prison. What I had better do," he added with a sigh, "is to get to Maître Jacques; he will give me a corner in some of his burrows, where I can stay till my leg is well."

"But your master ?—and his daughters ?"

"The marquis won't go back yet awhile to Souday; and he is right."

"What will he do, then ?"

"Probably cross the channel with the young ladies."

"That 's a pretty idea of yours, Jean Oullier, to go and live among that crew of bandits who follow Maître Jacques! Fine care they 'll take of you !"

"They are the only ones who can take me in without being compromised."

"How about me ? You forget me, and that is n't nice of you, Jean."

"You ?"

"Yes, me !"

"But you forget the ordinance."

"What ordinance ?"

"About the penalties incurred by those who harbor Chouans."

"Pooh ! my Jean; such orders are not issued for honest folk, but for scoundrels !"

"Besides, you hate Chouans."

"No; it is only brigands I hate, whichever side they are. They were brigands who killed my poor Pascal, and on those brigands I 'll avenge his death if I can. But you, Jean Oullier, your cockade, be it white or tricolor, is that of an honest man, and I 'll save you."

"But I can't walk a step."

"That 's no matter. Even if you could walk, Jean, I 'd be afraid to take you to my house by daylight,—not that I fear for myself; but ever since the death of that young man I fear treachery. Get back under those bushes; hide as best you can; wait till dark, and I 'll come back with a cart and fetch you. Then, to-morrow, I 'll go for the bone-setter at Machecoul; he 'll rub his hand over the nerves of your foot, and in three days you 'll run like a rabbit."

"Hang it! I know that would be best, but—"

"Would n't you do as much for me?"

"You know, Marianne, I 'd go through fire and water for you."

"Then don't say another word. I shall be back after dark."

"Thank you; I accept your offer. You may be very sure you are not helping an ungrateful man."

"It is not to get your gratitude I am doing it, Jean Oullier; but to fulfil my duty as an honest woman."

She looked about her.

"What are you looking for?" asked Jean.

"I was thinking if you tried to get farther back among the bushes you would be safer than in this ditch."

"I think it is impossible," said Oullier, showing his ankle, now swelled to the size of a man's head, and his torn hands and face. "Besides, I am not badly off here; you passed close by these bushes and did not suspect they hid a man."

"Yes, but a dog might pass and smell you out, just as mine did. Remember, my Jean, the war is over, and the days of denunciation and vengeance will begin, if they have not already begun."

"Bah!" said Jean Oullier, "we must leave something for the good God to do."

The widow was no less of a believer than the old Chouan. She gave him a piece of bread, cut an armful of ferns with which she made him a bed, and then, after carefully raising the branches of the briers and brambles about him, and satisfying herself that the eye of no passer would detect him, she departed, exhorting him to patience.

Jean Oullier settled himself as comfortably as he could, offered a fervent thanksgiving to the Lord, munched his bread, and presently went to sleep in that heavy sleep which follows great prostration.

He must have been lying there several hours when the sound of voices woke him. In the species of somnolence which followed the state of torpor he had been in, he fancied he heard the name of his young mistresses; suspicious as all men of his stamp are in the matter of their affections, he fancied some danger must be threatening either Bertha or Mary, and the thought was like a lever, which lifted in a second the torpor of his mind. He rose on his elbow, gently moved the brambles which made a thick rampart before him, and looked through them into the road.

It was dark, but not dark enough to prevent him from seeing the outline of two men who were sitting on a fallen tree on the other side of the road.

"Why did n't you continue to follow her, as you recognized her?" said one of them whom, from his strong German accent, Jean Oullier judged to be a stranger in these regions.

"Ha! damn it!" said the other. "She-wolf as she is, I never thought her so wily; but she gave me the slip, fool that I was."

"You might have been certain that the one we were after was in that group of peasant-women, and that Mary de Souday only stayed behind to meet and detain you."

"As for that, you are right enough; for when I asked that same group of women where the young girl was they said that she and her companion had lagged behind and left them on the road."

"What did you do then?"

"Hang it! I put up the pony at an inn, and hid myself at the farther end of Pirmile and waited for them."

"In vain, I suppose."

"In vain, — for more than two hours."

"They must have taken a cross-road and entered Nantes by the other bridge."

"Probably."

"It is very unfortunate. Who knows if such a piece of luck will ever happen to you again? Perhaps you may never find her now."

"Oh, yes, I shall. Let me alone for that."

"How will you do it?"

"Oh! — as my neighbor the Marquis de Souday, or my friend Jean Oullier would say — 'God wants her soul;' and I have at home just the bloodhound we need for the hunt."

"Bloodhound?"

"Yes, a regular bloodhound. There is something the matter with one of his front paws, but as soon as that is well I'll put a chain round his neck and he'll take us straight in the direction we want to go, without any trouble to us, except taking care he does not pull too hard on the chain and break it in his hurry to get there."

"Come, stop joking; these are serious matters."

"Joking! what do you take me for? Do you suppose I joke in presence of the fifty thousand francs you have promised me? — for you really did say fifty thousand, did n't you?"

"You ought to be sure of it, for you have made me tell you a score of times."

"I know that; but I am never tired of hearing it, any more than I shall be tired of fingering the louis when I get them."

"Deliver us the person we want, and you shall have them."

"Bless me! I hear those yellow-boys chinking in my ears, — dzing! dzing!"

"Meantime, tell me what you mean by a bloodhound."

"Oh! I'd tell you willingly, but —"

"But what?"

"Give and take, you know."

"What do you mean by 'give and take'?"

"Well, as I told you the other day, I wish to oblige the government, partly because I respect it, and partly because I like to harass the nobles and all that belong to them — for I hate 'em all. But, all the same, while obliging the government of my choice, I should be glad to see the color of its money, — for, don't you see, thus far I have given it much more than I receive. Besides, how do I know that if the government lays hold of that person for whom they offer her weight in gold, how do I know, I say, that they will pay what they promised me, or rather promised you?"

"You are a fool."

"I should be a fool if I did not say what I am saying to you now. I like to make myself secure; and if I must speak frankly, I don't see much security in this affair."

"You run the same risks that I do. I have received from an eminent person the promise of one hundred thousand francs if I succeed."

"One hundred thousand francs! That 's very little to have come so far to get. Come, own that it is two hundred thousand, and that you give me a quarter of it; because I am on the spot and don't have to travel for the money as you do. Two hundred thousand francs! You are pretty lucky! A good round sum and rings well. So be it, I 'll have confidence in the government; but, let me ask, why should I have it in you? How can I be sure you won't slip off with the money when the government pays it? And if you should, where 's the court or the judge before whom I could sue you, I 'd like to know?"

"My good sir, political associates must trust each other; faith signs their contract."

"Is that why they are so wonderfully well kept? Frankly, I 'd prefer another signature."

"Whose?"

"Yours, or that of the minister with whom you are dealing."

"Well, we'll try to satisfy you."

"Hush!"

"What?"

"Don't you hear something?"

"Yes; some one is coming this way. I think I hear the wheels of a cart."

The two men rose at once, and by the light of the moon,

which was then shining, Jean Oullier, who had not lost a single word of the conversation, saw their faces. One of the men was a stranger to him; the other proved to be Courtin, — a fact he knew already by the tones of the farmer's voice and the mention he had made of Michel and the "she-wolves."

"Let us go," said the stranger.

"No," replied Courtin; "I 've a number of things to say to you. Let us hide in this bush till the cart has gone by, and then we can finish our business."

They walked toward the ditch. Jean knew he was lost; but, unwilling to be caught like a hare on its form, he rose to his knees, and pulled his knife from his belt. It was blunt, to be sure, but in a hand to hand struggle could still be of use. He had no other weapon and supposed the two men to be unarmed. But Courtin, who had seen a man's form rise in the bush and heard the rustle of the reeds and brambles, made three steps backward, seized his gun hidden behind the fallen tree, cocked one barrel, lifted the weapon to his shoulder, and fired. A stifled cry followed the explosion.

"What have you done?" cried the stranger, who seemed to think Courtin's action rather too expeditious.

"See! see!" replied Courtin, trembling and very pale; "a man was watching us."

The stranger went to the bushes and parted the branches.

"Take care! take care!" said Courtin; "if it is a Chouan and he is not quite dead, he 'll attack you."

So saying, Courtin, with his other barrel cocked, held himself ready to fire at a safe distance.

"It is a peasant," said the stranger, "but I think he is dead."

So saying, he took Jean Oullier by the arm and dragged him out of the ditch. Courtin, seeing that the man was motionless and apparently dead, ventured to approach.

"Jean Oullier!" he cried out, recognizing the Vendéan, "Jean Oullier! My faith! I never expected to kill a man, but since it was to be, it is a grand thing it was he instead of another. That, I can truly say, deserves to be called a lucky shot."

"Meantime," said the stranger, "here comes the cart."

"Yes, it is at the top of the hill, for the horse is trotting. Come, there 's no time to lose; we had better be off. Is he really dead?"

"He seems so."

"Very good; forward then."

The stranger dropped Jean Oullier's arm, and the head fell back upon the ground with the heavy thud of a dead-weight.

"Yes, yes, he 's dead, sure enough!" said Courtin. Then, not daring to go nearer, he pointed his finger at the body. "There," said he, "that secures us our pay better than any signature; that dead body is worth two hundred thousand francs to us."

"How so?"

"He was the only man who could get that bloodhound I told you about away from me. I thought he was dead. I was mistaken. Now that I know it with my own eyes, we are safe. Forward! forward!"

"Yes, for here comes the cart."

The vehicle was now not a hundred steps from the body. The two men sprang into the bushes and disappeared in the darkness, while the widow Picaut, who was coming for Jean Oullier, alarmed by the shot, ran forward to the place where she had left him.

XXIV.

MAÎTRE COURTIN'S BATTERIES.

A FEW weeks had sufficed to bring about a radical upsetting of the lives of all those personages who, from the beginning of this narrative, have successively passed under the eyes of the reader.

Martial law was proclaimed in the four departments of La Vendée. The general who commanded them issued a proclamation inviting the country-people to give in their submission, promising to receive it with indulgence. The attempt at insurrection had so miserably failed that the greater part of the Vendéans abandoned all hope for the future. A few of them, who were openly compromised, followed the advice of their own leaders, given when they disbanded them, and gave up their arms. But the civil authorities would not accept this capitulation; they seized the offered arms and arrested their owners. A goodly number of these confiding persons were thrown into prison, and this impolitic severity paralyzed the pacific intentions of those who with greater prudence were awaiting events.

Maître Jacques owed to these proceedings a large increase in the number of his troop; he made so much, and made it so cleverly, out of the conduct of his adversaries, that he finally gathered about him a body of men large enough to still hold out in the forests while the rest of La Vendée disarmed itself.

Gaspard, Louis Renaud, Bras-d'Acier, and other leaders put the sea between them and a stern government. The Marquis de Souday alone could not resolve upon that step. Ever since he had parted from Petit-Pierre — that is, ever since Petit-Pierre had left him — the unfortunate gentleman had completely lost the jovial good-humor with which, as a matter of honor, he had, up to the last moment, opposed the gloomy views of his co-leaders; but as soon as duty no longer forced him to be gay, the marquis dropped to the lower extreme and became, as we may say, sad unto death. The defeat at Chêne not only wounded him in his political sympathies, but it knocked over to their foundations all the castles in Spain he had been so gleefully erecting. He now saw in this partisan existence, which his imagination had been endowing with romantic charm, things he had never dreamed of, — reverses which overwhelmed him, obscure poverty, the mean and trivial privations of an exile's life. He reached a point, — even he, who so recently had thought life in his little castle insufferably insipid, — he reached a point at which he regretted the good, pleasant evenings which the caresses and chatter of his girls made so pleasant, — above all, he missed his gossip with Jean Oullier; and he was so unhappy over the latter's continued absence that he made inquiries about his huntsman's fate with a solicitude not in any way customary with him.

The marquis was in this frame of mind when he one day encountered Maître Jacques loitering about the environs of Grand-Lieu and watching the movements of a column of soldiers. The Marquis de Souday had never had much liking for the master of "rabbits," whose first act of discipline had been to defy his authority. The independent spirit displayed by Maître Jacques had always seemed to the old gentleman a fatal example set to the Vendéans. Maître Jacques, on the other hand, hated the marquis, as he hated all whose birth or social position gave them naturally the position of leaders; and yet he was so touched by the misery to which he saw the old gentleman reduced in the cottage where, after Petit-Pierre's departure, the marquis had taken refuge, that he offered to hide him in the forest of Touvois; promising, besides the good cheer which always reigned in his little camp, and which he proposed to share with him, some amusement in occasional frays indulged in with the soldiers of King Louis-Philippe. Needless to say that the marquis always bluntly called that king "Philippe."

It was the last consideration we have mentioned which determined Monsieur de Souday to accept Maître Jacques' proposals. He burned to avenge the ruin of his hopes, and to make some one pay for his disappointments, for the annoyance his separation from his daughters caused him, and for the grief he felt at Jean Oullier's disappearance. He accordingly accompanied the lord of the burrows, who, from being his subordinate — or rather his insubordinate — now became his protector; and the latter, really touched by the simplicity and good-nature of the marquis, showed him much more considerate attention than his rough exterior and ways of life would seem to promise.

As for Bertha, the day after her retreat to Courtin's house, and as soon as she recovered some strength, she plainly perceived that to be under the same roof with the man she loved, far from the protection of her father, and without Jean Oullier, who could in a way replace him, was, to say the least of it, an impropriety; and, in spite of the fact that Michel was wounded, might be interpreted in a way to injure her reputation. She therefore left the farmhouse and installed herself with Rosine in the Tinguy cottage. This was about three quarters of a mile distant from Courtin's house, where she went daily to give Michel all the care of a sister, and the delicate attentions of a loving woman.

The tenderness, devotion, and self-abnegation of which Bertha gave Michel so many proofs touched the young man deeply; but as they did not in any degree affect his feelings for Mary, his situation became more and more difficult and embarrassing. He dared not think of the despair he might bring into the heart of the young girl to whom he owed his life. Nevertheless, little by little, a gentle resignation did succeed the bitter and violent repulsion he had felt at first, and without habituating himself to the idea of the sacrifice Mary demanded of him, he replied by smiles, which he tried to make affectionate, to the attentions which Bertha showered on him; and when she left his bedside the sigh that escaped him, and which she interpreted as meant for her, alone testified to his inward feelings.

If it had not been for Courtin, who always came to his room as soon as Bertha had disappeared through the trees of the garden, and sitting beside him talked of Mary, Michel's tender and impressionable soul might have ended in resigning itself to the necessities of the situation, and in accepting the fate they made for him. But Courtin talked to his young master so incessantly of Mary, he showed so earnest a wish to see him happy according to his heart's desire, that Michel, as the wound in his arm healed and his strength returned, felt his inward wound reopening, and his gratitude to Bertha disappearing before the image of her sister.

Courtin was doing a work analogous to that of Penelope; he undid at night that which Bertha, with so much care, had done by day. When he brought the young baron to his house the latter's feebleness precluded all necessity of asking pardon for his former conduct; and now, having, as we have heard him tell, got possession of Michel's secret, he managed, by protestations of devotion to his interests and by cleverly encouraging the young man's love for Bertha's sister, to worm himself back entirely into his master's confidence. Michel had suffered as much from not being able to tell his woes as from the woes themselves. Courtin seemed to be so sympathizing, he flattered his dreams so pleasantly, he seemed to admire Mary so truly, that, little by little, he led Michel to betray, if not to confess, what had passed between him and the sisters.

Courtin was very careful, however, not to assume a position hostile to Bertha. He managed, cleverly enough, to make her think he was devoted to the idea of her marriage with his young master. When they met away from Michel he always spoke to her as though to his future mistress; and he did this so well that Bertha, knowing nothing of his antecedents, was constantly talking to Michel of the great devotion of his farmer, whom she called "our good Courtin."

But no sooner was he alone with Michel than he entered, as we have said, into all the latter's secret feelings. He pitied him; and Michel, under the influence of that pity, allowed himself to tell his farmer the incidents of his relation to Mary. Courtin constantly repeated to him, "She loves you;" insinuating that he, Michel, ought to force Mary with a gentle violence, for which she would certainly be grateful, to follow the dictates of her own heart. He even went beyond Michel's own hopes and assured him that as soon as he was well and communications were once more open, he could so arrange matters that, without ingratitude to Bertha, she could be brought to renounce, of herself, the projected marriage.

Michel's convalescence did not progress as rapidly as Courtin desired. He saw, with deep anxiety, the days go by without affording any clue as to Petit-Pierre's actual hiding-place; and he restlessly awaited the moment when he could let loose his young master on Mary's traces, — for, of course, the reader has understood that Michel was the "bloodhound" he had talked of using.

Bertha, relieved of all anxiety about Michel's wound, had made, with Rosine, several trips into the forest of Touvois to see her father in his present refuge. Two or three times after such excursions Courtin had led the conversation to persons concerned in the insurrection in whom the sisters would probably take an interest; but Bertha remained impenetrable; and the farmer was too well aware that the topic was dangerous, and that the slightest imprudence on his part would speedily awaken suspicion, to press such inquiries. Still, as Michel grew better and stronger, he urged him, whenever they were alone together, to come to a determination; offering to take a letter at any time to Mary and bring back her answer, doing his best to make it favorable.

This state of things lasted six weeks. At the end of that time Michel was almost well; his wound had healed and his strength returned. The neighborhood of the post which the general had established at La Logerie prevented the young man from showing himself during the daytime; but as soon as it was dark he walked about the orchard leaning on Bertha's arm. These evening promenades annoyed Courtin, who, so long as Bertha and Michel talked together in the house, could overhear what they said by eavesdropping; and one day he told them positively that their nocturnal rambles must cease. On being asked why, he produced a judgment by default which condemned Michel de la Logerie to death.

This communication produced but little effect on Michel, but Bertha was terror-stricken. She almost flung herself at the young man's feet, and begged his pardon for having enticed him into this fatal position; and that night when she left the farmhouse she was in a state of pitiable agitation.

The next day she came early. All night she had dreamed dreadful dreams, and they followed her waking. She saw Michel discovered, arrested, shot! Two hours earlier than usual she was at the farmhouse. Nothing had happened; nothing seemed to make that day more alarming than other days. It passed as usual, — full of charm mingled with anguish for Bertha; full of melancholy internal aspirations for Michel.

Evening came, — a beautiful summer's evening. Bertha was leaning against a little window looking out into the orchard; she was watching the sunset beyond the great trees of the forest of Machecoul, the tops of which were undulating like waves of verdure. Michel was sitting on his bed breathing in the soft odors of the coming night.

Suddenly they heard the wheels of a carriage coming up the avenue.

The young man darted to the window. Both saw a calèche entering the court-yard. Courtin ran to the carriage, hat in hand; a head looked out, — it was that of the Baronne de la Logerie.

Michel, on seeing his mother, felt a cold chill run through his veins; it was evident that she had come for him. Bertha questioned him with her eyes to ask what she ought to do. Michel pointed to a dark corner, — a sort of closet or recess without a door, — where she might hide, and hear all without being seen herself. He thought he should gather strength from her secret presence. Five minutes later the stairs creaked under his mother's step.

Bertha had rushed to her hiding-place and Michel had seated himself near the window, as if he had neither seen nor heard anything. The door opened and the baroness appeared.

Perhaps she had come with the intention of being harsh and stern as usual; but on seeing Michel by the paling light, pale himself as the twilight, she abandoned all severity, and opening her arms, cried out: —

"Oh, my unhappy child! have I found you?"

Michel, who did not expect this reception, was greatly moved; and he flung himself into his mother's open arms crying: —

"Oh, mother, — mother! My good mother!"

She, too, was greatly changed; traces were plainly to be seen upon her face of incessant tears and sleepless nights.

XXV.

MADAME LA BARONNE DE LA LOGERIE, THINKING TO SERVE HER SON'S INTERESTS, SERVES THOSE OF PETIT-PIERRE.

THE baroness sat down, or rather, fell into a chair, drawing Michel to his knees before her, and taking his head, which she pressed to her lips. At last the words which she seemed unable to bring out came to her.

"Is it possible that you are here in this place, not a hundred steps away from the château, which is full of soldiers?"

"The nearer I am to them, mother," replied Michel, "the less they'll look for me here."

"But don't you know what has taken place in Nantes?"

"What has taken place there?"

"The military courts have passed sentence after sentence."

"That only signifies to those they catch," said Michel, laughing.

"It signifies to every one," said his mother; "for those who are not taken may be taken at any moment."

"Not when they are hiding in the house of a mayor well-known for his Philippist opinions."

"You are none the less —"

The baroness stopped, as if her mouth refused to utter the words.

"Go on, mother!"

"You are none the less condemned —"

"Condemned to death; I know that."

"What! you know it, unhappy boy, and you stay here quietly?"

"I tell you, mother, that as long as I am with Courtin I 'm quite safe."

"Then he has been kind to you, has he, that man?"

"He has been simply a second providence. He found me wounded and dying of hunger; he brought me home, and since then he has fed and hidden me."

"I must own I have distrusted him."

"Then you are wrong, mother."

"Maybe so. But talk of our own affairs, my dear child. No matter how well hidden you may be, you cannot stay here."

"Why not?"

"Because a mere chance, the slightest imprudence would betray you." Michel shook his head. "You don't want me to die of terror, do you?" said his mother.

"No no; I will listen to you."

"Well, I shall die of terror if you stay in France."

"But, mother, have you reflected on the difficulties of flight?"

"Yes; and I have surmounted them."

"How so?"

"I have chartered a small Dutch vessel which is now lying in the river opposite to Couéron. Get on board of her and go. God grant that you are strong enough for the journey." Michel did not answer. "You will go to England," continued his mother. "You will leave this cursèd land which drank your father's blood; say you will, my son! So long as you stay here I cannot have an easy moment; I fancy at all hours I see the hand of the executioner stretched out to tear you from my arms." Still Michel kept silence. "Here," continued the baroness, "is a letter to the captain; and here too is an order for fifty thousand francs to your credit in England or America. Wherever you are, write to me, so that I may follow and join you. But what is the matter? Why don't you answer me?"

The fact is, Michel received this proposal with an insensibility which almost amounted to stupor. Go away? why, that was to part from Mary! At the mere idea of that separation his heart was so wrung that he fancied he would rather face the death to which he was condemned. Since Courtin had assisted in reviving his passion, he had in his heart conceived new hopes, and without saying a word of them to his farmer, he thought day and night on the means of getting to her. He could not endure the idea of once more renouncing her; and instead of replying to his mother as she developed her plan, he was simply strengthening his determination to be Mary's husband. Hence the silence which, naturally, made the baroness uneasy.

"Mother," said Michel at last, "I do not answer you because I cannot answer as I wish."

"How do you mean, as you wish?"

"Listen to me, mother," said the young man, with a firmness of which at any other time she would have thought him, and perhaps he might have thought himself, incapable.

"You don't refuse to go, I hope?"

"I don't refuse to go," said Michel, "but I put conditions to my going."

"Conditions where it concerns your life, your safety? Conditions before you consent to relieve your mother's agony?"

"Mother," said Michel, "since we last saw each other I have suffered much, and consequently I have learned much. I have learned, above all, that there are moments which decide the whole future happiness or misery of our lives. I am now in one of those moments, mother."

"And you mean to decide for my misery?"

"No; I shall speak to you as a man, that is all. Do not be surprised at that; I was thrown, a child, into the midst of these events, and I have come out of them a man. I know the duties I owe my mother; those duties are respect, tenderness, gratitude, — and those duties I will never evade. But in passing from youth to manhood, mother, horizons open and broaden the farther we go; there we find duties, succeeding those of youth, not exclusively to our family, but also to society. When a man reaches that stage in his life, though he still loves his mother, he must inevitably love another woman, who will be to him the mother of his children."

"Ah!" exclaimed the baroness, starting back from her son with an impulse that was stronger than her will.

"Yes, mother," said the young man, rising, "I have given that love; another love has replied to mine; our lives are indissolubly united; if I go, I will not go alone."

"You will go with your mistress?"

"I will go with my wife, mother."

"Do you suppose that I shall give my consent to that marriage?"

"You are free not to give your consent, mother, but I am free not to leave this place."

"Oh, wretched boy!" cried the baroness; "is this my reward for twenty years of care, and tenderness, and love?"

"That reward, mother," said Michel, his firmness increased by the knowledge that another ear was listening to his words, "you have in the respect I bear you, and the devotion of which I will give you proofs on every occasion. But true maternal love is not a usurer; it does not say, 'I will be twenty years thy mother in order to be thy tyrant;' it does not say, 'I will give thee life, youth, strength, intelligence, in order that all those powers shall be obedient to my will.' No, mother, true maternal love says: 'While thou wert feeble I supported thee; while thou wert ignorant I taught thee; while thou wert blind I led thee. To-day thou art strong and capable; make thy future life, not according to my will, but thine own; choose one among the many paths before thee, and wherever it may lead, love, bless, reverence the mother who made and trained thee to be strong;' that is the power of a mother over her son, as I see it; that is the respect and the duty which he owes to her."

The baroness was speechless; she would sooner have expected the skies to fall than to hear such firm and argumentative language from her son. She looked at him in stupefaction.

Proudly satisfied with himself, Michel looked at her calmly, with a smile upon his lips.

"So," she said, "nothing will induce you to give up this folly?"

"Say rather that nothing will induce me to break my word."

"Oh!" cried the baroness, pressing her hands upon her eyes, "unhappy mother that I am!"

Michel knelt beside her.

"I say to you: blessed mother you will be on the day you make the happiness of your son!"

"What is there so seductive about those *wolves?*" cried the baroness.

"By whatever name you call the woman I love," said Michel, "I shall reply to you: she has every quality that a man should seek in a wife; and it is not for you and me, mother, who have suffered so much from calumny, to seize, as readily as you have done, on the calumnies told of others."

"No, no, no!" cried the baroness, "never will I consent to such a marriage!"

"In that case, mother," said Michel, "take back those cheques and the letter to the captain of the vessel; they are useless to me, for I will not leave this place."

"What else can you do, you miserable boy?"

"Oh, that's simple enough. I'd rather die than live separated from her I love. I am cured. I am able to shoulder a musket. The remains of the insurrectionary army are collected in the forest of Touvois under command of the Marquis de Souday. I will join them, and fight with them, and get myself killed at the first chance. This is the second time death has missed me," he added with a pallid smile. "The third time his aim may be true and his hand steady."

The young man laid the letters and cheques on his mother's knees. In his tones and gestures there was such resolution and firmness that his mother saw that she cherished in vain the hope of changing him. In presence of that conviction her strength gave way.

"Well," she said, "be it according to your will, and may God forget that you have forced your mother to yield to you."

"God will forget it, mother; and when you see the happiness of your son you will forget it yourself."

The baroness shook her head.

"Go," she said, "marry, far away from me, a stranger I do not know and have never seen."

"I shall marry, I hope, a woman whom you will know and appreciate, mother; and that great day of my happiness will be blessed by your sanction. You have offered to join me wherever I go; wherever that may be I shall expect you, mother."

The baroness rose and made a few steps toward the door.

"Going without a word of farewell, without a kiss, mother? Are you not afraid it may bring me evil?"

"My unhappy boy, come to my arms, to my heart!"

And she said the words with that maternal cry which, sooner or later, must come from a mother's heart. Michel pressed her tenderly to his breast.

"When will you go, my child?" she said.

"That must depend on her, mother."

"As soon as possible, will you not?"

"To-night, I hope."

"You will find a peasant's dress below in the carriage. Disguise yourself as best you can. It is twenty-four miles from here to Couëron. You could get there by five in the morning. Don't forget the vessel's name, — the 'Jeune Charles.'"

"Don't be anxious, mother. The moment I know my end is happiness I shall take every precaution to reach it."

"As for me, I shall go back to Paris and use all my influence to get that fatal sentence revoked. But you — I entreat you, and I repeat it — take care of your life, and remember that my life is wrapped up in yours."

Mother and son again kissed each other, and Michel took his mother to the door. Courtin, as a faithful servitor, was keeping watch below. Madame de la Logerie begged him to accompany her to the château.

When Michel, after locking the door, turned round he saw Bertha, with a smile of happiness on her lips, and a halo of love about her head. She was waiting the moment to throw herself into his arms. Michel received her in them; and if the little room had not been dark she must have seen the embarrassment on the young baron's face.

"And now," she said, "nothing can part us; we have my father's consent, and now your mother's."

Michel was silent.

"Shall we start to-night?"

Still Michel said nothing.

"Well," she said, "why don't you answer me?"

"Because nothing is less sure than our departure," he replied.

"But you promised your mother to go to-night."

"I told my mother it depended on *her*."

"That is, on *me*," said Bertha.

"What!" exclaimed Michel, "would Bertha, true royalist and so devoted to the cause, leave France without thinking of those she leaves behind her?"

"What can you mean?" asked Bertha.

"I mean something grander and more useful to the country than my own escape, my personal safety," said the young man.

Bertha looked at him in astonishment.

"I mean the escape and safety of Madame," added Michel.

Bertha gave a cry; she began to understand.

"Ah!" she ejaculated.

"That vessel my mother has chartered for me can take from France not only you and me, but the princess, your father, and," he added in a lower voice, "your sister."

"Oh, Michel, Michel!" cried the young girl, "forgive me for not thinking of that! Just now I loved you; now I admire you! Yes, yes, you are right; Providence itself inspired your mother; yes, I will forget all the hard and cruel things she said of me, for I see in her an instrument of God sent to our succor to save us all. Oh, my friend, how good you are! — more than that, you are grand for having thought of it."

The young man stammered unintelligible words.

"Ah!" continued Bertha, in her enthusiasm, "I knew you were the bravest and most loyal of men; but to-day you have gone beyond my hopes and expectations. Poor child! wounded, condemned to death, he thinks of others before he thinks of himself! Ah, friend, I was happy, now I am proud in my love!"

If the room had been lighted Bertha must have seen the flush on Michel's cheek; he knew what his disinterestedness really was. It is true that after obtaining his mother's consent to marry the woman he loved, Michel had really dreamed of something else, — namely, the idea of rendering to Petit-Pierre the greatest service the most devoted follower could do for her at that moment, and afterward avow all and ask her, as a reward for that service, to procure for him Mary's hand. We can readily imagine his shame and confusion of face in Bertha's presence, and why, to all these demonstrations of the young girl the baron, cold in spite of himself, replied merely: —

"Now that all is arranged for us, Bertha, we have no time to lose."

"No," she said, "you are right. Give your orders. Now that I recognize the superiority not only of your heart but of your mind, I am ready to obey."

"Well," said Michel, "we must part here."

"Why so?" asked Bertha.

"Because you must go to the forest of Touvois and notify your father of what has happened, and bring him away with you. From there you must get to the bay of Bourgneuf, where the 'Jeune Charles' shall stop and pick you up. I shall go to Nantes and tell the duchess."

"You, in Nantes! Do you forget that you are condemned to death and that the authorities are watching for you? It is I who must go to Nantes and you to Touvois."

"But the 'Jeune Charles' expects me, Bertha, and in all probability the captain would obey no one but me; seeing a woman in place of a man he might suspect some trap and throw us into inextricable difficulties."

"But just reflect on the dangers you run in Nantes."

"On the contrary, it may be, if you think of it, Bertha, the very place where I should run the least. They will never suppose that, being condemned to death in Nantes, I should enter the town which condemned me. You know very well that there are times when the greatest boldness is the greatest safety. This is one of those times; and you must let me do as I choose."

"I told you I would obey you, Michel; I obey."

And the proud and beautiful young girl, submissive as a child, awaited the orders of the man who, thanks to an appearance of devotion, had just acquired almost gigantic proportions in her eyes.

Nothing was simpler than the decision they had made and its mode of execution. Bertha gave Michel the address of the duchess in Nantes and the different passwords by which he could gain admittance to her. She herself, dressed in Rosine's clothes, was to reach the forest of Touvois. Michel, of course, was to wear the peasant's costume brought to him by his mother. If nothing occurred to interfere with these arrangements the "Jeune Charles" would be able to sail at five o'clock on the following morning, carrying Petit-Pierre away from France, and with her the last vestiges of civil war.

Ten minutes later Michel was astride of Courtin's pony, saddled and bridled by himself, and taking leave, by a wave of his hand, of Bertha, who returned to the Tinguy cottage, from which she intended to start immediately by a cross-road toward the Touvois forest.

XXVI.

MARCHES AND COUNTER-MARCHES.

In spite of the adornment of wind-galls and spavin, with which age and toil had favored Maître Courtin's pony, that brave beast showed energy enough in the amble which served him for a trot to bring Michel into Nantes before nine o'clock at night. His first stopping-place was to be the tavern of the Point du Jour.

He had hardly crossed the pont Rousseau before he began to look about him for the said tavern. Recognizing its sign, — a star lengthened by a ray of the most beautiful yellow ochre painter ever used, — he stopped his pony, or rather the pony of Maître Courtin, before a wooden trough where the horses of the wagoners, who wanted to halt without unharnessing, were watered.

No one appeared at the door of the inn. Forgetting the humble clothes which he wore, and remembering only the alacrity with which the servants at La Logerie welcomed his arrival, Michel rapped impatiently on the trough with the heavy stick he held in his hand. At the sound a man in his shirt-sleeves came out of the court-yard and advanced to Michel; he wore on his head a blue cotton cap pulled down to his eyes. Michel fancied that what he saw of the face was not unknown to him.

"The devil!" cried the man in a grumbling tone; "are you too much of a lord, my young *gars*, to take your horse to the stable yourself? However, no matter; you shall be served as well as any."

"Serve me as you please, but answer a question."

"Ask it," said the man, folding his arms.

"I want to see Père Eustache," added Michel, sinking his voice.

Low as the tone was, the man showed signs of annoyance; he looked furtively about him, and though there was no one to be seen but a few children who were gazing with their hands behind their backs in naïve curiosity at the new-comer, he took the horse hastily by the bridle and led him into the court-yard.

"I told you I wanted to see Père Eustache," said Michel, getting off the pony as soon as the man in the blue cap had led him to the shed which served as stable to the hôtel Point du Jour.

"I know that," said the latter. "I heard it, confound you; but I don't keep your Père Eustache in my oat-bin. Besides, before I tell you where to find him I'd like to know where you come from."

"The South."

"Where are you going?"

"To Rosny."

"Very good; then you must go to the church of Saint-Sauveur, and there you will find the man you want. Go; and try not to speak so loud, Monsieur de la Logerie, when you talk in the street — if you want to gain the object of your journey."

"Ah, ha!" cried Michel, somewhat astonished; "so you know me?"

"I should think so!" said the man.

"I must have that horse taken back to its home."

"It shall be done."

Michel put a louis into the man's hand, who seemed delighted with the fee and made him many offers of service; then he boldly went out into the town. When he reached the church of Saint-Sauveur the sexton was in the act of shutting the gates. The lesson the young baron had just received at the gate of the inn bore fruits; Michel waited cautiously and looked about him before putting any questions.

Cathedral of Nantes.

Four or five beggars, before leaving the church porch, where they had asked alms all day of the faithful, were kneeling beneath the organ to say their evening prayer. No doubt Père Eustache was among them; for besides two or three women with their cotton capes, patched with various colors, thrown over their heads, there were three male beggars, each with a holy-water sprinkler in his hand. Either of the three might be the man Michel was in search of; luckily he knew the sign of recognition. He took the branch of holly that was fastened in his hat, which Bertha had told him was the sign by which Père Eustache would know him, and let it drop before the door. Two of the beggars passed without taking the least notice of it; the third, who was a little old man, thin and weakly, whose enormous nose projected boldly beyond a black silk cap, stopped when he saw the holly on the pavement, picked it up, and looked about him uneasily. Michel issued from behind the pillar which concealed him.

Père Eustache (for it was he) cast a sidelong look at the young man; then, without a word, he walked toward the cloister. Michel understood that the holly was not a sufficient sign to the distrustful giver of holy water; after following for about ten yards, he hastened his steps and accosted him, saying: —

"I am from the South."

The beggar stopped.

"Where are you going?" he asked.

"To Rosny," replied Michel.

The beggar turned round and retraced his steps; this time he went toward the town. A look from a corner of his eye told Michel it was all right. The latter then let his guide pass him and followed him at a distance of five or six paces. They returned past the portal of the church, and soon after, having entered a dark and narrow alley, the beggar stopped for a few seconds before a low door placed in the wall of a garden; then he continued his way.

Michel was about to follow him; but the beggar made

him a sign as if to point out the little door, and rapidly disappeared. The young man then saw that Père Eustache had slipped the holly branch he had picked up through the iron ring that served as a knocker.

So this was the end of his journey. He raised the knocker and let it fall. At the sound a small wicket made in the door itself opened and a man's voice was heard asking what was wanted. Michel repeated the passwords, and he was shown into a room on the ground-floor, where a gentleman, whom he recognized as having seen at the château de Souday on the evening when General Dermoncourt ate the supper prepared for Petit-Pierre, and seen again, gun in hand, before the fight at Chêne, was quietly reading a newspaper, sitting before a large fire with his feet on the fender, wrapped in his dressing-gown.

In spite of his very pacific appearance and occupation, a pair of pistols lay within reach of his hand on a table where there were also, laid out for use, pens, ink, and paper. The gentleman recognized Michel at once and rose to receive him.

"I think I have seen you in our ranks, monsieur," he said.

"Yes, monsieur," replied Michel, "the evening before the fight at Chêne."

"And the day of the fight?" asked he of the dressing-gown, smiling.

"I was fighting at La Pénissière, where I was wounded."

The gentleman bowed.

"Will you have the goodness to tell me your name?" he said.

Michel told his name; the gentleman in the dressing-gown consulted a pocket-book, gave signs of satisfaction, and turning to the young man asked: —

"Will you now tell me what has brought you?"

"The wish to see Petit-Pierre, and do her a great service."

"Pardon me, monsieur; but no one can see the person of

whom you speak, at least not so easily. You are indeed one of us; I know that you may be relied on so far; but you will readily understand that all going and coming about a retreat which has hitherto been able to keep its secret successfully, would soon attract the attention of the police. Have the kindness, therefore, to tell me your plans, and I will see that you receive an answer."

Michel then related what had passed between himself and his mother; how she had chartered a vessel for his escape, and how the idea had occurred to him that it might be used to put Petit-Pierre in safety. The man in the dressing-gown listened with ever-increasing interest, and as soon as the young baron had given full information he exclaimed: —

"It really seems as though Providence had sent you. It is impossible — no matter what precautions we take to conceal the place where Petit-Pierre is hidden — it is really impossible to escape the police investigations much longer. For the good of the cause, for Petit-Pierre's own sake and for ours, it is much better that she should leave the country; and as the difficulty of chartering a vessel is thus removed, I will at once see Petit-Pierre, explain the circumstances, and receive her orders."

"Shall I go with you ?" asked Michel.

"No; your peasant's dress beside me would immediately attract the attention of the police spies, by whom we are surrounded. What inn are you stopping at ?"

"The Point du Jour."

"That is where Joseph Picaut is hostler; there is nothing to fear there."

"Ah !" exclaimed Michel, "I knew his face was not unknown to me; but I thought he lived in the open country between the river Boulogne and the forest of Machecoul !"

"You were right; he is only a tavern hostler as occasion demands. Wait there for me. I will go to you in two hours from now, — either alone, or accompanied by Petit-

Pierre, — alone, if Petit-Pierre rejects your proposal; with her, if she accepts."

"Are you perfectly sure of that man Picaut?" asked Michel.

"Yes, as we are of ourselves. If there is any fault to find with him it is that he is too zealous. Remember that since Petit-Pierre has been in La Vendée more than six hundred peasants have known at different times of her various hiding-places; and the noblest claim of those poor people to honor, is that not one, poor as he was, thought of betraying her. Let Joseph know that you expect friends, and that he must be on the watch for them. If you merely say to him the words, 'Rue du Château, No. 3,' you will obtain from him, and all connected with the inn, the most absolute and also the most passive obedience."

"Have you any other advice to give me?"

"Perhaps it may be prudent for the persons who will accompany Petit-Pierre to leave the house where she is hidden singly, and go singly to the tavern of the Point du Jour. Ask them to give you a room with a window looking on the quay; have no light in your room, but keep the window open."

"You have forgotten nothing?"

"Nothing. Adieu, monsieur, or rather, au revoir! If we succeed in reaching your vessel safely you will have done an immense service to the cause. As for me, I am in continual fear. They say enormous sums have been offered for the betrayal of the princess, and I tremble lest some one may yet be tempted to sacrifice her."

Michel was ushered out; but instead of taking him by the door through which he had entered, they took him through an entrance which opened on another street. Thence he rapidly crossed the town and returned to the quay. When he reached the tavern of the Point du Jour he found that Joseph Picaut had engaged a boy to take Courtin's pony back to the farmhouse as Michel had requested.

On entering the stable Michel made Joseph a sign, which the latter understood perfectly; he sent the boy away, postponing the return of the horse till the next day.

"You said you knew me," remarked Michel as soon as they were alone.

"I did more, Monsieur de la Logerie; I called you by your name."

"Well, I 'm not sorry to know that we have equal advantages in that respect. I know your name; it is Joseph Picaut."

"I don't say it is n't," said the peasant, with a sly look.

"Are you to be trusted, Joseph?"

"That depends on who trusts me,—blues and reds, no; whites, yes."

"Then you are white?"

Picaut shrugged his shoulders.

"If I were not, should I be here,—I who am condemned to death as you are? That 's so; they have done me the honor of a sentence by default. Yes, you and I are equal before the law now."

"And you are here—"

"As hostler, neither more nor less."

"Then take me to the master of the inn."

Picaut woke up the inn-keeper, who was in bed. The latter received Michel with some distrust; and the young man, feeling there was no time to lose, decided on striking the great blow, and said deliberately the five words:—

"Rue du Château, No. 3."

The words were scarcely heard by the inn-keeper before his distrust disappeared and his whole manner changed. From that moment he and his house were at Michel's disposal. It was now Michel's turn to make inquiries.

"Have you other travellers in the house?"

"Only one."

"Of what kind?"

"The very worst,—a man to fear."

"You know him, then?"

"It is the mayor of La Logerie, Courtin, a vile cur."

"Courtin!" exclaimed Michel. "Courtin here! Are you sure?"

"I don't know him; but Picaut says it is he."

"When did he get here?"

"About fifteen minutes ago."

"Where is he?"

"He has just gone out. He got something to eat and went off immediately, telling me he should not be in till late, — not before two in the morning. He said he had business in Nantes."

"Does he know you knew him?"

"I think not; unless he recognized Joseph Picaut just as Picaut recognized him. But I doubt if he did, for he stood in the light and Joseph kept in the shade."

Michel reflected a moment.

"I don't think Courtin is as bad as you suppose him to be," he said; "but never mind, it is as well to distrust him, and on no account must he know of my presence in your inn."

Picaut, who had hitherto been standing on the threshold of the door, here came forward and joined in the conversation.

"Oh!" he said, "if he is likely to trouble you, say so; we can settle him so that he shall know nothing, or if he does know anything he shall be made to hold his tongue. I have old scores against him which I've long wanted a pretext to —"

"No, no!" cried Michel, hastily, "Courtin is my farmer. I am under obligations to him which make me anxious that no harm shall happen to him; besides," he hastened to add, seeing the frown on Picaut's brow, "he is not what you think he is."

Joseph Picaut shook his head; but Michel did not notice the gesture.

"Don't trouble yourself," said the inn-keeper. "If he comes in I'll look after him."

"Very good. As for you, Joseph, take the horse on which I came. I want you to do an errand. By the bye, Courtin must not see that horse in the stable; he would certainly recognize it, inasmuch as it is his own beast."

"What next?"

"You know the river, don't you?"

"There 's not a corner of the left bank I 've not shot over. I know less of the right."

"That 's all right; it is the left bank you 'll have to follow."

"Follow where?"

"To Couéron. Opposite to the second island, between the two old wrecks, you will see a vessel called the 'Jeune Charles.' Though at anchor its foretopsail will be set; you 'll know it by that."

"Trust me to know it."

"Take a boat and row out to her. They 'll call to you, 'Who 's there?' Answer, 'Belle-Isle en Mer.' Then they 'll let you go aboard. You 'll give the captain this handkerchief, just as it is, — that is to say, knotted at three corners, — and you will tell him to be all ready to weigh anchor at one o'clock to-night."

"Is that all?"

"Yes — or rather, no, it is not all. If I am satisfied with you, Picaut, you shall have five pieces of gold such as the one I gave you to-night."

"Well, well," said Joseph Picaut, "leaving out the chance of being hung, it is not such a bad business; and if I can only get a shot now and then at the Blues, or revenge myself on Courtin, I sha'n't regret Maître Jacques and his burrows. What next?"

"How do you mean?"

"Why, after I have done the errand?"

"Then you will hide somewhere on the bank of the river, and wait for us; whistle to let us know where you are. If all goes well imitate a cuckoo; if on the contrary you see anything that ought to make us uneasy, give the owl's cry."

"Ha! Monsieur de la Logerie," said Joseph, "I see you've been well trained. All you've ordered is clear, and seems to me well arranged. It is a pity, though, you have n't a better horse to put between my legs; otherwise the matter could be quickly done."

Joseph Picaut departed on his mission. The inn-keeper then took Michel to a poor-looking room on the first floor, which served as an annex to the dining-room, and had two windows opening on the main-road; then he put himself on the watch for Courtin.

Michel opened one of the windows as agreed upon with the gentleman in the dressing-gown; after which he sat down on a stool, placing himself so that his head could not be seen from the road he was watching.

XXVII.

MICHEL'S LOVE AFFAIRS SEEM TO BE TAKING A HAPPIER TURN.

MICHEL, under his apparent composure, was really in a state of extreme anxiety. He was about to meet Mary; and, at the mere idea his breast tightened, his heart swelled, his blood coursed in leaps along his veins; he felt himself trembling with emotion. He formed no hopes as to what the result might be, but the firmness which, contrary to all his habits, he had shown in presence of his mother and also of Bertha had answered so well that he now resolved to be equally firm with Mary. He saw very plainly that he had come to a crisis in this singular situation, and that eternal happiness or irreparable misery would result from his present conduct.

He had been on the watch about an hour and a half, following anxiously with his eyes all the human forms which seemed to be approaching the little inn, looking to see if they came toward the door, feeling wretched when they passed it and his hopes vanished, thinking minutes eternities, and wondering whether his heart would not burst in his bosom when he was actually in Mary's presence.

All of a sudden he saw a shadow coming from the direction of the rue du Château, walking rapidly, skirting the house, and making no sound with its motions. By the clothing he recognized a woman; but it could not, of course, be Petit-Pierre, or Mary, for it was not to be supposed that either would venture there alone.

And yet, it seemed to the baron as if the woman were looking up at the house trying to recognize it; next he saw her stop before the inn, and then he heard the three little raps, the signal, struck on the door. With one bound he sprang from his post of observation to the staircase, rushed hastily down, opened the door, and in the woman, closely wrapped in a mantle, he recognized Mary.

Their two names were all the young pair dared to say when they found themselves face to face; then Michel seized the young girl by the arm, guided her through the darkness, and took her to the chamber on the first floor. But scarcely had they entered it, when, falling on his knees, he burst forth: —

"Oh, Mary, Mary ! is it really you ? Am I not dreaming ? I have dreamt so often of this blessèd moment, so often have I tasted this infinite joy in imagination only, that I fancy I am still the plaything of a dream. Mary, my angel, my life, my love, oh ! let me hold you to my heart ! "

"Michel, my friend," said the young girl, sighing to feel she could not conquer the emotion that now seized upon her, "I, too, am happy that we meet again. But tell me, poor, dear friend, you have been wounded, have you not ? "

"Yes, yes; but it was not my wound that made me suffer; it was the misery of being parted from all I love in this world. Oh, Mary ! believe me, death was deaf and obstinate, or it would have come at my call."

"Michel, how can you say such things ? How can you forget all that my poor Bertha has done for you ? We have heard all; and I have only loved and admired my dear sister the more for the devotion she has proved to you at every instant."

But at Bertha's name Michel, who was resolved not to let Mary impose her will upon his any longer, rose abruptly and walked about the room with a step which betrayed his emotion. Mary saw what was passing in his soul and she made one last effort.

"Michel," she said, "I ask you, I conjure you, in the

name of all the tears I have shed to your memory, speak to me only as though to a sister; remember that you are soon to become my brother."

"Your brother! I, Mary?" said the young man, shaking his head. "As for that, my decision is made, and firmly made. Never, never, will I be your brother, I swear it!"

"Michel, do you forget that you once swore otherwise?"

"I did not swear it; no! you wrung the promise from me, you wrung it cruelly; you took advantage of the love I bear you to compel me to renounce it. But all that is within me rises against that promise; there 's not a fibre in my body that does not refuse to keep it. And I here say to you, Mary, that for two months, ever since we have been parted, I have thought of you only! Buried in the blazing ruins at La Pénissière and near to death, I thought of you only! Wounded with a ball through my shoulder, which just missed my heart, I thought of you only! Dying of hunger, weariness, and weakness, I thought of you only — of you alone! Bertha is my sister, Mary; you are my beloved, my precious treasure; and you, Mary, you *shall* be my wife!"

"Oh, my God! how can you say it, Michel; are you mad?"

"I was for a moment, Mary — when I thought I could obey you. But absence, grief, despair, have made another man of me. Count no longer on the poor, weak reed which bent at your breath; whatever you may say or do, you shall be mine, Mary! — because I love you, because you love me, because I will no longer lie to God or to my own heart."

"You forget, Michel," said Mary, "that my resolutions do not change as yours do. I swore to a course of conduct, and I shall keep my oath."

"So be it; then I will leave Bertha forever; Bertha shall never see me again!"

"My friend —"

"Seriously, Mary, for whose sake do you suppose I am here now?"

"You are here to save the princess, to whom we are all devoted, body and soul."

"I am here, Mary, to meet you. Don't think more of my devotion to the princess than it deserves. I am devoted to you, Mary, and to no other. What inspired in my mind the thought of saving Petit-Pierre? My love for you! Should I have thought of it, think you, if it had not been that in saving her I should see you? Don't make me either a hero or a demigod; I am a man, and a man who loves you ardently and is ready to risk his head for you! Why should I care, otherwise, for these quarrels of dynasty against dynasty? What have I to do with the Bourbons of the elder branch or the Bourbons of the younger branch, — I, whose past has nothing to do with either of them; I, who have not a single memory connecting me with theirs? My opinions are — you; my beliefs are — you. If you were for Louis Philippe, I should be for Louis Philippe. You are for Henri V. and I am for Henri V. Ask for my blood and I shall say, 'There it is, take it!' but don't ask me to lend myself any longer to an impossible state of things."

"What do you mean to do, then?"

"Tell Bertha the truth."

"The truth! impossible! you will never dare to?"

"Mary, I declare to you —"

"No, no!"

"Yes, I declare to you that I shall do it. Every day I am shaking off the swaddling-clothes of my weak youth. There's a vast distance already between me and that child you met in the sunken road, scratched and weeping with fear at the very name and thought of his mother. It is to my love that I owe this new strength. I have borne, without blenching, a look which formerly made me bow my head and bend my knees. I have told all to my mother, and my mother has replied to me, 'I see you are a man; do as you will!' My will is to consecrate my life to you; but I also will that you shall be mine. See, therefore, in what a senseless struggle you have plunged us. I, the husband of Bertha! let us suppose it for a moment; why, there could be no greater misery on earth than that poor creature would endure, not to speak of mine. They told me tales in my infancy of Carrier's 'republican marriages,' when living bodies were tied to dead ones and flung into the Loire. That, Mary, would be our marriage, Bertha's and mine; and you, you would stand by and see our agony! Mary, would you be glad of your work then? No, I am resolved; either I will never see Bertha again, or the first time that I do see her I will tell her how my stupid timidity misled Petit-Pierre, and how courage has always failed me until now to speak the truth; and then—then—no, I will not tell her that I do not love her, but I will tell her that I love you."

"Good God!" cried Mary, "but don't you know, Michel, that if you do that she will die of it?"

"No, Bertha will not die of it," said the voice of Petit-Pierre, who had entered the room behind them without their hearing her. The two young people turned round hurriedly with a cry. "Bertha," continued Petit-Pierre, "is a noble and courageous girl, who will understand the language you propose to address her, Monsieur de la Logerie, and who will also know how to sacrifice her happiness to that of the sister she loves. But you shall not have the pain of telling her. It is I who did the wrong,—or rather, who made the mistake,—and it is I who will repair it; begging Monsieur Michel," she added, smiling, "to be in future a little more explicit in his confidences."

At the first sound of Petit-Pierre's voice, which had startled them into a cry, the lovers hastily stepped apart from each other; but the princess caught them by the arm, drew them once more together, and joined their hands.

"Love each other without remorse!" she said. "You have both been more generous than any one has the right to expect of our poor human race. Love each other without stint! for blessed are they who have no other ambition in this world."

Mary lowered her eyes, but as she lowered them her hand pressed Michel's. The young man knelt at the feet of the little peasant lad.

"It needs all the happiness you order me to take, to console me for not dying for you," he said in a spasm of gratitude.

"Oh, don't talk of being killed or dying! Alas! I see how useless it is to be killed or to die. Look at my poor Bonneville! What good did all his great devotion do me? No, Monsieur de la Logerie, live for those you love; and you have given me the right to place myself among them! Live for Mary, and — I will take upon myself to declare that Mary will live for you!"

"Ah! madame," cried Michel, "if all Frenchmen had seen you as I have seen you, if they knew you as I know you —"

"I should have some chance of returning in triumph — especially if they were lovers! However, let us, if you please, talk of other things; before dreaming of future triumphs we must think of present retreat. See if our friends have arrived. I must blame you, my brave sentinel, for being so absorbed in Mademoiselle Mary that you failed to make me the concerted signal; and I might have waited in the street till morning if I had not heard your voice through the window; happily, you had left the door open and I was able to get in."

As Petit-Pierre uttered this reproach in a laughing tone two other persons who were to accompany her in her flight arrived; but after a short consultation it was decided that her safety might be endangered by the presence of too many persons, and they stayed behind. Petit-Pierre, Michel, and Mary started alone.

The quay was deserted; the pont Rousseau seemed absolutely solitary. Michel led the way. They crossed the bridge without incident. Michel took a path along the bank; Petit-Pierre and Mary followed him, walking side by side. The night was splendid, — so splendid that they feared to continue along this open way. Michel proposed to take the road to Pèlerin, which ran parallel with the river, but was less exposed than the path along the bank.

Thanks to the moonlight, they could see the river from time to time, like a broad and brilliant silver sheet, marked here and there with wooded islets, their tree-tops clearly defined against the sky. This clearness of the night, though it had its inconveniences, had on the other hand, some advantages. Michel, who served as guide, was sure of not losing his way; and, as they walked along, they could even see the schooner itself at intervals.

When they had passed, or rather gone round the village of Pèlerin, the young baron hid the duchess and Marie in a rocky hollow of the shore, and going to a little distance along the bank he gave the whistle which was to signal Joseph Picaut.

As Joseph did not reply with the owl's cry, — the cry of alarm, — Michel, who, up to that time had been very anxious, felt more easy. He felt sure that, as he received no answer, the Chouan would soon come to him.

He waited five minutes; nothing stirred. He whistled again, more sharply than before; still nothing answered, no one came. He thought he might have been mistaken as to the place of meeting, and he hurried along the bank. But no! a hundred steps farther took him past the isle of Couéron; and there was no other island within sight where a vessel could lie, — yet the vessel was not visible.

It certainly was the spot agreed upon, and he returned upon his steps. The vessel must be within sight where he had first stopped; but even so, he could not explain to himself Joseph Picaut's absence.

An idea came to him. Had the enormous sum promised to whoever would deliver up the person passing under the name of Petit-Pierre tempted the Chouan, whose cast of countenance had not impressed him favorably? He communicated his suspicions to Petit-Pierre and Mary, who now joined him.

But Petit-Pierre shook her head.

"It is not possible," she said. "If that man had betrayed us we should have been arrested before now; besides, that does n't explain the absence of the vessel."

"You are right. The captain was to send a boat ashore, and I don't see it."

"Perhaps it is not yet time."

Just then the church clock at Pèlerin struck two, as though it was ordered to make answer to her words.

"There!" said Michel, "it is two o'clock!"

"Was there any fixed hour with the captain?"

"My mother could only act on probabilities, and she told him it might be as late as five o'clock."

"He had, then, no reason to be impatient, for we have got here three hours too soon."

"What shall we do?" asked Michel. "My responsibility is so great I dare not act by myself."

"We must take a boat and look for the ship. As the captain is aware we know his anchorage, very likely he expects us to go to him."

Michel went a few hundred feet toward Pèlerin and found a boat made fast to the shore. Evidently, it had been lately used, for the oars, which were lying in the bottom of it, were still wet. He came back with the news to his companions, asking them to go back into their hiding-place while he crossed the river.

"Do you know how to row?" asked Petit-Pierre.

"I own to you," replied Michel, blushing for his ignorance, "that I am not very good at it."

"Then," said Petit-Pierre, "we will go with you. I will steer the boat; many a time I have done that in the bay of Naples for amusement."

"And I 'll help him to row," said Mary. "My sister and I often row over the lake of Grand-Lieu."

All three embarked. When they reached the middle of the river Petit-Pierre, looking forward in the direction of the current, cried out: —

"There she is ! there she is ! "

"Who ? What?" exclaimed Mary and Michel together.

"The ship ! the ship ! There, don't you see ?"

And Petit-Pierre pointed down the river in the direction of Paimbœuf.

"No," said Michel, "that can't be the ship !"

"Why not ?"

"Because it is sailing away from us !"

Just then they reached the extremity of the island. Michel jumped ashore, helped his two companions to land, and ran with all speed to the other side.

"It is our vessel !" he cried, returning. "To the boat ! to the boat, and row as fast as we can !"

All three sprang again into the boat; Mary and Michel strained at the oars while Petit-Pierre took the helm. Helped by the current the little boat flew along rapidly; there was still a chance of overtaking the schooner if she kept on her present course.

But presently a black shadow came between their eyes and the lines of the masts and cordage standing out against the sky; she had hoisted her mainsail. Soon another bit of canvas, the foretopsail, rose into the air; the jib followed; and then the "Jeune Charles," profiting by the breeze which was steadily rising, hoisted her other sails, one by one.

Michel took the second oar from Mary's tired hands and bent to the thwarts like a convict on the galleys. Despair had seized him ; for in that second of time he had seen all the consequences which would follow on the loss of the schooner. He began to shout and hail her; but Petit-Pierre stopped him, exhorting him to prudence.

"Ah !" she cried, her gayety surmounting all vicissitudes of fortune, "Providence evidently does not choose that I shall leave this glorious land of France !"

"God grant it may be Providence!" said Michel.

"What do you mean by that?" asked Petit-Pierre.

"I fear there is some horrible machination under all this."

"Nonsense, my poor friend; it is only a bit of ill-luck. They mistook the day or the hour, that's all. Besides, how do we know whether we could have slipped through the cruisers at the mouth of the Loire? All's for the best, perhaps."

But Michel was not convinced by Petit-Pierre's reasoning; he continued to lament; talked of throwing himself into the river and swimming to the schooner, which was now gently widening the distance and beginning to disappear in the mists on the horizon. It was, in fact, with much difficulty that Petit-Pierre succeeded in calming him; perhaps she might not have done so without Mary's help.

Three o'clock was now ringing from the steeples at Couéron; in another hour it would be daylight. There was no time to lose. Michel and Mary took up the oars; they regained the shore and left the boat about where they found it. It then became a question whether they should return to Nantes. This being decided upon, it was most important to get there before daybreak.

Suddenly Michel, as they walked along, stopped and struck his forehead.

"I'm afraid I have committed a great folly," he said.

"What folly?" asked the duchess.

"I ought to have returned to Nantes by the other bank."

"Pooh! all roads are safe if you follow them cautiously; besides, what should we have done with the boat?"

"Left it on the other shore."

"So that the poor fisherman to whom it belongs would have lost a whole day in looking for it! No, no! better take more trouble ourselves than snatch the bread out of the mouth of some poor fellow who has little enough as it is."

They reached the pont Rousseau. Here Petit-Pierre

insisted that Michel should let her return to the house alone in company with Mary; but Michel would not consent. Perhaps he was too happy in the sense of Mary's presence; for she, under the influence of Petit-Pierre's promise, replied (with sighs, it is true, but still she replied) to the tender words her lover said to her. For this reason, perhaps, he positively refused to leave them, and all they could induce him to do was to walk behind them, at some distance.

They had just crossed the place du Bouffai when Michel, as he turned the corner of the rue Saint-Sauveur, felt certain that he heard a step behind him. He turned and saw a man, who, perceiving that he was noticed, darted hastily into a doorway. Michel's first idea was to follow him; but he reflected that if he did so he should lose sight of Petit-Pierre and Mary. He therefore hurried on and overtook them.

"We are followed!" he said to Petit-Pierre.

"Well, let them follow us!" said the duchess, with her usual serenity. "We have plenty of ways of evading them."

Petit-Pierre signed to Michel to follow her up a cross-street, where, after taking about a hundred steps, they reached the end of the little alley which Michel had once before taken, and where he had recognized a door by the branch of holly hung there by Père Eustache.

Petit-Pierre lifted the knocker and struck three blows at varying intervals. At this signal the door opened as though by magic. Petit-Pierre made Mary enter the court-yard and then she entered herself.

"Good!" said Michel. "Now I will see if that man is still watching us."

"No, no!" cried Petit-Pierre, "you are condemned to death. If you forget it, I don't; and as you and I are running the same danger, you will be good enough to take the same precautions. Come in — quick!"

During this time the man whom Michel had seen reading his paper the evening before, appeared on the portico, wearing the same dressing-gown and apparently half asleep. He raised his arms to heaven on seeing Petit-Pierre.

"Never mind! never mind!" said the latter, "don't lose time in lamentation. It is all a failure, and we are followed. Open the door, my dear Pascal!"

He turned to the half-open door behind him.

"No, not the house door," said Petit-Pierre, "the garden door. In ten minutes the house will be surrounded; we must make for the hiding-place at once!"

"Follow me, then."

"We will follow. So sorry to disturb you, my poor Pascal, at such an early hour; and all the more distressed because my visit will force you to come too, if you don't want to be arrested."

The garden door was now open. Before passing through, Michel stretched out his hand to take Mary's. Petit-Pierre saw the action and gently pushed the girl into the young man's arms.

"Come," she said, "kiss him, or, at any rate, let him kiss you! Before me, it is quite permissible; I stand to you as a mother, and I think the poor lad has fully earned it. There! Now go your way, Monsieur de la Logerie, and we will go ours; but remember that the care of my own interests will not prevent me from looking after yours."

"When may I see her again?" said Michel, timidly.

"It will be dangerous, I know that," replied Petit-Pierre; "but after all, they say there's a God who protects both lovers and drunkards, and if so, I'll rely on him. You shall pay one visit at least to the rue du Château, No. 3. I intend, if I can, to return your Mary to you."

So saying, Petit-Pierre gave Michel a hand, which he kissed respectfully; then Petit-Pierre and Mary turned in the direction of the upper town, while Michel took his way back toward the pont Rousseau.

XXVIII.

SHOWING HOW THERE MAY BE FISHERMEN AND FISHERMEN.

Maître Courtin had been very unhappy in mind during the whole evening Madame de la Logerie had compelled him to pass with her. By gluing his ear to the door he had heard every word the baroness had said to her son, and he knew, therefore, of the scheme of the schooner.

Michel's departure would, of course, upset all his projects for the discovery of Petit-Pierre; consequently, he was little desirous of the honor the baroness did him in taking him home with her. He was, in fact, most anxious to get back to the farmhouse. He hoped, by evoking the image of Mary, to prevent, or at least delay, the flight of his young master; for if the latter departed he lost, of course, the thread by which he expected to penetrate the labyrinth in which Petit-Pierre was hidden.

Unluckily for him, as soon as Madame de la Logerie reached the château she struck another vein of ideas. In taking Courtin from the farmhouse her only idea had been to hide her son's departure and protect him from the farmer's curiosity; but on reaching the château she found the house, occupied for the last few weeks by a band of soldiers, in such deplorable disorder that she forgot, in presence of a devastation which assumed to her eyes the proportions of a catastrophe, all her natural distrust of Courtin, and she kept him with her as the recipient and echo of her lamentations. Her despair, expressed with the energy of conviction, prevented Courtin from leaving her, without some decided pretext, and therefore delayed his return to the farmhouse.

He was too shrewd not to suspect that the baroness had brought him to keep him away from her son; but her despair was so genuine at the sight of her broken china, shattered mirrors, greasy carpets, and her salon transformed into a guardroom and adorned with primitive but most expressive designs, that he began to doubt his first suspicion, and to think that if his young master had really not been cautioned against him it would be an easy matter to join him before he could board the vessel.

It was nine o'clock before the baroness, after shedding a last tear over the filthy defacements of the château, got into her carriage and Courtin was enabled to give the order to the postilion to drive on: "Road to Paris!" No sooner had he done so than he turned round rapidly and ran with all his might toward the farmhouse.

It was empty; the servant told him that Monsieur Michel and Mademoiselle Bertha had been gone two hours, and had taken the road to Nantes.

Courtin at once thought of following them, and ran to the stable to get his pony, — that, too, had gone! In his hurry he had forgotten to ask the servant by what manner of locomotion his young master had started. The recollection of his pony's extremely slow method of progression reassured him somewhat; but, at any rate, he only stopped in his own house long enough to get some money and the insignia of his dignity as mayor; then he started bravely afoot in quest of him whom by this time he regarded as a fugitive and almost as the embezzler of a hundred thousand francs, which his imagination had already discounted through the person of Mary de Souday's lover.

Maître Courtin ran like one who sees the wind whirling away his bank-notes; in fact, he went almost as fast as the wind. But his haste did not prevent him from stopping to make inquiries of every one he passed. The mayor of La Logerie was innately prying at all times, and on this occasion, as may well be supposed, he was not backward with his questions.

At Saint-Philbert-de-Grand-Lieu, he was told that his pony had been seen about half-past seven o'clock that evening. He asked who rode it; but he got no satisfactory answer on that point, — the inn-keeper, of whom he inquired, having taken notice only of the obstinacy of the animal in refusing to pass the tavern sign (a branch of holly and three apples saltierwise) where his master usually baited him on the way to Nantes.

A little farther on, however, the farmer was luckier; the rider was described to him so exactly that he could have no doubt about his being the young baron; and he was also told that the traveller was alone. The mayor, a prudent man if ever there was one, supposed that the two young people had parted company out of prudence, meaning to rejoin each other by different roads. Luck was evidently on his side; the pair were parted, and he knew, if he could only meet Michel alone, the game was won.

He felt so sure that the young baron had not deviated from the road and was now in Nantes that when he reached the inn of the Point-du-Jour he did not trouble himself to ask the inn-keeper for further information, which, by the bye, he doubted if the man would give him. He stopped only long enough to eat a mouthful, and then, instead of following Michel into Nantes, he turned back over the pont Rousseau and then to the right, in the direction of Pèlerin. The wily farmer had his plan.

We have already explained the hopes which Courtin had founded on Michel. Mary's lover would sooner or later betray to him, for some personal end, the secret hiding-place of the woman he loved; and as that beloved woman was living with Petit-Pierre, Michel's betrayal of Mary's retreat would also betray the duchess. But if Michel contrived to escape, all Courtin's hopes went with him. Consequently, at any cost Michel must not escape. Now, if Michel did not find the "Jeune Charles" at her anchorage Michel would be forced to remain.

As for Madame de la Logerie, she being well on the

road to Paris, it would be some days at least before she could hear that her son had not sailed, and could take other measures to remove him from La Vendée. Courtin was confident that this delay would suffice him to obtain from Michel the clue he sought.

The only difficulty was that he did not know in what way to reach the captain of the "Jeune Charles," the name of the schooner which he had heard the baroness tell to Michel; but — without dreaming of his likeness in this to the greatest man of antiquity — Courtin resolved to run for luck.

Luck did not escape him. When he reached the top of the hill above Couéron he saw, above the poplar-trees on the islet, the masts of the schooner; the foretopsail was hoisted and was flapping to the breeze. Undoubtedly, it was the vessel he was in search of. In the lessening twilight, which was beginning to make all things indistinct, Maître Courtin, glancing along the shore, saw at about ten paces from him a fishing-rod held horizontally over the river with a line at the end, and a cork at the end of the line which floated on the current.

The rod seemed to come from a small hillock, but the arm that held it was invisible. Maître Courtin was not a man to remain in ignorance of what he wanted to know; he walked straight to the hillock and round it; there he discovered a man crouching in a hollow between two rocks, absorbed in contemplation of the swaying of his float at the will of the current.

The man was dressed as a sailor, — that is, he wore trousers of tarred-cloth and a pea-jacket; on his head was a species of Scotch-cap. A few feet from him the stern of a boat, fastened by its bow to the shore, swayed gently to the wash of the water. The fisherman did not turn his head as Courtin approached him, although the latter took the precaution to cough, and make his cough significant of a desire to enter into conversation. The fisherman not only kept an obstinate silence, but he did not even look Courtin's way.

"It is pretty late to be fishing," remarked the mayor of La Logerie at last.

"That shows you know nothing about it," replied the fisherman, with a contemptuous grimace. "I think, on the contrary, that it is rather too early. Night is the time it is worth while to fish; you can catch something better than the young fry at night."

"Yes; but if it is dark how can you see your float?"

"What matter?" replied the fisherman, shrugging his shoulders. "My night eyes are here," he added, showing the palm of his hand.

"I understand; you mean you feel a bite," said Courtin, sitting down beside him. "I 'm fond of fishing myself; and little as you think so, I know a good deal about it."

"You? fishing with a line?" said the other, with a doubtful air.

"No, not that," replied Courtin. "I depopulate the river about La Logerie with nets."

Courtin dropped this hint of his locality, hoping that the fisherman, whom he took to be a sailor stationed there by the captain of the schooner to take Monsieur Michel de la Logerie on board, would catch it up; but he was mistaken; the man gave no sign of recognizing the name; on the contrary he remarked coolly: —

"You boast of your talent for the great art of fishing, but I don't believe in it."

"Pray why?" asked Courtin. "Have you the monopoly?"

"Because you seem to me, my good sir, to be ignorant of the first principle of that art."

"And what may that principle be?" asked Courtin.

"When you want to catch fish avoid four things."

"What are they?"

"Wind, dogs, women, and chatterers. It is true, I might say three," added the man in the pea-jacket, philosophically, "for women and chatterers are one."

"Pshaw! you'll soon find out that my chattering, as you call it, is not out of season, for I am going to propose to you to earn a couple of francs."

"When I've caught half a dozen fish I shall have earned more than a couple of francs, and amused myself into the bargain."

"Well, I'll go as far as four, or even five francs," continued Courtin; "and you will have the chance to do a service to your neighbor, which counts for something, does n't it?"

"Come," said the fisherman, "don't beat round the bush; what do you want of me?"

"I want you to take me on board your schooner, the 'Jeune Charles,' the masts of which I see over there beyond the trees."

"The 'Jeune Charles,' said the sailor, reflectively, "what's the 'Jeune Charles'?"

"Here," said Maître Courtin, giving the fisherman an oil-skin hat he had picked up on the shore, on which appeared the words, in gilt letters: "LE JEUNE CHARLES."

"Well, I admit you must be a fisherman, my friend," said the sailor. "The devil take me if your eyes are not in your fingers, like mine; otherwise you never could have read that in the darkness! Now, then, what have you to do with the 'Jeune Charles'?"

"Did n't I mention something just now that struck your ear?"

"My good man," said the fisherman, "I'm like a well-bred dog; I don't yelp when bitten. Heave your own log and don't trouble yourself about my keel."

"Well, I am Madame la Baronne de la Logerie's farmer."

"What of it?"

"I am sent by her," said Courtin, growing more and more audacious as he went on.

"What of that?" asked the sailor, in the same tone, but more impatiently. "You come from Madame de la Logerie; well, what have you got to say for her?"

"I came to tell you that the thing is a failure; it is all discovered, and you must get away as fast as you can."

"That may be," replied the fisherman; "but it does n't concern me. I am only the mate of the 'Jeune Charles;' though I do know enough of the matter to put you aboard and let you talk with the captain."

So saying, he tranquilly wound up his line and threw it into the boat, which he pulled toward him. Making a sign to Courtin to sit down in the stern, he put twenty feet between him and the shore with one stroke of the oars. After rowing five minutes he turned his head and found they were close alongside the "Jeune Charles," which, being in ballast, rose some twelve feet above them out of the water.

At the sound of oars a curiously modulated whistle came from the schooner, to which the mate replied in somewhat the same manner. A figure then appeared in the bows; the boat came up on the starboard side and a rope was thrown to it. The man with the pea-jacket climbed aboard with the agility of a cat, then he hauled up Courtin, who was less used to such nautical scrambling.

XXIX.

INTERROGATORIES AND CONFRONTINGS.

When, to his great joy, the mayor of La Logerie found himself safely on the deck of the vessel, he saw a human form whose features he could not distinguish, so hidden were they in a thick woollen muffler which was wound around the collar of an oil-skin coat; but whom, by the respectful attitude of the cabin-boy, who had summoned him on deck, Courtin took to be the captain of the schooner himself.

"What 's all this?" said the latter, addressing the mate and swinging the light of a lantern, which he took from the cabin-boy, full in the face of the new-comer.

"He comes from you know who," replied the mate.

"Nonsense!" returned the captain. "What are your eyes good for if they can't tell the difference between the cut of a young fellow of twenty and an old hulk like that?"

"I am not Monsieur de la Logerie, that 's a fact," said Courtin. "I am only his farmer and confidential man."

"Very good; that 's something, but not all."

"He has ordered me —"

"In the name of all the porpoises! I don't ask what he ordered you, you miserable land-lubber," cried the captain, squirting a black jet of saliva, — an action which somewhat hindered the explosion of his evident wrath. "I tell you that 's something, but not all."

Courtin looked at the captain with an amazed air.

"Don't you understand, — yes or no?" demanded the latter. "If no, say so at once, and you shall be put ashore with the honors you deserve, — and that 's a good taste of the cat-o'-nine-tails round your loins."

Courtin now perceived that in all probability Madame de la Logerie had agreed with the captain of the "Jeune Charles" on a password, or sign of recognition; that sign he did not know. He felt he was lost; all his plans crumbled to naught, his hopes vanished; besides which, caught in a trap like a fox, he would appear in the young master's eyes when he came aboard for what he really was. His only way of escape from the luckless position he had put himself into was to pretend that simplicity of a peasant which sometimes amounts to idiocy and to empty his face of all intelligence.

"Hang it, my dear gentleman," he said, "I don't know a thing more, myself. My good mistress said to me, says she: 'Courtin, my good friend, you know the young baron is condemned to death. I 've arranged with a worthy sailor to get him out of France; but we 've been denounced by some traitor. Go and tell this to the captain of the "Jeune Charles," which you 'll find at anchor opposite Couéron, behind the islands!' and I came just as hard as I could, and that 's all I know."

Just then a vigorous "Ahoy!" was given from the bows of the vessel and diverted the captain's mind from the violent reply he was doubtless about to make. He turned to the cabin-boy, who, lantern in hand and mouth open, was listening to the conversation between his master and Courtin.

"What are you doing there, you shirk, booby, whelp?" cried the captain, accompanying his words with a pantomine which — thanks to the rapid evolutions of the young aspirant to a broad pennant — touched him only on the fleshy parts, though it sent him whirling into the gangway. "Is that how you mind your work?" Then, turning to the mate he added: "Don't let any one aboard without knowing him."

But the words were hardly out of his mouth before the

new-comer, using the rope which had hoisted Courtin, and which was still hanging, appeared on deck. The captain picked up the lantern which the cabin-boy had dropped in his skurry, and which, providentially, was not extinguished; and then, light in hand, he advanced to his visitor.

"By what right do you come aboard my vessel without hailing me, you!" cried the angry captain, seizing the stranger by the collar.

"I came aboard because I have business with you," replied the other, with the confident air of a man who is sure of his facts.

"What is it, then? Out with it, quick!"

"Let go of me, first. You may be sure I sha'n't get away, as I came of my own accord."

"Ten thousand millions of whales!" cried the captain, "holding you by the collar does n't choke the words in your throat, does it?"

"But I can't talk when I 'm embarrassed!" said the new-comer, without showing the least timidity at the tone of his questioner.

"Captain," said the mate, intervening, "it seems to me, *sacredie!* that you are mistaken. You ask the fellow who is backing and filling to show his colors, and you are tying the halliards of the other when he wants to run his up."

"True," said the captain, loosening his hold of the new-comer, whom our readers of course know to be Jean Picaut, Michel's real messenger.

The latter now felt in his pocket, pulled out the handkerchief given to him by Michel, and offered it to the captain, who carefully unfolded it and counted the three knots with as much particularity as though they were so much money. Courtin, to whom no one was paying attention, watched the whole scene and lost nothing of it.

"Good!" said the captain; "you are all right. We 'll talk presently; but first, I must get rid of that fellow aft. You, Antoine," he added, addressing the mate, "take this one to the steward's pantry and give him a quantum of grog."

The captain returned aft and found Courtin sitting on a coil of rope. The mayor of La Logerie held his head in his hands as if he were paying not the slightest attention to the scene forward. He seemed stupefied, whereas, as we know, he had not lost a word of the conversation between the captain and Joseph Picaut.

"Oh, do have me put ashore, captain!" he said, as soon as he saw the latter approaching him. "I don't know what's the matter with me; but for the last few minutes I have felt very ill — as if I were going to die!"

"Pooh! if you are like that in a river swell you'll have a hard time of it before we cross the line!"

"Cross the line? good God!"

"Yes, my fine fellow; your conversation strikes me as so agreeable that I sha'n't part company with you. You'll stay aboard of me during the little trip half round the world I'm bound for."

"Stay aboard! what, here?" cried Courtin, feigning more terror than he really felt. "And my farm, and my good mistress, what'll become of them?"

"As for the farm, I'll engage to show you such sights in foreign lands that you can make it a model farm when you get back. And as for your good mistress, I'll replace her advantageously."

"But why, monsieur? What makes you take this sudden resolution to carry me off? Just think, if my stomach turns with this river swell, as you call it, I sha'n't be fit for anything all the way!"

"That will teach you to fool the captain of the 'Jeune Charles,' lubberly thief that you are!"

"But how have I offended you, my worthy captain?"

"Come," said the officer, apparently resolved to cut short the dialogue, "answer plainly; it is your only chance to escape going to the sharks. Who sent you here?"

"I told you," cried Courtin, "it was Madame de la

Logerie ! and when I tell you that I am her farmer, it is as true as it is that there 's a God in heaven ! "

"But," said the captain, "if Madame de la Logerie sent you, she must have given you something by which you could be recognized, — a note, a letter, a scrap of paper. If you have nothing to show, you don't come from her; and if you don't come from her, you are a spy! — in which case, beware! The moment I 'm sure of it, I 'll treat you as spies should be treated! "

"Ah! my God!" cried Courtin, pretending to be more and more terrified; "I can't allow myself to be so suspected. There, take these; they are letters to me which I happen to have about me; they 'll show you I really am Courtin, as I told you; and there 's my scarf, as mayor of La Logerie. My God! what can I do to convince you I speak the truth?"

"Your mayor's scarf!" cried the captain. "How is it, you rascal, that if you are a public functionary under oath to the government, how is it, I say, that you are aiding and abetting a man who has borne arms against the government, and is now condemned to death?"

"Ah! my dear monsieur, that 's because I am so attached to my masters that my feelings for them are stronger than my sense of duty. Well, — if I must tell you, — it was in my capacity as mayor that I knew the plan was betrayed, and that you were to be boarded to-night. I told Madame de la Logerie of the danger; and it was then she said to me: 'Take that handkerchief and find the captain of the "Jeune Charles" — ' "

"She gave you a handkerchief ?"

"Yes, upon my word!"

"Where is it ?"

"In my pocket."

"Fool, idiot, jackass, give it to me!"

"Give it to you ?"

"Yes."

"Oh, I'm willing, — there it is!"

And Courtin slowly drew a handkerchief from his pocket.

"Give it me, you dog!" cried the captain, snatching the handkerchief from Courtin's hand and convincing himself by a rapid examination that the three knots were really there.

"But, you stupid brute, you idiot, beast!" continued the captain, "did n't Madame de la Logerie tell you to give me that handkerchief?"

"Yes, she told me," replied Courtin, making his expression of face as vacant as possible.

"Then why did n't you give it to me?"

"Hang it!" said Courtin; "when I was hoisted on to the deck I saw you blowing your nose with your fingers, and I said to myself, 'Bless me! if the captain does that he won't need a handkerchief.'"

"Ha!" said the captain, scratching his head, with some remains of doubt in his mind, "either you are a clumsy trickster or a downright imbecile. In either case, as there is more chance of your being imbecile, I prefer to settle on that. Now, tell me over again what you are here for, and what the person who sent you told you say to me."

"Well, here 's word for word what my good mistress said to me: 'Courtin,' says she, 'I know I can trust you, can't I?' 'Yes, that you can,' says I. 'Well,' says she, 'you must know that my son, whom you 've watched over, and nursed, and hidden in your house at the risk of your life, is to escape to-night on board of the "Jeune Charles." But, as I have heard, and as you have told me yourself, the plan is discovered. You have only just time to go and tell the worthy captain that he must not wait for my son, but had better sail away as fast as he can, or he will be arrested this very night for aiding and abetting the escape of a political prisoner — and also, for other things.'"

Maître Courtin added the conclusion of his speech, presuming from the general appearance of the captain of the "Jeune Charles" that he might have other peccadilloes on his conscience than the one in question. Perhaps the mayor's astute mind was not mistaken, for the worthy sailor was somewhat pensive for a few moments.

"Come," he said at last, "follow me."

The farmer passively obeyed; the captain took him to his own cabin, put him in, and double-locked the door. A few minutes later Courtin, who was in darkness and not a little uneasy at the turn that matters were taking, heard a tramp of footsteps on the deck which presently approached the cabin door. The door was unlocked, the captain entered first; he was followed by Joseph Picaut, behind whom came the mate, bearing a lantern.

"Ah, *ça!*" cried the captain of the "Jeune Charles," "now we 'll get at the bottom of this matter! We 'll unravel the thread which seems to me pretty well tangled up, or, by the hull of my ship, I 'll brush the shoulders of both of you with the cat-o'-nine-tails till the devil himself would pity you!"

"As for me, captain, I have said all I have to say!" exclaimed Courtin.

Picaut quivered at the sound of that voice; he had not yet seen his enemy, and was not aware that he was on board the vessel. He made one step forward to convince himself.

"Courtin!" he cried, "the mayor of La Logerie! Captain, if that man knows our secret, we are lost!"

"Who is he, then?" demanded the captain.

"A traitor, a spy, a sneak!"

"The devil he is!" cried the captain. "You need n't tell it me fifty times before I believe it; for there 's something sly and false in the fellow's face which does n't a bit suit me."

"Ha!" continued Joseph Picaut, "you are not mistaken. He 's the damnedest cur and lowest scum in the whole Retz district!"

"What have you got to say to that, come now?" said the captain to Courtin.

"He can't say anything; I defy him!" continued Picaut.

Courtin was silent.

"Well, well, I see I shall have to take strong measures to make you speak, my fine fellow!" said the captain, who, thereupon, pulled from his bosom a little silver whistle hanging to a silver chain, and produced therefrom a prolonged and piercing sound. At the signal two sailors entered the cabin.

At sight of them a diabolical smile crossed Courtin's face.

"Good!" said he; "that 's just what I wanted before speaking."

Taking the captain by the arm he led him to a corner of the cabin and said a few words in his ear.

"Is that true, actually true?" asked the captain.

"Easy enough to prove it!" replied Courtin.

"You are right there," said the captain.

At a word from him the mate and the two sailors seized Joseph Picaut, pulled off his jacket and tore open his shirt. The captain then came up to him and gave him a smart blow on the shoulder. Instantly the two letters branded on the Chouan when he went to the galleys were visible on his rugged skin.

Picaut had been so suddenly and violently seized and handled by the three men that he had no time to defend himself in the first instance; but he no sooner perceived the object of the assault than he made the most desperate efforts to escape the clutches by which he was held; of course, however, he was mastered by the triple strength against him and could only roar with rage and blaspheme.

"Lash his hands and feet!" cried the captain, judging of the man's honesty by the tell-tale certificate on his shoulder, "and down with him to the hold between two hogsheads!" Then, turning to Maître Courtin, who gave a sigh of relief, "I beg your pardon, my worthy mayor," he said, "for confounding you with a scoundrel of that kind; but don't be uneasy, I 'll guarantee that if any one sets fire to your barn within the next three years it won't be that fellow's hand that applies the match!"

Then, without losing a moment he went on deck, and Courtin, to his great satisfaction, heard him call all hands to get the vessel under way.

Once convinced of the danger he was in, the worthy sailor seemed in so great a hurry to put as much space as possible between the law and himself, that he excused himself to the mayor of La Logerie without even the civility of offering him a glass of brandy, shoved him into the boat with a hasty good-bye, and left him to find his way to the shore as best he could.

Maître Courtin rowed as directly to the bank as the current would let him; and just as the boat's keel touched the sandy shore he saw the "Jeune Charles" slowly moving as sail after sail was hoisted to the breeze.

Courtin then hid himself in the same nook of the rocks where he had found the mate of the vessel fishing, and there he waited.

But not for long; he had hardly been there half an hour before Michel arrived, and he saw, to his great astonishment, that neither of the two women who accompanied him was Bertha. A moment later, and he discovered that they were Mary and Petit-Pierre.

Then, indeed, he congratulated himself on the success of his trick, so wonderfully seconded by chance, and he now bent all his mind to profit by the rare good luck which providence had bestowed upon him.

It will readily be understood that he never lost sight of Michel, Mary, and Petit-Pierre as long as they waited on the shore, and that when the three embarked in the boat to overtake the ship, he watched them with his eyes every inch of their way; that he saw them return and land, and followed them back to Nantes with such precautions that the three fugitives were wholly unaware they were spied upon.

And yet, cautious as Courtin was, it was actually he whom Michel had caught sight of at the corner of the place du Bouffai; it was he who followed the trio to the house which he saw them enter.

When the door into the court-yard closed after them, and they disappeared from sight, he was certain that he now knew the duchess's hiding-place. He passed before the door, and as he did so, he drew from his pocket a bit of chalk and made a cross upon the wall beside it; then, certain that he had the fish in his net, he felt he had only to draw it in and put his hand on a hundred thousand francs.

XXX.

WE AGAIN MEET THE GENERAL, AND FIND HE IS NOT CHANGED.

Maître Courtin was not a little excited. As the last of the three persons he had followed from Couéron disappeared into the court-yard a vision danced before his eyes, such as he had seen that night on the moor returning from Aigrefeuille, — a vision that seemed to him the most beautiful of all possible visions: he saw before his dazzled eyes the sparkling of a pyramid of coins, casting their adorable gold reflections into the far, far future.

Only, the pyramid was double the size of the one he had then seen; for his first thought on finding the fish in his net was that he should be a monstrous fool if he let that mysterious man at Aigrefeuille share in the benefits of his catch. He resolved on the spot not to let him know of the discovery, but to go himself straight to the authorities of Nantes and reveal the matter to them. To do him justice, however, it must be said that Maître Courtin did think, in this first flush of his hopes, of his young master, and of the fact that he was about to deprive him of liberty, perhaps of life; but he instantly smothered that sentiment of untimely remorse, and, in order not to let his conscience send forth another such cry, he began to run with all his might toward the Prefecture.

He had hardly gone fifty yards before, just as he turned the corner of the rue du Marché, a man, running from the opposite direction, bolted against him and knocked him to the wall. Courtin gave a cry, not of pain, but amazement, for the man was no other than Monsieur Michel de la Logerie, whom he thought he had left safely behind the green door he had carefully marked with a white cross.

His stupefaction was so great that Michel would certainly have noticed it had he not himself been so preoccupied; but at the moment he was only delighted to see a man he thought to be his friend, and who, as he believed, might now be of use to him.

"Oh, Courtin!" he cried, "tell me, did you come down the rue du Marché?"

"Yes, Monsieur le baron."

"Then you must have met a man running away."

"No, Monsieur le baron."

"Why, yes, you must! It is impossible that you did not see him, — a man who seemed to be on the watch for some one?"

Maître Courtin reddened; but he instantly recovered himself.

"Wait! stop! yes, I did," he said, suddenly resolving to profit by this unexpected chance of averting all suspicion from himself. "There was a man walking in front of me, but I saw him stop at that green door you see down there."

"That's it!" cried Michel, forgetting everything except his desire to discover the man who had followed them. "Courtin, will you give me a proof of your fidelity and devotion? I positively must discover that man. Which way do you think he went?"

"That way," replied Courtin, pointing to the first street his eyes lighted on.

"Come on, then, and follow me."

Michel started to run in the direction Courtin had pointed out; but the latter, as he followed, began to reflect. For an instant he thought of leaving his master to run where he liked, and going himself about the business he was engaged in; but the next instant he thought otherwise and congratulated himself heartily for not following his first idea.

It was evident to his mind that the house had two issues; and as Michel had discovered they were watched, both must have been used to throw the pursuer off the scent. Petit-Pierre had probably gone out as Michel did, by another door. Michel must surely know, by this time, the real retreat where Mary lived with Petit-Pierre; he would therefore stay by Michel, from whom he could undoubtedly obtain the information he wanted; whereas he might lose all by pushing matters too hastily. He therefore resigned himself to the loss of his expected catch and possessed his soul in patience.

He hastened his pace and rejoined Michel.

"Monsieur le baron," he said, "I must remind you to be cautious. It is getting to be daylight; the streets will soon be full of people, and they will all look at you if you run in this way with your clothes all wet and muddy. If we meet a police-agent he will certainly think it suspicious and arrest you; and what will your mother say then? She has given me so many cautions about you!"

"My mother? why, she thinks me at sea, on my way to England!"

"Were you going away?" asked Courtin, with the most innocent air in the world.

"Yes; did n't she tell you so?"

"No, Monsieur de la Logerie," replied the farmer, giving an expression of deep and bitter sadness to his countenance, "no. I see that, in spite of all I have done for you, the baroness distrusts me; and I tell you that cuts me to the heart as a ploughshare cuts into the ground."

"Oh, nonsense! don't trouble about that, my good Courtin; but your change of front has been rather sudden and needs explanation. In fact, when I think of that night you cut the girths of my horse's saddle, I ask myself why you have become so kind and attentive and devoted."

"Oh, hang it, Monsieur Michel! that 's easy told. At that time I was fighting for my political opinions; now that all danger of insurrection is over, and I am certain the government I love can't be overthrown, I don't see anything in Chouans and *she-wolves* but friends of my master; and it makes me sorry to be so little understood."

"Well," said Michel, "I am going to give you a proof that I appreciate your return to better ideas by confiding to you a secret I believe you have already guessed. Courtin, it is probable that the new Baronne de la Logerie will not be the one who, till now, people think it is."

"You mean you won't marry Mademoiselle de Souday ?"

"Quite the contrary; only, my wife's name may be Mary, and not Bertha."

"Ah, I 'm glad for you ! for you know I helped that on as much as I could; and if I did n't do more it was because you would n't let me. Ah, *ça !* have you seen Mademoiselle Mary since you came to Nantes ?"

"Yes, I have seen her; and the few minutes I spent with her sufficed, I hope, to secure my happiness," cried Michel, giving way to the intoxication of his joy. Then he added: "Are you obliged to go back to La Logerie to-night ?"

"Monsieur le baron ought to feel that I am at his service," replied Courtin.

"Very good; then you shall see her yourself, Courtin; for to-night I 'm to meet her again."

"Where ?"

"Where I met you just now."

"Oh, that 's good !" said Courtin, his face brightening with a satisfaction equal to that on Michel's own face. "That 's good ! you don't know how happy I am to have you marry according to your own likings. Faith ! if your mother consents, you are right enough to take the one you love. You see, now, I gave you good advice."

And the worthy farmer rubbed his hands as though he were on a pinnacle of satisfaction.

"My good Courtin," said Michel, touched by his farmer's sympathy, "where shall I find you this evening ?"

"Where you please."

"Did n't you put up, as I did, at the Point du Jour ?"

"Yes, Monsieur le baron."

"Well, then, we can pass the day there. To-night you can go with me when I meet Mary, and keep watch for us."

"But," said Courtin, much embarrassed by a proposal which interfered with all his plans, "I 've got a good deal to do in town."

"Well, I 'll go with you; it will help me to kill time."

"No, that won't do; my business as mayor will take me to the Prefecture, and you must n't go there. No, do you go back to the inn and keep quiet, and to-night at ten o'clock I 'll be on hand to start, — you as happy as a king, and I very glad of your happiness."

Courtin was most anxious to be rid of Michel for the present. The idea of gaining the whole reward for the capture of Petit-Pierre so filled his mind that he was determined not to leave Nantes without knowing the exact amount offered, and laying some plan to obtain it all himself and not divide it with any one.

Michel yielded to Courtin's reasoning, and giving a glance at his muddy clothing he decided to take leave of him then and there and go back to the tavern.

As soon as his young master had left him Courtin made his way to the quarters of General Dermoncourt. He gave his name to the orderly, and after a few minutes' delay he was shown into the presence of the man he came to see.

The general was a good deal dissatisfied with the turn matters were taking; he had sent to Paris plans of pacification, somewhat like those which had succeeded so well under General Hoche. These plans had not been approved; the general saw the civil authority encroaching everywhere on the powers which martial law assigned to the military alone; and his susceptibilities as an old soldier, wounded at every turn, together with his patriotic feelings, made him deeply dissatisfied.

"What do you want?" he said to Courtin, looking him over from head to foot.

Courtin bowed as low as he was able.

"General," he said, "perhaps you remember the fair at Montaigu ?"

"*Parbleu*, as if it were yesterday! and especially the night after it. Ha! that expedition would have been a success, and I might have strangled the insurrection at its birth if a scoundrelly keeper had n't inveigled one of my troopers. By the bye, what was that man's name ?"

"Jean Oullier."

"What became of him ?"

Courtin could not help turning pale.

"He died," he said.

"The best thing he could do, poor devil; and yet, I 'm sorry too,— he was a brave fellow."

"If you remember the man who defeated the affair, general, it seems strange you have forgotten the one who helped you with information."

The general looked at Courtin.

"Jean Oullier was a soldier, a comrade, and soldiers remember each other; the rest — I mean spies and informers — they forget as soon as possible."

"Very well," said Courtin. "Then I shall have to refresh your memory, general, and tell you that I am the man who informed you of Petit-Pierre's hiding-place."

"Oh, are you ?" said the general. "Well, what do you want to say now ? Speak out, and briefly !"

"I want to do you exactly the same service over again."

"As for that, times are changed, my good friend. We are no longer among the sunken roads of the Retz region, where a tiny foot, a fair skin, and a soft voice are remarkable because they are rare in the country. Here, all the women look like great ladies; and a score of men of your kind have been to me to sell their mare's-nests. My soldiers have been kept on the *qui-vive* all the time; we have searched a dozen different places, and all to no purpose."

"General, I have a right to expect you to put faith in me, because the information I gave you first was correct."

"Upon my word," muttered the general, in a low tone, "it would be rather pleasant to discover, all by myself, what that man from Paris with his squads of spies, and sneaks, and pimps, and criminal and detective police can't find out. Are you sure of what you say?" he continued, raising his voice.

"I am sure that within twenty-four hours I shall know the street and the number of the house —"

"Then come and see me."

"But, general, I should wish to know —" Courtin stopped.

"Know what?" asked the general.

"I have heard talk of reward, and I wish to know —"

"Ah, true!" said the general, looking at Courtin with sovereign contempt. "I forgot, though you are a public functionary, that you are one of those who don't neglect their private interests."

"You said yourself, general, that we were the ones that were soonest forgotten."

"And you want money to take the place of public gratitude? Well, that 's logical. So, then, you don't give, my worthy mayor, you sell, you traffic, you trade in human flesh; and to-day, having something to sell, you come to what you think the best market, — is that it?"

"You have said it. Oh, don't feel embarrassed, general, business is business; and I am not ashamed to attend to mine!"

"So much the better; but I 'm not the man you ought to go to. They 've sent down a gentleman from Paris who is specially charged to attend to this matter. When you can lay hands on your prey, you had better go to him and sell it."

"So I will, general. But," continued Courtin, "as I did you such a service that first time, don't you feel inclined to give me some reward?"

"My good fellow, if you think I owe you anything I am ready to pay it. Speak out! I 'm listening."

"It will be all the easier because I don't ask much."

"Go on."

"Tell me the sum the government has promised to the man who delivers Petit-Pierre into your hands."

"Fifty thousand francs, perhaps; I did n't pay much attention to it, any way."

"Fifty thousand francs!" exclaimed Courtin, stepping back as if he had been struck. "Why, fifty thousand francs is nothing!"

"I agree with you there; it is n't worth while to be infamous for such a sum as that. But you can say that to those it concerns; as for you and me, we have done with each other, I think. Take yourself away. Good-day to you!"

And the general, resuming the work he had laid aside to receive Courtin, paid not the slightest attention to the bows and civilities with which the mayor of La Logerie endeavored to make a proper retreat.

The latter departed far less satisfied in mind than he was when he entered. He had no doubt whatever that the general knew correctly the exact amount of the reward, and he could not reconcile what he had just heard with what the mysterious man at Aigrefeuille had told him, — unless it might be that the said mysterious man was the agent sent by the government from Paris. He now gave up all idea of acting without him, and he resolved, while practising the utmost caution, to let him know as soon as possible what had happened.

Until now the man had come to Courtin; but the farmer had his address, and was directed to write to him if anything important occurred. Courtin did not write; he went in person. After a good deal of trouble he managed to find, in the lowest quarter of the town, at the farther end of a damp and muddy blind alley full of the sordid booths of rag-pickers and old-clothes men, a tiny shop, where, following certain directions, he asked for Monsieur Hyacinthe. He was told to go up a ladder, and was then shown into a small room, much cleaner and more decent than might have been expected from the general appearance of this lair.

There he found the man from Aigrefeuille, who received him far better than the general had done; and with whom he had a long conference.

XXXI.

COURTIN MEETS WITH ANOTHER DISAPPOINTMENT.

If the day seemed long to Michel, to Courtin its length was intolerable; he thought that night would never come. And though he felt he ought to keep away from the rue du Marché and the adjacent streets, it was impossible to avoid airing his impatience in their neighborhood.

When evening came, mindful of his engagement with Michel, he returned to the tavern of the Point du Jour. There he found Michel awaiting him eagerly. As soon as the young man saw him he exclaimed: —

"Ah, Courtin, I am thankful to see you. I have discovered the man who followed us last night."

"Hein! what? what did you say?" asked Courtin, making, in spite of himself, a step backward.

"I have discovered him, I tell you!"

"But the man — who is he?" asked Courtin.

"A man in whom I felt sure I might trust; and you would have trusted him too in my position, — Joseph Picaut."

"Joseph Picaut!" repeated Courtin, feigning astonishment.

"Yes."

"Where did you meet him?"

"At this inn, where he is hostler, or rather, where he is playing the part of hostler."

"Why did he follow you? You can't have had the imprudence to tell him your secret? Ah, young man, young man!" exclaimed Courtin; "they may well say youth and imprudence go together. A former galley-slave!"

"That 's the very reason. Don't you know why he was sent to the galleys ?"

"Damn it, yes! for highway robbery."

"But it was in the time of the great war. However, that 's neither here nor there. I gave him an errand to do."

"If I were to ask you what errand, you 'd think me inquisitive; and yet it is my real interest in you that makes me ask, and nothing else."

"Oh! I have no reason for concealing the matter from you. I sent him to let the captain of the 'Jeune Charles' know that I should be on board at three o'clock in the morning. Well, no one has since seen Picaut or the horse — and, by the bye," added the young baron, laughing, "the horse was your pony, my poor Courtin; your pony, which I took from the farm and rode to Nantes."

"Oh! oh!" exclaimed Courtin, "then Sweetheart is —"

"Sweetheart is probably lost to you forever."

"Perhaps he has gone back to his stable," said Courtin, who, even in presence of the grand financial horizon which was opening before him, felt a profound regret for the twenty or twenty-five pistoles at which he valued his pony.

"Well, what I want to tell you is, that if, as I suppose, Joseph Picaut followed us he must now be on the watch about the neighborhood."

"What object has he?" inquired Courtin. "If he wanted to deliver you up nothing could have been easier than to bring the gendarmes here."

Michel shook his head.

"No, — do you say no?"

"I say it is not I whom he is after, Courtin; it is not on my account he watched us yesterday."

"Why so?"

"Because the price on my head would not pay him for his treachery."

"But whom else can he be spying on?" said the farmer,

calling up all the vacant simplicity he was capable of imprinting on his face and accent.

"A Vendéan leader whom I was anxious to save while making my own escape," replied Michel, beginning to perceive whither Courtin's questions were leading him, — though he was not sorry to admit the latter into half his secret in order to use him when occasion came.

"Ah, ha!" exclaimed Courtin; "and you think he has discovered the hiding-place of the Vendéan leader? That would be a misfortune, Monsieur Michel."

"No; he only got to the outworks, as it were; but I am afraid, now that he is once on the scent, he may have better luck this time."

"This time, — how do you mean?"

"Why, to-night, if he watches us, he will find out I have a meeting with Mademoiselle Mary."

"*Mordieu!* you 're right."

"And that makes me very uneasy," said Michel.

"But I shall be on the watch; and if you are followed I 'll whistle in time for you to get away."

"And you?"

Courtin laughed.

"Oh! I — I don't risk anything. My opinions are well-known, thank God; and in my capacity as mayor I can have all the dangerous companions I choose."

"Evil is good sometimes," said Michel, laughing in his turn. "But listen, what time is that?"

"Striking nine from the clock at Bouffai."

"Then, come on, Courtin."

Courtin took his hat, Michel his, and they both went out and were soon at the corner where Michel had met his farmer the night before. The latter stood with his right to the rue du Marché and his left toward the alley into which opened the green door he had marked with a cross.

"Stay there, Courtin," said Michel. "I 'll wait at the farther end of this alley; I don't know which way Mary means to come. If she passes you, direct her toward me;

if she comes my way, do you move up nearer to us, so as to be ready in case of need."

"Don't trouble about that," said Courtin, as he settled himself on the watch.

Courtin was now at the summit of happiness; his plan had completely succeeded. In one way or another he was certain to come in contact with Mary; Mary was the intimate attendant on Petit-Pierre; he would follow Mary when she left Michel, and he had no doubt that the young girl, unconscious of being tracked, would herself betray the hiding-place of the princess by going there.

Half-past nine o'clock ringing from all the belfries in Nantes surprised Courtin in the midst of these reflections. Their metallic vibrations were hardly stilled before he heard a light step coming up on his right; he went in that direction, and saw a young peasant-woman wrapped in a mantle and carrying a package in her hand, whom he recognized to be Mary. The young girl, seeing a strange man apparently on the watch, hesitated. Courtin went up to her and made her recognize him.

"It is all right, Mademoiselle Mary," he said, replying to her relieved gesture; "but I 'm not the one you are looking for, am I? You want Monsieur le baron; well, there he is, waiting for you down there."

And he pointed with his finger to the alley. The girl thanked him with a gesture of her head and moved hastily away in the direction given her. As for Courtin, convinced that the interview would be a long one, he sat down, philosophically, on a milestone, prepared to wait. From that milestone, however, he could keep the two young people in sight while dreaming of his coming fortune, which now seemed a certainty, — for he held in Mary one end of the thread that would lead him through the labyrinth; and this time, he vowed, the thread should not break.

But he had scarcely begun to set up the scaffolding of glorious dreams on the golden clouds of his imagination, when the two young people, after exchanging a few sentences, returned in his direction. They passed in front of him; the young baron had Mary on his arm and was carrying the little package the farmer had lately seen in Mary's hand. Michel nodded to him.

"Ho, ho!" thought Courtin, "is it going to be as easy as this? There 's absolutely no credit in it." And he followed the lovers on a sign from Michel, keeping at a short distance behind them.

Presently, however, he began to feel a slight uneasiness. Instead of going to the upper town, where Courtin felt instinctively that the princess was hidden, the pair turned down toward the river. The farmer followed their movements with deep anxiety. Soon, however, he began to fancy that Mary had some errand in that direction, and that Michel was only accompanying her.

Nevertheless, his anxiety again deepened when, on turning the corner of the quay, he saw the young pair making straight for the tavern of the Point du Jour, which they presently entered. Unable to restrain himself any longer, he ran hastily forward and overtook the baron.

"Ah, here you are, — just in time!" said Michel.

"What is it?" asked the spy.

"Courtin, my dear fellow, I 'm the happiest man on earth!"

"Why so?"

"Quick! saddle me two horses!"

"Two horses?"

"Yes."

"And Mademoiselle Mary? don't you mean to take her back?"

"No, Courtin, I shall carry her off!"

"Where?"

"To Banlœuvre; where we shall make some plan to get away together."

"But will Mademoiselle Mary desert — "

Courtin stopped short; he was about to betray himself. But Michel was much too happy and excited to be distrustful.

"Mademoiselle Mary will not desert any one, my dear Courtin; we are to send Bertha in her place. Don't you see that I can't be the one to tell Bertha I do not love her?"

"Then who will tell her?"

"Don't trouble yourself about that, Courtin; somebody will tell her. Now, quick! saddle those horses!"

"Have you any horses here?"

"No, none of my own; but there are always horses, don't you understand, for those who travel for the good of the cause."

And Michel pushed Courtin toward the stable, where, in fact, two horses were munching their oats as if awaiting the young people.

Just as Michel was putting the saddle on the second horse the master of the inn came down, followed by Mary.

"I come from the South and am going to Rosny," Michel said to him, continuing to saddle one of the horses, while Courtin was saddling, but more slowly, the other. Courtin heard the password, but did not comprehend it.

"Very good," said the master of the inn, nodding his head in sign of intelligence.

Then, as Courtin seemed rather behindhand, he helped him to saddle the other horse and rejoin Michel.

"Monsieur Michel," said Courtin, making a last effort, "why go to Banlœuvre instead of to La Logerie? You would be more comfortable at my house."

Michel questioned Mary by a look.

"Oh! no, no, no!" she said. "Remember, my dear friend," she whispered, "that Bertha will be certain to return there to get news of us, and to know why the vessel was not at the place agreed upon; and I would n't for all the world see her before the friend you know of speaks to her. I think I should die of shame and grief if I saw her just now."

At Bertha's name, which he overheard, Courtin raised his head as a horse raises his to the sound of trumpets.

"Mademoiselle does not want to go to La Logerie ?" he said.

"But, Mary," said Michel, hesitating.

"What ?" asked the girl.

"Who will give your sister the letter that summons her to Nantes ?"

"As for that," said Courtin, "it is n't hard to find a messenger. If there is anything you want said or done, Monsieur Michel, I 'll undertake it."

Michel hesitated; but he, like Mary, dreaded Bertha's first outbreak of anger. Again he looked at Mary; she replied with an assenting sign.

"Then we will go to Banlœuvre; and you must take the letter," said Michel, giving Courtin a paper. "If you have anything to say to us, Courtin, you will find us there for the present."

"Ah, poor Bertha ! poor Bertha !" said Mary, springing on her horse. "How shall I ever console myself for my happiness ?"

The two young people were now in their saddles; they made a friendly sign to the master of the inn; Michel commended the letter once more to Courtin's care, and then they both rode away from the tavern of the Point du Jour.

At the end of the pont Rousseau they came near riding over a man who, in spite of the heat of the weather, was wrapped in a sort of mantle which almost hid his face. This sombre apparition alarmed Michel; he quickened his horse's pace and told Mary to do the same. After going about a hundred yards Michel turned round. The stranger had stopped, and, in spite of the darkness, was watching them.

"He is looking at us !" said Michel, feeling instinctively that they had just passed some great danger.

After the unkncwn man had lost sight of the riders he

continued his way to Nantes. At the door of the Point du Jour he stopped, looked about him as if in search of some one, and saw a man reading a letter by the light of a lantern. He went up to the man, who, at the sound of his steps, looked round.

"Ah, it 's you!" said Courtin. "Faith, you 've just missed getting here too soon; a minute earlier and you would have found yourself in company you would n't have liked."

"Who were those two young people who nearly knocked me over on the bridge?"

"The very ones I mean."

"Well, what 's the news, — good, or bad?"

"Both; but more good than bad."

"Is it to be to-night?"

"No; the affair is postponed."

"You mean failed, blunderer!"

Courtin smiled.

"It is true that luck has been against me since yesterday; but no matter! we must be satisfied with walking, not running, that 's all. Though to-day is a failure, in view of immediate results, I would n't take twenty thousand francs for it."

"Ah, ha! you are sure of that?"

"Yes, very sure. The proof is that I 've got hold of something already."

"What?"

"This," said Courtin, showing the letter he had just unsealed and read.

"A letter?"

"A letter."

"What 's in it?" said the man in the cloak, putting out his hand to take the paper.

"One moment. We will read it together. I prefer to hold it, because it is intrusted to me for delivery."

"Well, let us read it," said the man.

They both went up to the lantern and read as follows: —

Come to me as soon as possible; you know the passwords.
Your affectionate

PETIT-PIERRE.

"To whom is that letter addressed?" asked the man in the cloak.

"To Mademoiselle Bertha de Souday."

"Her name is not on the cover, nor at the bottom of the page."

"Because a letter might be lost."

"And you are commissioned to deliver that letter?"

"Yes."

The man gave a second glance at the paper.

"The writing is certainly hers," he said. "Ah! if you had only allowed me to accompany you we should have her by this time."

"What does that matter, if you are sure of her later?"

"Yes, true. When shall I see you again?"

"Day after to-morrow."

"Here, or in the country?"

"At Saint-Philbert-de-Grand-Lieu; that is half way between Nantes and my house."

"I hope next time you won't stir me up for nothing."

"I promise you that."

"Try to keep your word; I keep mine. Here's the money. See, I hold it ready, so that you may not have to wait for it."

He opened his wallet and showed the farmer, complacently, a mass of bank-bills amounting probably to a hundred thousand francs.

"Oh," said Courtin, "only paper!"

"Paper, of course, but signed 'Garat;' that is a good signature."

"No matter," said Courtin; "I prefer gold."

"Well, gold you shall have," said the other, replacing the portfolio in his pocket and crossing his mantle over his coat.

If the pair had not been so engrossed in their conversation they would have seen that a peasant had climbed the wall between the street and the court-yard by the help of a cart which stood outside, and was listening to what they said, and gazing at the bank-notes with an air which implied that in Courtin's place he would have been quite satisfied with Garat's signature.

"Very good; then the day after to-morrow at Saint-Philbert," repeated the man in the cloak.

"Day after to-morrow."

"What time?"

"Evening, of course."

"Say seven o'clock. The first comer will wait for the other."

"But you 'll bring the money?"

"You mean the gold? yes."

"All right."

"Do you expect to bring the matter to conclusion then?"

"I hope to. It costs nothing to hope."

"Day after to-morrow, at Saint-Philbert, seven o'clock," muttered the peasant on the wall, letting himself gently down into the street. "We 'll be there." Then he added with a laugh that sounded terribly like the grinding of teeth: "When a man is branded he ought to earn his label."

XXXII.

THE MARQUIS DE SOUDAY DRAGS FOR OYSTERS AND BRINGS UP PICAUT.

Bertha, who had left the farmhouse at La Logerie at the same time as Michel, reached her father after a tramp of about two hours. She found him extraordinarily depressed and utterly disgusted with the hermit's life he was leading in Maître Jacques' warren, though the latter had arranged it for his personal comfort and installed him safely in it.

From a feeling that was purely chivalrous, Monsieur de Souday had not been willing to leave the country so long as Petit-Pierre was in it, and in danger. Therefore, when Bertha came to him with the news of the duchess's probable departure, the old Vendéan gentleman resigned himself, though without heartiness, to follow the advice of General Dermoncourt and depart for the third time to foreign lands.

He and his daughter left the forest of Touvois at once. Maître Jacques, whose hand was now nearly well, though it lacked two fingers, wished to accompany them to the coast and assist in their embarkation.

It was midnight when the three travellers, following the high-road from Machecoul, reached the heights above the valley of Souday. As the marquis looked at the four weathercocks on his four towers, which were shimmering in the moonlight above the sea of verdure which surrounded them, he sighed. Bertha heard him and came nearer to his side.

"What is it, father?" she said. "What are you thinking of?"

"Of many things, my poor child," he answered, shaking his head.

"Don't take gloomy thoughts into your head, father. You are still young and vigorous; you 'll see the house again some day."

"Yes," said the marquis, with another sigh, "but —" he stopped, half choking.

"But what ?" asked Bertha.

"I shall never see my poor Jean Oullier again."

"Alas !" said the girl.

"Oh, house, — poor house !" said the marquis; "how empty you will seem to me without him !"

Though there was really more of egotism than attachment to his faithful servant in the marquis's regret, if Jean Oullier could have heard that lament it would certainly have touched him deeply.

Bertha resumed the subject.

"Do you know, father," she said, "I can't help fancying, though I am sure I don't know why, that our poor friend, in spite of all they say, is not dead. It seems to me that if he were really dead I should have wept more for him; a secret hope, which I can't explain, comes and stops my tears."

"That 's odd," interrupted Maître Jacques; "but I have just the same feeling. No, Jean Oullier is not dead; and I have something better than presumption to go upon, — I saw the body they said was his, and I could n't recognize it."

"Then what has become of him ?" asked the marquis.

"Faith, I don't know !" replied Maître Jacques; "but I keep expecting every day to get news of him."

The marquis sighed again. At this moment they were passing through an angle of the forest. Perhaps he was thinking of the hecatombs of game he and his faithful keeper had piled beneath those verdant arches, — a sight, alas! he might never see again. Perhaps the few words said by Maître Jacques had opened his heart to a renewed hope of recovering his old friend. The latter supposition is the more probable, for he urged the master of rabbits to make most particular inquiries about Jean Oullier's fate, and to let him know the result.

When they reached the seashore the marquis would not wholly conform to the plan laid down by Michel and Bertha for his embarkation. He feared that if they followed the shore along the bay of Bourgneuf, as agreed upon, they might draw the attention of the coast-guard cutter to the schooner; nothing would induce him to incur the reproach of compromising Petit-Pierre's safety for personal considerations, and he decided that the proper thing to do was for himself and daughter to go out to sea and meet the "Jeune Charles."

Maître Jacques, who had friends and accomplices everywhere, soon found a fisherman who was willing, for the consideration of a few louis, to take them in his boat to the schooner. The little craft was drawn up on the shore. The marquis and Bertha, instructed by Maître Jacques, who was familiar with all smuggling manœuvres, slipped into it and escaped the eyes of the custom-house officers who watched the coast. An hour later the tide floated the boat; the owner and his two sons, who served as crew, got into her and put out to sea.

As it still wanted half an hour till daybreak, the marquis did not wait till the boat was in the offing to come out of his hiding-place in the little deck cabin, where he was even more cribbed and confined than in Maître Jacques' burrow. As soon as the fisherman saw him he began to ask questions.

"You say, monsieur, that the vessel you expect is coming from the mouth of the Loire?"

"Yes," replied the marquis.

"At what hour was she to leave Nantes?"

"From three to five this morning," said Bertha.

The fisherman consulted the wind.

"The wind is southwest," he said; "the tide was high

at three o'clock. We ought to meet them between eight and nine; it will take them four hours to get here. Meantime, in order not to attract attention from the coast-guard, we had better throw over some drag-nets and make a pretence of fishing, to explain our being here."

"Make a pretence!" cried the marquis; "why, I should like to fish in good earnest! All my life I have wanted the opportunity for that sport; and faith, as I can't hunt in Machecoul this year, it is a fine compensation which Heaven sends me, — too fine to miss it!"

In spite of Bertha's cautions — for she feared her father's great height might attract attention — the marquis began to work with the fisherman at once.

The net was thrown out and allowed to drag for some time at the bottom of the sea; but before long, the Marquis de Souday, who had valiantly hauled on the ropes to bring the net to the surface, was as delighted as a child with the shining mass of eels, turbot, plaice, skate, and oysters which came up palpitating from the depths of the sea. He at once forgot his griefs, his hopes, his memories; he forgot Souday and the forest of Machecoul, the marches of Saint-Philbert, the great moors; and with them he forgot wild-boars, deer, foxes, hares, partridges, and snipe, and thought only of the shining population with smooth or scaly skins which each throw of the net produced before his eyes.

Daylight came.

Bertha, who till then had sat in the bows absorbed in thought, watching the waves as they parted at the prow of the little vessel and floated away in two phosphorescent furrows, — Bertha now climbed on a coil of rope to examine the horizon.

Through the morning mists, thicker at the mouth of the river than elsewhere, she could see the tall masts and spars of several vessels; but none of them carried the blue pennant by which they were to recognize the "Jeune Charles." She observed this to the fisherman, who assured her, with an oath, that it was impossible for the schooner, if she left Nantes during the night, to have made the open sea already.

The marquis did not give the worthy fisherman and his men much time for discussion, for he was so pleased with his taste of their trade that he allowed no spare time between the throws of the net; and any little pause that occurred he filled up with questions to the old sailor on the rudiments of nautical science.

It was in the course of this instructive conversation that the fisherman requested him to observe that by throwing the net as a drag they were forced to make long tacks, and that this method of proceeding would end by leading them astray from their post of observation. But the marquis, with that careless indifference which was the basis of his character, paid no attention to the skipper's argument, and continued to fill the hold of the boat with the products of the haul.

The morning went by. It was ten o'clock, and still no vessel approached them. Bertha became very uneasy; she mentioned her fears to her father several times, and at last with so much urgency that the marquis could do no less than consent to go nearer to the mouth of the river. He profited by the manœuvre, however, to make the old sailor teach him how to haul his wind, — that is to say, how to trim his sails so as to make as slight an angle with the keel as the rigging would allow. They were in the most tangled part of the demonstration when Bertha uttered a cry.

She had just seen at a few hundred feet from the boat a large vessel with all sail spread, to which she had hitherto paid no attention, as it did not fly the promised signal, and was now partly hidden by the jib of the boat.

"Look out! look out!" she cried; "there 's a ship coming down upon us!"

The fisherman saw in an instant the danger that threatened them, and springing to the helm he wrenched it from the hand of the marquis, then, without observing that he knocked the latter flat on the deck, he managed to get the boat round to windward of the ship, which was close upon them. Rapid as the manœuvre was, he could not prevent a slight collision; the boom of the lugger's mainsail grazed the side of the schooner with a loud noise, her gaff was entangled for a moment with the latter's bowsprit; the boat heeled over, shipped a sea, and if the skipper's rapid manœuvre had not enabled him to catch the wind, she might not have righted as rapidly as she did, or perhaps not have righted at all.

"The devil take that damned coaster!" cried the old fisherman. "Another minute and we should have gone to the bottom in exchange for the fish we 've just caught!"

"Go about! go about!" cried the marquis, exasperated by his fall. "After him! the devil take me if I don't board him and ask the captain what he means by such insolence!"

"Do you expect me," said the old sailor, "with my one sail and two poor jibs, to overhaul a craft of that kind? Look at his canvas, the villain! — every stitch set! And see how it draws!"

"Yet we must overtake him!" cried Bertha, running aft. "It is the 'Jeune Charles!'"

And she showed her father a broad, white band at the stern of the other vessel on which could be read, in letters of gold, "LE JEUNE CHARLES."

"Faith, you are right, Bertha!" cried the marquis. "Go about, my friend, go about! But why does n't he carry the signal agreed upon with Monsieur de la Logerie? And why, instead of steering for the bay of Bourgneuf, is he heading east?"

"Perhaps some accident has happened," said Bertha, turning pale.

"God grant it may not be to Petit-Pierre!" muttered the marquis.

Bertha admired her father's stoicism, but in her heart she murmured: "God grant it may not be to Michel!"

"Never mind!" said the marquis, "we must find out what all this means."

The lugger had meantime gone about, and again catching the wind, began to move rapidly through the water; this manœuvre on a vessel of her size could be done so quickly that the schooner, in spite of her volume of sail, did not get far in advance. The fisherman was able to hail her.

The captain appeared on the poop.

"Are you the 'Jeune Charles' from Nantes?" asked the skipper of the boat, making a trumpet of his two hands.

"What 's that to you?" answered the captain of the schooner, whose good humor did not seem to be restored by the certainty of having evaded the clutches of the law.

"I have folks aboard for you!" cried the fisherman.

"More messengers! A thousand devils! I tell you if you bring me any more such fellows like those I have had this night, I 'll run you down, you old oyster-dredger, before I let 'em aboard!"

"No, they are passengers! Are n't you looking out for passengers?"

"I 'm looking out for a good wind to take me round Cape Finisterre!"

"Let me come alongside," said the fisherman, at Bertha's suggestion.

The captain of the "Jeune Charles" looked at the sea, and not perceiving between himself and the coast anything to warrant apprehension, and desirous, moreover, to know if the passengers asking to come aboard were those for whom his vessel was chartered, he did as the fisherman requested, hauled down his foresail and mainsail and brought-to his vessel sufficiently to throw a line to the lugger and bring her alongside.

"Now, then!" cried the captain, leaning over his bulwarks, "what 's all this about?"

"Ask Monsieur de la Logerie to come and speak to us," said Bertha.

"Monsieur de la Logerie is not aboard of me," replied the captain.

"But," returned Bertha, in a troubled voice, "at any rate, you have two ladies, have n't you?"

"Ladies or passengers, I have n't any," said the captain; "except a rascal in irons down in the hold, where he is cursing and swearing fit to take the masts out of the ship and make the bulkhead he 's lashed to tremble."

"Good God!" cried Bertha, trembling herself. "Do you know if any accident has happened to the persons who were to embark on your ship?"

"Faith, my pretty young lady," said the captain, "if you would tell me what all this means you would oblige me greatly; for the devil is in it if I can make out anything about it. Last night two men came on board, both from Monsieur de la Logerie, with two different messages: one ordered me to sail at once; the other told me to stay where I was. One of these men was an honest farmer, — a mayor, I think, for he showed me a bit of a tricolor scarf. It was he who told me to up anchor and be off as fast as I could. The other, who wanted me to stay, was an old galley-slave. I put faith in the most respectable of the two, for, after all, his advice was safest, and I came away."

"My God!" exclaimed Bertha, "it must have been Courtin; some accident has happened to Monsieur de la Logerie!"

"Do you want to see the other man?" asked the captain.

"What man?" said the marquis.

"The one I 've got below in irons. You may recognize him, and then we shall get at the truth of this business, — though it is too late now to do any good."

"Too late to get away, — yes, that may be," said the marquis; "but not too late to save our friends if they are in any peril. Show us the man!"

The captain gave an order, and a few seconds later Joseph Picaut was brought on deck. He was still chained and bound; but, in spite of his bonds, he had no sooner caught sight of the coast of La Vendée, which he thought he was fated never to see again, than, without reckoning distance, or the impossibility of swimming, bound as he was, he tried to escape his captors and fling himself into the sea.

This happened on the starboard side forward, so that the passengers in the lugger, which was now to leeward near the stern of the vessel, could not see what happened; but they heard Joseph Picaut's cry and knew that a struggle of some kind was taking place on the schooner. The fisherman pushed his boat along the side of the ship, and they then saw Joseph Picaut struggling in the grasp of four men.

"Let me jump into the water!" he was shouting. "I'd rather die at once than rot in that hole!"

He might possibly have succeeded in flinging himself overboard if he had not at that instant recognized the faces of the Marquis de Souday and Bertha, who were looking up at him in amazement. "Ah, Monsieur le marquis! ah, Mademoiselle Bertha!" cried Picaut; "you will save me, won't you? It is for executing Monsieur Michel's orders that this brute of a captain treats me as he does; and the lies of that scoundrel Courtin are at the bottom of it."

"Now, then, I want to know the truth about all this," interposed the captain. "If you can relieve me of that blaspheming fellow I shall be glad enough; for I'm not bound for either Botany-Bay or Cayenne."

"Alas!" said Bertha, "it is all true, captain. I don't know what motive the mayor of La Logerie could have had to send you to sea without your passengers; but it is very certain that this man is the one who told you the truth."

"Unbind him, then! Ten thousand cat-o'-nine-tails! let him go hang where he pleases! Now, as for you, what do you want? Are you coming with me, or are you not? It won't cost any more to take you or leave you. I was paid in advance; and to ease my conscience I 'd rather like to take somebody."

"Captain," said Bertha, "is n't it possible to go back up the river and let our friends embark to-night as they meant to do last night?"

"Impossible!" replied the captain, shrugging his shoulders. "Think of the custom-house officers and the river-police! No, no; a plan postponed is a plan defeated. Only, I say again, if you wish to use my vessel to get over to England, I am at your service, and it shall cost you nothing."

The marquis looked at his daughter, but she shook her head.

"Thank you, captain, thanks," replied the marquis. "It is impossible."

"Then we had better part company at once," said the captain. "But before we do so, let me ask you to do me a service."

"What is it?"

"It is about a little note of hand which I will give you, duly signed, requesting you to draw my share of it when you draw your own."

"I 'll do anything to please you, captain," said the marquis, affably.

"Very good; then add one hundred lashes on the back of the fellow who fooled me last night, in addition to your own."

"It shall be done," replied the marquis.

"If he has any strength to bear them after he has paid what he owes to me," said a voice.

At the same instant a heavy body fell into the water, and the head of Joseph Picaut was seen about ten paces off, its owner swimming vigorously to the lugger. Once freed of his irons, the Chouan, fearful, no doubt, that some unforeseen circumstance should detain him on the vessel, had plunged head foremost over the schooner's bulwark.

The skipper and the marquis gave him each a hand, and Joseph Picaut clambered into the boat. He was scarcely there before he shouted: —

"Monsieur le marquis, tell that old whale up there that the brand on my shoulder is a cross of honor!"

"Yes, captain, that's true!" cried the marquis. "This peasant was sent to the galleys for doing his duty in the days of the Empire, — his duty as we see it, I mean; and though I don't wholly approve of the means he took, I can declare to you that he has not deserved the treatment you gave him."

"Very well," said the captain, "that's all right. Once, twice, thrice, will you come aboard, or will you not?"

"No, captain, thank you."

"Then good-bye, and better luck."

So saying, the captain signed to the helmsman, the schooner paid off into the wind, the sails were squared again, and the vessel sailed rapidly away, leaving the lugger stationary.

While the old fisherman was working his boat to shore, Bertha and her father held counsel together. In spite of Picaut's explanations (and those explanations were brief, the Chouan having only seen Courtin at the moment when he was seized and bound) they could not understand the motives of the mayor of La Logerie. His conduct, however, was plain enough, and seemed to them extremely suspicious, — although, as Bertha now told her father, he had shown a true devotion to Michel during his illness, and had often expressed to her the utmost attachment to his young master. The marquis, however, was strongly of opinion that his present tortuous behavior concealed some scheme that was not only dangerous to Michel's safety, but to that of their other friends.

As for Picaut, he declared plainly that he lived and breathed for vengeance only, and that if Monsieur de Souday would give him a suit of sailor's clothes to replace those which were torn from his back in the struggles he had gone through, he would start for Nantes the instant he touched land.

The marquis, convinced that Courtin's treachery was in some way connected with Petit-Pierre, wished to go to the town himself; but Bertha, who believed that Michel, finding the escape a failure, would return to the farmhouse at La Logerie, where he would expect her to join him, persuaded her father to put off entering Nantes till he could get some more definite information.

The fisherman landed his passengers at the Pornic point. Picaut, for whose benefit the skipper's son had given up his spencer and his oilskin cap, started across country in a bee-line for Nantes, swearing in every key that Courtin had better look out for himself. But before leaving the marquis he begged him to tell Maître Jacques all the particulars of his adventure, feeling quite certain that the master of the warren would fraternally assist in his revenge.

It was thus that, thanks to his knowledge of localities, he was able to reach Nantes about nine that evening; and going, naturally, to his old post at the Point du Jour, he overheard a part at least of the conversation between Courtin and the mysterious individual of Aigrefeuille, and saw the money, or rather the bank-bills, which Courtin did not regard as valuable until they were changed into coin.

As for the marquis and his daughter, it was not until nightfall that they ventured, notwithstanding Bertha's impatience, to start for the forest of Touvois; and it was not without actual grief of heart that the old gentleman thought of the happy morning he had spent among the fishes, reflecting that it would have no morrow, and that he was fatally condemned to live, for an indefinite time, like a rat in his hole.

XXXIII.

THAT WHICH HAPPENED IN TWO DWELLINGS.

Maître Jacques was not mistaken in his presentiments; Jean Oullier was living. The ball which Courtin had fired at random into the bush — on chance, as it were — had entered his breast; and when the widow Picaut (the wheels of whose cart had alarmed Courtin and his companion) reached him, she felt sure she was lifting a dead body. With a charitable sentiment, very natural to a peasant-woman, she did not choose that the body of a man for whom her husband had always, in spite of their political differences, expressed the utmost respect, should be left as food for the buzzards and jackals; she was determined that the good Vendéan should lie in holy ground, and she therefore placed him on her cart to take him home.

Only, instead of hiding him in the cart, as she had intended doing, she now laid him on it uncovered, and several of the peasants whom she met on the way stopped to look at and touch the bloody remains of the Marquis de Souday's old keeper. In this way the news of Jean Oullier's death was spread about the canton; and this was how the marquis and his daughters heard of it, and why Courtin, — who, the next day, wanted to make sure that the man he most feared was no longer living to terrify him, — why Courtin had been deceived and misled like the rest.

It was to the old cottage where she had formerly lived with her husband that Marianne Picaut now took the body. Since Pascal's death she had, in her loneliness, removed to the inn kept by her mother at Saint-Philbert. The cottage was nearer to Machecoul, Jean Oullier's parish, than the inn; to which, had he been living, she intended to take him and keep him safely concealed till he was well.

Just as the cart reached the open crossway we have often mentioned, one road of which led to the dwelling of the two Picaut brothers, it met a man on horseback following the road to Machecoul. This man, who was no other than our old acquaintance, Monsieur Roger, the doctor at Légé, questioned some of the little ragamuffins who, with the persistency and curiosity of their age, were following the cart. When the doctor heard that it contained the body of Jean Oullier, he left his present direction and followed the cart to the Picaut dwelling.

The widow placed Jean Oullier on the bed where Pascal Picaut and the poor Comte de Bonneville had lain side by side. While thus busy in doing him the last offices, and wiping the blood and dust which covered his face and matted his hair, the widow suddenly looked up and saw the doctor.

"Alas ! dear Monsieur Roger," she said, "the poor *gars* is beyond your help, more 's the pity. There are so many left on this earth who are not worth their salt that it is doubly sad when one like Jean Oullier is carried off before his time."

The doctor made the widow tell him all she knew of Jean Oullier's death. The presence of her sister-in-law and the children and women who had followed the cart out of curiosity, prevented the widow from relating how she had met him and left him a few hours earlier, full of life, except for his broken ankle; and how, returning after dark, she heard a pistol-shot and the footsteps of men who were running away, having no doubt murdered him. She merely said that coming from the moor she had found the body on the road.

"Poor, brave man !" said the doctor. "But after all, better such a death — the death of a soldier — than the fate that awaited him had he lived. He was seriously compromised, and if taken, they would have sent him, no doubt, to the cells on Mont Saint-Michel."

As he said the words the doctor went nearer to the body and mechanically took the inert arm to lay it over the breast; but his hand had no sooner come in contact with the flesh than the doctor started.

"What is it?" asked the widow.

"Nothing," replied the doctor, coldly. "The man is dead and only needs the last offices."

"Why did you bring his body here?" said the wife of Joseph Picaut, angrily. "We shall have the Blues down upon us! You know what happened the first time, and can judge by that."

"What does that signify to you," said the widow, "as neither you nor your husband live here any longer?"

"It is the very reason we don't live here," replied Joseph's wife. "We are afraid the Blues may be after us and destroy the little property that is left."

"You would do well to have him recognized before you bury him," interrupted the doctor; "and if that will be any trouble to you I'll undertake to remove the body to the château of the Marquis de Souday, whose physician I am." Then, seizing a moment when the widow passed close beside him, he whispered, "Get rid of these people." This was easy to do, as it was then near midnight. As soon as they were alone the doctor said, going close up to Marianne: —

"Jean Oullier is not dead."

"Not dead?" she cried.

"No. I said nothing before those people, because, in my opinion, it is of the utmost consequence that no one shall come here and disturb you in the care I am sure you will give him."

"God bless you!" said the good woman, joyfully. "If I can help to cure him you may count on me; I'll do it with the greatest happiness, for I shall never forget the friendship my poor husband felt for him. Neither shall I cease to remember that though I was then working against him and his, Jean Oullier would n't let me die by the hand of a murderer."

Then, having carefully closed all the shutters and the door of her room, the widow lighted a fire, heated water, and while the doctor examined the wound and tried to discover what, if any, vital organs were involved, she said good-bye to a few old gossips still lingering about the house, saying she was on her way back to Saint-Philbert. Then at the first turn of the road she darted into the woods and returned to the cottage by way of the orchard.

She listened at Joseph Picaut's part of the house; it was closed and she heard no sound. Evidently her sister-in-law and the children had returned to the hiding-place in which they lived while the husband and father continued to keep up, under Maître Jacques, the partisan warfare.

Marianne re-entered her own part of the house by the back door. The doctor had finished dressing the wound; the signs of life in the body were becoming more and more evident. Not only the heart, but the pulses too were beating; and on putting a hand before the lips the breath could be distinctly felt. The widow listened joyfully to what the doctor told her.

"Do you think you can save him?" she asked.

"That 's in God's hands," replied the doctor. "All I can say is that no vital organ is involved, but the loss of blood has been enormous; and I have also found it impossible to extract the ball."

"But," said Marianne, "I have heard that men can be cured and live to old age with a ball in the body."

"So they can," replied the doctor. "But now, how are you going to manage?"

"I did mean to take the poor fellow to Saint-Philbert and hide him there till he died or recovered."

"You can't do that now," said the doctor. "He must have been saved by what we call a clot, which has plugged the artery. The slightest jar now would prove fatal. Besides, in your mother's inn at Saint-Philbert, with so many going and coming, you could never conceal his presence."

"Good God! do you believe that in such a state they would have the cruelty to arrest him?"

"They would not put him in prison, of course; but they would take him to some hospital, and as soon as he recovers they would try him, and condemn him either to death or to the galleys. Jean Oullier is one of those obscure leaders who are so dangerous through their influence on the body of the people that the government will be pitiless toward him. Why don't you confide in your sister-in-law? Jean Oullier and she hold the same opinions."

"You heard what she said?"

"That 's true. I see you can't have much confidence in her pity. And yet, God knows, she of all people ought to be merciful to her neighbor, for if her husband were taken it might go far worse with him than with Jean Oullier."

"Yes, I know that," said the widow, in a gloomy voice. "Death is upon them all."

"Well," said the doctor, "the question is, can you hide him here?"

"Here? Yes, of course I can; he will even be safer here than elsewhere, because the house is thought to be empty. But who would take care of him?"

"Jean Oullier is not a girl or a baby," replied the doctor. "Two or three days hence, after the fever subsides, he can be left alone all day; and I 'll promise you to visit him at night."

"Very good; and I 'll be here all the time I can without exciting suspicion."

Marianne, with the doctor's help, carried the wounded man into the stable adjoining her room; she bolted the door carefully, placed her own mattress on a pile of straw, and then, appointing to meet the doctor there the following night, and knowing that the sick man would need only a little fresh water at first, she threw herself on a heap of straw beside him and waited patiently till he showed some signs of returning life, either by words or even by a sigh.

The next day she showed herself at Saint-Philbert; and when asked about Jean Oullier, replied that she had followed the advice of her sister-in-law, and fearing to be molested, had taken the dead body back to the moor where she had found it. Then she returned to her house on pretence of putting it in order. The following evening she again closed it carefully and went back to Saint-Philbert before dark, so that all the town might see her. But no sooner was it really night than she returned to Jean Oullier.

She nursed him in this way for three days and nights, shut up with him in the stable, fearing to make the slightest noise that might betray her presence; and though at the end of those three days Jean Oullier was still in the state of torpor which follows great physical commotions and loss of blood, the doctor advised her to stay at home during the day and return to him only at night.

Jean Oullier's wound was so severe that he really hung for a fortnight between life and death; fragments of his clothing carried in by the ball remained in the wound, where they kept up the inflammation, and it was not till Nature herself eliminated them that the doctor, to the widow's great joy, declared him out of danger. The good woman's care redoubled as soon as she felt he would recover; and though her patient was still weak and could hardly articulate more than a few words, and the signs were few of his being any better, she never failed to spend the night beside him and supply all his wants, taking at the same time the utmost precautions.

In spite of all drawbacks, however, no sooner were the foreign substances expelled from the wound, and a steady and healthful suppuration set up, than he made rapid strides to recovery. As his strength returned he began to worry greatly about those he loved; and he now implored the widow to bring him some news of the Marquis de Souday, Bertha, Mary, and even Michel, — Michel, who had actually triumphed over the old Vendéan's antipathies and conquered a place, however small, in his affections. Marianne did as he requested, and made some inquiries of the royalist travellers who stopped at her mother's inn; and she was soon able to relieve Jean Oullier's mind by telling him that his friends were all living and well; that the marquis was in the forest of Touvois, Bertha and Michel at Courtin's farmhouse, and Mary, in all probability, at Nantes.

But the widow had no sooner uttered the name of Courtin than a total change came over her patient's face; he passed his hand across his forehead as if to clear his thought, and rose in his bed for the first time without assistance. Friendship and tenderness had occupied his first returning thoughts; hatred and thoughts of vengeance now filled his hitherto empty brain, and over-excited it with all the more violence because it had been torpid so long.

To her terror, Marianne Picaut heard Jean Oullier again uttering phrases he had cried out in his fever, and which she had then taken for delirium; she heard him mingle Courtin's name with accusations of treachery and murder and of fabulous sums paid for some crime. Talking thus, her patient became violently excited; with flashing eyes, and in a voice trembling with emotion he implored her to go and find Bertha and bring her to his bedside. The poor woman believed his excitement was caused by a return of the fever, and was all the more uneasy because the doctor had told her that he should not return for two nights. She nevertheless promised the patient to do as he requested.

On this promise Jean Oullier calmed down, and little by little, overcome with the violence of the emotions he had just passed through, he went to sleep.

The widow, sitting on the straw beside the bed, and conscious of her own fatigue, felt her eyes closing and sleep overtaking her in spite of herself, when, all of a sudden she heard, or fancied she heard, some unusual sound in the court-yard. She listened attentively; it was certainly a man's step on the pavement which surrounded the pile of manure which lay in the yard of the two dwellings. Presently a hand unfastened the latch of the adjoining door, and Marianne heard a voice, which she recognized as that of her brother-in-law, cry out: "This way, this way!" and then the steps went up to Joseph's house.

Marianne knew that the house was empty; this nocturnal visit of her brother-in-law excited her curiosity. She did not doubt it concerned some scheme of violence such as all Chouans cherish traditionally, and she resolved to listen.

She softly raised the shutter of a hole through which the cows, when in the stable, poked their heads to eat the provender laid for them on the floor of the room itself. Through this narrow opening she crawled into her own room; then she climbed noiselessly up the ladder on which the Comte de Bonneville had met his death, entered the garret, which, as we know, was common to the two houses, and there, with her ear to the floor above her brother-in-law's room, listened attentively.

She came into the midst of a conversation already begun.

"Did you see the sum?" said a voice which was not completely unknown to her, though she could not recall the owner of it.

"As plain as I see you," replied Joseph Picaut. "It was all in bank-bills; but he insisted on having it in gold."

"So much the better! for bills, I must say, don't attract me much; it is difficult to get them taken in country places."

"I tell you he is to have gold."

"Good! and where are they to meet?"

"At Saint-Philbert, to-morrow night. You have plenty of time to collect your *gars*."

"My *gars!* are you crazy? How many did you say they were?"

"Two; that villain and his companion."

"Well, then, two against two; that 's the right kind of war, as Georges Cadoudal of glorious memory used to say."

"But you have only one hand now, Maître Jacques."

"That does n't matter, if the one hand is a good one. I 'll settle the strongest of the pair."

"No, no! that 's not in the agreement!"

"What do you mean?"

"I want the mayor for myself."

"You are exacting!"

"Oh, the villain! it will be little enough satisfaction for all he has made me suffer."

"If they have the money you say they have, there 'll be enough to compensate you, even if he had sold you on the shambles like a negro. Twenty-five thousand francs! You are not worth all that, my good fellow, I know!"

"Perhaps not; but revenge is what I am after, and I 've long wanted to get my hand on him, the damned cur. It was he who caused —"

"Caused what?"

"No matter; I know."

Joseph Picaut's meaning was unintelligible to every one except Marianne. She was certain that the recollection in the Chouan's mind related to the killing of her poor husband, and a shudder ran through her frame.

"Well," said Joseph's companion, "you shall have your man. But, before undertaking the matter, will you swear that all you have said is true, and that it is really a government agent on whom I am to lay hands? Otherwise, you understand, the affair won't suit me."

"The devil! Do you suppose any private man is rich enough to make presents like that to such a villain? Besides, those fifty thousand francs are only on account; I heard that plainly."

"And you could n't find out what they were paying such a large sum for?"

"No, but I can guess."

"Tell me."

"It is my opinion, Maître Jacques, that in ridding the earth of that pair of rascals we shall be killing two birds with one stone,—a private matter first, and a political stroke next. But don't be uneasy; I'll know more by to-morrow night, and let you know."

"*Sacredié!*" exclaimed Maître Jacques; "you make my mouth water. Look here! I retract my word; you can only have your man if I leave a bit of him!"

"Leave a bit of him! what do you mean?"

"Why, before you settle with him I want my share in the conversation."

"Pooh! do you suppose you could get his secret out of him?"

"Yes, if he is once my prisoner."

"He's a sly one!"

"Nonsense. You, who knew the old days, don't you remember how we used to make 'em speak,—those who did n't want to?" said Maître Jacques, with a dangerous look.

"Ha, yes! how we roasted their paws! Faith, you are right; that will serve my vengeance better still," replied Joseph Picaut.

"And then we shall find out why and wherefore the government sends those little gifts of fifty thousand francs, on account, to a country mayor. That knowledge may be worth more to us than the gold we pocket."

"Hey! gold has its value, especially to us who are old offenders and likely to leave our heads on the place du Bouffai. With my share, that is, twenty-five thousand francs, I can get away and live elsewhere."

"You shall do as you like. But come! tell me exactly where your pair are to meet; it is important not to miss them."

"At the inn of Saint-Philbert."

"Then that's all right. Is n't that inn kept by your sister-in-law, or pretty nearly? She shall have her share; it will be in the family."

"Oh, no, no!" cried Joseph. "In the first place she is not one of ours; and besides, she does n't speak to me since —"

"Since what?"

"My brother's death, there! since you force me to tell you."

"Ah, ha! so it was true, what they said, that if you did not strike the blow, you at least held the candle?"

"Who said that, — who said that?" shouted Joseph Picaut. "Name him, Maître Jacques, and I 'll hack him into pieces like that stool!" And suiting the action to the word, he dashed the stool on which he was sitting to the stone hearth and shivered it to fragments.

"Quiet! quiet!" said Maître Jacques; "what 's all that to me? You know I never meddle in family affairs. Come back to our own business. You were saying?"

"I was saying, don't mix the matter up with my sister-in-law."

"Then it must be settled in the open country. But where? They 'll be sure to come by different roads."

"Yes, but they will go away together. In order to get home, the mayor will have to take the road to Nantes as far as the Tiercet."

"Well, then, let 's ambush by the road to Nantes among the reeds; it is a good hiding-place. For my part, I 've made more than one good stroke just there."

"So be it. Where shall we meet? I shall leave here to-morrow, before daylight," said Joseph.

"Well, then, meet me at the Ragot crossways in the forest of Machecoul," said the master of warrens.

Joseph agreed to the place and promised to be there. The widow heard him offer Maître Jacques a night's lodging under his roof; but the old Chouan, who had his burrows in every forest of the canton, preferred those asylums to all the houses in the world, if not for comfort, at least for security.

He departed therefore, and all was silent in Joseph's part of the house.

Marianne returned to her stable and found Jean Oullier fast asleep; she did not wake him. The night was far advanced, — so advanced that she had only time to get back to Saint-Philbert before daylight. After arranging, as usual, everything that her patient might want during the morrow, she left the stable through the window.

As she walked thoughtfully along, the hatred she felt to her brother-in-law, because of her firm conviction that he had shared in the death of Pascal, and her deep desire for vengeance, which the loneliness and sufferings of her widowhood made daily more imperious, came over her. It seemed to her that heaven, by calling her providentially to the discovery of Joseph's secret intention of crime, put itself on her side; she believed she would be serving its designs (while satisfying her hatred) in preventing the accomplishment of this crime and the ruin and death of those she considered innocent. Her first idea had been to denounce Maître Jacques and Joseph either to the police or to those they intended to attack; but she now renounced that scheme and resolved to be herself, and all alone, the intermediary between fate and the victims of the intended crime.

XXXIV.

COURTIN FINGERS AT LAST HIS FIFTY THOUSAND FRANCS.

Petit-Pierre's letter to Bertha had not told Courtin much, except that Petit-Pierre was in Nantes and awaited Bertha. As to her hiding-place and the means of reaching it, the letter left him in the dark.

He did, however, possess an important piece of information in his knowledge of the house with two entrances, through which Michel, Mary, and the duchess had undoubtedly passed. For a moment he thought of continuing his method of spying, and of following Bertha when, in obedience to Petit-Pierre's injunction, she should seek the princess in Nantes; and he also thought of discounting to his profit the distress of the girl's mind when she should discover the true relations of Michel and her sister. But the farmer had now come to doubt the efficacy of the means he had hitherto employed; he felt he might lose, without recovery, his last chance of success, if accident or the vigilance of those he watched were to baffle once more his sagacity and cunning. He therefore decided to try another means and take the initiative.

Was the house which opened on the nameless alley to which we have several times taken the reader, and also on the rue du Marché, actually inhabited? If so, who lived there? Through that person, or persons, might it not be possible to reach Petit-Pierre? Such were the questions which reflection placed before the mind of the mayor of La Logerie.

In order to solve them it was necessary that he should stay in Nantes; and Maître Courtin at once resolved to give up returning to his farm, where it was very probable that Bertha had already gone to meet Michel on learning of the failure of his attempt to escape. He therefore boldly decided on his new course.

The next day, at ten o'clock in the morning, he knocked at the door of the mysterious house; but instead of presenting himself at the door on the alley, he went to that on the rue du Marché,—his intention being to convince himself that the two doors gave entrance to the same house.

When the person who answered the knock had satisfied himself through a little iron grating that the person knocking was alone, he opened, or rather half-opened the door. The two heads now came face to face.

"Where do you come from ?" asked the man inside.

Taken aback by the suddenness with which this question was put, Courtin hesitated.

"*Pardieu !*" he said, "from Touvois."

"No one is expected from there," replied the man, attempting to close the door; but it was not so easy to do this, for Courtin had his foot against it.

A ray of light darted into the farmer's mind; he remembered the words Michel had used to obtain the two horses from the landlord of the Point du Jour, and he felt certain that those words, which he had not understood at the time, were the countersign.

The man continued to push the door; but Courtin held firm.

"Wait, wait !" he said. "When I said I came from Touvois I was only trying to find out if you were in the secret; one can't take too many precautions in these devilish times. Well, there ! I don't come from Touvois, I come from the South."

"And where are you going ?" asked his questioner, without, however, yielding one inch of the way.

"Where do you expect me to go, if I come from the South, but to Rosny ?"

"That 's all right," said the servant; "but don't you see, my fine friend, that no one can come in here without showing a white paw?"

"For those who are all white, that is n't difficult."

"Hum! so much the better," said the man, a peasant of Lower Brittany, who was running over the beads of a chaplet in his hand while speaking.

But inasmuch as Courtin had really answered with the proper passwords, he showed him, though with evident reluctance, into a small room, and said, pointing to a chair: —

"Monsieur is engaged just now. I will announce you as soon as he has finished with the person who is now in his office. Sit down, — unless you want to spend the time more usefully."

Courtin saw that he had gained more than he expected. He had hoped to meet some subordinate agent from whom he could extract, either by trickery or corruption, the clues he wanted. When the man who admitted him spoke of announcing him to his master, he felt that the matter was becoming serious, and that he ought to be ready with some tale to meet the necessities of the situation. He refrained from questioning the servant, whose stern and gloomy countenance showed him to be one of those rigid fanatics who are still to be found on the Celtic peninsula. Courtin instantly perceived the tone he ought to take.

"Yes," he said, giving to his countenance a humble and sanctimonious expression, "I will wait Monsieur's leisure and employ the time in prayer. May I take one of those prayer-books?" he added, glancing at the table.

"Don't touch those books if you are what you pretend to be; they are not prayer-books, they are profane books," replied the Breton. "I 'll lend you mine," he continued, drawing from the pocket of his embroidered jacket a little book, the cover and edges of which were blackened by time and usage.

The movement he made in carrying his hand to his

pocket disclosed the shining handles of two pistols stuck into his wide belt, and Courtin congratulated himself on not having risked any attempt on the fidelity of the Breton, whom he now felt to be a man who would have answered it in some dangerous way.

"Thank you," he said, as he received the book and knelt down with such humility and contrition that the Breton, much edified, removed the hat from his long hair, made the sign of the cross, and closed the door very softly, that he might not trouble the devotions of so saintly a person.

As soon as he was alone, the farmer felt a desire to examine in detail the room in which he found himself; but he was not the man to commit such a blunder as that. He reflected that the Breton's eye might be fixed on him through the keyhole; he therefore controlled himself and remained absorbed in prayer.

Nevertheless, while mumbling his pater-nosters, Courtin's eyes did rove about the floor below him. The room was not more than a dozen feet square, and was separated from an adjoining room by a partition, in which there was a door. This little room was plainly furnished in walnut, and was lighted by a window on the court-yard, the lower panes of which were provided with a very delicate iron grating painted green, which prevented any one on the outside from seeing into the apartment.

He listened attentively to hear if any sound of voices could reach him; but as to this, precautions had doubtless been taken, for though Maître Courtin strained his ears toward the door and toward the chimney, near which he was kneeling, not a sound reached him.

But, as he stooped beneath the chimney-piece to listen better, Courtin caught sight, among the ashes, of several bits of crumpled paper lying in a heap, as if placed there to be burned. These papers tempted him; he dropped his arm, and then, leaning his head against the chimney-piece, he slowly stretched out his hand and took up the papers, one by one. Without changing his position he managed to open them, confident that his movements at that level were hidden from any eye at the keyhole by a table in the middle of the room.

He had examined and thrown away as of no interest several of these papers, when on the back of one (among a number of insignificant bills which he was about to crumple up on his knee and return to the ashes) he spied certain words in a delicate and refined handwriting, which struck him; they were as follows: —

"If you feel uneasy, come at once. Our friend desires me to say that there is an empty room in our retreat which is at your service."

The note was signed M. de S. Evidently, as the initials indicated, it was signed by Mary de Souday. Courtin put it carefully away in his pocket; his peasant craftiness had instantly perceived the possible good he might get out of its possession.

He continued his investigations, however, and came to the conclusion, from sundry bills for large payments, that the owner or lessee of the house must be intrusted with the management of the duchess's money-matters. Just then he heard the sound of voices and of steps in the passage. He rose hastily and went to the window. Through the grating we have mentioned he saw the servant escorting a gentleman to the door. The latter held in his hand an empty money-bag, and before leaving the premises he folded it up and put it in his pocket. Until then Courtin had not been able to see his face; but, just as he passed in front of the servant to go out of the door, Courtin recognized Maître Loriot.

"Ah, ha!" he said. "So he 's in it, is he? It is he who brings them money. Decidedly, I made a good stroke in coming here."

He returned to his place near the chimney, thinking that the time for his interview had probably arrived. When the Breton opened the door he found the visitor so absorbed in his orisons that he never stirred. The peasant went to him, touched him gently on the shoulder, and asked him to follow him; Courtin obeyed, after ending his prayer as he began it, by making the sign of the cross, which the Breton imitated.

The farmer was now shown into the same room where Maître Pascal had formerly received Michel; on this occasion, however, Maître Pascal was much more seriously employed. Before him was a table covered with papers, and Courtin fancied he saw the shining of various gold-pieces among a pile of opened letters, which seemed to have been lately heaped there as if to hide them.

Maître Pascal intercepted the farmer's glance; at first he was not displeased, attributing it to nothing more than the inquisitive interest which the peasantry always attach to the sight of gold and silver. Nevertheless, as he did not choose to allow that curiosity to go too far, he pretended to search for something in a drawer, and in order to do so threw up an end of the long green table-cloth so that it covered the pile of papers effectually. Then, turning to his visitor he said roughly: —

"What do you want?"

"To fulfil an errand."

"Who sends you?"

"Monsieur de la Logerie."

"Ah, do you belong to that young man?"

"I am his farmer, his confidential man."

"Then say what you have to say."

"But I don't know that I can do that," said Courtin, boldly.

"Why not?"

"Because you are not the person to whom Monsieur de la Logerie sent me."

"Who was it, then?" asked Maître Pascal, frowning with some uneasiness.

"Another person, to whom you were to take me."

"I don't know what you mean," returned Maître Pascal,

unable to conceal the impatience he felt at what he supposed to be an unpardonable piece of heedlessness on Michel's part.

Courtin, noticing his annoyance, saw that he had gone too far; but it was dangerous to beat too rapid a retreat.

"Come," said Pascal, "will you, or will you not tell me what you are here for? I have no time to waste."

"Bless me! I don't know what to do, my good gentleman," said Courtin. "I love my young master enough to jump into the fire for him. When he says to me 'do this' or 'do that,' I always try to execute his orders just as he gives them, so as to deserve his confidence; and he did not tell me to give his message to you."

"What is your name, my good man?"

"Courtin, at your service."

"What parish do you belong to?"

"La Logerie."

Maître Pascal took up a note-book, and looked it over for a few moments; then he fixed an investigating and distrustful eye on Courtin.

"You are the mayor of La Logerie?" he asked.

"Yes, since 1830." Then, observing Maître Pascal's increasing coldness, "It was my mistress, Madame la baronne, who had me nominated," he added.

"Did Monsieur de la Logerie only give you a verbal message for the person to whom he sent you?"

"Yes; I have a bit of a letter here, but it is n't for that person."

"Can I see that bit of a letter?"

"Of course; there 's no secret in it, because it is n't sealed."

And Courtin held out to Maître Pascal the paper Michel had given him for Bertha, in which Petit-Pierre begged her to come to Nantes.

"How happens it that this paper is still in your hands?" asked Maître Pascal. "It is dated some days ago."

"Because one can't do everything all at once; and I am

not going back our way just yet, and till I do I can't meet the person to whom I 'm to give the note."

Maître Pascal's eyes had never left the farmer's face from the moment he had failed to find Courtin's name on the list of those whose loyalty could be trusted. The latter was now affecting the same idiotic simplicity that had succeeded so well with the captain of the "Jeune Charles."

"Come, my good man," said Maître Pascal, "it is impossible for you to give your message to any one but me. Do so if you think proper; if not, go back to your master, and tell him he must come himself."

"I sha'n't do that, my dear monsieur," replied Courtin. "My master is condemned to death, and I don't wish to say a word to bring him back to Nantes. He is better off with us. I 'll tell the whole thing to you; you can do what you think best about it, and if Monsieur is not pleased, he may scold me; I 'd rather that than bring him here."

This artless expression of devotion reconciled Maître Pascal in a degree to the farmer, whose first answer had seriously alarmed him.

"Go on, my good man, and I will answer for it your master will not blame you."

"The matter is soon told: Monsieur Michel wants me to tell you, or rather tell Monsieur Petit-Pierre, — for that is the name of the person he sent me to find, — "

"Go on!" said Maître Pascal, smiling.

"I was to tell him that he had discovered the man who ordered the ship to sail a few moments before Monsieur Petit-Pierre, Mademoiselle Mary, and himself reached the rendezvous."

"And who may that man be?"

"One named Joseph Picaut, lately hostler at the Point du Jour."

"True; the man whom we placed there has disappeared since yesterday," said Maître Pascal. "Go on, Courtin!"

"I was to warn Monsieur Petit-Pierre to beware of this Picaut in town, and to say he would look out for him in the country. And that 's all."

"Very good; thank Monsieur de la Logerie for his information. And now that I have received it, I can assure you that it was intended for me."

"That 's enough to satisfy me," said Courtin, rising.

Maître Pascal accompanied the farmer as he went out with much civility, and did for him what Courtin had noticed that he did not do for Maître Loriot, — he followed him to the very door of the street.

Courtin was too wily himself to mistake the meaning of these attentions; and he was not surprised, when he had gone about twenty paces from the house, to hear the door open and close behind him. He did not turn round; but, certain that he was followed, he walked slowly, like a man at leisure, stopping to gaze like a countryman into all the shop-windows, reading the posters on the walls, and carefully avoiding everything that might confirm the suspicions he had not been able to destroy in Maître Pascal's mind. This constraint was no annoyance to him; in fact, he enjoyed his morning, feeling that he was on the verge of obtaining the reward of his trouble.

Just as he arrived in front of the hôtel des Colonies he saw Maître Loriot under the portico, talking to a stranger. Courtin, affecting great surprise, went straight to the notary, and inquired how he came to be at Nantes when it was not the market-day. Then he asked the notary if he would give him a seat in his cabriolet back to Légé, to which the latter very willingly assented, saying, however, that he still had a few errands to do and should not be ready to leave Nantes for four or five hours, and advising Courtin to wait in some café.

Now, a café was a luxury the farmer would not allow himself under any circumstances, and that day least of all. In his religious fervor he went devoutly to church, where he assisted at vespers said for the canons; after which he returned to Maître Loriot's hotel, sat down on a stone bench under a yew-tree, and went to sleep, or pretended to do so, in the calm and peaceful slumber of an easy conscience.

Two hours later the notary returned; he told Courtin that unexpected business would detain him at Nantes, and that he could not start for Légé before ten o'clock. This did not suit the farmer, whose appointment with Monsieur Hyacinthe (the name, it will be remembered, of the mysterious man of Aigrefeuille) was from seven to eight o'clock at Saint-Philbert-de-Grand-Lieu. He therefore told Monsieur Loriot that he must give up the honor of his company and go on foot, for the sun was getting low and he wanted to get home before night-fall.

When Courtin, sitting on the bench, had first opened his eyes, he saw the Breton servant watching him; he now paid no attention to him and seemed not to see him as he started to keep his rendezvous. The Breton followed him over the river; but Courtin never once betrayed, by looking backward, the usual uneasiness of those whose consciences are ill at ease. The result was that the Breton returned to his master and assured him that it was a great mistake to distrust the worthy peasant, who spent his leisure hours in the most innocent amusements and pious practices; so that even Maître Pascal, cautious as he was, began to think Michel less to blame for confiding in so faithful a servant.

XXXV.

THE TAVERN OF THE GRAND SAINT-JACQUES.

One word on the lay of the land about the village of Saint-Philbert. Without this little topographical preface, which shall be short, like all our prefaces, it would be difficult for our readers to follow in detail the scenes we are now about to lay before their eyes.

The village of Saint-Philbert stands at the angle formed by the river Boulogne as it falls into the lake of Grand-Lieu; the village is on the left bank of the river. The church and the principal houses are somewhere about fifteen hundred yards from the lake; the main, in fact the only street follows the river-bank, and the lower it goes to the lake, the fewer and poorer the houses; so that when the vast blue sheet of water, framed in reeds, which forms the terminus of the street is reached, there is nothing to be seen but a few thatched huts occupied by men who are employed in the fisheries.

Yet there is, or rather was at the time of which we write, one exception to this decadence of the lower end of the village street. About thirty steps away from the huts we have mentioned stood a brick and stone house, with red roofs and green shutters, surrounded with hay and straw stacks, like sentinels round a camp, and peopled with a world of cows, sheep, chickens, ducks, — all either lowing and bleating in the stables or clucking and gabbling before the door as they preened themselves in the dust of the road.

The road served as the court-yard of the house, which, if deprived of that useful resort, could still fall back upon its gardens, which are simply the most magnificent and productive of all the country round. From the road the crests of the fruit-trees can be seen above the farm-buildings, covered in spring-time with the rosy snow of their blossoms; in summer, with fruits of all kinds; and during nine months of the year, with verdure. These trees spread in a semi-circle about a thousand feet southerly, to a little hill crowned with ruins which looks down upon the waters of the lake of Grand-Lieu.

This house is the inn kept by the mother of Marianne Picaut. These ruins are those of the château de Saint-Philbert-de-Grand-Lieu.

The high walls and gigantic towers of this the most celebrated baronial castle in the province, built to hold the country in check and command the waters of the lake, the gloomy arches that once echoed to the clanking spurs of Comte Gilles de Retz as he trod its paved floors, meditating on those monstrous debauches which surpassed all that Rome in its decadence ever invented, — now, dismantled, dilapidated, swathed in ivy, overgrown with gilliflowers, crumbling on all sides, have descended, from degradation to degradation, to the lowest of all; grand, savage, terrible as they once were, they are now humbly utilitarian; they have been reduced at last to making a living for a family of peasants, descendants of poor serfs who in former days regarded them, no doubt, with fear and trembling.

These ruins shelter the gardens from the northwest wind, so fatal to fertility, and make this little corner of earth a perfect Eldorado, where all things grow and prosper, — from the native pear to the grape, the fruiting sorbus to the fig-tree.

But this was not the only service which the old feudal castle did to its new proprietors. In the lower halls, cooled by currents of impetuous air, they kept their fruits and garden products, preserving them in good condition after the ordinary season had passed; thus doubling their value. And besides this source of profit, the dungeons, where Gilles de Retz had piled his victims, were now a dairy, the butter and cheese of which were justly celebrated. This is what time has done with the Titanic works of the former lords of Saint-Philbert.

One word now on what they once were.

The château de Saint-Philbert consisted originally of a vast parallelogram enclosed with walls, bathed on one side by the waters of the lake and protected on the other side by a broad moat hollowed in the rock. Four square towers flanked the four corners of this enormous mass of stone; a citadel in the centre, with its portcullis bristling with spikes, defended the entrance. Opposite to the citadel, on the other side of the castle, a fifth square tower, taller and more imposing than the rest, commanded the whole structure, and the lake, which surrounded it on three sides.

With the exception of this fifth tower and the citadel, or keep, all the rest of the fortress, walls and main-buildings, had pretty much crumbled away, and time had not entirely spared the great tower itself. The rotten beams of the first floor, unable to support the stones which year by year slid down upon them in greater numbers, had sunk to the ground-floor, raising it by over a foot, leaving no other ceiling in the tower than the rafters of the roof.

It was in this lower room that the grandfather of the widow Picaut had principally kept his fruit, and the walls were lined with shelves on which the good man spread in winter the various products of his garden. The doors and windows of this portion of the tower had remained more or less intact, and at one of these windows could still be seen an iron bar covered with rust, which undoubtedly dated from the days of Comte Gilles.

The other towers and the walls of the main building were completely in ruins; the masses of masonry which had fallen had rolled either into the court-yard, which they obstructed, or into the lake, which covered them with its reeds at all times and its foam in stormy weather. The citadel, about as intact as the great tower, was crowned with an enormous mass of ivy which took the place of a roof; in it were two small chambers, which, notwithstanding the colossal appearance of the structure, were not more than eight or ten feet square, owing to the enormous thickness of the walls.

The inner court-yard, used in feudal days as the barrack-ground of the castle's defenders, obstructed by the rubbish which time had heaped there, — fragments of columns and battlements, broken arches, dilapidated statues, — was now impassable. A narrow path led to the great tower; another, less carefully cleared, led to a remaining vestige of the east tower, where a stone staircase was actually left standing, by which all persons desirous of enjoying a beautiful view could, after a series of acrobatic feats, reach the platform of the main tower by following a gallery which ran along the wall like those Alpine paths cut on the face of the rock between precipice and mountain.

It is unnecessary to say that, except during the period of the year when the fruits were stored there, no one frequented these ruins of the château de Saint-Philbert. At that period a watchman was stationed there, who slept in the keep; all the rest of the year the gates of the tower were locked and the place was abandoned to lovers of historical reminiscences, and to the boys of the village, who pervaded the old ruins, where they found nests to pillage, flowers to pick, dangers to brave, — all things of eager attraction to children.

It was in these ruins that Courtin had appointed to meet Monsieur Hyacinthe. He knew they would be absolutely deserted at the hour he named to his associate, inasmuch as the lingering ill-repute of the place drove away at night all the village urchins who, as long as the sun was above the horizon, scampered like lizards among the dentelled ridges of the old ruin.

The mayor of La Logerie left Nantes about five o'clock; he was on foot, and yet he walked so fast that he was an hour earlier than he needed to be when he crossed the bridge which led into the village of Saint-Philbert. Maître Courtin was somewhat of a personage in the village. To see him desert the Grand Saint-Jacques (the inn before which he usually tied his pony Sweetheart) in favor of the Pomme de Pin, the tavern kept by the mother of the widow Picaut, would have been an event which, as he very well knew, would have set the village tongues a-wagging. He was so convinced of this that, although, being deprived of his pony and never taking any refreshment except what was offered to him, it seemed a useless matter to go to an inn at all, the mayor of La Logerie stopped, as usual, before the door of the Grand Saint-Jacques, where he held with the inhabitants of the village (who, since the double defeat at Chêne and La Pénissière, had drawn closer to him) a conversation which, under present circumstances, was not unimportant to him.

"Maître Courtin," said one man, "is it true what they say?"

"What do they say, Matthieu?" replied Courtin. "Tell me; I 'd like to know."

"Hang it! they say you 've turned your coat, and nothing can be seen but the lining of it, — so that what was blue is now white."

"Well done!" said Courtin; "if that is n't nonsense!"

"You 've given occasion for it, my man; and since your young master went over to the Whites it is a fact that you 've stopped gabbling against them as you once did."

"Gabbling!" exclaimed Courtin, with his slyest look, "what 's the good of that? I have something better to do than gabble, and — and you 'll hear of it soon, my lad."

"So much the better! for, don't you see, Maître Courtin, all these public troubles are death to business. If patriots can't agree, they 'll die of poverty and hunger instead of being shot like our forefathers. Whereas, if we could only get rid of those troublesome *gars* who roam the forests about here and make trouble, business would soon pick up, and that 's all we want."

"Roaming?" repeated Courtin, "who are roaming? Seems to me that none but ghosts are left to roam now."

"Pooh! there 's plenty of them left. It is n't ten minutes since I saw the boldest of them go by, gun in hand, pistols in his belt, — just as if there were n't any red-breeches in the land."

"Who was he?"

"Joseph Picaut, by God! — the man who killed his brother."

"Joseph Picaut! here?" exclaimed Courtin, turning livid. "It is n't possible!"

"It 's as true as you live, Maître Courtin! as true as there is a God! He did have on a sailor's hat and jacket, but never mind, I recognized him all the same."

Maître Courtin reflected a moment. The plan he had laid in his head, which rested on the existence of the house with two issues, and the daily intercourse of Maître Pascal with Petit-Pierre, might fail; in which case, he had Bertha to fall back upon as a last resource. There would then remain, in order to discover Petit-Pierre's retreat, one means open to him, — the means he had already failed in with Mary, — namely, to follow Bertha when she went to Nantes. If Bertha saw Joseph Picaut all was lost; still worse would it be if Bertha put Picaut in communication with Michel! Then the part he had played in stopping the embarkation would be disclosed to the young baron, and the farmer was a ruined man.

Courtin asked for pen, ink, and paper, wrote a few lines, and gave them to the man who had spoken to him.

"Here, *gars* Matthieu," he said, "here 's a proof that I 'm a patriot and that I don't turn round like a weather-cock to the wind of any master. You accuse me of following my young landlord in all his performances; well, the fact is that I have only known within the last hour where he is hiding, and now I am going to lay hands on him. The more occasion I have to destroy the enemies of the nation, the better pleased I am, and the more I hasten to take advantage of it; and what 's more, I do it without inquiring whether it is to my advantage or disadvantage, or whether the persons I denounce are my friends or not."

The peasant, who was a double-dyed Blue, shook Courtin's hand heartily.

"Are your legs good?" continued the latter.

"I should think so!" said the peasant.

"Well, then, carry that to Nantes at once; and as I have a good many haystacks out, I rely on you to keep my secret; for, you understand, if I 'm suspected of having the young baron arrested, those stacks will never get into my barn."

The peasant made a promise of secrecy, and Courtin, as it was now dusk, left the inn on the right, made a tack across the fields, and then, returning cautiously on his steps, took a path which led to the ruins of Saint-Philbert.

He reached them by the shore of the lake, followed the moat, and entered the court-yard by a stone bridge which had long replaced the portcullis that gave entrance to the citadel.

As he entered the court-yard he whistled softly. At the signal a man sitting on the fallen masonry rose and came to him. The man was Monsieur Hyacinthe.

"Is that you?" he said, as he approached with some caution.

"Yes," said Courtin, "don't be alarmed."

"What news?"

"Good; but this is not the place to tell it."

"Why not?"

"Because it is as dark as a pocket. I almost walked over you before I knew it. A man might be hidden here at our feet and we not be the wiser. Come! the affair is in too good shape just now to risk anything."

"Very good; but where will you find a lonelier place than this?"

"We must find one. If I knew of an open desert in the neighborhood I 'd go there and speak low. But, for want of a desert, we 'll find some place where we are certain of being alone."

"Go on; I 'll follow you."

XXXVI.

JUDAS AND JUDAS.

It was toward the great middle tower that Courtin now guided his companion, not without stopping once or twice to listen; for, whether it was reality or fancy, the mayor of La Logerie thought he saw shadows gliding near them. But as Monsieur Hyacinthe reassured him after every pause, he ended by thinking it an effect of imagination; and when they reached the tower he opened a door, entered first, took from his pocket a wax candle and a sulphur match, lighted the candle and carried it cautiously into all the corners and angularities of the room to make sure that no one was hidden there.

A door, cut in the wall to the right and partly broken down by the rubbish of the ceiling, excited his fears and also his curiosity. He pushed it open and found himself in front of a yawning space from which a damp vapor was rising.

"Look there!" said Monsieur Hyacinthe, who followed him, showing Courtin a wide breach in the outer wall, through which they could see the lake sparkling in the moonlight. "Look at that!"

"I see it plain enough," said Courtin, laughing. "Yes, Mère Chompré's dairy needs repairing; since I was here last the hole in that wall is double the size it used to be. One might get a boat in now."

Raising his light and holding it outward he tried to look into the depths below; not succeeding, he took a stone and flung it into the water, where it fell with a sonorous noise that sounded like a threat, while the wash of the ruffled water against the steps and the foundations gave an answering ripple.

"Well," said Courtin, "there is evidently nothing there that can hear us but the fish of the lake; and the old proverb says, you know, 'Mute as a fish.'"

Just then a stone came rolling down from the roof along the tower wall and fell into the court-yard.

"Did you hear that?" asked Monsieur Hyacinthe, uneasily.

"Yes," replied Courtin. Unlike his companion, who seemed to grow more timorous in the gigantic shadow thrown by the ruins, the farmer recovered courage after convincing himself that no human being could possibly be lurking in the court-yard. "I 've seen large bits of masonry fall from the top of that old tower just from the blow of a bat's wing."

"Hé, hé!" exclaimed Monsieur Hyacinthe, with his nasal laugh, which was like that of a German Jew; "it is precisely the night-birds we have to fear."

"Yes, the Chouans," replied Courtin. "But no! these ruins are too near the village; and though a villain I thought I had got rid of has been seen roaming about here to-day, I feel sure he won't dare to risk a visit by night."

"Put out your light, then!"

"No, no; we don't need it to talk by, that 's true, but we have something else to do than talk, I 'm thinking."

"Have we?" said Monsieur Hyacinthe, eagerly.

"Yes. Come into this recess, where we shall be sheltered, and where the light can be hidden."

So saying he led Monsieur Hyacinthe beneath the archway that led down to the gate of the cellars, placed the light behind a fallen stone, and sat down himself on the cellar steps.

"Do you mean to say," said Monsieur Hyacinthe, planting himself in front of Courtin, "that you are going to give me the name of the street and the number of the house in which the duchess is hidden?"

"That, or something like it," replied Courtin, who had heard the clinking of gold on Monsieur Hyacinthe's person, his eyes sparkling with greed.

"Come, don't lose time in useless words. Do you know where she is living?"

"No."

"Then why have you brought me here? Ha! if I have a regret it is that I ever committed myself to a dawdler like you."

For all answer Courtin took the paper he had picked from the ashes of the hearth in the rue du Marché and held it out to Monsieur Hyacinthe, raising the light that he might see to read it.

"Who wrote that?" asked the Jew.

"The young girl I told you about, who was with the person we are in search of."

"Yes, but she is not with her now."

"That is true."

"Therefore I should be glad to know what good this letter is. What does it prove? How can it help our purpose?"

Courtin shrugged his shoulders and replaced the candle beside the stone.

"Really, for a city gentleman," he said, "you are not very sharp."

"What do you mean by that?"

"Don't you see that the duchess offers an asylum to the man to whom the letter is addressed, in case he is in any danger?"

"Yes, what next?"

"Next? Why, if we put him in danger he is certain to take it."

"And then?"

"Then we can search the house he goes to, and catch them all together."

Monsieur Hyacinthe reflected.

"Yes, the scheme is a good one," he said, turning the

letter over and over in his hand and holding it near the candle to make sure it contained no other writing.

"I should think it was a good one!" exclaimed Courtin.

"Where does that man live?" asked Monsieur Hyacinthe, carelessly.

"Oh, as for telling you where he lives, that 's another matter. I 've told you the scheme, and you think it a good one, — you said so yourself; if I told you how to carry it out I should just be giving myself away for nothing."

"But suppose the man does not accept the retreat offered to him, and does not go to the house where she is hidden?" said Monsieur Hyacinthe.

"Oh, that 's impossible if we follow a plan I 'll explain to you. His own house has two issues. We go to one with a posse of soldiers; he escapes by the other, which we leave clear; he sees no danger that way, but we follow him from a distance. You see for yourself the thing can't fail. And now, unfasten your belt and pay me the money."

"Will you come with me?"

"Of course I will."

"From now till the game is played you will not leave me a single instant?"

"I don't wish to, inasmuch as you only pay me half now."

"But remember this," said Monsieur Hyacinthe, with a determination scarcely to be expected from his pacific demeanor, "I warn you that if you make even one suspicious gesture, if I have the slightest reason to think you are deceiving me, I will blow your brains out."

So saying Monsieur Hyacinthe drew a pistol from his pocket and showed it to his companion. The face of the man who made the threat was cold and calm, but a dangerous flash in his eye convinced the other that he was a man to keep his word.

"As you please," said Courtin; "and all the easier for you because I have no weapon."

"That's a blunder," remarked Monsieur Hyacinthe.

"Come," said Courtin, "pay me what you promised, and swear to me that if the thing succeeds you will pay me as much more."

"You may rely upon my word, which is sacred; a man is honest, or he is not honest. But why do you want to carry this gold yourself, as you and I are not to part?" continued Monsieur Hyacinthe, who seemed to have as much reluctance to part with his belt as Courtin had eagerness to grasp it.

"What!" exclaimed the latter; "don't you see I'm in a fever to touch that gold, to feel it, to handle it? I am dying to know if it is really there, even if I don't touch it. Why, for the joy of that, for that one moment of happiness when I feel it in my fingers, I've risked all! You *shall* give it to me now, or I'll not say another word. Yes! for this one moment I've braved everything, I've summoned courage, — I who am afraid of my shadow, I who trembled and shook when I walked up our avenue at night. Give me that gold, give me that gold, monsieur! We have many dangers to face, many risks to run yet; that gold will give me courage. Give me that gold if you wish me to be as calm, as relentless as yourself."

"Yes," replied Monsieur Hyacinthe, who had watched the vivid lighting up of the peasant's dull, wan face as he said these words. "Yes, you shall have the money the instant you give me the address; but I will have the address, the address!"

One was as eager as the other for the thing each desired. Monsieur Hyacinthe rose, and took off his belt; Courtin, intoxicated with the metallic sound he heard, again stretched forth his hand to seize it.

"One moment!" cried Monsieur Hyacinthe; "give and take!"

"Yes, but let me first see if it is really gold you have there."

The Jew shrugged his shoulders, but he yielded to the

wishes of his accomplice; he pulled the iron chain that closed the mouth of the leathern bag, and Courtin, dazzled by the gleam of gold, felt a shudder pass through all his body, while with elongated neck, and fixed eyes, and trembling lips, he plunged his hands with ineffable, indescribable pleasure into the heap of coin which rippled through his fingers.

"He lives," he said, "rue du Marché, No. 22; the other door is in an alley running parallel with the rue du Marché."

Maître Hyacinthe released his hold on the belt, which Courtin seized with a deep sigh of satisfaction. But almost at the same instant he raised his head with a terrified look.

"What is it ?" asked Monsieur Hyacinthe.

"I heard steps," said the farmer, his face convulsed.

"No, no," said the Jew, "I heard nothing. I 've been a fool to give you that money."

"Why ?" said Courtin, clasping the belt to his breast as if afraid the other might snatch it back.

"Because it seems to double your fears."

With a rapid movement Courtin clutched his companion's arm.

"What is the matter ?" asked Monsieur Hyacinthe again, beginning to feel uneasy.

"I tell you I hear steps overhead !" said Courtin, looking up to the dark and gloomy space above them.

"Nonsense; perhaps you are ill."

"I don't feel well, that 's true."

"Then let 's leave the place; we have nothing more to do here, and it is time we were on the way to Nantes."

"No, no, not yet."

"Why not yet ?"

"Let us hide here and listen. People are about, and they are watching for us; and if they are watching for us they 'll guard the door. Oh, my God ! my God ! can it be that they are after my gold already?" moaned the farmer, trying to fasten the belt about his waist, but trembling so violently that he could not do it.

"My good friend, you are certainly losing your head," said Monsieur Hyacinthe, who proved to be the more courageous man of the two. "Let us put out the light and hide in the cellar. We can see from there if you are mistaken."

"You are right, you are right," said Courtin, blowing out the candle as he opened the cellar door and went down the first step into the inundated vault.

But he went no farther. A cry of terror burst from him, in which could be heard the words: —

"Help, help! Monsieur Hyacinthe!"

The latter laid a hand on his pistol, when a powerful hand seized his arm and twisted it as if to break it. The pain was so great that the Jew fell on his knees, the sweat pouring from his face as he cried out for mercy.

"One word, and I'll kill you like the dog you are!" said the voice of Maître Jacques. Then, addressing Joseph Picaut, who was just behind him, he went on: "Well, do-nothing, have n't you got him? What are you about?"

"Oh, the villain!" exclaimed Joseph, in a voice that was broken and breathless from his efforts to hold Courtin, whom he had seized the moment the latter opened the door to go down the cellar stairs, and who was now making desperate efforts to save, not himself, but his gold. "Oh, the traitor! he is biting me, tearing me. If you had n't forbidden me to bleed him, I'd soon have done for him."

At the same instant two bodies fell within six feet of Monsieur Hyacinthe, whom Maître Jacques was pinning to the ground.

"If he kicks too long, kill him, kill him!" said Maître Jacques. "Now that I know all I want to know, I don't see why not."

"Damn it! why did n't you say so before, and I'd have finished him at once!"

By a violent effort Picaut threw Courtin under him and

got a knee upon his breast, pulling a long-bladed knife from his belt, on which, dark as it was, Courtin saw the light flashing.

"Mercy! mercy!" cried the mayor. "I 'll tell all, I 'll confess all; but don't kill me!"

Maître Jacques' hand stayed Picaut's arm, which, in spite of Courtin's offer, was in the act of descending upon him.

"Don't kill him!" said Maître Jacques, "on reflection, he may still be useful. Tie him up like a sausage, and don't let him stir, paws or toes!"

The luckless Courtin was so terrified that he actually held out his hands to Joseph, who bound them with a slender, loose rope Maître Jacques had made his companion bring with him. Nevertheless, the wretched man would not release his clutch on the belt full of gold, which he held pressed to his stomach by his elbow.

"Have n't you bound him yet?" cried Maître Jacques, impatiently.

"Let me finish roping this paw," replied Joseph.

"Very good; and when you 've done bind this fellow, too," continued Maître Jacques, pointing to Monsieur Hyacinthe, whom he had allowed to get upon his knees, in which posture the Jew remained silent and motionless.

"I could do it faster if there were any light," said Joseph Picaut, provoked to find a knot in his rope, which in the darkness he could not undo.

"Well, after all," said Maître Jacques, "why the devil are we in a hurry? Why not light the lantern? It would do my soul good to see the faces of these sellers of kings and princes."

Suiting the action to the word, Maître Jacques pulled out a little lantern and lighted it with a sulphur match as imperturbably as if he had been in the depths of his forest of Touvois; then he turned the light full on the faces of Monsieur Hyacinthe and Courtin. By the gleam of that light Joseph Picaut saw the leather belt the farmer was hugging to his breast, and he sprang forward to tear it from him. Maître Jacques mistook the object of his action. Thinking that the Chouan's hatred to Courtin had got the better of him, and that he meant to kill him, the master of rabbits sprang forward to prevent it.

As he did so a line of fire darted from the upper part of the tower and shot through the darkness; a dull explosion was heard and Maître Jacques fell head foremost on Courtin's body, who felt his face covered with a warm and fetid liquid.

"Ha! villain!" cried Maître Jacques, rising on one knee and addressing Joseph, "ha! you have led me into a trap. I forgave you your lie, but you shall pay for your treachery!"

Raising his pistol, he fired at close quarters on Pascal Picaut's brother. The lantern rolled down the steps into the waters below and was extinguished; the smoke of the two shots made the darkness deeper.

Monsieur Hyacinthe, when Maître Jacques fell, rose pale, mute, mad with terror, and ran hither and thither about the tower, endeavoring to find an exit. At last he saw through a narrow window the sparkle of a star on the black vault of heaven, and with the strength of terror he climbed to the opening, giving no heed to the fate of his accomplice, and plunged head foremost into the lake.

The immersion into cold water calmed the blood which was rushing violently to his brain, and he recovered his self-control. He came to the surface of the water, where he kept himself by swimming. Then he looked about him to see in which direction he had better turn, and his eyes lighted on a boat moored at the breach in the wall through which the waters of the lake had forced their way into the tower. Shuddering, he swam for it, making as little noise as he could, climbed in, seized the oars, and was five hundred feet away from the shore before he even thought of his companion.

"Rue du Marché, No. 22," he cried. "No, terror has n't made me forget it. Success depends now on the rapidity with which I get to Nantes. Poor Courtin! — I may now consider myself heir to the last fifty thousand francs; but what a fool I was to give him the first! I might at this very moment have had the address and the money both. What a blunder! what a blunder!"

Then, to stifle his remorse, the Jew bent to his oars and made the boat spin across the lake with a vigor which seemed quite incompatible with his weakly appearance.

XXXVII.

AN EYE FOR AN EYE, AND A TOOTH FOR A TOOTH.

In order to follow Monsieur Hyacinthe for a moment we were obliged to leave our older acquaintance, Courtin, stretched on the ground, legs and arms tied, in thickest darkness, between the two wounded bandits.

The sound of Maître Jacques' heavy breathing and Joseph's moans terrified him as much as their threats had done. He trembled lest one or the other might revive and remember he was here, and execute summary vengeance on him; he held his breath, lest even its tremor might recall him to their minds.

And yet, another feeling was even more powerful in him than the love of life. He was resolved to keep to the very last moment the precious belt from those who might be his murderers, and he continued to hug it to his breast, even daring, in order to hide it, that which he would not have dared to save his life; he gently suffered the belt to slip to the ground beside him, and then with an almost imperceptible motion he crept in the same direction until he had covered it with his body.

Just as he had managed to execute this difficult manœuvre he heard the door of the tower rolling and creaking on its rusty hinges, and he saw a sort of phantom clothed in black advancing toward him, holding a torch in one hand, and dragging with the other a heavy musket, the butt-end of which resounded on the stones.

Though the shades of death were already darkening his eyes, Joseph Picaut saw the apparition; for he cried out, in a voice broken with agony: —

"The widow! the widow!"

The widow of Pascal Picaut, for it was she, walked slowly forward, without a glance at Courtin or Maître Jacques, who, pressing his left hand on a wound in his breast, was striving to rise upon his right; then she stopped in front of her brother-in-law and gazed at him with an eye that was still threatening.

"A priest! a priest!" cried the dying man, horrified by that awful phantom, which roused a hitherto unknown feeling in his breast, — that of remorse.

"A priest! What good will a priest do you, miserable man? Can he bring back to life your brother whom you murdered?"

"No, no!" cried Joseph; "no, I did not murder Pascal. I swear it by eternity, to which I am now going!"

"You did not kill him, but you let others do so, — if, indeed, you did not urge them to the crime. Not content with that, you fired at me. You would have been twice a fratricide in one day if the hand of a brave man had not pushed aside your weapon. But be sure of this: it is not the harm you tried to do to me that I am avenging. It is the hand of God that strikes you through me — Cain!"

"What!" exclaimed Joseph Picaut and Maître Jacques, "that shot — "

"I fired it; I knew I should surprise you here in the commission of another crime, and it was I who shot you in the act. Yes, Joseph, yes; you so brave, you so proud of your strength, bow down before God's judgment! — you die by a woman's hand."

"What matters it to me how I die? Death comes from God. I implore you, woman, give my repentance chance for efficacy; let me be reconciled to the Heaven I have offended; bring me a priest, I implore you!"

"Did your brother have a priest in his last hour? Did you give him, you, the time to lift his soul to God when he fell beneath the blows of your accomplices at the ford of the Boulogne? No, an eye for an eye, and a tooth for a tooth! Die a violent death; die without help temporal or spiritual, as your brother died. And may all brigands," she added, turning to Maître Jacques, "all brigands who, in the name of any flag, no matter which it is, bring ruin to their country and mourning to their homes, descend with you to the lowest hell!"

"Woman!" cried Maître Jacques, who had succeeded in raising himself, "whatever be his crime, whatever he may have done to you, it is not good that you should speak to him thus. Forgive him, that you may yourself be forgiven!"

"I?" said the widow. "Who dares to raise a voice against me?"

"The man whom, without intending it, you have sent to his grave; he who received the ball you meant for your brother-in-law; the man who speaks to you, I — I whom you have killed. And yet I am not angry with you; for, by the way the world wags now, the best thing men of heart can do is to go and see if that three-colored rag which seems to be to the fore here waves in God's heaven."

Marianne gave a cry of astonishment, almost of horror, when she heard what Maître Jacques told her. As the reader has doubtless understood, she had watched for the arrival of Courtin; then when he and his companion had entered the tower she went up the old staircase and along the outer gallery till she reached the platform of the tower; thence, through the rafters of the roof, she had fired on her brother-in-law.

We have seen how, in consequence of the movement made by Maître Jacques to save Courtin, he was the one to receive the shot.

This miscarriage of her hatred had, as we have said, bewildered the widow; but quickly recovering herself as she remembered what bandits these men really were, she said: —

"Even if that is true, if I did shoot one intending to shoot the other, my shot struck you as you were both about to commit another crime. I have saved the life of an innocent man."

A savage smile curled the pale lips of Maître Jacques on hearing her last words. He turned toward Courtin and felt in his belt for the handle of his second pistol.

"Ha! yes!" he said with a dangerous laugh; "here's an innocent man; I had almost forgotten him. Well, that innocent, since you remind me of him, I'll give him his brevet as martyr. I won't die without accomplishing my mission."

"You shall not stain your last hour with blood, as you have stained your whole life, Maître Jacques!" cried the widow, placing herself between Courtin and the Chouan. "I know how to prevent it."

And she turned the muzzle of her gun full on Maître Jacques.

"Very good," said Maître Jacques, as if he resigned himself. "Presently, if God allows me time and strength, I will make you know the two scoundrels whom you call innocent; but, for the time being, I will let this one live. In exchange, and to deserve the absolution I gave you just now, forgive your poor brother. Don't you hear the rattle in his throat? He will be dead in ten minutes, and then it will be too late."

"No, never! never!" said the widow, in a muffled voice.

Not only the voice but the rattle in Joseph's throat grew perceptibly weaker, and yet he did not cease to use his last remaining strength in beseeching his sister's pardon.

"It is God and not I whom you must implore," she said.

"No," said the dying man, shaking his head; "I dare not pray to God so long as your curse is upon me."

"Then address your brother, and pray to him to forgive you."

"My brother!" murmured Joseph, closing his eyes as if a terrible spectre were before him; "my brother! I shall see him! I shall be face to face with him!"

And he strove to push away with his hand the bloody

phantom which seemed to beckon to him. Then, in a voice that was hardly intelligible, and was indeed scarcely more than a whisper, —

"Brother! brother!" he murmured, "why do you turn away your head when I pray to you? In the name of our mother, Pascal, let me clasp your knees. Remember the tears we shed together in our childhood, which the first Blues made so bitter. Forgive me for having followed the terrible path our father enjoined on both of us. Alas! alas! how could I know it would bring you and me face to face as enemies? My God! my God! he does not answer me! Oh, Pascal, why do you turn away your head? Oh! my poor child, my little Louis, whom I shall never see again," continued the Chouan, "pray to your uncle, pray to him for me! He loved you as his own child; ask him, in the name of your dying father, to help a repentant sinner to reach the throne of God! Ah, brother! brother!" he murmured, with a sudden expression of joy that bordered on ecstasy, "you hear him, you pardon me, you stretch your hand to the child. My God! my God! take my soul now, for my brother has forgiven me!"

He fell back upon the ground from which, by a mighty effort, he had risen to stretch his arms toward the vision.

During this time, and gradually, the hatred and vengeance in the widow's face subsided. When Joseph spoke of the little boy whom Pascal loved as his own child, a tear forced its way from her eyelids; and when at last, by the gleam of her torch, she saw the face of the dying man illuminated, not with an earthly light, but by a sacred halo, she fell upon her knees, and pressing the hand of her wounded brother, she cried out: —

"I believe you, I believe you, Joseph! God unseals the eyes of the dying and lets them see into the heights of heaven. If Pascal pardons you, I pardon you. As he forgets, so I forget. Yes, I forget all to remember one thing only, — that you were his brother. Brother of Pascal, die in peace!"

"Thank you, thank you," stammered Joseph, whose voice now hissed through his lips, which were stained with a bloody froth. "Thank you! but — the wife, the children?"

"Your wife shall be my sister, and your children are my children," said the widow, solemnly. "Die in peace, Joseph!"

The hand of the Chouan went to his forehead as though he meant to make the sign of the cross; his lips murmured a few words, doubtless not said for human ears, for no one understood them. Then he opened his eyes unnaturally wide, stretched out his arm, and gave a sigh; it was his last.

"Amen!" said Maître Jacques.

The widow knelt down and prayed beside the body for some instants, — quite amazed that her eyes should be filled with tears for him who had made her weep so bitterly.

A long silence followed. No doubt this silence oppressed Maître Jacques, for he suddenly called out: —

"*Sacrediè!* who would suppose there was one living Christian still here? I say one, for I don't call Judas a Christian."

The widow quivered; beside the dead she had indeed forgotten the dying.

"I 'll go back to the house and send help," she said.

"Help? Don't do anything of the kind; they 'd only cure me for the guillotine; and, thank you, la Picaut, I 'd rather die the death of a soldier. I 've got it, and I won't let go of it now."

"Do you suppose I 'd give you up to the authorities?"

"Yes; for you are a Blue and the wife of a Blue. Damn it! the capture of Maître Jacques would make a fine figure on your record-book."

"My husband was a patriot, and I shared his feelings, that is true. But I have a horror, above all things, of traitors and treachery. For all the gold in the world I would not betray a person, not even you."

"You say you have a horror of treachery. Do you hear that, you cur?"

"Come, Jacques, let me send help," said the widow.

"No," said the Chouan bandit, "I 'm at the end of my tether; I feel it and I know it. I 've made too many such holes not to know all about it. In two hours, or three at most, I shall be disporting myself on the great open moor, — the last, grand, beautiful moor of the good God. But listen to me now."

"I am listening."

"This man whom you see here," he continued, pushing Courtin with his foot as he might a noxious animal, "this man, for a few gold coins, has sold a head which ought to be sacred to all, not only because it is of those who are destined to wear a crown, but because her heart is noble and kind and generous."

"That head," replied the widow, "I have sheltered beneath my roof."

In the portrait Maître Jacques had drawn she recognized the duchess.

"Yes, you saved her that time, la Picaut, I know it; and it is that which makes you so great in my eyes; it is that which leads me to make you my last request."

"Tell me what it is."

"Come nearer and stoop down; you alone must know what I have to say."

The widow went close to Maître Jacques and leaned over him and listened attentively.

"You must," he said in a very low voice, "tell all this to the man you have in your house."

"Who is that?" asked the widow, thunderstruck.

"The man you are hiding in your stable; the one you go every night to nurse and comfort."

"But who told you?"

"Pooh! do you think anything can be hidden from Maître Jacques? All I say is true, la Picaut, and it makes Maître Jacques the Chouan, Maître Jacques the Chauffeur, proud to be among your friends."

"But the *gars* is a very sick man; he has hardly strength to stand, and then only by leaning on the wall."

"He 'll find strength, never fear; he 's a man, — a man indeed such as there 'll be no more of after we have gone," said the Vendéan, with savage pride; "and if he can't take the field himself he 'll make others do so. Tell him merely that he must warn Nantes instantly, without losing a minute, a second; he must warn *he knows who.* That other man who was here is already on the march while we are talking."

"It shall be done, Maître Jacques."

"Ah ! if that rascal Joseph had only spoken sooner!" resumed Maître Jacques, raising his body to stop the blood which was rushing violently to his chest. "He knew, I am certain, what was plotting between these two villains; but he had them in his power and he never thought to die. Well! man proposes, and God disposes. It must have been the booty that tempted him. By the bye, widow, you ought to be able to find that booty somewhere."

"What must I do with it ?"

"Divide it in two parts; give one to the orphans this war has made, white as well as blue; that 's my share. The other belongs to Joseph; give that to his children."

Courtin gave a sigh of anguish; for the words were spoken loud enough for him to hear.

"No," said the widow, "no, it is the money of Judas; it would bring evil. I will not take that money for those poor children, innocent as they are."

"You are right; then give it all to the poor. The hands that receive alms cleanse everything, even crime."

"And he ?" said the widow, motioning toward Courtin but not looking at him, "what is to be done with him ?"

"He 's well bound and gagged, is n't he ?"

"He seems to be."

"Well, leave it to the man you have at your house to say what shall be done with him."

"So be it."

"By the bye, la Picaut, when you go for him, give him this roll of tobacco. I have no further use for it, and I think it will please him mightily. I declare, though," continued the master of warrens, "it makes me half sorry to die. Ha! I 'd give my twenty-five thousand francs prize-money to see the meeting of our man and this one; droll enough, that will be!"

"But you must not stay here," said Marianne Picaut. "We have a little bedroom in the citadel, where I will carry you. There, at any rate, you can see a priest."

"As you please, widow; but first, do me the kindness to make sure that my scoundrel is securely bound. It would embitter my last moments, don't you see, if I thought he would get loose before the shaking up he is going to have presently."

The widow bent over Courtin. The ropes were so tightly bound around his arms that they entered the flesh which was red and swollen on each side of them. The farmer's face, above all, betrayed the misery he was enduring and was paler than that of Maître Jacques.

"He can't stir," said Marianne. "See! Besides, I'll turn the key on him."

"Very good; it won't be for long. You will go at once, won't you, la Picaut?"

"Yes, I promise."

"Thank you. Ah! the thanks I give you are nothing to those the man you have over there will give when you tell him all."

"Well, well! Now let me carry you to the citadel, where you can have the care you need. The confessor and the doctor will both hold their tongues, don't be afraid of that."

"Very good; carry me along. It will be queer to see Maître Jacques die in a bed, when he never, in all his life, slept on anything but ferns and heather."

The widow took him in her arms and carried him to the little room we have mentioned, and laid him on a pallet that was kept there. Maître Jacques, in spite of the suffering he must have endured, in spite of the gravity of his position, continued, in the presence of death, the same merry but sardonic being he had been all his life. The nature of this man, totally unlike that of his compatriots, never belied itself for a single instant. But, in the midst of his lively sarcasms, flung at the things he had defended quite as much as at those he had attacked, he never ceased to urge the widow Picaut to go at once and fulfil the errand to Jean Oullier which he had intrusted to her.

Thus urged, Marianne only took time to lock the door and push the bolts of the fruit-room in which she left Courtin a prisoner. She crossed the garden, re-entered the inn, and found her old mother greatly alarmed by the noise of the shots which had reached her. Her daughter's absence increased the old woman's fears, and she was beginning to be terribly alarmed lest the widow had been made the victim of some trap by her brother-in-law, when Marianne returned.

The widow, without telling her mother a word of what had happened, begged her not to let any one pass into the ruins; then, flinging her mantle over her shoulders, she prepared to go out. Just as she laid her hand on the latch of the door a light knock was given without. Marianne turned back to her mother.

"Mother," she said, "if any stranger asks to pass the night at the inn say we have no room. No one must enter the house this night; the hand of God is upon it."

The person outside rapped again.

"Who 's there ?" said the widow, opening the door, but barring the way with her own person.

Bertha appeared on the threshold.

"You sent me word this morning, madame," said the young girl, "that you had an important communication to make to me."

"You are right," said the widow. "I had wholly forgotten it."

"Good God!" cried Bertha, noticing that Marianne's kerchief was stained with blood, "has any harm happened to my people, — to Mary, my father, Michel?"

And in spite of her strength of mind, this last thought shook her so terribly that she leaned against the wall to keep herself from falling.

"Don't be uneasy," answered the widow. "I have no misfortune to tell you; on the contrary, I am to say that an old friend whom you thought lost is living, and wants to see you."

"Jean Oullier!" cried Bertha, instantly guessing whom she meant, "Jean Oullier! It is he whom you mean, is n't it? He is living? Oh, God be thanked! my father will be so glad! Take me to him at once, — at once, I entreat you!"

"It was my intention to do so this morning; but since then events have happened which lay upon you a duty more pressing still."

"A duty!" exclaimed Bertha, astonished. "What duty?"

"That of going to Nantes immediately; for I doubt if poor Jean Oullier, exhausted as he is, can possibly do what Maître Jacques requests of him."

"What am I to do in Nantes?"

"Tell him, or her, whom you call Petit-Pierre that the secret of her present hiding-place has been sold and bought, and she must leave it instantly. Any place is safer than the one she is now in. Betrayal is close upon her; God grant you may get there in time!"

"Betrayed!" cried Bertha, "betrayed by whom?"

"By the man who once before sent the soldiers to my house to capture her, — by Courtin, the mayor of La Logerie."

"Courtin! Have you seen him?"

"Yes," replied Marianne, laconically.

"Oh!" cried Bertha, clasping her hands, "let me see him!"

"Young girl, young girl," said the widow, evading a reply to this request, "it is I, whom the partisans of that woman have made a widow, who urge you to make haste and save her; and it is you, who boast of being faithful to her, who hesitate to go!"

"No, no; that is not so!" cried Bertha. "I do not hesitate; I am going."

She made a motion to go out; the widow stopped her.

"You cannot go to Nantes on foot; you would get there too late. In the stable of this house you will find two horses; take either you please, and tell the hostler to saddle him."

"Oh," said Bertha, "I can saddle him myself. But what can we ever do for you, my poor widow, who have twice saved her life?"

"Tell her to remember what I said to her in my cottage beside the bodies of two men killed for her sake; tell her that it is a crime to bring discord and civil war into a region where her enemies themselves protect her from treachery. Go, mademoiselle, go! and may God guide you."

So saying, the widow left the house hurriedly, — going first to the rector of Saint-Philbert, whom she asked to visit the citadel, and then, as rapidly as possible, she struck across the fields to her own house.

XXXVIII.

THE RED-BREECHES.

For the last twenty-four hours Bertha's anxiety had been extreme. It was not only on Courtin that her suspicions fell; they extended to Michel himself.

Her recollections of that evening preceding the fight at Chêne, the apparition of a man at her sister's window, had never entirely left Bertha's mind; from time to time they crossed it like a flash of flame, leaving behind them a painful furrow, which the passive attitude taken toward her by Michel during his convalescence was far from soothing. But when she learned that Courtin, whom she supposed to have acted under Michel's directions, had ordered the schooner to sail, and when, above all, she returned, frightened and breathless with love, to the farmhouse at La Logerie, and did not find him whom she came to seek, then indeed her jealous suspicions became intense.

Nevertheless, she forgot all to obey the duty laid upon her by the widow; before that duty all considerations must give way, even those of her love. She ran to the stable without losing another moment; chose the horse that seemed to her most fit to do the distance rapidly; gave him a double feed of oats to put into his legs the elasticity they needed; threw upon his back, as he ate, the sort of pack-saddle used in those regions; and, bridle in hand, waited until the animal had finished eating.

As she stood there waiting, a sound, well-known in those days, reached her ears. It was that of the regular tramp of a troop of armed men. At the same moment a loud knocking was heard on the inn door.

Through a glazed sash, which looked into a bake-house that opened into the kitchen, the young girl saw the soldiers, and discovered at the first words they said that they wanted a guide. At that moment everything was significant to Bertha; she trembled for her father, for Michel, for Petit-Pierre. She therefore would not start until she had found out what these men were after. Confident of not being recognized in the peasant-woman's dress she wore, she passed through the bake-house and entered the kitchen. A lieutenant was in command of the little squad.

"Do you mean," he was saying to Mère Chompré, "that there 's not a man in the house, — not one ?"

"No, monsieur; my daughter is a widow; and the only hostler we have is out somewhere, but I don't know where."

"Well, your daughter is the person I want. If she were here she would serve us as guide, as she did at the Springs of Baugé one famous night; or, if she could n't come herself, she might tell us of some one to take her place. I know I could trust her; but these miserable peasants, half Chouans, whom we compel to guide us against their will, never leave us an easy moment."

"Mistress Picaut is absent; but perhaps we can supply some one in her place," said Bertha, advancing resolutely. "Are you going far, gentlemen ?"

"Bless my soul! a pretty girl!" said the young officer, approaching her. "Guide me where you will, my beauty, and the devil take me if I don't follow you!"

Bertha lowered her eyes and twisted the corner of her apron like a bashful village-girl, as she answered: —

"If it is n't very far from here, and the mistress is willing, I 'll go with you myself. I know the neighborhood."

"Agreed!" cried the lieutenant.

"But on one condition," continued Bertha, — "that some one shall bring me back here. I am afraid to be out in the roads alone."

"God forbid I should yield that privilege to any one, my dear, even if it costs me my epaulets!" said the officer. "Do you know the way to Banlœuvre?"

At the name of the farmhouse belonging to Michel, where she had lived herself for some days with the marquis and Petit-Pierre, Bertha felt a shudder run through her body, a cold sweat came upon her forehead, her heart beat violently, but she managed to master her emotion.

"Banlœuvre?" she repeated. "No, that 's not in our parts. Is it a village or a château, Banlœuvre?"

"It is a farmhouse."

"A farmhouse! Whom does it belong to?"

"To a gentleman of your neighborhood."

"Are you billeted at Banlœuvre?"

"No; we have an expedition there."

"What is an expedition?"

"Well done!" cried the lieutenant. "Here 's a pretty girl who wants information!"

"Natural enough, too. If I take you, or get some one to take you to Banlœuvre, of course I want to know why you are going there."

"We are going," said the sub-lieutenant, joining in the conversation for the sake of showing his wit, "to give a white such a dose of lead that he 'll turn blue."

"Ah!" cried Bertha, unable to repress the exclamation.

"Hey! what 's the matter with you?" asked the lieutenant. "If we had told you the name of the man we are going to arrest, I should have said you were in love with him."

"I?" said Bertha, calling up her strength of mind to hide the terror in her heart. "I, in love with a gentleman?"

"Kings have married shepherdesses," said the sub-lieutenant, who seemed to be of a comic humor.

"Well, well!" cried the lieutenant; "here 's the shepherdess fainting away like a fine lady."

"I? fainting!" exclaimed Bertha, endeavoring to laugh. "Nonsense, we don't have city manners here!"

"Nevertheless, you are as pale as your linen, my pretty girl."

"Goodness! you talk of shooting a man as you would a rabbit in a hedge!"

"Not at all the same thing," said the sub-lieutenant; "for a rabbit is good to eat, whereas a dead Chouan is good for nothing."

Bertha could not prevent her proud, energetic face from betraying, by its expression, the disgust she felt at the jokes of the young officer.

"Ah, *ça!*" said the lieutenant, "you are not as patriotic as your mistress. I see we sha'n't get much help from you."

"I am patriotic; but much as I hate my enemies, I can't see them killed with a dry eye."

"Pooh!" said the officer, "you 'll get accustomed to it, just as we soldiers get accustomed to sleeping on the high-roads instead of our beds. To-night, when the letter of that cursèd peasant came to the guard-house at Saint-Martin, and obliged me to start off at once, I damned the State to all the devils. Well, I now see I was wrong, for it has its compensations, — in fact, instead of cursing and swearing, I find the expedition charming."

So saying, and as if to add to the pleasures of the situation, he stooped and tried to snatch a kiss from the neck of the young girl. Bertha, who did not suspect his amorous intention, felt the young man's breath upon her face and started away, red as a pomegranate, her nostrils quivering, her eyes sparkling with indignation.

"Oh, oh!" continued the lieutenant, "you are not going to get angry for a silly kiss, are you, my beauty?"

"Do you think, because I am a poor country-girl, that I can be insulted with impunity?"

"'Insulted with impunity'! hey, what fine language!" said the sub-lieutenant; "and they told us we were coming to a land of savages."

"Do you know," said the lieutenant, looking fixedly at Bertha, "that I 've a great mind to do something."

"Do what?"

"Arrest you on suspicion, and not let you off till you pay me the ransom I would set upon your liberty."

"What would that be?"

"A kiss."

"I can't let you kiss me, because you are neither my father, nor brother, nor husband."

"Are they the only ones who will have the right to put their lips to those pretty cheeks?"

"Of course they are."

"Why so?"

"I don't wish to forget my duty."

"Your duty! oh, you little joker!"

"Don't you think we peasant-girls have our duties as well as you soldiers have yours? Come" (Bertha tried to laugh), "if I were to ask you the name of the man you are going to arrest, and it would be against your duty to tell it, would you tell it to me?"

"Faith," said the young man, "I should n't fail much in duty if I did tell you; for there is n't, I think, the slightest harm in your knowing it."

"But suppose there were any harm?"

"Oh, then — but I declare I don't know; your eyes have turned my head, and I really can't say what I should do. Well, yes, if you are really as curious as I am weak, I 'll tell you that name and betray the country; only, I must be paid for it with a kiss."

Bertha's apprehensions were so great, — she was so convinced that Michel was the object of the expedition, — that she forgot, with her usual impetuosity, all caution, and without reflecting on the suspicions she gave rise to by her persistency, she abruptly offered him her cheek. He took two resounding kisses.

"Give and take," he said, laughing. "The name of the man we are going to arrest is Monsieur de Vincé."

Bertha drew back and looked at the officer. A misgiving crossed her mind that he had tricked her.

"Come, let 's start," said the lieutenant to his subordinate. "I shall go and ask the mayor for the guide we evidently can't get here." Turning to Bertha he added, "Any guide he may give me won't please me as you do, my dear," and he gave an affected sigh. Then he called to his men: "Forward there, march!"

Before starting himself he asked for a match to light his cigar. Bertha searched in vain on the mantel-piece. The officer then took a paper from his pocket and lighted it at the lamp. Bertha watched his movements and threw a glance at the paper, which the flames were beginning to shrivel up, and she distinctly saw there Michel's name.

"I suspected it," thought she. "He lied to me. Yes, yes, it is Michel they are going to arrest."

As the officer threw down the half-burned paper, she put her foot upon it with some difficulty, and the officer took advantage of her motions to seize another kiss.

"Hush!" he said, putting his finger on his lip; "you are not a peasant-girl. Look out for yourself, if you have any reason for hiding. If you play your part as badly with those who are seeking you as you have with me, who am not instructed to arrest you, you are lost."

So saying, he hastily turned away, fearing perhaps to be lost himself. He was no sooner out of sight than Bertha seized the remains of the paper. It contained the denunciation that Courtin had sent to Nantes by the peasant Matthieu, which the latter, to save himself trouble, had put into the first post-office he came to. This post-office was that of Saint-Martin, the next village to Saint-Philbert.

Enough remained unburned of Courtin's writing to enlighten Bertha as to the object of the troop now advancing on Banlœuvre. Her head swam. If the sentence already pronounced on the young man were executed by the soldiers, Michel would be dead in two hours; she saw him, a bloody corpse, reddening the earth about him. Her mind gave way.

"Where is Jean Oullier?" she cried to the old landlady.

"Jean Oullier?" said the latter, gazing stolidly at the girl. "I don't know what you mean."

"I ask you, where is Jean Oullier?"

"Is n't Jean Oullier dead?" replied Mère Chompré.

"But your daughter, where has your daughter gone?"

"I 'm sure I don't know; she never tells me where she is going when she goes out. She is old enough to be the mistress of her own actions."

Bertha thought of the Picaut cottage; but to go there would take her an hour, and it might prove a waste of time. That hour would suffice to insure Michel's death.

"She will be back in a minute," she said to the old woman. "When she comes tell her I could not go as soon as she expected to the place she knows of; but I will be there before daylight."

Running to the stables, she slipped the bridle on the horse, sprang upon his back, rode him out of the building, and giving him a vigorous blow with a switch, put him at once into a gait that was neither trot nor gallop, but fast enough to gain half an hour at least on the soldiers. As she crossed the market-place of Saint-Philbert she heard on her right the receding footsteps of the little troop.

Then she took her bearings, passed the houses, dashed her horse into the river Boulogne, and came out to join the road a little above the forest of Machecoul.

XXXIX.

A WOUNDED SOUL.

Fortunately for Bertha the horse she was riding had better qualities than his appearance denoted. He was a little Breton beast which, when quiet, seemed gloomy, sad, depressed, like the men of his native region; but once warmed to action (like them again) he increased every moment in vigor and energy. With flaring nostrils, and his tangled mane floating in the wind, he attained to a gallop; presently his gallop became a run. Plains, valleys, and hedges passed and disappeared behind him with fantastic rapidity, while Bertha, bending low upon his neck, gave rein and urged him onward with voice and whip.

The belated peasants whom she met, seeing the horse and its rider fade into the distance as quickly as they had seen them appear, took them for phantoms, and signed themselves devoutly behind them.

Rapid as this going was, it was not as fast as Bertha's heart demanded; to her a second seemed a week, a minute a year. She felt the terrible responsibility that rested on her, — the responsibility of blood and death and shame. Could she save Michel, and, having saved him, should she still have time to avert the danger that threatened Petit-Pierre? That was the question.

A thousand confused ideas coursed through her brain; she blamed herself for not having given Marianne's mother more careful instructions; she was seized with vertigo at the thought that after the headlong rush of that mad ride, the poor little Breton horse would surely be unable to return from Banlœuvre to Nantes; she reproached herself for using in the interests of her love the time and resources which might be necessary to save the noblest head in France; then she reflected that unless others possessed, as she did, the passwords, it would be impossible for any one to reach the illustrious fugitive. So thinking, and torn by a thousand conflicting emotions, culminating in a sort of intoxication or madness, she pressed her horse with her heel and continued her wild ride, which, at any rate, cooled her brain, burning with thoughts that were like to burst it.

At the end of an hour she reached the forest of Touvois. There she was compelled to slacken speed; the way was full of quagmires. Twice the little horse plunged into them. She was forced to let him walk, calculating that in any case she had gained sufficiently on the soldiers to give Michel time to escape.

She hoped; she breathed. A moment of joyful satisfaction came to quench the all-consuming anguish of her fears; once more Michel would owe to her his life!

We must have loved, we must have known the ineffable joy of sacrifice, to comprehend what there was of happiness in this immolation of herself to the man she loved, and the proud joy with which Bertha thought for an instant that Michel's life, which she was now about to save, might cost her dear.

Her mind was full of these thoughts when she saw the white walls of the farmhouse shining in the moonlight, framed by the dark tufts of the nut-trees. The gate of the farmyard was open. Bertha dismounted, fastened her horse to a ring in the outer wall, and crossed the yard on foot.

The manure which covered the ground deadened the sound of her steps; no dog barked to welcome her, or to signify her presence to the inmates. To her great surprise Bertha noticed a horse standing, saddled and bridled, by the door of the house. The horse might belong to Michel;

but then again it might belong to a stranger. Bertha was determined to make sure before entering the house.

One of the shutters in the room where Petit-Pierre had asked her hand of her father in Michel's name stood open. Bertha went softly up to it and looked within.

Hardly had her eyes rested on the interior of the room when she gave a stifled cry and almost fainted. She had seen Michel at Mary's knees; one hand was round her sister's waist, and the latter's hand was toying with his hair; their lips were smiling to each other; their eyes shone with that expression of joy which can never be mistaken by hearts that have loved.

The prostration caused by this discovery lasted but a second. Bertha rushed to the door of the room, pushed it open violently, and appeared on the threshold like an embodiment of Vengeance, her hair dishevelled, her eyes flaming, her face livid, her breast heaving.

Mary gave a cry and fell on her knees with her face in her hands. She had guessed the whole at a single glance, so frightfully convulsed was Bertha's face.

Michel, horrified by Bertha's look, rose hastily, and, as though he found himself suddenly in presence of an enemy, he mechanically put his hand on his arms.

"Strike!" cried Bertha, who saw his action; "strike, miserable man! It will be a fit conclusion to your baseness and your treachery!"

"Bertha," stammered Michel, "let me tell you, let me explain to you!"

"To your knees! to your knees! — you and your accomplice!" cried Bertha. "Say on your knees the lies you will invent for your defence! Oh, the vile wretch! And I have flown here to save his life! I, half mad with terror and despair for the fate that was hanging over him; I, who have forgotten all, all, honor, duty; I, who laid my life at his feet, who had but one thought, one object, one desire, one wish, — that of saying to him, 'Michel, look! see how I love you!' — I come, and I find him betraying his word, denying his promises, faithless to sacred ties — I will not say of love, but of gratitude — and with whom? for whom? The being I loved next to him in this world, the companion of my childhood, — my sister! Was there no other woman to seduce? Speak! speak, wretch!" went on Bertha, seizing the young man's arm and shaking it with violence. "Or did you wish, in deserting me, to take away my only consolation, — the heart of that second self I called a sister?"

"Bertha, listen to me!" said Michel. "Listen to me, I implore you! We are not, thank God, as guilty as you think us. Oh, if you did but know, Bertha!"

"I will hear nothing; I listen only to my heart, which grief is breaking, which despair has crushed; I listen only to the voice within me which says you are a coward! base! My God! my God!" she cried, grasping her hair in her clenched hands, "my God! is this the reward of my tenderness, which was so blind that my eyes refused to see, my ears to hear when they told me that this child, this timid, trembling, wavering, unmanly creature, was not worthy of my love? Oh, poor fool that I have been! I hoped that gratitude would bind him to her who took pity on his weakness, who braved all prejudice and public opinion to drag him from the bog of infamy and make his name, his degraded name, an honorable and honored one!"

"Ah!" cried Michel, rising, "enough! enough!"

"Yes, enough of a degraded name!" repeated Bertha. "That touches you, does it? So much the better; I will say it again and again. Yes, a name soiled and degraded by all that is most odious, cowardly, infamous, — by treachery! Oh, family of betrayers! The son continues in the way of the father; I ought to have expected it."

"Mademoiselle, mademoiselle!" said Michel, "you abuse the privilege of your sex in thus insulting me; and not only me, but all that a man holds most sacred, — the memory of his father!"

"Sex! sex! So I have a sex now, have I? I had none

when you were betraying me at the feet of that poor fool, none when you were making me the most miserable of creatures; but now, because I do not lament and tear my hair and beat my breast and drag myself to your feet, now, now you suddenly discover I am a woman, a being to be respected because she is gentle, to whom suffering must be spared because she is weak! No, no! for you I have no longer a sex. You have before you, from this hour, a being whom you have mortally offended, and who returns you insult for insult. Baron de la Logerie, coward and traitor double-dyed is he who seduces the sister of his betrothed wife, — yes, I was the affianced wife of that man! Baron de la Logerie, not only are you a traitor and a coward, but you are the son of a traitor and a coward; your father was the infamous wretch who sold and betrayed Charette. He, at least, paid the penalty of his crime, which he expiated with his life. You have been told that he was killed in hunting, — a benevolent lie, which I here refute. He was killed by one who saw him do his deed of treachery; he was killed by — "

"Sister!" cried Mary, springing forward and laying her hand on her sister's lips, "you are about to commit the crime you denounce in others; you are betraying secrets which do not belong to you!"

"Be it so; but that man shall speak! The contempt I cast upon him shall make him raise his head! He shall find, in his shame or in his pride, the strength to send me out of a life that is odious to me, a life which can be henceforth but a long delirium, an eternal despair. Let him complete with one blow the ruin he has begun! My God! my God!" continued Bertha, in whose eyes the tears were beginning to force their way, "why dost thou suffer men to break the hearts of thy living creatures? My God! my God! what can ever console me for this?"

"I will," said Mary. "I will, my sister, my good sister, my precious sister, if you will but hear me, if you will only pardon me."

"Pardon you! you?" cried Bertha, pushing Mary away from her. "No! you are the partner of that man; I know you no more! But, I warn you, watch each other mutually, for your treachery will bring evil on both of you."

"Bertha! Bertha! in God's name, do not say such things! Do not curse us, do not insult us thus!"

"Ha!" exclaimed Bertha, "you feel it, do you? Yes, it is not without good reason that we are called 'she-wolves'! And now they'll say: 'The Demoiselles de Souday both loved Monsieur de la Logerie, and after promising to marry' (for I suppose he promised it to you as he did to me) 'he deserted them and took a third!' Why, even for wolves it would be monstrous!"

"Bertha! Bertha!"

"If I scorned the epithet they gave us, as I scorn all empty considerations of mock propriety," continued the young girl, still at the height of her excitement, "if I laughed at the conventions of society and the world, it was because we both — both, do you hear that? — because we both had the right to walk proudly in a virtuous independence of unsullied honor; because we were so high in our inward consciousness that such miserable insults were beneath our notice. But to-day all that is changed, and I here declare that I will do for you, Mary, what I disdain to do for myself, — if that man will not marry you, I will kill him. It will at least save our father's name from dishonor."

"That name is not dishonored; I swear it, Bertha!" cried Mary, kneeling down before her sister, who, shaken at last beyond her strength, fell into a chair and clasped her head in her hands.

"So much the better; it is one pain the less for her whom you will never see again." Then, twisting her arms with a gesture of despair, "My God! my God!" she cried, "after having loved them so well, to be forced to hate them!"

"No, you shall not hate me, Bertha! Your tears, your

sufferings are worse to me than your anger. Forgive me! Oh, my God! what am I saying? You will think me guilty if I clasp your knees and ask your pardon. I am not guilty, I swear it. I will tell you — but oh! you must not suffer, you must not weep! Monsieur de la Logerie," continued Mary, turning to Michel a face that was bathed in tears, "Monsieur de la Logerie, all that has happened is a dream; the daylight has come. Go! go far away; forget me! Go at once!"

"Mary," said Bertha, who had suffered her sister to take her hand, which the latter covered with tears and kisses, "you do not reflect; it is too late; it is impossible."

"Yes, yes, it is possible, Bertha!" said Mary, with a heart-rending smile. "Bertha, we will each take a spouse whose name will protect us from the calumnies of the world."

"Whom do you mean, poor child?"

Mary raised her hand to heaven.

"God!" she said.

Bertha did not answer; grief was choking her; but she held Mary tightly clasped against her breast, while Michel, utterly overcome, fell on a bench in a corner of the room.

"Forgive us!" murmured Mary, in her sister's ear. "Do not crush him! Is it his fault if a mistaken education has made him so irresolute and timid that he had no courage to speak when it was his duty to do so? He has long wished to tell you the truth, but I have withheld him. I alone am to blame, I hoped we should forget each other. Alas, alas! God has made us very feeble against our own hearts! But now, we will never leave each other, you and I, dear sister. Look at me! let me kiss your eyes! No one shall ever come between us! no man shall bring trouble and discord between two sisters. No, no! we will live alone together, loving each other, — alone with ourselves and God, to whom we will consecrate our lives; and there will still be happiness, my Bertha, happiness in our solitude, for we can pray for him, we can pray for him!"

Mary uttered the last words in a heart-rending tone. Michel, convulsed with anguish, came and knelt beside her before Bertha, who, with her mind bent on her sister, did not notice him.

At this moment the soldiers appeared at the door which Bertha had left open, and the officer we have seen at the inn of Saint-Philbert advanced into the middle of the room and laid his hand on Michel's shoulder.

"You are Monsieur Michel de la Logerie ?" he said.

"Yes, monsieur."

"Then I arrest you, in the name of the law."

"Great God !" cried Bertha, recovering her senses. "I had forgotten it! Ah, it is I who have killed him! And the other! down there! down there! Oh, what is happening there ?"

"Michel, Michel !" said Mary, forgetting what she had just said to her sister. "Michel, if you die, I will die with you."

"No, no," cried Bertha, "he shall not die; I swear to you, sister, you shall still be happy! Make way, monsieur, make way!" she said to the officer.

"Mademoiselle," replied the latter, with painful politeness, "like you I cannot trifle with my duty. At Saint-Philbert you were only, to me, a suspicious person. I am not a commissary of police, and I was not called upon to interfere with you. Here I find you in flagrant rebellion against the laws, and I arrest you."

"Arrest me! arrest me at this moment! You may kill me, monsieur, but you shall not have me living!"

And before the officer could recover from his surprise Bertha climbed the window, sprang into the court-yard, and reached the gate. It was guarded by soldiers. Looking about her the girl saw Michel's horse, which, frightened by the noise and the apparition of the soldiers, had broken loose and was running hither and thither about the yard.

Profiting by the confidence that the officer felt in the precaution taken of surrounding the house, a security which prevented him from ordering violence against a woman, she went straight to the animal and sprang into the saddle with a bound, then passing like a thunderbolt before the eyes of the amazed officer, she reached a place in the wall which was slightly broken down; there with heel and bridle she urged on the horse, which was an excellent English hunter, made it jump the barrier which was still nearly five feet high, and darted away across the plain.

"Don't fire! don't fire upon that woman!" cried the officer, who did not think the prize worth taking dead if he could not get her living.

But the soldiers who formed the cordon outside the court-yard did not understand the order, and a rain of balls hissed around Bertha as the vigorous stride of her good English beast carried her toward Nantes.

XL.

THE CHIMNEY-BACK.

Let us now see what was happening in Nantes during this night which began with the death of Joseph Picaut, followed by the arrest of Monsieur Michel de la Logerie.

Toward nine o'clock that evening a man with his clothes soaked in water and soiled with mud presented himself at the Prefecture, and on refusal of the usher in charge to take him to the prefect, he sent in to that official a card, bearing, as it appeared, some all-powerful name, for the prefect immediately left his employment to receive this man, who was no other than the one known to us as Monsieur Hyacinthe.

Ten minutes after their interview a strong force of gendarmes and police officers was on its way to the house occupied by Maître Pascal in the rue du Marché, and soon appeared before the door of the house which opened on the street.

No precaution was taken to dull the sound of the column's advance, or to mislead any one as to its intentions; so that Maître Pascal, on becoming aware of its advance, had plenty of time to notice that the door into the alley was not guarded, and to escape in that way before the emissaries of the law could burst in the door on the rue du Marché, which was not opened to them.

He made at once for the rue du Château and entered No. 3. Monsieur Hyacinthe, whom he had not perceived, hidden as he was behind a stone block near the entrance of the alley, followed him with all the practised skill of a hunter stalking the game he covets.

During this preliminary operation, for the success of which Monsieur Hyacinthe had probably vouched, the authorities had taken strong military measures; and no sooner had the Jew made his report of what he had seen to the prefect of the Loire than twelve hundred men advanced upon the house into which the spy had seen Maître Pascal disappear. These twelve hundred men were divided into three columns. The first went down the Cours, leaving sentinels stationed along the walls of the Archbishop's garden and the adjoining houses, skirted the castle moat and came in front of No. 3 rue du Château, where it deployed. The second, following the rue de l'Évêché, crossed the place Saint-Pierre, went down the main street, and joined the first column by the rue Basse-du-Château. The third united with the two others from the upper end of the rue du Château, leaving, like the others, a long line of sentries with fixed bayonets behind it.

The investment was complete; the whole nest of houses, in the midst of which was No. 3, was securely surrounded.

The troops entered the ground-floor, preceded by the commissaries of police, who marched before them, pistol in hand. The soldiers spread themselves through the house and guarded all the exits; their mission was then fulfilled. That of the police began.

Four ladies were, apparently, the only occupants of the house. These ladies, who belonged to the upper aristocracy of Nantes, and were respected, not only for their social position, but for their honorable characters, were arrested.

Outside the house a crowd gathered, and formed another cordon behind that of the soldiers. The whole town seemed to have turned into the streets; but no sign of royalist sympathy was shown. The crowd was grave and curious, that was all.

Investigations began inside the house; and their first result confirmed the authorities in the conviction that Madame la Duchesse de Berry occupied it. A letter addressed to her Royal Highness was lying open on a table. The disappearance of Maître Pascal, who was seen to enter the house and known not to have left it, proved the existence of some hiding-place within its walls. That hiding-place must be found.

All articles of furniture were opened if the keys were in them; broken open if they were not. The sappers and masons sounded the walls and floors with their hammers; builders, who were taken from room to room, declared it impossible, comparing the internal with the external construction, that any hiding-place was made in the walls. In several of the rooms, however, articles were found, such as printed papers, jewels, articles of silver, which might, to be sure, have belonged to the owners of the house, but, under the circumstances, seemed to point to the presence of the princess within the walls. When the garret was reached the builders declared that there, less than elsewhere, was it possible for a hiding-place to exist.

The police then searched the neighboring houses, sounding the walls with such violence that fragments of masonry were detached, and at one time it was thought that the walls themselves were coming down.

While these things were happening about them the ladies of the house, who were under arrest, showed the greatest coolness; though kept in sight by their guards, they calmly sat down to dinner. Two other women, — and history ought, ere this, to have searched out their names and preserved them for posterity, — two other women were the special objects of police investigation; these women, the servants of the household, named Charlotte Moreau and Marie Boissy, were taken to the castle, thence to the barracks of the gendarmerie, where, finding that they resisted all threats, an attempt was made to corrupt them. Large and still larger sums of money were offered to them, but they answered steadily that they knew nothing whatever of the Duchesse de Berry.

After these ineffectual efforts the search relaxed: the

prefect was the first to retreat, leaving, by way of precaution, a sufficient number of men to guard each room in the house, while the commissaries of police took up their quarters on the ground-floor. The house was still surrounded and the National Guard sent a detachment to relieve the troops of the line, who took a rest.

In distributing sentries, two gendarmes were placed in two attic rooms, which had, of course, been carefully searched. The cold was so sharp that these men suffered from it. One of them went downstairs and returned with an armful of peat-fuel, and ten minutes later a fine fire was blazing in the chimney, the iron back of which was soon red-hot.

Almost at the same time, although it was scarcely daylight, the work of the masons began again; their crow-bars and mallets struck the walls of the attic rooms and made them tremble. In spite of this noisy racket, one of the gendarmes was fast asleep; his companion, now comfortably warm, had ceased to keep up the fire, and the masons, satisfied at last, gave up the search in this part of the house, which, with the instinct of their trade, they had carefully explored.

The gendarme who was awake, profiting by the silence that followed the diabolical uproar which had continued since early on the previous evening, went to sleep himself. His companion soon after waked up cold. His eyes were scarcely open before he thought of warming himself, and relighted the fire; but as the peat did not ignite very readily, he threw into the fireplace a number of copies of the "Quotidienne" which lay pell-mell upon the table. The flames from the newspapers produced a thicker smoke and greater heat than the peat had done at any time. The gendarme, feeling comfortable, was occupying his time by reading the "Quotidienne," when all of a sudden his pyrotechnic edifice came tumbling down, and the peat squares which he had set against the chimney-back rolled into the room.

At the same instant he heard from behind that back a noise which gave him an odd idea; he fancied there were rats in the chimney, and that the heat of his fire had forced them to decamp. On this he woke up his comrade, and together they made ready to chase the rodents, sabre in hand.

While their attention was wholly fixed on this new species of game, one of them noticed a decided movement of the chimney-back, and he called out: —

"Who 's there?"

A woman's voice replied: —

"We surrender, — we will open the door; put out your fire!"

The two gendarmes jumped to their fire and scattered it out with a few kicks. The chimney-back then slowly turned on a pivot and disclosed a hollow space, from which a woman, bareheaded, her face pale, her hair standing up from her forehead like that of a man, dressed in a simple Neapolitan gown of a brown color, scorched in many places, came forth, placing her feet and hands on the heated hearth.

This woman was Petit-Pierre, her Royal Highness Marie-Caroline, the Duchesse de Berry.

Her companions followed her. For sixteen hours they had been confined in that cramped place without food. The hole which was thus their asylum was made between the flue of the chimney and the wall of the adjoining house under the roof, the rafters of which served to conceal it.

At the moment when the troops surrounded the house her Royal Highness was listening to Maître Pascal, who gave her an amusing account of the scare which had led him to leave his house and come to hers. Through the windows of the room in which she sat the duchess could see the moon rising in the calm sky, and defining, like a brown silhouette, the massive towers, the silent, motionless towers of the old castle.

There are moments when nature seems so gentle, so

friendly, that it is impossible to believe a danger lurks and threatens us from the midst of such perfect quietude.

Suddenly Maître Pascal, coming nearer to the window, saw the flash of bayonets. Instantly he threw himself back, exclaiming: —

"Escape ! save yourself, Madame !"

The duchess at once rushed up the staircase, the others following her. Reaching the hiding-place, she turned and called to her companions. As they knew the place could only be entered on their hands and knees, the men went first; then, as the young lady who attended on her Royal Highness was unwilling to pass before her, the duchess said, laughing: —

"Go in, go in ! Good strategy requires that when a retreat is made the commander should always be in the rear."

The soldiers entered the door of the house just as that of the hiding-place was closed on the princess and her friends.

We have seen with what minute care the search had been made. Every blow struck on the walls resounded in the refuge of the duchess; the plaster fell in showers, the bricks were loosened, and the prisoners came near being buried in the mass of rubbish shaken down by the jar of the hammers and the iron-bars and joists of the searchers. When the gendarmes built their fire the back of the chimney and the wall gave forth a heat which made the little chamber almost insupportable. After a while those who were imprisoned in it could scarcely breathe, and they would have perished asphyxiated if they had not succeeded in getting a few slates off the roof, which made an opening that let in air.

The duchess suffered the most; for, having entered last, she was nearest to the chimney-back. Each of her companions begged her to change places, but she would not consent to it. To the danger of being suffocated was now added that of being burned alive. The door of the hiding-place was red-hot, and threatened at every moment to set fire to the clothing of the women. In fact, Madame's gown had been twice on fire and she had put it out with her hands, which were badly burned; the scars remained visible for many months.

Every minute exhausted the interior air, and the external air admitted through the tiny holes did not suffice to renew it. The breathing of the prisoners became more and more difficult; another ten minutes in that furnace might sacrifice the future life of the duchess. Her companions implored her to surrender; but she would not. Her eyes filled with tears of anger, which the scorching air dried upon her cheeks. The fire had again caught her gown and again she had extinguished it; but in the movement she thus made she chanced to touch the spring of the chimney-back, which moved and attracted the attention of the gendarme.

Supposing that this accident had betrayed her retreat, and pitying the sufferings of her companions, Madame consented to surrender, leaving the chimney as we have related. Her first words were a request to see General Dermoncourt. One of the gendarmes went to find him on the ground-floor, which he had not chosen to leave throughout the search.

XLI.

THREE BROKEN HEARTS.

As soon as the general's arrival was announced, Madame went hastily toward him.

"General," she said quickly, "I surrender to you; and I trust to your loyalty!"

"Madame," replied Dermoncourt, "your Royal Highness is under the safeguard of French honor!"

He led her to a chair, and as she seated herself she pressed his arm firmly and said: —

"General, I have nothing to reproach myself with. I have done my duty as a mother to recover my son's inheritance."

Her voice was clear and accentuated. Though pale, she was excited as if by fever. The general sent for a glass of water, in which she dipped her fingers; the refreshing coolness calmed her.

During this time the prefect and the commander of the National Guard were notified of what had happened. The prefect was the first to arrive. He entered the room in which Madame was sitting, with his hat on his head, ignoring that a woman was a prisoner there, — a woman whose rank and whose misfortunes deserved more respect than had ever been shown her.

He approached the duchess, looked at her, touched his hat cavalierly, and said: —

"Yes, that is really she."

Then he went out to give some orders.

"Who is that man?" asked the princess.

The question was a natural one, for the prefect had presented himself without any of the distinctive signs of his high administrative position.

"Madame can surely guess," said the general.

She looked at him with a slight laugh.

"I suppose it must be the prefect," she said.

"Madame could not have been more correct had she seen his license."

"Did that man serve under the Restoration?"

"No, Madame."

"I am glad for the Restoration."

The prefect now returned, entering without being announced, as before; and, as before, he did not remove his hat. Apparently, the prefect was hungry on that particular morning, for he brought with him, on a plate which he held in his hand, a slice of pâté. He put the plate on the table, asked for a knife and fork, and began to eat with his back to the princess.

Madame looked at him with an expression of mingled anger and contempt.

"General," she said, "do you know what I most regret in the station I once occupied?"

"No, Madame."

"Two ushers, to turn that man out."

When the prefect had finished his repast he turned round and asked the duchess for her papers.

Madame replied that he could look in her late hiding-place, where he would find a white portfolio she had left there.

The prefect went to fetch the portfolio and brought it back with him.

"Monsieur," said the duchess, opening it, "the papers in this portfolio are of very little consequence; but I wish to give them to you myself in order that I may explain their ownership."

So saying, she gave him one after the other the things that were in the portfolio.

"Does Madame know how much money she has here?" asked the prefect.

"Monsieur, there ought to be about thirty-six thousand francs; of which twelve thousand belong to persons whom I will designate."

The general here approached and said that if Madame felt better it was urgent that she should leave the house.

"To go where?" she said, looking at him fixedly.

"To the castle, Madame."

"Ah, yes, and from there to Blaye, no doubt?"

"General," said one of Madame's companions, "her Royal Highness cannot go on foot; it would not be proper."

"Monsieur," replied Dermoncourt, "a carriage would only encumber us. Madame can go on foot by throwing a mantle over her shoulders and wearing a hat."

On this the general's secretary and the prefect, who seemed to be suddenly pricked by gallantry, went down stairs and returned with three hats. The princess chose a black one, because, as she said, the color was analogous to the circumstances; after which she took the general's arm to leave the house. As she passed before the door of the garret she gave a glance at the chimney-back, which remained open.

"Ah, general!" she said, laughing, "if you had not treated me as they treated Saint Lawrence, — which by the bye is quite unworthy of your military generosity, — you would n't have me under your arm, now. Come, friends," she added, addressing her companions.

The princess went down the staircase on the general's arm. As she was about to cross the threshold into the street she heard a great noise among the crowd, who flocked behind the soldiers and formed a line ten times as deep as that of the military.

Madame may have thought that those cries and shouts were aimed at her; but she gave no sign of fear except that she pressed a little closer to the general's arm.

When the princess advanced between the double line of

soldiers and National Guards, who made a lane from the house to the castle, the cries and mutterings she had heard became louder and more violent than before. The general cast his eyes in the direction from which the tumult chiefly came, and there he saw a young peasant-woman trying to force her way through the ranks of the soldiers who opposed her passage; and yet, being struck by her beauty and the despair that was visible on her face, were refraining from violence in repulsing her.

Dermoncourt recognized Bertha, and called the duchess's attention to her. The latter gave a cry.

"General," she said eagerly, "you have promised not to separate me from my friends; let that young girl come to me."

On a sign from the general the ranks opened, and Bertha reached the august prisoner.

"Pardon, Madame! pardon for an unhappy woman who might have saved you, and did not! Oh, I would I could die, cursing that fatal love which has made me the involuntary accomplice of the traitors who have sold your Royal Highness!"

"I don't know what you mean, Bertha!" interrupted the princess, raising the young girl and giving her the arm that was free. "What you are doing at this moment proves that whatever else has happened I cannot doubt a devotion the memory of which will never leave me. But I have to talk to you of other things, dear child. I have to ask your pardon for contributing to an error which may, perhaps, have made you most unhappy; I have to tell you that —"

"I know all, Madame," said Bertha, lifting her eyes, that were red with tears, to the princess.

"Poor child!" exclaimed the duchess, pressing the girl's hand. "Then, follow me, come with me; time and my affection will calm a sorrow that I comprehend, that I respect —"

"I beg your Highness to forgive me for not obeying

her, but I have made a vow which I must fulfil. God alone is placed by duty above my princess."

"Then go, dear child!" said Madame, comprehending the young girl's meaning. "Go, and may the God you seek be with you! When you pray to Him remember Petit-Pierre; the prayers of a broken heart ascend to Him."[1]

They had now reached the gates of the prison. The duchess raised her eyes to the blackened walls of the old castle; then she held out her hand to Bertha, who, kneeling down, laid a kiss upon it, murmuring once more the words, "Forgive me!" Then Madame, after an instant's hesitation, passed through the postern, giving a last smile in token of farewell to Bertha.

The general withdrew his arm from the duchess to allow her to pass in; then he turned hastily to Bertha and said in a low voice: —

"Where is your father?"

"He is at Nantes."

"Tell him to return to the château, and stay there quietly; he shall not be disturbed. I'll break my sword sooner than allow him to be arrested, my old enemy!"

"Thank you for him, general."

"And you, if you have any need of my services, command them, mademoiselle."

"I want a passport to Paris."

"When?"

"At once."

"Where shall I send it to you?"

"To the other side of the pont Rousseau; to the inn of the Point du Jour."

[1] Hers was a gallant soul. She was privately married to an Italian nobleman of distinguished name and fame, and a child was born to her during her imprisonment at Blaye. The Bourbons never forgave her; they treated her, and so did the French people, as if she had disgraced herself. Justice has never been done to her brave, generous, gallant heart, — a royal heart that felt for others. Her second marriage was a most happy one. She survived her husband several years, and died in 1873. — Tr.

Chateau of Nantes.

"In an hour you shall have it, mademoiselle."

With a sign of farewell the general turned and disappeared beneath the gloomy portal.

Bertha worked her way through the close-pressed ranks of the crowd until she reached the nearest church, which she entered. There she remained a long time kneeling on the cold stone pavement.

When she rose the stones were wet with tears.

Then she crossed the town and the pont Rousseau. Approaching the inn of the Point du Jour, she saw her father sitting at the threshold of the door. Within the last few hours the Marquis de Souday had aged ten years; his eye had lost the humorous, bantering look which gave it such expression; he carried his head low, like a man whose burden was too heavy for him.

Warned by the priest who had received the last confession of Maître Jacques, and who went to the forest of Touvois to tell the marquis what had happened, the old man started at once for Nantes. A mile from the pont Rousseau he met Bertha, whose horse had fallen, having broken a tendon in the furious pace to which she had urged him.

The girl confessed to her father what had happened. The old man did not reproach her, but he broke the stick he held in his hand against the stones of the road.

When they reached the pont Rousseau public rumor informed them, though it was only seven in the morning, of the arrest of the princess before that arrest was actually accomplished. Bertha, not daring to raise her eyes to her father, rushed toward Nantes; the old man seated himself on the bench before the inn, where we find him four hours later.

This sorrow was the only one against which his selfish and epicurean philosophy was impotent. He would have pardoned his daughter many faults; but he could not think without despair that she had covered his name with the crime and shame of lèze-chivalry, and that a Souday, the last of the name, should have helped to fling royalty into the gulf.

When Bertha approached him he silently held out to her a paper a gendarme had given him. It was her passport from the general.

"Father, will you not forgive me as she forgave me?" said the girl, in a gentle, humble tone which contrasted strangely with her self-assuming manner in other days.

The old gentleman sadly shook his head.

"Where shall I find my poor Jean Oullier?" he said. "Since God has preserved him to me I want to see him. I want him to go with me out of this country!"

"Will you leave Souday, father?"

"Yes."

"Where will you go?"

"Where I can hide my name."

"And Mary, poor Mary, who is innocent!"

"Mary will be the wife of the man who is the cause of this execrable crime. I will never see Mary again!"

"You will be alone."

"No; I shall have Jean Oullier."

Bertha bowed her head; she entered the inn, where she changed her peasant dress for mourning garments, which she had bought on her way through the town. When she came out the old man had gone. Looking about her she saw him, with his hands clasped behind his back, his head sunk on his breast, sadly walking in the direction of Saint-Philbert.

Bertha sobbed; then she cast a lingering look at the verdant plain of the Retz region, which can be seen in the distance from Nantes, backed by the dark-blue line of the forest of Machecoul.

"Farewell, all that I love in this world!" she cried.

Then she turned and re-entered the town of Nantes.

XLII.

GOD'S EXECUTIONER.

During the three hours that Courtin spent bound hand and foot, and lying on the earth in the ruins of Saint-Philbert, side by side with the corpse of Joseph Picaut, his heart passed through all the agony that can rend and torture a human being.

He felt the precious belt beneath him, for he had managed to lie upon it; but the gold it contained only added more pangs to his other pangs, more terror to the countless terrors which assailed his brain. That gold, which was more to him than life itself, was he doomed to lose it? Who was this unknown man whom he had heard Maître Jacques tell the widow to summon? What was this mysterious vengeance he had now to fear? He passed in review before him all the persons to whom, in the course of his life, he had done harm; the list was long, and their threatening faces peopled the darkness of the tower.

And yet, at times, a ray of hope traversed his gloomy mind; vague and undecided at first, it presently took on consistency. Could it be that a man possessing that glorious gold should die? If vengeance rose before him would not a handful of those coins silence it? His imagination counted and re-counted the sum belonging to him, which was really, really his own, which was bruising his flesh delightfully, pressing into his loins as if the gold itself were becoming a part of his very body. Then he reflected that if he could only escape he should add fifty thousand more francs to the fifty thousand now beneath him; and, helpless as he was, a victim doomed to death, awaiting the fall of the sword of Damocles above his head, which might at any instant cut the thread of his life, his heart melted into such joy that it took the character of intoxication. But soon his ideas again changed their course. He asked himself if his accomplice — in whom he felt only the confidence of an accomplice — would not profit by his absence to cheat him of the share that belonged to him; he saw that man escaping, weighed down by the weight of the enormous sum he was carrying, and refusing to divide it with him, who, after all, had done the whole betrayal. He mentally prepared for such occasion; he thought of words of entreaty to reach the heart of that Jew, threats to intimidate him, reproaches that might move him; but suddenly, when he reflected that if Monsieur Hyacinthe loved gold as he loved it, — which was probable, inasmuch as he was a Jew, — when he measured his associate by his own measure, when he sounded in his own soul the depths of the sacrifice he demanded, he said to himself that tears, prayers, threats, reproaches would all be useless, and he fell into paroxysms of rage; he vented roars which shook the old arches of the feudal edifice; he struggled in his bonds, he bit the ropes, he tried to tear them with his teeth; but those ropes, slender and loosely twisted as they were, seemed to take on life, to become living things under his efforts; he fancied he felt them struggling against him, increasing their tangled snarl; the knots he undid seemed to tie themselves again, not singly as before, but in double, treble, quadruple turns; and then, as if to punish his efforts, they buried themselves in his flesh, where they made a burning furrow. All dreams of hope, all thought of riches and happiness vanished like clouds before the breath of a tempest; the phantoms of those whom the farmer had persecuted rose terrible before him; all things lurking in the shadow, stones, beams, fragments of broken wood-work, fallen cornices, all took form, and each of those threatening shapes looked at him with eyes which shone in the darkness like thousands of sparks dart-ing on the tissue of a black shroud. The mind of the wretched man began to wander. Mad with terror and despair he called to the corpse of Joseph Picaut, of which he could see the outline, stiff and stark, about four feet from him; he offered him a fourth, a third, a half of his gold if he would loose his bonds; but the echo of the arches alone replied in its funereal voice, and, exhausted by emotion, he fell back for a moment into dull insensibility.

He was in one of these moments of torpor when a noise without made him quiver. Some one was walking in the inner court-yard of the castle, and presently he heard the grinding of the rusty bolts of the old fruit-room. Courtin's heart beat as though it would burst his breast. He was breathless with fear, choking with anguish; he felt that the coming person was the avenger summoned by Maître Jacques.

The door opened. The flame of a torch lighted the rafters with its ruddy glare. Courtin had an instant of hope; it was the widow, bearing the torch, whom he first saw, and he thought she was alone; but she had scarcely made two steps into the tower before a man who was behind her appeared. The hair of the hapless farmer rose on his head; he dared not look at the man; he closed his eyes and was silent.

The man and the widow came nearer. Marianne gave the torch to her companion, pointing with her finger to Courtin; and then, as if indifferent to what was about to happen, she knelt down at the feet of Joseph Picaut's body and began to pray.

As for the man, he came close beside the farmer and, no doubt to convince himself that he was really the mayor of La Logerie, he cast the light of the torch across his face.

"Can he be asleep?" he said to himself, in a low voice. "No, he is too great a coward to sleep; no, his face is too pale — he 's not sleeping."

Then he stuck his torch into a fissure in the wall, sat

down on an enormous stone which had rolled from the top to the middle of the tower and, addressing Courtin, said to him: —

"Come, open your eyes, Monsieur le maire. We have something to say to each other, and I like to see the eyes of those who speak to me."

"Jean Oullier!" cried Courtin, turning livid, and making a desperate effort to burst his bonds and escape. "Jean Oullier living!"

"If it were only his ghost, Monsieur Courtin, it would be, I think, enough to terrify you; for you have a long account to settle with him."

"Oh, my God! my God!" exclaimed Courtin, letting himself drop back on the ground like a man who resigns himself to his fate.

"Our hatred dates far back, does n't it?" continued Jean Oullier; "and its instincts have not misled us; they have embittered you against me, and to-day, exhausted and half dead as I am, they have brought me back to you."

"I have never hated you," said Courtin, who the moment he perceived that Jean Oullier was not about to kill him on the spot, felt a gleam of hope in his heart and foresaw the possibility of saving his life by discussion. "I have never hated you; on the contrary! and if my ball did strike you it was not because I meant it for you. I did not know you were in that bush."

"Oh, my grievances against you go farther back than that, Monsieur Courtin!"

"Farther back?" replied Courtin, who, little by little, was recovering some energy. "But I swear that before that accident, which I deplore, I never put you in any danger, I never did you any harm."

"Your memory is short, and your offences weigh most on the soul of the offended person, it appears; for I remember the wrongs you have done me."

"What wrongs? What can you remember against me? Speak, Monsieur Jean Oullier! Do you think it right to kill a man without hearing him, without allowing him to say one word in his defence?"

"Who told you I meant to kill you?" said Jean Oullier, with the icy calmness he had not quitted for an instant. "Your conscience, perhaps."

"Speak out, Monsieur Jean! tell me of what I am accused! Except for that luckless shot, I know I am as white as the driven snow. Yes, I can prove to you that no one has been a better friend than I to the worthy family at Souday; no one has respected them more, or been more glad of this marriage which is to unite the families of your master and mine."

"Monsieur Courtin," said Jean Oullier, who had left free course to this flux of words, "it is, as you say, only fair that an accused person should defend himself. Defend yourself, therefore, if you can. Listen to me; I begin—"

"Oh, go on! I am not afraid of your questions!" replied Courtin.

"We shall soon see that. Who betrayed me to the gendarmes at the fair of Montaigu, so as to lay hands more securely on my master's guests, whom you rightly supposed I was defending? Who, having done that, basely hid himself behind the hedge of the last garden in Montaigu, and after borrowing a gun of the owner of that garden, fired at my dog and killed my poor companion? Answer, Monsieur Courtin!"

"Who dares to say he saw me do that?" cried the farmer.

"Three persons; among them the man from whom you borrowed the gun."

"How should I know the dog was yours? No, Monsieur Jean, upon my honor, I was ignorant of it."

Jean made a contemptuous gesture.

"Who," he continued, in the same calm but accusing voice, "who, having slipped into Pascal Picaut's house, sold to the Blues the secret he discovered there,—the secret of a sacred hospitality?"

"I bear testimony to that," said the deep voice of Pascal's widow, issuing from her silence and immobility.

The farmer shuddered and dared not defend himself.

"Whom have I constantly found," resumed Jean Oullier, "during the last four months, busy with shameful schemes, laying his plots and sheltering them under the name of his young master, proclaiming devotion and fidelity to him, and soiling the very name of those virtues by contact with his criminal intentions? Whom did I hear, on the Bouaimé moor, discussing the price of blood? Whom did I see weighing the gold offered him for the basest and most odious of treacheries? Who, I say, was that man, if not you?"

"I swear to you by all there is most sacred among men!" said Courtin, who still believed that Jean Oullier's principal grievance was the shot that wounded him. "I swear to you that I did not know you were in that luckless bush!"

"But I tell you I don't blame you for that! I have not said a word, I have not opened my lips to you about it! The list of your crimes is long enough without adding that!"

"You speak of my crimes, Jean Oullier, and you forget that my young master, who will soon become yours, owes me his life; and that if I had been the traitor that you call me I should have delivered him up to the soldiers who passed and repassed my house every day while he was there. You forget all that, while, on the contrary, you rake up every trifling circumstance against me."

"If you did save your master," continued Jean Oullier, in the same inexorable tone, "it is because that sham devotion was useful to your plans. Better for him, better for those two poor girls, if you had let them end their days honorably, gloriously, than to have mixed them up in these shameless intrigues. That is what I have against you, Courtin; that thought alone doubles the hatred I feel to you."

"The proof that I don't hate you, Jean Oullier, is that if I had chosen you would long ago have been put out of this world."

"What do you mean?"

"On the day of that hunt when the father of Monsieur Michel was killed — murdered, Monsieur Jean, we won't blink the word — a beater was not ten paces from him; and the name of that beater was Courtin."

Jean Oullier rose to his full height.

"Yes," continued the farmer, "and this beater saw it was Jean Oullier's ball that brought the traitor down."

"Yes," said Jean Oullier; "but it was not a crime, it was an expiation. I am proud to have been the man whom God selected to punish that criminal."

"God alone may punish, God alone may curse," said the mayor.

"No, I am not mistaken; it is He who has put into my heart this hatred of sin, this ineradicable recollection of treachery; it was the finger of God touching my heart when that heart quivered at the name of the traitor. When my shot struck that Judas I felt the breath of the divine Justice cross my face and cool it; and, from that moment to this I have found the peace and calmness I never had while that unpunished criminal prospered before my eyes. God was with me."

"God is never with a murderer."

"God is always with the executioner who lifts the sword of justice. Men have their laws, He has his. I was that day, as I am to-day, the sword of God."

"Do you mean to murder me as you murdered Baron Michel?"

"I mean to punish the man who sold Petit-Pierre as I punished him who sold Charette. I shall punish him without fear, without doubt, without remorse."

"Take care; remorse will come when your future master calls you to account for his father's death."

"That young man is just and loyal; if he is ever called

upon to judge my conduct I shall tell him what I saw in the wood of La Chabotière, and he will judge me rightly."

"Who can testify that you tell the truth? One man alone, and that is I. Let me live, Jean, let me live! and, as that woman did just now, I will rise and say: 'I bear testimony to that.'"

"Fear makes you foolish, Courtin. Monsieur Michel will ask for no other testimony when Jean Oullier says, 'This is the truth;' when Jean Oullier, baring his breast, says, 'If you wish to avenge your father, strike!' when Jean Oullier kneels before him and prays to God to send the expiation if He himself judges that the deed should be expiated. No, no! and you are wrong, wrong to evoke in your terror those bloody memories before my mind. You, Maître Courtin, you have done worse things than Michel did; for the blood you sold is nobler still than that he trafficked in. I did not spare Michel, why should I spare you? Never, never!"

"Pity! mercy! Jean Oullier. Do not kill me!" sobbed the wretched man.

"Implore those stones, ask pity of them! They may answer you; but nothing can move my will, or shake my resolution. You shall die!"

"Ah, my God! my God!" cried Courtin, "is there no one to help me? Widow Picaut! widow Picaut! here! here! will you let him cut my throat? Here! help me! protect me! If you want gold, I'll give it! I have gold, gold! No, what am I saying? My mind is wandering; I have no gold!" said the poor wretch, fearing to spur on the murder he saw glittering in the eyes of his enemy if he offered such hopes. "No, I have no gold, but I have property, estates. I'll give you all; I'll make you rich — both of you! Oh, mercy, Jean Oullier! Widow Picaut, defend me!"

The widow did not stir; except for the movement of her lips she might have been taken, as she knelt there in her mourning garments, pale as marble, mute and motionless beside the corpse, for one of those kneeling statues we often see at the foot of some ancient monument.

"What!" continued Courtin, "will you really kill me? kill me without a fight, without danger, when I cannot lift a foot to escape or a hand to defend myself? Will you cut my throat in my bonds like a beast that they drag to a slaughter-house? Oh, Jean Oullier, that 's not the work of a soldier; you are a butcher!"

"Who told you I would do it thus? No, no, no, Maître Courtin. Look, the wound you gave me has not healed; it still bleeds. I am weak, tottering, feeble; I am proscribed, a price is on my head! — well, in spite of all that, I am so certain of the justice of my cause that I do not hesitate to appeal to the judgment of God. Courtin, you are free!"

"Free?"

"Yes, I set you at liberty. Oh, you need not thank me; what I do, I do for myself, not you, — that it may never be said Jean Oullier struck a fallen man, an unarmed man. But don't mistake; the life I give you now, I will take some day."

"Oh, God!"

"Maître Courtin, you will go from here unbound and free; but, I warn you, beware! As soon as you have passed the threshold of these ruins I shall be upon your traces; and those traces I will never abandon until I have struck you down and made your body a corpse. Beware, Maître Courtin, beware!"

So saying, Jean Oullier took his knife and cut the cords that bound the farmer hand and foot. Courtin made a bound of almost frantic joy; but he instantly controlled it. In springing up he felt the belt; it seemed as though it called to him. Jean Oullier had given him life, but what was life without his gold?

He flung himself down upon it as quickly as he had risen.

Jean Oullier had seen, rapid as Courtin's movement was, the swollen leather of the belt, and he guessed what was passing in the farmer's mind.

"Why don't you go?" he said. "What are you waiting for? Yes, I understand; you are afraid that, seeing you free as myself and stronger than I, my wrath may revive; you are afraid I may throw you another knife like my own and say to you: 'Defend yourself, Maître Courtin, we are equal now!' No, Jean Oullier has but one word, and that he has given you. Make haste! depart! fly! If God is with you, He will protect you against me; if He condemns you, what care I for the start I give you? Take your cursèd gold, and begone!"

Maître Courtin did not answer. He rose, stumbling like a drunken man; he tried to fasten the belt around his waist, but could not; his fingers trembled as though they were shaken by an ague. Before departing he kept himself turned in terror toward Jean Oullier. The traitor feared treachery; he could not believe that the generosity of his enemy did not hide some trap.

Jean Oullier pointed with his finger to the door. Courtin rushed into the court; but before he reached the postern-gate he heard the voice of the Vendéan, sonorous as the clarion of battle, calling to him: —

"Beware, Courtin! beware!"

Maître Courtin, free as he was, shuddered; and in that moment of agitation he struck his foot against a stone, tripped, and fell forward. He uttered a cry of agony, fancying that the Vendéan was upon him; he thought he felt the cold steel of a knife piercing between his shoulders.

It was only an omen. Courtin rose, and a minute later, having passed the postern, he darted, a free man, into the open country he had not expected to see again.

When he had disappeared the widow went up to Jean Oullier and offered him her hand.

"Jean," she said, "as I listened to you, I thought how

right my Pascal was when he told me there were brave, strong souls under every flag."

Jean Oullier wrung the hand the worthy woman who had saved his life held out to him.

"How do you feel now?" she asked.

"Better; we are always stronger for a struggle."

"And where are you going?"

"To Nantes. After what your mother told us, I think Bertha may not have gone there; and I fear some disaster from the delay."

"Well, at any rate, take a boat; that will spare your legs the fatigue of half the distance."

"I will," replied Jean Oullier.

And he followed the widow to the place on the lakeside where the boats of the fishermen were drawn up on the sand.

XLIII.

SHOWS THAT A MAN WITH FIFTY THOUSAND FRANCS ABOUT HIM MAY BE MUCH EMBARRASSED.

As soon as Maître Courtin had crossed the bridge leading from the castle he began to run like a madman; terror lent him wings. He did not ask himself whither his steps led him; he fled to flee. If his strength had equalled his fear he would have put the world between himself and the threats of the Vendéan, — threats he continued to hear resounding in his ears like a funeral knell.

But after he had done about a couple of miles across country in the direction of Machecoul, exhausted, breathless, choked by the rapidity of his flight, he fell rather than seated himself on the bank of a ditch, where he came to his senses and began to reflect on what he had better do. His first idea was to go at once to his own house; but that idea he almost immediately abandoned. In the country, no matter what effort the authorities might make to protect the mayor of La Logerie, Jean Oullier — with his relations to the country-people and his perfect knowledge of roads, forests, and gorse moors, seconded by the sympathy that the whole community felt for him, and by the hatred they felt for Courtin — was all-powerful, and the game would be wholly on his side.

In Nantes alone could the farmer find refuge, — Nantes, where an able and numerous police would protect his life until such time as they could arrest Jean Oullier, — a result Courtin hoped to reach very soon by the information he was able to give as to the usual hiding-places of the insurrectionists.

As he sat there thinking these things his hand went to his belt to lift it; the weight of the mass of gold he carried hurt him, and had contributed not a little to the breathless fatigue of his hard run. That gesture decided his fate.

Surely he should find Monsieur Hyacinthe in Nantes. The thought of receiving from his associate, if their plot had succeeded (and this he did not doubt), an equal sum to that he carried, filled Courtin's heart with a joy that put him far above the tribulations he had lately undergone. He did not hesitate another moment, but turned at once in the direction of the town.

He resolved on getting there as the crow flies, across country. On the road he risked being watched; chance alone could put Jean Oullier on his traces if he kept to the plain. But his imagination, heated by the terrible vicissitudes of the night, was more powerful than his common-sense. No matter how carefully he glided beside the hedges, crouching in the shadows and stifling the sound of his steps, not daring to enter any field until certain it was deserted, a panic fear pursued him all the way.

In the trees with their pruned heads, which rose above the hedges, his fancy saw assassins; in their knotty branches extending above him, arms and hands with daggers ready to strike him. He stopped, chilled with fear; his legs refused to carry him farther, as though they were rooted to the ground; an icy sweat burst from his body; his teeth chattered convulsively; his shaking fingers clutched his gold, and it took him a long time to recover from his terror. He could not endure to continue in the fields, and made for the high-road.

Besides, he reflected that he might meet a vehicle of some kind on its way to Nantes and obtain a seat in it, which would shorten the way and also protect him.

After taking about five hundred steps he came out upon the road which follows for over a mile the shores of the lake of Grand-Lieu, to which it serves as a species of dike.

Courtin stopped every few minutes to listen; and presently he fancied he heard the trot of a horse's feet. He flung himself into the reeds which bordered the road on the lakeside, and crouched there, again enduring all the agonies of mind which we have just described.

But he now heard oars to his left dipping softly in the water. He crept through the reeds to look in the direction of the sound, and saw, in the shadow, a boat gliding slowly past the shore. It was, no doubt, some fisherman, intending to gather in his nets before daybreak.

The horse came nearer; the ring of his hoofs on the stones of the road terrified Courtin; danger was there, there! and he must flee from it. He whistled softly to attract the attention of the fisherman. The latter stopped rowing.

"This way! this way!" cried Courtin.

He had scarcely said the words before a vigorous stroke of the oars sent the boat within four feet of the fugitive.

"Can you put me across the lake and take me as far as Port-Saint-Martin?" asked Courtin. "I 'll pay you a franc for it."

The fisherman, who was wrapped in a sort of pea-jacket, with a hood which concealed his face, answered only by a nod; but he did better than reply. Using his boat-hook he drove the wherry in among the reeds, which bent and quivered under its prow; and just as the horse whose coming had so terrified Maître Courtin reached the point in the road he had lately left, the latter, with two springs, gained the boat and was safely in it.

The fisherman, as though he had shared his passenger's apprehensions, turned the boat toward the middle of the lake, while Courtin gave a sigh of relief. At the end of ten minutes the road and the trees that bordered it seemed merely a line upon the horizon.

Courtin could scarcely contain himself for joy. The boat, which some fortunate chance had brought to that spot, would enable him to crown his hopes and fulfil all wishes. Once at Port-Saint-Martin, he had only a three-mile walk to Nantes over a road frequented at every hour of the day or night; and once in Nantes he was safe.

Courtin's joy was so great that, in spite of himself, and as an effect of the reaction of his terror, he felt impelled to some outward manifestation of it. Sitting in the stern of the boat, he looked excitedly at the fisherman, as the latter bent to his oars and put at every stroke a stretch of water between him and danger. Those strokes, he counted them aloud; then he laughed a hollow laugh, fingered his belt, and made the gold slip forward and back inside it. This was not mere joy — it was intoxication.

Presently, however, he began to think the fisherman had gone far enough from the shore, and that it was high time to turn the boat's head to Port-Saint-Martin, which they were now leaving behind them on their right. He waited a few minutes, thinking it might be a manœuvre of the fisherman's to catch some current of which he would take advantage. But still the fisherman rowed on and on towards the middle of the lake.

"Hey, *gars*," cried the farmer at last, "you can't have heard me rightly; you are making for Port-Saint-Père, and I told you Port-Saint-Martin. Go the way I told you, and you 'll earn your money sooner!"

The fisherman was silent.

"Did you hear me? What are you about?" cried Courtin, impatiently. "Port-Saint-Martin, I say! Go to your right! It is very well not to keep too near the shore, out of reach of balls in these queer times; but I wish you to go in that direction if you please."

The boatman appeared not to hear him.

"Ah, *ça!* are you deaf?" exclaimed the farmer, beginning to get angry.

The fisherman replied only by a vigorous stroke of his oars, which sent the boat flying several paces farther out on the surface of the lake.

Courtin, beside himself, sprang to the bow, knocked off the hood which in the darkness concealed the fisherman's head, put his own face close to the man's face, and then, with a stifled cry, fell on his knees at the bottom of the boat.

The man let go his oars, but did not rise.

"God has spoken, Maître Courtin," he said; "His judgment is against you! I was not seeking you, but He sends you to me; I had forgotten you for a time, and He puts you in my way. God wills that you shall die, Maître Courtin."

"No, no, no! you won't kill me, Jean Oullier!" cried the wretched man, falling back into all his terrors.

"I will kill you as surely as those stars which are in the sky were placed there by God's hand. Therefore, if you have a soul, think of it; repent, and pray that your doom may not be too severe."

"Oh, you cannot do it, you will not do it, Jean Oullier! Think that you are killing a child of the good God, whose name you speak! Oh, not to tread the earth again, which is so beautiful in the sunlight! to sleep in an icy bed away forever from those I love! Oh, no, no, no! it is impossible!"

"If you were a father, if you had wife, mother, or sister expecting your return, your words might touch me; but no! useless among men, you have lived only to use them, and to return them evil for good. You blaspheme even now in lying, for you love no one. No one has ever loved you on this earth, and my knife will wound no heart but your own in killing you. Maître Courtin, you are now to appear before your Judge; once more, I say, commend your soul to Him."

"Can a few short moments suffice for that? A guilty man like me needs time, needs years of repentance to equal his crimes. You who are so pious, Jean Oullier, you will surely leave me time to sorrow for my sins."

"No; life would only enable you to commit others. Death is expiation; you fear it. Put your fears and your anguish at the feet of the Lord, and He will receive you in His mercy. Maître Courtin, time is passing, and as true as

God is there above those stars, in ten minutes you will be before Him!"

"Ten minutes, my God! ten minutes! Oh, pity! pity! mercy!"

"The time you employ in useless prayers is lost to your soul; think of that, Maître Courtin, think of that!"

Courtin did not answer; his hand had touched an oar, and a gleam of hope came into his mind. He gently seized it; then rising abruptly, he aimed a blow at the head of the Vendéan. The latter threw himself to the right and evaded it; the oar fell on the forward gunwale and was shivered into a thousand bits, leaving but a fragment in the farmer's hand.

Quick as lightning Jean Oullier sprang at Courtin's throat. Again the hapless man fell on his knees. Paralyzed by fear he rolled to the bottom of the boat; his choking voice could scarcely murmur the cry for "Mercy! mercy!"

"Ha, the fear of death did awaken a spark of courage in you!" cried Jean Oullier. "Ha, you found a weapon! Well, so much the better, — so much the better! Defend yourself, Courtin; and if the weapon you hold in your hand does n't suit you, take mine!" continued the old keeper, flinging his knife at the other's feet.

But Courtin was incapable of seizing it; all movement had become impossible to him. He stammered a few incoherent words; his whole body trembled as though he was shaken by an ague; his ears hummed and all his senses seemed to leave him in his awful dread of death.

"My God!" cried Jean Oullier, pushing the inert mass before him with his foot, "my God! I cannot put my knife into that dead body."

He looked about him as if in search of something.

Nature was calm; the night silent; the breeze scarcely ruffled the surface of the lake; the undulation of the water rippled softly against the sides of the boat; nothing was heard but the cry of the water-fowl flying eastward, their wings dotting with black the crimson lines of the dawn as it slowly ascended heavenward.

Jean Oullier turned abruptly to Courtin and shook him by the arm.

"Maître Courtin, I will not kill you without taking my share of the danger," he said. "Maître Courtin, I will force you to defend yourself; if not against me, at least against death. Death is coming, it is here; defend yourself!"

The farmer answered only by a moan. He rolled his haggard eyes about him, but it was plain he could not distinguish the objects that surrounded him. DEATH, terrible, hideous, menacing, effaced all else.

At the same instant Jean Oullier gave a vigorous stamp with his heel on the bottom of the boat. The rotten planks gave way and the water entered, boiling and foaming, into the boat.

Courtin was roused by the coldness of the flood as it reached him; he gave an awful cry, — a cry in which there was nothing human.

"I am lost!" he screamed.

"It is God's judgment!" said Jean Oullier, stretching his arm to heaven. "Once I did not strike you because you were bound; this time, my hand spares you again, Maître Courtin. If your good angel wants you, let him save you; I have not stained my hands with your blood."

Courtin had risen while Jean Oullier said these words, and he moved hither and thither in the boat, making the water plash about him. Jean Oullier, calm, impassible, knelt in the bow and prayed.

The water came higher and higher.

"Oh, who will save me? who will save me?" cried Courtin, now livid, and contemplating with terror the six inches of wood which alone remained above the surface of the lake.

"God, if it pleases Him! Your life, like mine, is in His hands; let Him take one or the other — or save, or condemn us both. We are in His hands; once more, Maître Courtin, I say to you, accept His will."

As Jean Oullier spoke the boat gave a lurch; the water had reached the level of the gunwale, the skiff whirled once round, sustained itself for a second on the surface, and then slowly sank beneath the feet of the two men and buried itself in the depths of the lake with dismal mutterings.

Courtin was dragged down by the suction of the boat; but he came to the surface of the water, and his fingers seized the second oar, which floated near him. This slender bit of light dry wood supported him on the water long enough for him to make another appeal to Jean Oullier. The latter did not answer; he was swimming gently in the direction of the dawn.

"Help! help!" cried the miserable Courtin. "Help me to get ashore, Jean Oullier, and I will give you all the gold I have upon me!"

"Throw that ill-gotten gold to the bottom of the lake!" said the Vendéan, seeing the farmer buoyed upon the oar. "That is your one chance of saving your life; and this advice is the only help I will give you!"

Courtin put his hand to the belt; but drew it back as though his fingers were burned by the contact, or as if the Vendéan had commanded him to rip open his bowels and sacrifice his flesh and blood.

"No, no!" he murmured, "I can save it, and myself too."

He began to swim; but he had neither the skill nor the practice of Jean Oullier in that exercise. Moreover, the weight of the gold upon him was too great; at every stroke he went beneath the water, which, in spite of him, got into his throat. Again he called to Jean, but Jean Oullier was now a hundred yards away.

In one of these immersions, which lasted longer than the others, he was seized with a sort of vertigo, and suddenly, with a rapid movement, he detached the belt. But, before letting his precious gold drop into the gulf, he resolved to handle it, to feel it for the last time; he did clasp it, he did feel it with his trembling fingers.

That last contact with the metal he loved decided his fate; he could not resolve to release his hold of it; he pressed it to his breast, and made a strong movement with his feet to tread the water; but the weight of the upper part of his body burdened with the coin threw him off his balance; he sank. After a few seconds passed under water, he rose half suffocated, flung a curse to the heaven he saw for the last time, and then, dragged down by his gold as by a demon, he went to the bottom.

Jean Oullier, turning at that moment, saw rings upon the surface of the water, — the last sign given by the mayor of La Logerie of his existence; the last movement ever made around him in the land of the living.

The Vendéan raised his eyes to heaven and worshipped God for the justice of his decrees.

Jean Oullier swam well; but his recent wound and the fatigues and emotions of this terrible night had exhausted him. When he was only a hundred strokes from the shore he felt that his strength betrayed his courage; nevertheless, calm and resolute in this crucial moment as he had been all his life, he resolved to struggle to the last. On he swam.

Soon he felt a sort of faintness; his limbs grew numb; he fancied a thousand pins were pricking and tearing his flesh; his muscles grew painful; the blood mounted violently to his brain, and a dull, confused humming, like the roaring of the sea against the rocks, clamored in his ears; black clouds filled with phosphorescent sparks danced before his eyes; he thought he was about to die, and yet his limbs, obedient in their impotence, continued the motion his will imposed upon them. He still swam.

His eyes closed in spite of himself; his limbs now stiffened entirely; he gave a last thought to those with whom he had crossed the sea of life, — to the children, to the wife, to the old man who had brightened his youth;

to the two young girls who had taken the places of those he loved; he desired that his last prayer, like his last thought, should be of them.

But at that instant, and in spite of himself, an idea suddenly crossed his brain. A phantom passed before his eyes; he saw the elder Michel bathed in his blood, dying on the mossy ground of the forest. Raising his arm from the water aloft to heaven he cried out: —

"God! if I was mistaken, if it was a crime, forgive me! not in this world but the next!"

Then, as if that solemn invocation had exhausted its last powers, the soul seemed to leave the body, which floated inert upon the current at the moment when the sun, rising above the mountains on the horizon, gilded with its earliest fires the waters of the lake, — the same moment when Courtin, sinking to the bottom, rendered his last breath; the same moment when Petit-Pierre, in Nantes, was driven from her hiding-place and arrested.

Michel, in charge of the soldiers, was making his way to Nantes.

After marching half an hour along the high-road, the lieutenant who commanded the little troop came up to his prisoner.

"Monsieur," he said, "you look like a gentleman; I have the honor to be one myself. It pains me to see you handcuffed. Will you give me your word of honor not to escape if I release you?"

"Gladly," said Michel; "and I thank you, monsieur, swearing to you that no matter from what direction succor may come to me, I will not leave your side without your permission."

After this they continued their way, arm in arm; so that any one who met them would little have suspected that one was a prisoner.

The night was fine, the sunrise splendid; all the flowers, moist with dew, sparkled like diamonds; the air was full of sweetest fragrance; the birds were singing in the branches. This march to Nantes was really a delightful promenade.

When they reached the extremity of the lake of Grand-Lieu the lieutenant stopped his prisoner, with whom he had advanced fully half a mile beyond the escort, and pointing to a black mass, which was floating on the surface of the water, about fifty feet from the shore, he asked him what he thought it was.

"It looks like the body of a man," answered Michel.

"Can you swim?"

"A little."

"Ah, if I knew how to swim I 'd be in the water now," said the officer, sighing, and turning as if to call up his men.

Michel waited for nothing more; he ran to the bank, threw off his clothes, and jumped into the lake. A few instants later he brought to shore a body he had already recognized as that of Jean Oullier.

During this time the soldiers had come up, and they at once set to work to revive the drowning man. One of them took out his flask, and prying open the Vendéan's teeth poured a few drops of brandy into his mouth.

This revived him. His first glance fell on Michel, who was holding his head, and such an expression of anguish came upon his face that the lieutenant noticed and mistook it.

"This is the man who saved you, my friend," he said, pointing to Michel.

"Saved me! he! his son!" exclaimed Jean Oullier. "Ah! I thank thee, O God, who art wonderful in thy mercy as thou art terrible in thy justice!"

EPILOGUE.

TOWARD seven o'clock in the evening of a day in the year 1842, ten years after the events we have here recorded, a heavy carriage stopped before the gate of the Carmelite convent at Chartres.

The carriage contained five persons: two children eight and nine years old, a gentleman and lady, — the first about thirty-five, the second thirty, — and a peasant, bent with age but still vigorous in spite of his white hair. Although his dress was humble, this peasant occupied the seat beside the lady; one of the children was sitting on his knee and playing with the rings of a thick steel chain which fastened his watch to the button-hole of his waistcoat, while he himself passed his brown and shrivelled hand through the silky hair of the little one.

At the jar of the carriage, as it turned from the paved high-road into the faubourg Saint-Jean, the lady put her head out of the window; then she drew it back with an expression of pain as she saw the high walls that surrounded the convent, and the gloomy portal which gave entrance to it.

The postilion dismounted, and going to the door of the carriage said: —

"This is the place."

The lady pressed the hand of her husband, who was seated opposite to her, while two large tears rolled down her cheeks.

"Go, Mary, and take courage," said the young man, in whom our readers will recognize Baron Michel de la

Logerie. "I regret that the convent rules will not let me share this duty with you. It is the first time in ten years we have suffered apart."

"You will speak to her of me, will you not?" said the old peasant.

"Yes, my Jean," answered Mary.

The young woman sprang from the carriage and knocked at the gate. The sound of the knocker gave a funeral note, which echoed through the vaulted portal.

"Mère Sainte-Marthe?" said the lady when her summons was answered.

"Are you the person our mother is expecting?" asked the Carmelite.

"Yes, sister."

"Then come in. You shall see her; but remember, our rule requires that, although she is our Superior, you can see her only in presence of a sister; and she forbids you absolutely to speak to her, even in these last moments, of the earthly things she has left behind her."

Mary bowed her head.

The Carmelite went first and conducted the Baronne de la Logerie along a damp, dark corridor, in which were a dozen doors; she opened one of these doors and stood aside to allow the lady to enter. Mary hesitated an instant; she was choking with emotion; then she regained her self-command, crossed the threshold, and found herself in a little cell about eight feet square.

In this cell, for all furniture, was a bed, a chair, and a *prie-dieu;* for all ornament, a few holy images fastened to the bare walls, and an ebony and brass crucifix, which stretched out its arms above the *prie-dieu.*

Mary saw nothing of all that. On the bed lay a woman whose face had taken the color and the transparency of wax, and whose discolored lips seemed about to exhale their parting breath.

This woman was, or rather, had been Bertha. She was now naught else than the Mère Sainte-Marthe, superior of the convent of the Carmelites at Chartres, — soon to be only a corpse.

When she saw the lady enter the dying woman stretched forth her arms, and Mary fled to them. Long they held themselves embraced; Mary bathing with tears her sister's face, Bertha gasping, — for in her eyes, hollowed by the austerities of the cloister, there seemed to be no more tears.

The Carmelite sister, who had seated herself on the chair and was reading her breviary, was, however, not so occupied with her prayers that she did not notice what was passing before her. She probably thought these embraces were lasting too long, for she coughed significantly..

Mère Sainte-Marthe gently pushed Mary away from her, but did not release her hand, which she held in hers.

"Sister! sister!" murmured Mary, "who could have told me we should meet thus?"

"It is God's will, to which we must submit," replied the Carmelite mother.

"His will is sometimes very stern," sighed Mary.

"How can you say so, sister? That will is gentle and most merciful to me. God, who might have left me longer on this earth, deigns to recall me to Him."

"You will meet our father above," said Mary.

"And whom do I leave behind me?"

"Our good Jean Oullier, who lives and loves you always, Bertha."

"Thank you; and whom else?"

"My husband, — and two children, who are named, the boy, Pierre, the girl, Bertha. I have taught them to bless you daily."

A faint color came upon the cheeks of the dying woman.

"Dear children!" she murmured, "if God grants me a place beside Him, I promise to pray for them above."

And the dying soul began on earth the prayer it was to end in heaven.

In the midst of that prayer and in the silence of that cell, the striking of a clock was heard, then the tinkling of a bell, and the sound of feet approaching along the corridor. They were bringing the viaticum.

Mary fell on her knees by Bertha's pillow. The priest entered, holding the sacred chalice in his left hand, and in his right the consecrated wafer.

At this moment Mary felt the hand of Bertha seeking hers; for the purpose, as she thought, of pressing it. She was mistaken; Bertha slipped into her sister's hand an object which she felt to be a locket. She tried to look at it.

"No no," said Bertha, "wait till I am dead."

Mary made a sign of obedience and bowed her head upon her clasped hands.

The cell was now filled with nuns, all kneeling; and as far as could be seen along the corridor were others in their gloomy robes kneeling and praying.

The dying woman seemed to recover some strength with which to go into the presence of her Creator; she lifted herself up, murmuring: —

"I am ready, my God!"

The priest laid the wafer on her lips, and she fell back gently on the bed with closed eyes and clasped hands. Except for the motion of her lips, she seemed to have died, so pale was her face, so feeble the breath that issued from her bosom.

The priest concluded the other ceremonies of the extreme unction, but she did not open her eyes. He left the cell, and the assistants followed him.

The Carmelite nun, who had first met Mary, now came to her where she knelt, and touching her gently on the shoulder, said: —

"My sister, the rule of our order forbids that you should stay any longer in this cell."

"Bertha! Bertha!" said Mary, sobbing, "do you hear what they say to me? My God! after living together twenty years without being parted for a single day, and then separated for eleven years, — not to be allowed one hour together when we are parting for eternity!"

"You may stay in the house until I am dead, my sister; and it will make me happy to think you are near me and praying for me."

Mary bent down to kiss her dying sister for the last time, but the nun interposed, saying: —

"Do not turn our blessed mother's mind from the celestial path she now has entered, by vain, earthly thoughts."

"Oh, I will not leave her thus!" cried Mary, flinging herself on Bertha's bed and putting her lips to those of her sister. Bertha's lips replied by a feeble quiver, then she gently pushed her sister away from her. But the hand that made this motion had no power to rejoin the other, and it fell inert upon the bed.

The nun advanced, and without a tear, without a sigh, without a sign of emotion upon her face, she took that dying hand, joined it to the other, and laid them clasped upon Bertha's breast. Then she gently pushed Mary to the door.

"Oh, Bertha! Bertha!" cried her sister, breaking into sobs.

It seemed to her that a murmur echoed back these sobs, and in that murmur she fancied that she heard the name of "Mary!"

She was in the corridor; the door of the cell was closed behind her.

"Oh, let me see her!" she cried. "Let me see her once more, — only once!"

But the nun stretched out her arms and barred the way.

"I submit," said Mary, blinded by her tears. "Take me where you choose, sister."

The nun led her to an empty cell, the occupant of which had died the night before. Mary saw through her tears a *prie-dieu* surmounted by a crucifix, and she went, half stumbling, to kneel there.

For an hour she remained absorbed in prayer. At the end of an hour the nun returned and said, in the same cold impassible voice: —

"Mère Sainte-Marthe is dead."

"May I see her?" asked Mary.

"The rule of our order forbids it," replied the Carmelite.

Mary dropped her head into her hands with a sigh. One of those hands still clasped the object Bertha had given her at the moment she was about to receive, for the last time, the blessed sacrament. Mère Sainte-Marthe was dead, and Mary was free to look at what she had given her.

It was, as she knew already from its shape, a locket. Mary opened it. It contained some hair and a paper. The hair was the color of Michel's hair; the paper contained these words: "Cut during his sleep on the night of June 5, 1832."

"O, my God!" murmured Mary, raising her eyes to the crucifix, "O my God! in thy mercy receive her! for thy passion lasted but forty days, and hers has lasted eleven years!"

Putting the locket upon her heart, Mary went down the cold, damp stairway of the convent.

The carriage and those it contained were still waiting before the gate.

"Well?" asked Michel, opening the door and making a step toward his wife.

"Alas, it is all over!" replied Mary, throwing herself into his arms. "She died promising to pray for us above."

"Happy children!" said Jean Oullier, laying his hands, one on the head of the little boy, the other on that of the little girl. "Happy children! walk fearlessly through life, for a martyr watches over you in heaven!"

THE END.

Printed in the United States
47284LVS00001B/3

9 781589 631748